RACE

THE

SANDS

ALSO BY SARAH BETH DURST

The Deepest Blue

THE QUEENS OF RENTHIA
The Queen of Blood
The Reluctant Queen
The Queen of Sorrow

RACE
THE
SANDS

A NOVEL

SARAH BETH DURST

HARPER Voyager
An Imprint of HarperCollins Publishers

RACE THE SANDS. Copyright © 2020 by Sarah Beth Durst. All rights reserved. Printed in the United States of America. No part of this book may be used or reproduced in any manner whatsoever without written permission except in the case of brief quotations embodied in critical articles and reviews. For information, address HarperCollins Publishers, 195 Broadway, New York, NY 10007.

HarperCollins books may be purchased for educational, business, or sales promotional use. For information, please email the Special Markets Department at SPsales@harpercollins.com.

Harper Voyager and design are trademarks of HarperCollins Publishers LLC.

FIRST EDITION

Designed by Paula Russell Szafranski
Frontispiece © lenka/Adobe Stock

Library of Congress Cataloging-in-Publication Data has been applied for.

ISBN 978-0-06-288861-7

20 21 22 23 24 LSC 10 9 8 7 6 5 4 3 2 1

For Tamora Pierce

RACE

THE

SANDS

PART ONE

THE

CITY

OF

PERON

CHAPTER 1

Call it what it is: monster racing.

Forget that, and you die.

Tamra thought she should have that tattooed on her fore-head so the idiots she was trying to train stood a chance of remembering it. Bellowing with every shred of voice she had left, she shouted at her newest crop of riders, "They're not your *pets*! They're not your *friends*! You falter, they will kill you! You lose focus, they will kill you! You do anything stu-pid, they will—say it with me now . . ."

Dutifully, the five riders-to-be chimed, "Kill us!"

"Yes!"

One of her students raised her hand, timidly, which was not a good sign. If a little shouting withered her, how was she going to survive a race? "But I thought you told us to befriend the kehoks? Earn their trust?"

Oh, by the River, was *that* how they interpreted it? "Did I?" She fixed her glare on each of them, letting it linger until they wilted under her gaze like a sprout beneath the full desert sun. "Can anyone tell me exactly what I told you to do?"

Another answered, "To, um, be kind to them? Serve their needs?"

For the last month, she'd had them mucking out the kehoks' stalls and piling them with fresh straw, dragging water from the Aur River to fill the kehoks' buckets, and selecting the highest quality feed. She'd instructed them to care for the kehoks as they would a beloved horse, albeit keeping away from their teeth and claws and, in some cases, spiked tails. "Exactly. Anyone want to tell me *why*?"

The first student, Amira, cleared her throat. "So they learn to trust us and will obey—"

"They are monsters," Tamra snapped. "They do not trust. They do not feel gratitude. Or mercy. They do not understand kindness." Kehoks didn't, *couldn't*, change. Unlike the rest of creation, they were what they were, condemned for all time.

"Then why—" a third began.

"Because *we* are not monsters!" Tamra bellowed. "The decency you display is for the sake of *your* souls. The kehoks are already doomed to their fates. I will *not* train riders only to have them come back as racers!"

They all looked shocked, and she had to resist rolling her eyes. *River save me from the innocent arrogance of youth.* All of them believed they were too pure to ever be reborn as a kehok. Only the darkest, most evil souls came back as those insults to nature, and so her young students believed themselves safe. They didn't understand that evil could grow if planted in a field of banal cruelty. They didn't see why it was important to diligently protect and preserve every scrap of honor. Then again, this wasn't a temple.

They'd either figure it out eventually or regret it for an eternity.

Besides, more than likely, they'll all turn out mediocre and come back as cows.

All she could do was give them the chance to improve their lot, both in this life and the next one. She couldn't control what they chose to do with that opportunity.

Tamra put her fists on her hips. "The ability to show kindness and mercy to those who do not deserve it is a strength! And that strength will give you an edge in the races."

And now they looked confused.

"Only the strongest win," Tamra said. "You've heard that a thousand times. But is it strength of muscle? Obviously not. No human alive can out-muscle a kehok. It's strength of mind, strength of heart, and strength of will."

The third student, a fifteen-year-old boy named Fetran, crossed his arms, as if that made him look tough and defiant. With his gangly limbs and pimply face, he just looked petulant. *Why, oh, why did I agree to train these children?* she asked herself. Oh, yes, their parents were paying her. Lousy way to pay the augurs' bills. Not that she had much of a choice. Because while she'd be far better off picking a potential winner, training him or her up with a brand-new kehok, and claiming her share of the prize money, there was the little problem that she couldn't afford the race entrance fees, not to mention the purchase price of a new kehok. . . .

"So, last season?" Fetran drawled. "Was your rider weak of mind, heart, or will?"

Low blow.

Tamra smiled.

He shrank back.

She smiled broader. She knew that when she smiled,

the scar that ran from her left eye to her neck stretched and paled. She'd gotten that scar during her final kehok race, a race she'd won, before she'd retired to raise her daughter and train future champions. Emphasizing that scar made people uncomfortable. She loved her scar. It was her favorite feature, a relic of a time when she was the one destined for greatness, with a wide future ahead of her.

In a falsely chipper voice, Tamra said, "Maybe it was a combination. But you seem to have everything sorted out, so how about you show us how it's done?"

Fetran looked as if he wanted to bolt. Or vomit. "I c-can't . . ."

She let him squirm a minute more, intending to let him off the hook, but then Amira stepped forward, cleared her throat, and said in a squeak, "I'll try."

Oh, kehoks. That was *not* what she'd meant to happen.

Tamra opened her mouth to say, *No, you're not ready.* But then she stopped. Studying Amira, she thought, *There's some strength in her. A spark, maybe. If it could be fed . . .*

Briefly, she allowed herself to imagine the glory, if she transformed one of these rich kids into a fierce competitor. She'd be the most sought-after trainer in all Becar, and her daughter would never again have to feel worry that they'd be separated.

No. It's a crazy idea. I can't turn one of them into a winner. It was widely known that the children of the wealthy dallied in racing but never won. None of them had the fire. You had to burn with the need to win, with the conviction that this is what you were meant to do. That was an aspect of racing that couldn't be taught, and these spoiled rich kids had never felt it. They'd never known the feeling of yearning for a future that vanished like a mirage before your eyes. Or the feeling of having all your dreams slip like sand through your fingers. They'd never tried to change their fate and discovered it was immutable.

They'd never been *thirsty*.

On the other hand . . . the girl *had* volunteered to try.

Maybe the answer to all Tamra's problems had been right here in front of her the whole time, and she'd been too stubborn to see it. The augurs preached that you could improve the quality of your soul by your choices, and thus grant meaning to your current life and hope for your next. Tamra might not be able to read the state of these kids' immortal souls . . .

But maybe I could give them a chance to shine.

"Follow me," Tamra said curtly.

"Hey, she asked *me*," Fetran butted in. "I'm first."

"You're going to break your neck," Amira told him.

"And you won't?"

"My kehok likes me."

Tamra heaved a sigh. Seriously, why did she bother talking? It wasn't as if they listened to her. Kehoks liked no one, because they loathed themselves. *I'm a terrible teacher. I should switch to raising potted plants.* "You'll race each other. And you'll use chains and harnesses." When Fetran began to object, she held up her hand. "I don't want to explain to your parents why their darlings are minus a few limbs."

Or have them explain to me why I'm not getting paid anymore.

Without looking back to see if they were following, Tamra stalked across the training grounds to the kehok stable, a prisonlike block, made of mud-brick and stone, that dominated half the practice area. Out of the corner of her eye she saw other trainers' students running obstacle courses, lifting weighted barrels, and wrestling each other on the sand. She didn't make eye contact with any of them. She knew what the other trainers would think of this—her students weren't ready for the track. But they would never be ready if they didn't take risks.

And if there was a chance she could shape them into what she needed them to be . . .

Closer to the stable, she heard the kehoks.

The worst part about a kehok scream was that it sounded almost human, as if a man or woman's vocal cords had been shredded and then patched up sloppily by an untrained doctor. It made your blood curdle and your bones shiver.

Tamra was used to it.

Her students still weren't.

Amira and Fetran huddled with the others in a clump as she flung open the doors. *This is a terrible idea,* she thought. Sunlight flooded the stalls, and the kehoks screamed louder. They kicked and bashed against their walls. There were eighteen kehoks in the stable, five of which were owned by Tamra's patron.

She halted in front of them.

The unnaturalness of the creatures made your skin crawl, even if you were accustomed to seeing them on a daily basis. Kehoks looked as if they'd been stitched together by a crazed god. There were dozens, even hundreds, of possible varieties, all of them with the same twisted wrongness to their bodies. In the batch before her, one had the heft of a rhino and the jaws of a croc. Another looked like a horse-size jackal with the teeth and venom of a king cobra. Another bore the head of a lizard and the hindquarters of a massive lion. According to the augurs, the shape of the kehok's body reflected the kind of depravity it had committed in its prior life.

Tamra picked the lion-lizard and the rhino-croc. She wasn't trusting newbies around venom, even in a practice race. Starting with the lion-lizard, she positioned herself in front of his stall and met his eyes.

Like all kehoks, he had sun-gold eyes.

The eyes were the only thing beautiful about any of them.

She let her gaze bore into his. Steadying her breathing, she shut out all other distractions: the whispers of her students, the screams of the other kehoks, even the muttering of other trainers, who had come to see what she was doing in the stalls so early in the training season.

She felt her heartbeat. Steady. *Thump, thump, thump.* Focusing on that, she willed the kehok's heart to beat at the same tempo.

He fought her. They always did.

Rearing back, he struggled against the shackles.

"Calm," she murmured. "Calm."

Moving slowly, Tamra gestured to Fetran to pass her a harness and saddle. He did, and Tamra kept her thoughts firmly fixed on the kehok. *Thump, thump, thump.*

She tossed the saddle onto the kehok's back. The monster shuddered but didn't try to bolt. Continuing to move deliberately, she attached the harness—both the harness and the saddle clipped onto a chain net that was fitted over the kehok's thick hide. The chain net allowed them to be shackled within their stall, as well as quickly saddled.

She repeated the process with the second mount.

When both were ready, she signaled her students: Fetran

and Amira to the starting gates and the rest to the viewing stands. Grasping one harness in each hand, she barked at the two kehoks, "Follow!"

Kehoks didn't respond to words.

They responded to intent. And will.

According to Becaran scientists who had studied the kehoks for ages, the kehoks read your conviction through a combination of your voice, your expression, and your body language. The augurs claimed they responded to your aura and its reflection of the purity of your purpose. But Tamra believed what most riders and former riders secretly believed: the kehoks read your heart and mind. Regardless of how they did it, though, the result was the same. Doubt yourself, and you'll be gored. Don't doubt . . . and they'll take you to the finish line.

In other words, the more stubborn you were, the better control you would have.

And Tamra was *very* stubborn.

She just had to hope these two teenagers were as stubborn as she'd been.

Everyone watched as she led the two kehoks to the racetrack. She was, she admitted to herself, showing off. Not many people could control two at once. It had been considered a useless parlor trick when she'd been a rider—you were allowed to influence only your own racer—but it had come in handy as a trainer.

Locking the kehoks into the starting shoots, Tamra beckoned Fetran and Amira. They slunk closer, clearly regretting having agreed to this. She thought about letting them back out, but then thought, *This is their chance at glory!* Or at least it was a step in the general vicinity of glory. Whether they knew it or not, she was offering them freedom from the lives that had been mapped out for them. And a chance to change the fate of their souls.

"One lap," she told them. "Loser mucks out the winner's stall for a week."

"Get ready to shovel," Fetran said to Amira, his bravado belied only by the adolescent cracking of his voice.

Amira's eyes were as wide as a hare who's caught sight of a hawk. But she said, "You're only saying that because you're scared I'll win."

You're both scared, Tamra wanted to say. "Mount up," she ordered instead. "Belt yourselves in. Fetran, take the rhino-croc. Amira, the lion-lizard."

The two students climbed the ladders into the starting shoots. Tamra moved around to the front, forcing the two kehoks to focus on her instead of the riders. Normally, an advanced rider would do this by him- or herself, but she wasn't taking chances. Her students had never run side by side before, on a shielded track. So far, all their experience with riding the kehoks had been solo, heavily supervised by her. She held the mounts steady with her will.

This is going to work, she thought. *I'm going to make them into winners! I'm going to change their destinies!* Instead of dilettantes who dabbled in racing before returning to run their parents' estates, they'd be champions. When they went for their annual augur readings—or however often rich kids went—they'd be told hawk or tiger, instead of cow or mouse. They'd be thrilled—the young always wanted to be reborn as something grand.

The two students lowered themselves into the saddles and belted themselves in with the harnesses—the straps should keep them on their kehok's back no matter what the monster did. In a professional race, there were no harnesses and no chain nets.

It added to the excitement.

She broke contact with the kehoks and climbed the ladders to check the straps. The second she switched her focus to the saddles, the kehoks began to buck and snort. Fetran and Amira clung to their backs.

Straps were secure.

She took a breath . . .

Reconsidered all her life choices that led her to this moment . . .

Decided it was too late to change her mind and run off into the desert to live a less stressful life subsisting on scorpions and camel dung . . .

She retreated to the stands, beyond the dampening shield that covered the track. All racetracks had an augur-created psychic shield that prevented anyone in the stands from influencing the racers, whether it was by concentrated determination or an overabundance of enthusiasm. From here on, it was up to her two students.

"You have one task," Tamra called to Fetran and Amira. "Fix this word in your mind:

"Run!"

Tamra then slapped the lever that unlatched the gates, and the two kehoks, with their riders still clinging to their backs, burst out of the starting shoots. They barreled forward—even at a cheap training facility like theirs, the practice track was hemmed in by high walls, so there was no place for the massive mounts to go except forward. But that didn't mean they wouldn't try to resist.

She jogged through the stands, parallel to the track.

The lion-lizard bashed against the wall, trying to knock his rider off. He didn't understand that the rider was attached. Tamra felt each blow in her memory—her bones still ached because of the number of times she'd been slammed against a training wall. Then there was the time a kehok had rolled on top of her in an attempt to unseat her. Her right leg had broken in three places, but she'd won that race. Some days—like today, with twinges of sympathy—her leg still hurt.

"Run!" she shouted at the two riders. "That's all that matters! That's all that exists! You are nothing but the sand beneath the hooves, the wind in your face, the sun on your back. You are this moment. Feel the moment. Feel the race!"

She missed it, the way the wind felt, the way the rest of the world fell away, the way life was distilled into a simple goal. Nothing about life was simple anymore.

She wished she could peel away everything else and just focus on this: a race. Just her and a monster that she understood and could control, rather than the monsters who wore human faces and believed they were purer of soul than she.

Maybe they are purer than me. But that doesn't make their actions right.

She couldn't dwell on that now, though, as Amira and Fetran demanded her attention. The other students and trainers cheered as the two kehoks and riders thundered around the track. Sand was kicked into the air in a cloud that billowed up toward the sky. She began to feel a shred of the old exhilaration—the barely bridled wildness of the kehoks, matched with the barely contained terror of the riders. It was intoxicating. Tamra cheered with the others as the riders rounded the third corner.

And then it happened—

Fetran lost control.

She knew it a split second before the crowd gasped. It was in the way the boy's kehok tossed his head, the sun glinting off his golden eyes—

Freedom.

The rhino-croc sensed that the boy's focus had slipped, and he pivoted on his back feet. Rising up, he struck the other kehok, the lion-lizard, in the face. The lion-lizard crashed to the wall, and the girl—pinned between her mount's back and the wall—cried out in pain. Shaking off the crash, the lion-lizard then charged at the rhino-croc. He lashed with his claws, and the croc clamped down with his massive jaws.

Tamra was already running. She leaped onto the sands of the track with no thought but to save her students. Ahead of her, the two kehoks were tearing into each other.

She threw herself forward, feetfirst, skidding between them on her back. Hands up, she roared with every fiber of her being: "STOP!"

Later, the other trainers would tell her what she did was suicidal.

You're crazy.

You don't throw yourself between out-of-control kehoks.

You don't lie prone beneath their hooves and claws.

But Tamra did.

What she didn't do was allow a shred of doubt or fear into her mind. They *would* stop because they *must* stop. Her livelihood depended on it. Her daughter depended on it. *I will not lose these students.*

You. Will. Stop.

And they did.

Snorting and snuffling, the two kehoks dropped back onto four feet and retreated from her. Rising to her feet, hands outstretched, one toward each, Tamra felt her whole body shaking with . . . She had no name for what she felt. But they would *calm*. Now.

She heard the others running toward them. Shouting for healers, the other trainers unstrapped her two riders. She heard the screams of her other students, their voices melding as if they were a single scared beast. One of the riders, Fetran, was howling in pain. The other, Amira, was frighteningly silent.

But Tamra kept her focus on the two kehoks.

She walked toward one and took his harness. Then she took the other. She led them along the racetrack, crossed the finish line, and then led them back across the training ground to their stalls. It felt ten times as far as it was.

Only when they were locked in did she allow other thoughts to enter her mind.

Her students.

Were they dead?

Was it her fault?

Yes, of course it is. She was their trainer. Part of her job was teaching them not to die.

For a moment, Tamra couldn't make her feet move. She'd rather face a herd of kehoks than exit the stables now and see what damage had been done.

One of the kehoks snorted as if it were mocking her cowardice.

Go, she ordered herself.

And she walked out of the stable to see how badly her students were broken, and to take responsibility for letting her hopes destroy their dreams—and possibly her own.

CHAPTER 2

Neither was dead, which was a miracle.

Both were broken, though. Badly. Left leg, one rib for Amira. Three ribs and a concussion for Fetran. Their parents had descended on the training ground, cleared out their belongings from their rooms, canceled their lessons, and demanded that Tamra compensate them for all healers' bills.

She'd argued they'd signed contracts, relieving her from responsibility for the cost of any injuries or funerals, except in cases of negligence.

Putting unprepared students onto the racetrack counted as negligence, they'd argued.

She had little defense against that.

The injuries proved she'd made the wrong choice.

It didn't matter that she couldn't afford the healers' fees, not on top of everything she owed the augurs for her daughter's training. And it didn't matter that if the riders-to-be had been talented enough to become real riders, they would have risen to the challenge. Instead of dreaming of glory, she should have coddled them—that's what their parents had wanted.

I misjudged that. I thought they'd want me to turn them into winners, if I could.

Riders got hurt. It was what happened in the Becaran Races. It was part of why the people loved them—there was true risk. And there were stiff penalties for anything the officials ruled as negligence. "Racing comes with risk," she told the parents.

They swore to go directly to her patron. Insist Lady Evara rescind her patronage. Kick Tamra off her training grounds. And then they'd file a complaint with the racing commission. Insist the commission charge her with overt negligence and revoke her training permit. Require her to submit proof of an acceptable augur reading before ever being allowed to work with children again, a demand usually made only of proven criminals. Or bar her from the tracks across all of Becar.

She should have groveled—as elite south-bank Becarans, they were used to the lower classes groveling at their feet—but she'd never been good at that. "Do what you need to do," she'd told them, and they'd stomped off to the ferry dock, following their injured offspring, whom Tamra was certain she was never going to see again, much less train.

By the end of the day, all the parents of her students had come to her, expressed their concern, listened to her apologies, and then politely withdrawn their children. One went as far as to say that they should have known better than to expect more from a lesser Becaran. As her last student left, she told herself, *You did this. In one misguided dream of glory, you lost them all.*

Avoiding the other trainers and their students, Tamra retreated to the stalls. She occupied herself with checking the locks on the doors and shackles. She didn't want to hear any snide comments or even accept any sympathy. *Says something about my life that I'm more comfortable being with monsters,* she thought. She patted one of the kehoks on her broad neck. The monster swung her golden eyes toward Tamra and then bared three rows of teeth and lunged forward to snap at her hand. Tamra was quick enough to avoid losing any fingers.

"Yeah, I feel the same way," she told the kehok, who was glaring at Tamra balefully. Drool dribbled from the kehok's jaws. "Ugh, people are the worst, right? Myself included. Good thing there's no chance I'll be reborn as one." It had been years since she'd paid for an official reading, but she had no illusions about the state of her soul. Being reborn as human, even as a lesser Becaran, required a kind of balance that most did not have. There was no shame in that. Unless you were destined to be a slug.

Or a kehok.

She should never have let those children try to race. Closing her eyes, she let the guilt swamp her. *They trusted me. And I failed them.*

She prayed to her ancestors and theirs that they healed quickly. Even if she never saw them again. Even if she never had another student. Even if their parents did take the revenge they'd promised and had her barred from the track. She'd wanted more than those kids could give, and that hadn't been fair to them. She'd pushed fish to fly like birds, and she should have known better.

Only when she was certain that the grounds were deserted did she begin the trudge home. The desert wind had shifted—the evening wind coming from the east, with a bite of chill. Stars were beginning to poke through the graying sky, and she took comfort in the familiar constellations: the Crocodile, the Emperor's Robe, and the Lady with the Sword. The lady's sword was ascendant this time of year, and the three stars that made the blade shone brighter than anything else in the sky. She used to tell her daughter, Shalla, the story of the Lady with the Sword, who saved an emperor from an army of assassins, suffered a mortal wound, and was reborn as a constellation.

Oh, Shalla, what am I going to do?

She had until the next augur payment to figure it out.

Set apart from the city, the training grounds and their practice racetrack were two miles from the closest nest of houses, far enough away to warrant their own river dock but close enough that the road between was well-worn, hardened sand. Beside the road was the mighty Aur River, black without the sun shining on it. Ahead, Tamra saw the soft amber glow from the tightly packed clusters of houses on the northern bank, all with the traditional white walls and blue-tile roofs. On the other side of the river, the southern bank, the palaces of the wealthy were lit with blue-glass lanterns, bathing their white walls in faux moonlight.

You couldn't tell there had been another riot there yesterday.

According to the other trainers, who loved to gossip, a group of textile workers had gone unpaid, and the business owners had blamed the emperor-to-be for unsigned contracts. Last week it had been dockworkers. Thankfully, both times the augurs had been on hand to help the city guard calm everyone down before the riot got out of control. But the turmoil was only going to get worse until Becar had an actual emperor again. Fun times.

At least tonight seemed peaceful. The night herons were calling to one another, a low croon so soothing that it unknotted the muscles in Tamra's neck and shoulders. She loved her home at night: the sweetness of the cool air, the serenity of the stars, and the knowledge that she'd be able to see her daughter in the brief moments they were allowed to visit before Shalla returned to the augur temple for another day of lessons.

Tamra picked up her pace, anxious to see her.

She and her daughter lived in a patchwork kind of house, two mud-walled huts that had been shoved together and painted white to create a two-room home, between a spice shop and a weaver's workroom. It smelled like a mix of cinnamon and citrus all the time, and there was the continuous comforting *whoosh-thump* sound of the shuttles on the weaver's loom. Their house was too small to hold a shop plus living quarters, so the rent was cheap. Wedged between the other buildings, it didn't look like much. But it was their home, and the recent unrest in other parts of the city hadn't touched it yet. She wondered if the discontent would reach such a boiling point that it would stop being safe to let Shalla walk to and from temple. She hoped it didn't come to that. Surely, the emperor-to-be would be crowned soon.

Tamra let herself in and breathed in the scent of baking onion bread, her favorite. "Shalla? Shalla, I'm back!" Shutting the door behind her, she braced herself.

A second later, an eleven-year-old girl bounded out of the second room and launched herself toward Tamra. Shalla had shiny black hair, burnished bronze skin, and brilliant purple eyes—her eyes were a legacy from a man that Tamra barely remembered, though she once thought she loved him. She'd named her Shalla, which meant "star," because she was the light that guided Tamra through the darkest parts of life.

Shalla launched herself into Tamra's arms, hugging her so tight that Tamra let out an "Oof!"

"Mama, you will not guess what happened!" Grabbing Tamra's hands, Shalla skipped in a circle as if she were again five years old. A memory flashed into Tamra's mind of her daughter that young, pudgy-cheeked and mud-spattered, contrasting with the polished young student she was being groomed to become, and Tamra felt like laughing and crying at the same time.

Shalla often made her feel that way, especially these days.

"You sprouted wings and learned to fly," Tamra guessed.

Stifling a laugh, Shalla rolled her eyes. "Mama."

"You tamed an elephant and want to keep him as a pet."

"Mama."

"You met the Lady with the Sword, and she promised you a ride across the desert on her magical cheetah, but first you had to eat a lake of honey."

"Mama! I passed the level eight exam!" For the past three weeks, Shalla had barely slept, worried about the exam and consumed by the fear that the augurs had made a mistake in choosing her—only the best souls were reborn as potential augurs. *An irrational fear,* Tamra thought. *Of course my Shalla was glorious in her past life.* But now all that worry had vanished, and Shalla was beaming joy with every bit of her body. Tamra wouldn't have been surprised if she started to glow bright enough to drown out the city lights.

Beaming back at her, Tamra kissed her on both cheeks. "Knew it! You are the most clever, most wise, most brilliant, most talented, most—"

Shalla laughed again. "Only in your eyes."

"My eyes are the only ones that matter. I see you clearly." Tamra cupped her daughter's face in her hands and met her gaze, hoping her daughter could read her sincerity. She meant every word. Shalla was a miracle and a marvel.

Pulling back, Shalla batted her mother's hands away. "Gah! You're looking at me like you look at kehoks!"

"I'm looking at you with adoration and admiration!"

"Exactly what I said." Then she yelped, "Oh, no, I burned it!" She scampered across the room to the brick oven and yanked the door open.

"You didn't," Tamra said reassuringly. No smoke. No burning smell. "It's perfect. Like you." If she told her daughter that often enough, maybe someday she'd believe it. Her worth wasn't measured in exam grades or in the approval of the augurs. She was worthy no matter how well she did or didn't do. Tamra wanted her daughter to understand that at the very core of her being.

Growing up, no one had ever told Tamra she had any worth. In fact, it was always the opposite.

Her one driving force from the second Shalla was born was to make sure that girl knew she was loved. *And then the augurs saw her value, too, and took her away from me.*

At least she had her back at night. *For now,* a tiny fear whispered inside her. Tamra pushed the fear back. She wasn't going to waste a moment bemoaning the fact that Shalla was destined for a higher purpose. Tamra spent enough time in the day drowning in bitterness and regret. Nights were for joy.

Shalla poked at the crust of the bread. She'd been cooking on her own for nearly a year now, and Tamra thought she had a talent for it. "You're right. Not burnt!" Shalla cheered.

"Mama . . ." Her shining face began to frown. "Augur Clari said to tell you that the fee for level nine lessons is thirty pieces higher than for level eights. But you have enough students, don't you? It won't be a problem, will it?" She gazed at Tamra with hopeful eyes.

For a moment, Tamra felt as if a desert wraith had stolen her breath. They wanted *more* gold? She'd been warned training was expensive, but Tamra had said she could handle it. She hadn't had much choice.

To be chosen to become an augur was considered one of the highest honors in Becar. It was also an honor you couldn't refuse—if the augurs deemed you worthy, you had to train. Becoming an augur required a pure soul, and those were rare. Becar couldn't afford to waste a single one.

Augurs possessed the rare ability to read souls. A trained augur could tell what kind of creature you had been in your past life and what kind of creature you would become when you were reborn. By the end of her studies, Shalla would be able to look at a night heron and tell you if it had once been the baker down the street, or the emperor's pet cat. Her skills would be in high demand and her future determined. She'd be granted a palace on the southern bank and the vast coffers of the temple would be open to her, in exchange for performing an augur's duties, and she'd be both respected and feared. The augurs were the moral compass of the empire, ensuring its greatness continued as it had for centuries, keeping Becarans on the path to embrace their destinies. In practical terms, they helped solve disputes, soothed grieving families, and guided people's behavior on a day-to-day basis.

Augurs were the heart and soul of Becar, which was lovely. Just not cheap.

By law, every trainee's family was offered the "honor" of paying for the cost of training. In return for regular payments, Shalla was allowed to continue to live with her mother.

If her family failed to pay, though, Shalla would be taken away. She would become a ward of the augur temple, required to live there and work for them every minute she wasn't in lessons. Tamra would not even be allowed to see her. Not until her training was complete, and her childhood was over. Shalla would emerge a stranger, formally "severed" from her.

I won't let that happen.

"It won't be a problem," Tamra lied.

Somehow she'd make it true.

AT DAWN, TAMRA SAT ALONE AT THE TABLE AND ATE A slice of onion bread. Last night it had been warm with melted onion. Today it crunched, cold in her mouth. She swallowed it down with her tea. Shalla was gone, back across the river for her daily augur lessons, and the house felt empty and bereft. And the specter of thirty additional pieces of gold hung over Tamra's head.

She'd have to grovel before the parents of her former students. Beg them to come back. Also, try to drum up more business, which would be hard with Fetran's and Amira's parents positioned against her, poisoning her reputation. At least the parts of it that weren't already poisoned.

And even if a miracle occurred and she won a full class of students, she still wasn't going to be able to pay Shalla's increased tuition. She was barely making the payments before. *It's not possible,* she thought. The math didn't work.

She took another swig of her tea. She hadn't added enough honey, and the bitter taste made her nose wrinkle.

So did the thought she'd been trying to ignore all night. Because there was, of course, one obvious way.

Train a rider who could win.

Pair him or her with the fastest racer she could find.

Win a few races, even minor ones, and that's tuition for months.

There were plenty of races each season, all with prize money: first the qualifiers, which were regional races held on tracks up and down the Aur River, and then the main races in the Heart of Becar, the capital of the empire. Both the minor and major main races offered pots of gold of various sizes for any top-three placement.

Thing was, none of the kehoks that her patron owned this season were fast enough, and the River knew none of her former students were strong enough—yesterday's fiasco had made that clear.

I have to go to the auction. Today. Before any more time is lost.

She had to find a new rider and a new racer. But first . . . she needed her patron to back her, for both money to purchase the kehok and for the race entrance fees. And this was easier said than done. After last season, she'd been lucky just to be able to teach using Lady Evara's kehoks. *Maybe her attitude will have mellowed. And maybe she won't have heard about yesterday's fiasco.* Besides, it had been several months since Tamra had last approached her.

And there's no better option. I have to try.

As much as she despised begging for gold, she'd do it. For Shalla.

It took nearly an hour to cross the city by foot, another half hour of waiting to pay a bronze coin to cross the Aur River by ferry, fifteen minutes on the crowded ferry pressed up against workers who smelled like lye and soot and spent the entire trip complaining about how the emperor-to-be *still* wasn't crowned yet, and gossiping about fears of foreign invaders while Becar was emperor-less—no treaties could be signed, no troops could be moved, no laws could be passed until Prince Dar was coronated, and that couldn't happen until he found the vessel for his predecessor's soul. By the time the ferry docked on the southern bank, Tamra felt as if her shoulders were up at her ears and every back muscle was a knot of tension. She didn't even want to think about what would happen if the emperor-to-be couldn't be crowned. She had enough of her own problems, thank you very much, without worrying about the world falling apart around her.

After the ferry, it took another half hour to wind through the back streets of the palaces. Men and women from the north bank, "lesser Becarans," weren't allowed to use the wide palm-tree-lined streets that connected the palaces. If they needed to get someplace on the southern bank, they had to use the narrow, covered alleys that hid them and their inferior clothes from the eyes of the wealthy.

More than once, Tamra had imagined riding a kehok down one of the thoroughfares, in full sight of the rich. *They watch and cheer loudly enough during the races, the same as the poor. Yet we're somehow unviewable where they live.*

Centuries ago, when the first augurs built the first temple, wealth was bestowed on the worthy and pure of soul. Their descendants were fond of believing that was still true—that the wealthy were naturally superior, even though there was no proof of that anymore. By law, all augur readings were private, shielding the nobility from charges of hypocrisy. She could guess who'd made that law: some rich parent who wanted their spoiled, rat-souled kid to inherit their land, gold, and title.

But she shoved her resentment down where it wouldn't show on her face as she approached her patron's palace. Over the past few months, ever since the death of the last emperor, the number of city guards patrolling these streets had doubled—it wouldn't do to look like a troublemaker.

Lady Evara possessed what she would have called a "modest" home, a sprawling complex of "only" six buildings and three gardens. The unrest throughout Becar, the threats brewing beyond the empire's borders . . . none of it appeared to have touched this oasis in the slightest. But that had to be an illusion. Even the aristocracy needed the empire to function in order to maintain their wealth and power. The rich were merely better at hiding any hint of strain, due to the fact that they, by definition, had absurd amounts of money.

Each building looked like a temple of polished white marble with a blue-tiled dome that gleamed against the cloudless sky. Strikingly beautiful, yes, but it was the gardens that were extraordinary. Entering through one of the servant archways, Tamra marveled at the gorgeous sprays of purple, blue, and yellow flowers that were suspended on impossible-to-see trellises so that they appeared to be floating. She inhaled the perfume of the blossoms, so thick that it made her head feel as if it were spinning. Reaching up, she trailed her fingers across the petals of the velvet-soft blossoms. Imagine having enough gold to create floating gardens. *Surely, Lady Evara will spend a bit of her fortune on a has-been rider's dreams of lost glory.*

Maybe she should think of a better sales pitch than that.

Trouble was, she wasn't good at asking for money. Or

for anything. She'd become a rider to prove her worth, and that hadn't changed—she wanted this patronage because she deserved it, not because anyone pitied her.

After giving her name to one of Lady Evara's servants, Tamra waited as instructed by a pond that was overstuffed with lilies and shimmering silver fish. A waterfall fed the stream, pouring from bronze vases. Even though she knew it cycled back through hidden hoses, it still felt like a frivolous waste of money.

But then, I suppose, so am I.

Last season her patron had showered her with enough money to buy the best racer at the auction and hire the most promising rider. Both had died when she'd pushed them too hard in their final race in the Heart of Becar.

Even worse, they'd taken down multiple racers and riders around them.

A high-profile disaster like that, accompanied by so many fines that Tamra had lost all her savings from her champion years, should have been enough for her patron to abandon her entirely. Tamra should just be grateful that she hadn't. *Yet here I am, about to ask her to trust me again.*

This is never going to work.

She fixed her thoughts on Shalla, attempting to firm up her resolve once more.

It was funny, but she'd never once felt this kind of self-doubt on the racetrack.

It's age, Tamra thought. *The youth can be confident because they don't know how many doors are closing with each passing day.* The youth had the illusion of limitless possibilities, whereas Tamra had already had her fate, her failure, shoved down her throat.

I can't fail again. I won't.

"My petal!" Lady Evara swept across the garden, looking as if she were wearing a garden on her body. She was draped in gauzy layers of fabric embroidered with a riot of flowers, all in gold- and emerald-colored threads. Her hair was dyed emerald and gold as well, and was wrapped around a puzzle of golden trellises so high and wide that Tamra didn't know how she managed to walk without tipping over. "Such a delight to see you, my dear, especially after what happened yesterday. Losing all your students at once. Tut-tut."

She shouldn't have been surprised that Lady Evara knew, but it still caught her off guard. Even with so many city services hamstrung by the lack of an emperor, the rich still found ways to get news faster than anyone else. She wondered whether one of the other trainers had sent a messenger wight with the humiliating details. Or it could have been one of her students' parents. Tamra tried not to let her dismay show on her face as she bowed low. "Gracious One, you look as beautiful as your garden."

Lady Evara laughed, a tinkling sound that resembled a wind chime. Tamra knew she'd cultivated that laugh—she'd once interrupted the great lady practicing when she thought no one could hear her. Or maybe she simply hadn't cared if Tamra had.

"You have probably guessed why I have come, Gracious One."

The laugh died as if it were a fire doused with water. "You *want*. Isn't that why you always come? Your wants. Your needs. Your dreams. But does anyone ever ask what I want and need?"

Oh, spectacular. It's going to be one of those *visits.* "What do you want and need?" Tamra asked dutifully, though what she really wanted to ask was how could Lady Evara need anything, living in such splendor? Her every whim was catered to. She'd never known true need. Maybe want, though. Even the rich had wants.

"Absolutely nothing. All my dreams have been fulfilled."

That . . . wasn't the answer she expected, even if she suspected it was true.

"That's a lie, of course," Lady Evara said airily. "I want to sponsor a winner. You promised me one. You were so very certain." She pouted, and Tamra tried to guess what the appropriate response was. An apology? Bravado? She went with truth:

"I can make a winner."

"Oh? So confident, sweet petal? You're cursed, they say, after last year's catastrophe. They call me foolish to encourage you. They'd rather I toss you to the jackals. But I'm not so fickle in my judgments. And I judge that you can do as you say."

Tamra allowed herself a hint of hope. Maybe this would be simpler than she'd thought it would. Maybe she'd be given another chance. Maybe . . .

"Still, I don't like to be considered a fool. *You* don't consider me a fool, do you?" Lady Evara looked at her then with piercing eyes, as if Tamra's answer were vitally important.

Someone else might have lied. Someone who played the games of the wealthy, who knew how to flatter, who knew how to handle people. Tamra wasn't good at reading people.

She was, though, *excellent* at reading monsters.

"Foolish, yes," Tamra said. "But a fool? Never."

Lady Evara laughed, clearly pleased with that answer. "Then I have a bargain for you. Last year, I gave you unlimited access to my funds to purchase your mount and woo your rider. This year, you may have two hundred gold pieces. Plus I will sponsor your entrance fees."

Two hundred! That was barely enough to—

"Standard cut of the prize money. But . . ." Lady Evara paused dramatically. "Succeed in training a rider and racer who can place top three in a race in the Heart of Becar, and I will not only continue to be your patron, but I will also pay your family's debts to the augurs for the next three years. I will see that your daughter continues in your care while fulfilling her destiny."

The offer was grand enough to make Tamra's head spin. Top three . . . It wasn't impossible. After all, Lady Evara hadn't said she needed to compete in the final championship race. Just in *a* race in the Heart of Becar. There were dozens of those—you just needed to win one of two regional qualifiers to be allowed to run. But with only two hundred gold pieces to begin with . . . "Five hundred," Tamra countered. "You can't purchase any reasonable mount—"

Lady Evara cut her off. "Then purchase the unreasonable. Win with a beast that others undervalue. Choose a rider who hasn't yet proven his or her worth. You must find yourself an uncut emerald and polish it until it gleams." She flashed her rings, catching glints of sunlight that filtered in between the flowers. Several of her jewels *were* emeralds. Others, rubies. One, a priceless black diamond. "Think, Tamra, what do you have to lose by accepting my offer? And think what you have to gain."

"What do *you* have to gain?" Tamra asked bluntly.

"Why, amusement, my petal," Lady Evara cooed. "I will have the pleasure of shaping the greatest triumph-against-adversity story that the Becaran Races has ever seen. Or I will have the entertainment of watching you destroy yourself in the effort. Either way, I will not be bored. And boredom, my dear, is the greatest enemy of all."

Tamra stared at her for a moment, speechless. *That wins for the most horrible thing I've heard a human say to another, at least recently.* How empty did your soul have to be to take joy in the destruction of another's hopes and dreams?

How rich did you have to be?

"Well?" Lady Evara asked. "This is a onetime offer. There are other river leeches who desire my money too, you know, especially in this time of uncertainty, and they may prove even more entertaining than you. Come, Tamra, will you seize your destiny and dare the sands once again?" There was a mocking lilt to her voice, but her eyes were fixed on Tamra like a jackal on its prey.

Gathering her dignity, Tamra tried not to feel as if she were making a deal with a kehok. "I accept your offer, Gracious One."

"Splendid!" Lady Evara beamed at her. Like her laugh, her smile vanished as quickly as it had come. "Now leave, and don't break anything—or anyone—on your way out."

Tamra gritted her teeth against the insult. "The gold pieces?"

"Oh, I don't handle such trifling amounts myself. One of my servants will meet you by the gate with my tokens." She made a shooing motion with her hand.

Tamra held on to her manners. Barely. "May your next rebirth bring you peace." Silently, she added, *Even though I'm certain you'll be reborn as a river slug.*

CHAPTER 3

Tamra traveled by river to the famed Gea Market. She both heard and smelled the market long before she saw it: the sound of the musicians' drums, the cheers from the gambling pits, the pervasive scent of garlic and the irresistible smell of baked pastries. Closer, she joined the other passengers near the front of the riverboat to see the riot of colors come into view.

Unlike her home city of Peron, where every building had white walls and blue-tiled roofs, Gea Market boasted buildings painted in every color under the sun, and between the poppy-red and sky-blue houses were clusters of tents made from rich purple, green, and gold fabrics. It was all so bright and beautiful that it made Tamra's eyes ache.

Shalla would have loved this.

She used to come with Tamra, before the augurs swooped in and changed their lives. Tamra would sneak her out of her reading and math lessons, and they'd travel together on the ferry. Shalla would point out everything she thought was interesting: the smooth curve of a hippo beneath the water, a stick floating by that looked like a crocodile, a man who wore bracelets from his wrists to his armpits, a woman with a leashed monkey on her shoulder that might have once been the woman's cousin. At the market, Shalla would be running in a dozen directions at once, so much to look at and see that she'd collapse exhausted in Tamra's arms before the sun was at its zenith, and they'd squeeze themselves into an unused bit of shade and rest until Shalla was ready to run and point and shout again. Often, they wouldn't even buy anything—it was just the joy and the spectacle that made the trip worthwhile.

Now, as she was jostled by other passengers eager to taste the wonders of the marketplace, she disembarked the ferry with a very different sense of purpose. Most of her fellow shoppers would return home with far less than they'd come with, but they'd be sticky with honey and bone-weary with dancing and draped in silks they didn't need and didn't mean to buy, and they'd be happy.

She wasn't looking for happiness, though.

She needed a miracle.

Specifically a two-hundred-gold-piece miracle.

After giving her name to the dockmaster, Tamra strode through the market, weaving between flocks of laughing customers, vendors hawking fragrant perfume vials, and dancers who'd tied bells to their wrists and ankles. Everywhere vendors sold tokens in the shape of birds and animals to honor one's ancestors, as well as lucky charms said to brighten one's aura (which there was no evidence actually worked). She evaded the usual pickpockets, keeping a tight grip on her purse with Lady Evara's tokens. A thief wouldn't get much use out of them without Lady Evara's approval, but the hassle of having them replaced would take time Tamra didn't have (and earn further ire from her patron). The auction closed at sundown, and she intended to spend every minute seeking out the best bargain.

The market had other ideas, though, and even the focused found themselves distracted. As she neared a purple tent selling jewelry, she saw a customer shove the shop owner. The owner grabbed a hammer used for pounding silver flat and waved it at the customer, who was screaming in his face about higher prices. The owner screamed back that the increase wasn't his fault—instead he blamed everyone else under the sun: the River-blasted trade agreements were on hold because the River-blasted emperor-to-be, Prince Dar, couldn't sign, and the corrupt Ranirans were milking the mess for every coin they could, and on and on . . . A crowd began to gather, making it impossible for Tamra to pass. She looked for another way around, trying to worm her way backward.

I don't have time for this!

As the crowd began to join the shouting, the market guards converged, bringing with them an augur. The robe-clad augur, with his pendant displayed, weaved through the crowd, murmuring to the men and women, calming them. You didn't misbehave when there was an augur nearby to bear witness—which made them excellent at diffusing escalating situations. The holy presence was enough to remind people to do better, to be the best version of themselves, for the sake of their future lives.

"Be as peaceful as the heron," the augur said. "Let your anger wash beneath you. Anger is an unworthy emotion, born of powerlessness. Choose instead to embrace your own inner strength and find serenity . . ."

Thanks to the augur and his string of crowd-soothing platitudes, Tamra was able to squeeze by.

Someday that could be Shalla, she thought. She wasn't sure how she felt about that—no, that wasn't true. Shalla would be an amazing augur. Even without a robe and pendant, she already made Tamra want to be a better person.

Halfway across the market, Tamra smelled the auction—the stench of kehok was unmistakable, undercutting even the sweetest baked goods. She heard the shrill screams of the trapped beasts, the shouts of the owners trying to keep them from savaging potential customers, and the crash of the kehoks thrashing against their cages and shackles.

The kehok auction was marked with black flags embroidered with the symbol of the Becaran Races, the victory charm given to the winning kehok. Imbued with rare and complex magic, the kind that few (if any) understood, much less mastered, the Becaran victory charm allowed the winner to do what no other monster could: be reborn as human.

Without the charm, kehoks were only ever reborn as kehoks, nature-defying monsters sired by muck and filth, who sprang into the world fully grown and deadly. It was an endless punishment for the worst of souls.

Tamra had the likeness of the victory charm tattooed on her right shoulder. It looked like a blue ring around a golden sun, to represent the life-giving River Aur that circles the world and the death-granting sun that scorches everything. It was faded now, after years of sun exposure, but she liked that—its age proved her decades-long commitment to the races. She wore a shirt that bared her shoulders to show off the tattoo to the sellers at the auction. She hoped it would dissuade those who thought she was a newbie they could cheat.

I can do this, she told herself. She was experienced. She

was wise. She was shrewd. She was . . . never going to find what she needed for two hundred gold pieces. Really, this was a hopeless task.

Shalla . . .

Squaring her shoulders, Tamra plunged into the auction.

Cage after cage lined the street, some of them stacked three or four tall, each with a kehok raging inside. A few slept, clearly drugged into complacency, but most were left alert to show off their strength and presumable speed.

The auction was far more chaotic than the word implied—there was no auctioneer or orderly presentation of beasts, like at one of the farm auctions. Instead, everyone was buying and selling all at once, deals made beneath the screams of the monsters. With the start of the races only a few weeks away, it was especially busy. The sellers scooted between the cages, shouting the statistics for each of their creatures: height, weight, age, number of races run, number of races won. You wanted fast and strong, with a will that could be bent without breaking.

The stronger the kehok, the harder to control, but the greater the payoff if the rider was skilled enough. It was a balance—what you thought you could train versus what would kill you.

Tamra skipped over the kehoks who had already proven themselves in races. Those would be automatically out of her price range. She let the other trainers haggle over them. She also skipped the ones whose sellers promised obedience. Those were fine for students, lousy for winners. She needed a kehok with fire in its soul.

A seller grabbed her arm. "I know who you are and what you want." His breath was rancid, stinking of overripe fish, and his fingers were as greasy as a sausage.

"I want your hand off of me," Tamra said, yanking back hard enough that the seller stumbled. He recovered quickly and launched into his sales pitch, but Tamra was already walking on.

She ignored the whispers around her and the swirl of gossip. The seller hadn't been the only one to recognize her, clearly. But it didn't matter what he or anyone said—she knew she wasn't going to buy from the likes of him. So eager to sell, he'd tell any lie about his kehoks.

She was on the lookout for a particular kind of seller. One that didn't want to be at the auction. One that didn't care about the sale as much as the hunt. One just like . . . him. Tamra set her sights on an overmuscled man with three cages behind him. He wasn't calling out to any of the shoppers. In fact, his arms were crossed over his beefy chest, and he was glaring at the potential customers as if daring them to come closer.

This was the kind of man who saw the kehoks as prizes to be won. The kind who trapped the most terrifying monsters he could find without any regard to their tractability. He didn't care if anyone bought his kehoks for a decent price. He just cared that everyone admired the fact that he'd caught such vicious brutes. *Presumably by himself, barehanded, with his eyes shut and while hopping on one foot.*

Coming closer, she eyed his prizes: three vicious bruisers. One was slick with slime, dripping from its jaws and the ripples in its thick, scarred skin. Another was a two-legged beast that wore skin covered in spikes from its neck down to a deadly-looking tail that terminated in a ball of flesh with spikes as long as Tamra's arm. The third was a massive lion. It was sheathed in black scales instead of tawny fur, its mane looked as if it were made from black metal, and its tail was split into three muscular whips.

"Which one's your strongest?" she asked.

He pointed to the third, the metallic-black lion. "Killed a man."

"While you were hunting him?" So, not by himself. And probably not while hopping on one foot either.

"Yesterday, at the market."

She didn't want a known killer. Once they had a taste for human death, more often than not it became their sole obsession. You couldn't race a beast that cared only about death. The desire to cause death was too closely linked to the desire to feel it. Dismissing the black lion, Tamra moved on to the spiked kehok. "Has this one been tested with a saddle?"

"No."

Not exactly practical for racing. She wasn't certain how a saddle would fit between the spikes. The hunter had clearly caught this one just for the fun of it.

As she stepped forward for a closer look at its back full of spikes, the two-legged kehok swung its macelike tail at the cage bars. *CRACK*. It hit hard, but the bars held. Expecting it, Tamra didn't flinch.

Behind her, she heard the gasps of other shoppers.

She ignored them and moved on to the kehok that oozed with its own goo. She wasn't bothered by the thick layer of slime, though she thought it would take a special kind of rider to sit in that filth every day for hours at a time. It wouldn't matter, though, if the beast could win. You can get used to anything if it'll bring you what you want.

She suppressed a grin, imagining what the augurs would

say about that sentiment. You were supposed to always seek to better yourself, but they probably never thought that meant subjecting yourself to daily goo.

Walking around the cage, Tamra examined each of its limbs. "Uneven legs," she noted. One hind leg had bunches of muscles, while the other seemed to be shriveled.

The seller grunted. She couldn't tell if that was agreement or an objection, or if he was just grunting at the heat or the stench or a hundred other things.

"This one didn't outrun you," she guessed.

"Caught up to it quickly. Problem was caging it. See the ooze? Burns to the touch."

"You're going to have trouble selling that one."

He shrugged. "All of them are trouble. Be slaughtering them after the auction. Hunt them down again in their new bodies. Might fetch better prices next time around. Plus it's how I test myself against them. I win if I re-catch them."

"You know odds are they won't remember you, right?" Except in rare cases, you couldn't remember your past lives. Restoring your memory of your past life usually required extensive exposure to your old home and family. Most never got that chance. It was a circle: you couldn't remember who you'd been, so you didn't return to where you'd remember, so you couldn't remember . . . and so on. This was part of why the augurs were so necessary—they could read both your past and future for you, and tell you whether you were on the right route or not. In the case of kehoks, who'd forfeited all rights to improving their fate, that amnesia was most likely a blessing.

Another shrug. "*I* remember. And the augurs back me up, when the market recordkeepers use them to do their tallies. Caught that one"—he nodded to the spiked kehok—"fifteen times."

She didn't want a kehok who could be caught so easily. Or one that would burn its rider. Reluctantly, she returned to the first kehok, the black-scaled lion. "And this one?"

"Augur hasn't been by to read it yet. Most of them have been reassigned to help the guards keep things calm, you know? Can't afford to have the market shut down. But I don't need any augur to tell me about this monster. First time catching it. It's got so I can tell—this is this one's first spin as a kehok. Might be why it's so full of rage. It took me three days to track it down, and the clever thing turned the tables on me—I would've been food for its stomach if I hadn't carried Ebzer." He patted the sword at his hilt.

Cute. He names his blades.

"How much?" she asked.

His eyes widened. "You don't want to buy him."

"I might." She crossed her arms. "Depends on the price."

"Told you he killed a man when we were moving him in here. Gored him trying to escape. He'll gore you too, given half the chance."

She said nothing, but continued to study the kehok. He was one of the strongest kehoks she'd ever seen, with leg muscles that looked as if they could kick down a tree in one blow. He'd be fast. Very fast. And it made a difference that he'd killed in an escape attempt, not purely out of a desire for violence—there was a chance he hadn't yet acquired a love of death.

He was watching her with golden eyes that held a hint of intelligence.

Intelligent kehoks could win races.

"Killed a man, you said?"

The seller nodded vigorously. "He has the heart of a killer. Must have been a murderer in his last life." Most of the lion-shaped kehoks had a predatory history, so Tamra wasn't surprised to hear that.

"He won't kill or gore me," Tamra said, pinning the kehok with her gaze. "I won't give him the chance." *You might be strong*, she said with her eyes, *but I'm stronger*. "One hundred gold pieces."

"Nuh-uh, a kehok this size? Least one thousand."

Tamra snorted. Seriously? He was trying to bargain with her, after first trying to talk her out of it? Looking at the seller, she could tell his heart wasn't in it. He was saying it because he thought he should be saying it. A hunter, not a businessman. He needed to partner with someone if he wanted to make any money. But it wasn't her job to tell him how to do his. "A killer kehok that no one has proven can be controlled? A kehok you plan to kill at sunset anyway? Anything I give you is more than he's worth. One hundred fifty, plus you throw in the cage." She'd need the cage to bring him home. She doubted she'd be able to control him on a crowded riverboat, not with zero time to train him.

"Can't figure out if you're stupid or crazy to want him at all."

Neither, she thought. *I'm desperate.* "I know what I want. And I get it."

That was a lie, but it was one she told herself daily. It made her feel as if her fate were more in her hands, rather than subject to the whims of those more powerful than she was and their rigid laws and traditions, and taxes, fines, and fees.

"Meet me at two hundred, and he's yours."

"One hundred seventy-five *and* the cage." She needed some left over to tempt a rider, though there was no rider with any level of experience who would be enticed by that low a starter fee. She could be stuck with a rider who was no more skilled than her paying students. And look how well *that* had turned out.

The seller spat on his hand and held it out.

She shook it and handed over Lady Evara's tokens.

She turned to the kehok. "You're mine," she told him.

He bared his lion teeth, each one as deadly as a knife. She understood him as clearly as if he'd spoken: *Then I am your death.*

"Your need to kill me is not greater than my need to use you," Tamra informed the kehok.

She thought she saw him flinch, but she must have imagined it. Kehoks were smart, but she didn't think he could have understood that.

Bargaining again with the seller, she arranged for him to transport the kehok to the riverboat docks. That required a bit more of Lady Evara's gold. Securing passage for her patron's newest purchase would require more. And she still needed a rider—one who had the strength of will to tame a creature as wild as this one. But Tamra felt more hopeful than she had in days.

Maybe I've found my miracle.

Or my death.

Either way, things were going to change.

CHAPTER 4

Hidden behind a stack of crates, Raia watched the trainer bargain for the killer kehok. She didn't need to hide to stay unnoticed—she wasn't the type of person whom anyone noticed, especially in a market. She was seventeen years old, old enough to be in Gea Market without parents but not old enough to be taken seriously as a buyer. Ordinary height, with a pretty but unmemorable face, nice enough skin, her black hair styled in multiple braids that were only just beginning to unravel. She'd picked clothes that were clean and simple—clothes that said both "I'm not worth kidnapping" and "Of course I didn't run away from my family and my future." But she hid out of habit anyway.

It was something she'd gotten far too good at lately.

Like stealing fruit.

A grapefruit weighed down one of her pockets, tugging at her tunic as well as her conscience. Raia knew what her former teachers would say about theft, but, she reminded herself yet again, they weren't here, and her stomach was.

She'd have time to balance out the harm she'd done to her soul *after* she did what she came here to do, which was to find a new future for herself.

And also find someplace not completely terrifying to sleep tonight, she thought.

Last night she'd bedded down in a toolshed behind an overcrowded house outside Gea Market. She'd woken every few minutes, convinced every creak and crack in the night was someone coming out to the shed in search of a trowel for a bit of late-night, can't-wait-until-morning gardening. She hadn't been caught. But she certainly hadn't slept well.

At dawn, when the market opened, she'd screwed up her courage and started approaching trainers. All morning, she'd tried. All morning, she'd failed. One look at her—her unmuscled arms and her uncalloused palms—and they'd turned away. She couldn't blame them. With all the uncertainty in Becar these days, no one wanted to take any kind of risk. The continued lack of an emperor was putting everyone on edge. But this trainer felt different.

Tamra Verlas.

Raia knew who she was, of course. Everyone did. She recognized the tattoo and the scar, even the way she walked.

The cursed trainer.

Last flood season, Trainer Verlas had made a mistake in one of the final races—given bad advice or . . . the rumors hadn't been clear on what exactly she'd done. Only that it was her fault that her rider and his kehok had died, as well as several other riders and even a few bystanders. It had been such a dramatic disaster that it was said she'd never sponsor a winner again. She'd been reduced to training the children of the wealthy, for their amusement, in one of the many low-end training facilities.

Yet here she was, at the market, clearly buying a racer.

Talk to her, Raia encouraged herself.

If Trainer Verlas needed a new racer, maybe she needed a new rider.

And if that's the case, maybe she'll be desperate enough to pick me.

Studying the trainer, though, Raia didn't think that was likely to happen. She didn't look like the kind to make decisions out of desperation.

Well, then maybe I'm desperate enough to make her pick me.

Cursed or not, this woman had trained a rider who'd nearly won the Becaran Races. Her racing style was said to have been unique, and her training style supposedly matched that. Unique enough to train a newbie? All Raia needed to do was win a few races. Not the whole thing. The prize money from just a few wins, even a string of minor races, should be enough . . .

But how to impress Tamra Verlas, when she'd never impressed anyone in her life? Especially not someone as impressive as the trainer.

Raia watched as Trainer Verlas approached the killer kehok with no fear. Her face, which Raia could see in profile, was placid. Her arms hung by her sides, muscles loose. She didn't look prepared to defend herself or jump out of the way. If the kehok attacked . . . Even from within his cage, he could do some damage.

Raia couldn't hope to ever look that fearless. She felt full of fear every second of every day, so much fear that sometimes she thought she'd choke on it. She felt fear right now, *for* Trainer Verlas.

The kehok bared his lion teeth, each tooth the size of

Raia's hand, and she felt prickles walk all over her skin. *Why am I even considering this? This is crazy!* She didn't know anything about racing, and she'd never even met anyone who'd ridden one of the monsters. There had to be another way to come up with enough gold to appease her family.

Except there wasn't. Not quickly. And not with her lack of any kind of useful skills.

She knew what was said: *Anyone can become a rider.* And what was also said: *But only those who don't fear death dare try.*

Raia did fear death, of course.

I just fear other things more.

She heard the trainer say to the kehok, "Your need to kill me is not greater than my need to use you." It wasn't said as a threat—Raia knew very well what those sounded like—and it wasn't a boast either. Trainer Verlas spoke as if she were stating a fact.

And Raia knew what she had to do.

I have to prove my *need.*

Taking a deep breath, she slunk out of her hiding place. No one noticed her. No one even glanced at her. She crossed the stream of people flowing in both directions past the cages. Her legs shook as if they were made of custard, but she didn't stop. She walked past the seller and Trainer Verlas. She kept her eyes fixed on the golden eyes of the black lion— the one everyone was calling the killer kehok.

He watched her like a cat watches his prey.

Alert. Amused. Hungry.

She felt her heart thump faster and harder, as if it wanted to burst out of her rib cage. It was beating so hard it nearly hurt. Her palms were sweating, and she knew she must look as terrified as she felt.

But it didn't matter what she felt. Because she *had* to do this. It was her best chance at freedom from her family and from a life she didn't want. And she wasn't going to let this opportunity slip away, no matter how scared she felt, no matter how bad an idea it was. Because it was her *only* idea.

Raia halted in front of the cage. Behind her, she dimly heard the seller barking at her to get back, it wasn't safe. She ignored him. She ignored all the buzzing and chatter, the cries and the thumps and the screams from the other cages. She focused only on the kehok.

"You won't kill me," she said softly, "because you need me as much as I need you."

She expected him to try to maul her. She was tense, ready to run—unlike Trainer Verlas—and she couldn't pretend to be otherwise. If the kehok swiped at her with those massive knife-sharp claws, she'd be a fool not to try to avoid its attack.

The kehok pressed his face closer to the bars, and she felt the sour heat of his breath.

He hasn't killed me yet. That's good, isn't it?

Louder, she said, "You want your freedom as much as I want mine. And the only way they'll ever let you out of this cage alive is if there's a chance you'll win races. And the only way you'll ever win races is if *I'm* your rider." She believed that, because she didn't think there was anyone else in this whole market, maybe in all of Becar, who needed to win badly enough to risk their life like this.

"You, girl? *You* want to be *his* rider?" That was Trainer Verlas, behind her.

If Raia hadn't been standing just a few inches from a killer, she'd have jumped on the chance to convince the trainer that yes, she was serious, and yes, she would work hard, and yes, she was ready, and *yes yes yes*—she'd said that speech a dozen times today already.

But this time . . . it wasn't the trainer she had to convince. It was the monster.

Win him, and she'd win the trainer.

She understood that instinctively. And she'd learned to trust her instincts, like she did a few weeks ago when she got the very strong sense to climb out her window and down the trellis and hide in the shadows of the topiary garden. . . . Those instincts hadn't steered her wrong. Her parents had come through her door only minutes later. She'd watched them, lit by the candles they carried, and seen that they'd brought ropes—ropes!—to tie her up, as if she were a disobedient dog.

But she couldn't think about them now. Only the kehok.

"We're alike, you and I," Raia told him, softly this time. She was aware an audience had gathered behind her. She saw them out of the corners of her eyes. "We both hate cages."

He snorted, almost as if he understood her.

"I have a proposition for you. You don't kill me, and I won't let them kill you. They will, you know. Even *she* won't stop them, if you don't accept a rider. Let me be that rider, and I will make sure you live." Raia took a deep breath and stepped even closer, raising up her hand palm out. Slowly, with every bit of her body screaming at her to flee—and a number of spectators yelling the same thing—she reached in between the bars and laid her hand on the kehok's cheek. It felt as smooth and cool as beaten metal.

Maybe this would work!

The kehok held still.

For about a second and a half.

Then he lunged forward with a horrific roar, and she felt

a strong arm around her waist hauling her back, so fast that she fell to the ground, flat on her back, as the kehok raged against the bars.

"Idiot," Trainer Verlas snarled at her. "You could have lost your arm. Or your life. What were you *thinking*? Are you that eager to start your next life?"

On her back, looking up at the furious trainer framed by the blazing noon sun, Raia felt her heart beating faster than a hummingbird's wings. She felt like screaming, crying, and laughing all at the same time, as four words chased around and around in her head: *I could have died!*

"But I didn't."

"What?"

Meeting Trainer Verlas's eyes, Raia said with as much fake confidence as she could muster, "I was thinking you're going to train me. And I'm going to race the sands."

CHAPTER 5

*B*est part about traveling with a deadly monster, Tamra thought, *is you don't have to chat with idiots.* She paid the dockworkers who maneuvered the kehok cage onto the ferry, then plopped herself down next to her prize and propped her feet up. With a sigh of contentment, she tilted her head back so she felt the warmth of the midday sun caress her face.

Across the ferry, the other twenty or so passengers, mostly north-bank laborers but a few river merchants as well, squeezed together as tightly as they could, leaving a wide patch of empty deck between them and the kehok.

She ignored them.

She also ignored the kehok bashing against the cage bars.

"What should I do?" a nervous voice asked.

Tamra squinted at her. *Oh, right. My new student.* "What did you say your name was?"

"Raia." She was eyeing the kehok as if she expected it to lunge through the bars and swipe at her jugular, which,

Tamra thought, was at least a sign that the girl had some common sense, as the lion would absolutely do that given half a chance. He screamed at them.

"You should ride the ferry, Raia. Like the rest of us." Did she expect to start training instantly? It wasn't a terrible idea. But Tamra's leg was throbbing, her old injury acting up the way it did sometimes, and she still wasn't sure what to make of her new ward.

She watched as Raia's eyes flicked back to the monster, then to the other passengers, then to the receding market, as if she couldn't decide which was more terrifying. The girl adjusted her hood so it shadowed more of her face. *She's hiding from someone,* Tamra thought. *Runaway?*

Probably.

That could be a problem. Especially if whomever she was running from was dangerous. "Why don't you have a seat, make yourself comfortable, and tell me why you're on the run?"

Raia answered promptly, "I didn't run from anywhere. I just don't have a home anymore. I've been orphaned, and my parents didn't set aside enough money for me. The creditors took our home, and I've been looking for a way to support myself."

Poor thing. She must have been practicing that speech for days. She seemed so nervous that Tamra said encouragingly, "You're a good liar. That was plausible."

"I'm not lying!" Raia's voice squeaked, making Tamra even more confident that yes, she was absolutely lying. On the plus side, she hadn't bolted yet.

Granted, it's difficult to bolt when you're in the middle of a river.

The river licked at the sides of the boat. A nice breeze carried the scent of lilies that clustered on the banks. When the breeze faltered, the sails flapped, and the ferryman shoved a pole into the water to push them along. Except for the kehok's horrifically bone-chilling screams, it was peaceful.

"Is he in pain?" Raia asked, unsubtly changing the subject.

"Don't feel sorry for him," Tamra said. "Given half a chance, he'll gore you."

"I can feel sorry for him and fear him at the same time." Raia was gazing into the cage. She'd drifted a few inches closer. "I wonder what terrible thing he did to be reborn like this."

"Calculate the distance from his shoulder to his paw, then double it," Tamra advised.

Raia looked at her blankly.

"Any closer than that, and he'll reach you."

As if to prove her point, the kehok slammed against the cage, rocking it forward, and swiped with his paw. His obsidian claws raked the air as Raia squealed and jumped back.

A few of the other passengers shrieked, huddling closer. A man from within the clump called out, "Hey! We deserve to travel without abominations! We pay our way!"

"We pay more!" Tamra hollered back.

There was a significant extra charge for transporting murderous cargo.

Raia scooted a safe distance away from the cage. Behind her, the other passengers were beginning to grumble about their right to a safe passage. The man in the middle was egging them on, but also, Tamra noticed, keeping about three peoples' worth of buffer between him and the kehok. *Very brave,* she thought. Perhaps he was hoping to spend his next life as a meerkat, hiding within his pack. Around him, the grumbles began to escalate.

Conversationally, Tamra said to Raia, "This happens sometimes. You get one or two scared people, and they'll run from danger. You get a bunch of scared people, and they'll *make* danger."

"You think they'll attack us?" She was quivering, but she didn't retreat behind Tamra. "Even with the harm that will cause their souls?"

"I know they will. Unless we reason with them." Raising her voice louder than the growing mob, Tamra said, "You either have a nice trip with an abomination, or I have a nice trip without *you*." She eyed the lock on the cage, as if she were thinking about opening it. Then she tilted her head so the other passengers couldn't see her mouth move, focused her will on the kehok, and whispered, "Fight."

He went into a frenzy, bashing from side to side in the cage, raking his claws against the bars, throwing his maned head back and roaring loud enough to shake the sail. The other passengers screamed and cowered.

One of them, pushed to the edge, fell into the water with a splash.

"Stop!" Tamra ordered the kehok.

He didn't respond right away, lost in his rage, but she bore her thoughts into him until at last he quieted. Out of the corner of her eye she saw Raia was staring at her. She was glad—and a little surprised—to see that the girl hadn't moved. She continued to stay a safe distance from the black lion's paws, but she hadn't retreated any farther than that.

The kehok backed to the far corner of his cage, crouched, and let out a whimper as if she were hurting him. She switched her attention back to the passengers—they'd fished the one who had fallen overboard out of the water and were clustered around her, comforting her. A few shot Tamra terrified, hate-filled looks, but the fire that had fueled the near-mob had been quenched.

In a soft voice, Raia asked, "*That* was reasoning with them?"

"Absolutely. I gave them a reason to behave themselves."

A grin—so fleeting that Tamra wasn't entirely sure she saw it—flickered across Raia's face; then she went back to staring at the kehok. *She has a sense of humor,* Tamra thought. *One more thing in her favor.*

There may be hope for her.

But common sense and the ability to take a joke weren't the only things. Tamra needed Raia to have hidden strength. Certainly the girl didn't have much in the way of visible strength. She was scrawny. Zero muscles. Soft skin. Whatever put her on the streets was recent. She didn't look like someone who'd been born to the kind of life Tamra had known. On instinct, Tamra commanded, "Show me your hands."

Raia startled like a hare in the grasses.

"Your hands. Palms up."

Raia held out her hands, and Tamra studied them. Soft, no calluses and no scars. No surprises. Ink stains between two of her fingers. Her wrists were just bone—Tamra could have wrapped one finger around them. A rich girl. Or at least well-off. Educated enough to write. Definitely a runaway. Tamra judged her to be about seventeen years old, give or take a year. *Old enough to know to run away from a bad situation,* she thought, *but not old enough to know where to run to.* "Your hands won't be as pretty by the end of this."

"I don't need pretty hands," Raia said.

"What do you need?" Tamra asked.

"Teach me how to do that." Raia nodded at the cage, where the kehok lurked, glaring at them with his golden eyes, waiting for them to show weakness. "You controlled him. How did you do it?"

"Tell me the truth about why you're running, and I'll give you your first lesson."

Raia was silent, and for a moment, Tamra thought she wasn't going to answer. But then the girl spoke in a voice so soft it was nearly swallowed up by the waves of the river. "I was told I was to be an augur, that I'd been identified by my aura as one who was worthy enough to be blessed with the power of inner sight. I didn't choose it. They chose me. That's how it always is, I guess. They said I was going to do wonderful things, that it was my destiny, because of the purity of my soul from my prior life. My parents were so proud."

"I'm sure they were." Tamra kept her voice neutral, but inside she began to calculate how quickly she could pay Raia's ferry fare to send her as far from Shalla as possible. If Raia had run from the augurs . . . *I can't harbor a fugitive from the augurs while my daughter is in training!*

At best, Tamra could give her a head start. There was a little leftover gold from Lady Evara—not much, but a few tokens could buy Raia a bit of distance.

She'd never heard of an augur trainee running from their duty before. It wasn't supposed to be part of their makeup. But Raia was right that trainees had no choice, and it wasn't an easy life. If Shalla had ever wanted to run, Tamra would have helped her, never mind the cost to her soul. She'd do the same for Raia. *Just . . . she can't stay here.*

"As it turns out, I wasn't special enough. After four

years, I was still failing to master the basic skills. So they cut me loose. Returned me to my parents as unteachable. Said they'd expected me to fulfill the potential they'd read in me, but unfortunately, I'd failed to become the kind of student I was supposed to be."

Tamra breathed again.

The augurs weren't the ones after her.

"So why run away?"

"Because my parents want their money back. All the gold they spent for my tuition since I was chosen. They want me to repay them. Since I have no money of my own—I was a student, so how could I have any?—they want to recoup their loss by marrying me to a man who'll pay for the privilege." She spat out the words as if they tasted rank.

Tamra had heard of such things happening—children treated as commodities, essentially sold into marriage, trading their future for their family's comfort—but she hadn't met anyone who'd experienced it. Hearing Raia's story made her wish that Raia's parents were here so she could unleash her kehok on them. Not to hurt them, of course, since that was strictly illegal, as well as immoral. *But, oh, I could scare them!*

"I take it this isn't a man you want to marry." She tried to keep the rage out of her voice—Raia seemed to be having a hard enough time telling her story as it was. She hadn't once made eye contact with Tamra. All her attention was on the shimmering river. An egret skimmed low over the ripples, its white feathers bright against the blue.

"He's not a man anyone should marry," Raia said. "Rumors say he beat his last wife to death. Of course my parents say not to believe rumors. He wasn't read by any augur after her death—her family had no money to pay for one, and there wasn't enough evidence to force one. So he's innocent, in their eyes. And wealthy."

"For the record, your parents are selfish and evil and have placed themselves on the path to be reborn as kehoks. Or at least dung beetles."

So much for not showing her rage.

Raia flashed her a bit of a smile. It faded quickly. "I told them I'd rather die than marry him. But the truth is that I'd rather live and not marry him. So that's why I'm with you. If I can earn enough money through the races, then I can repay my parents every cent they paid the augurs. They'll cancel the engagement. And I'll be free."

"Good," Tamra said fiercely.

At last Raia met her eyes. "What part of that is 'good'?"

"It means you have enough fire to face the sands," Tamra said. "It means I can teach you to win. You asked me how I controlled the black lion. It's as simple as this: I wanted it more than he wanted it." She watched Raia's face to see if she understood that. Everyone acted as if they got it, but only a few understood it in a bone-deep way—only the ones who truly *wanted* to seize control of their lives. "Any idiot can command a kehok, if they can learn to focus their thoughts. The trick is that you need to be fully in the moment. You can't think about the past, the future, what you ate for breakfast this morning, whether you'll eat breakfast tomorrow. . . . Most people can't do that, especially not for any extended length of time. Minds are unruly things, and most can't control theirs—and if you can't control yourself, you can't control a kehok. That's why you don't see kehoks used for labor. Or war."

Many had tried. It rarely went well.

You needed a fire inside you, the kind that kept you passionately invested in the here and now, the kind that made you want to shape what was happening rather than letting it shape you. Tamra had seen a glimpse of that fire inside Raia back at Gea Market. The key would be if Raia could call on that determination even when she wasn't in desperate need. "You'll help me unload the kehok," Tamra decided.

"But I can't lift—"

"There's a winch to lift the cage from the boat to the dock. Then we'll walk him from the dock to the stables. Or more accurately, you will."

Raia stared at her.

Looking at her expression, Tamra laughed.

"Good, you're joking." Raia sagged in relief. "I thought you meant you were going to unlock the cage and let him out."

"Oh, that is exactly what I meant. It's just your expression was hilarious."

JUST BEFORE SUNSET, THE FERRY DOCKED AT THE TRAINing grounds. Tamra helped the ferryman use the winch to swing the cage with the black lion from the boat to the dock, and then she watched as he booked it back into the middle of the river as fast as he could pole.

From the dock, she waved cheerfully at the remaining passengers. None of them were getting off until Tamra, Raia, and the kehok were as far away as possible.

They didn't wave back.

"Exactly how do we do this?" Raia asked.

"Carefully."

Tamra was confident she could train this kehok to be a racer and equally confident that she could transform a determined girl like Raia into a competent rider. But she didn't expect to accomplish either before nightfall. "Also, we'll use chains."

Crossing to a box, she opened it and hauled out one of the special kehok nets, made out of iron chains, that all racers wore. Tamra felt a throbbing in her leg and an ache in her back—the net weighed more than she did—as she hooked it up to a set of pulleys and raised it above the entrance to the cage.

It was a maneuver she'd done dozens of times. Each time got a little harder. Someday she wouldn't be able to do it at all. She refused to think about that day.

As she caught her breath, the kehok watched her with unblinking eyes.

"Here's what's going to happen," she told the kehok. "I am going to open the cage door. You are going to run forward, thinking this is your chance to escape, I'll drop the net on you, thereby ruining all your dreams of freedom, and then we're all going to proceed to the stable." She didn't expect him to understand all of that, but it helped focus her thoughts.

"And what do you need me to do?" Raia asked.

"Conquer your fear." Tamra approached the cage. The kehok was eyeing her as if he were far more interested in mauling her than allowing her to chain him. "And call him to you."

"Do *what*?"

Most kehoks would be happy to be presented with a willing target—he'd forget about the danger of the net in his eagerness to reach Raia.

"Call to him," Tamra repeated.

"I can't do that and not be afraid!"

Tamra rolled her eyes. "I didn't say *banish* your fear. I

said *conquer* it. You are right to fear the kehoks. They will always be stronger, faster, and far more deadly than you, and given the opportunity, they will kill you. Only idiots stop being afraid of what can kill them. Dead idiots. You shouldn't stop being afraid. But you shouldn't let your fear control you. Choose to be brave. Stand there. Don't run. And call to him."

Without waiting for a response, Tamra turned to the kehok. "Go to Raia. Go to the girl." She kept repeating the command—silently now, concentrating on it as if it were all she wanted in the world—as she unhooked the lock on the cage. Kicking the door open, she sprang back, ready to dive into the river if need be.

But the kehok didn't move.

Catlike, he lay down inside his cage.

A minute passed.

Then another.

"Call him," Tamra told Raia.

"Come to me," Raia said weakly.

River protect us . . .

"Like you mean it."

Raia clenched her fists, planted her feet wide, and commanded, "Come!"

Go to her, Tamra pushed.

He shifted his weight onto his hind legs, like a cat in the bushes about to hunt. She tensed, ready to leap toward the pulley. *Go,* Tamra thought. She ignored the niggling worry: it shouldn't be this hard to command him. Her order alone should have been enough to compel the beast. She'd controlled plenty of resistant kehoks before and never had trouble. Or at least rarely had trouble.

Something's wrong, a voice inside Tamra whispered.

Firmly, she pushed the doubt away. It had no place when dealing with kehoks.

"Come! Now!" Raia called.

The black lion launched himself forward with a furious roar. Tamra lunged for the pulley, smacked the release, and braced herself as the iron net plummeted down.

It landed with a smack on the kehok, the surprise of the sudden weight dropping him to the ground and pinning him to the dock. *Perfect*, Tamra thought. She hurried to him as the kehok pushed up onto his feet.

Grabbing one of the dangling chains, Tamra pulled, and the net tightened. It squeezed over his face and around his legs. The kehok net was a special design: it worked both to muzzle a kehok's jaws and hamper his movements. It wasn't heavy enough to stop them, but it was enough to slow them.

"Tell him to follow," Tamra said to Raia.

"Follow," Raia said in a quavering voice.

He chewed on the chains, trying to gnaw through the iron, but while he was focusing on freeing himself, he wasn't resisting their commands. He shuffled after them toward the stables.

It was slow, and Tamra was very aware that the net wasn't a perfect solution. Many a trainer and rider had died while a kehok was in chains, thinking they were safe. With a monster this strong, if his need to attack them overrode his need to be free of the net, they'd be in danger. And so they proceeded slowly, calmly, and alertly until they reached the stables.

Inside, the other kehoks screamed, sensing their approach.

That caught the attention of the black lion. He quit chewing on the chains. A low growl started in the back of his throat. *Oh, sweet Lady.* She'd hoped they could get him all the way in before he noticed. It usually worked.

Tamra quickly grabbed a hook from the wall of the stable. As the lion began to retreat, she latched the hook onto a loop of chain. "Grab one!" she called to Raia.

Raia obeyed, taking a second hook and sticking the end into the net.

Both of them leaned back, pulling the kehok toward the stable.

But the kehok was stronger. Still retreating, it dragged them away from the stables, their heels plowing through the dirt. *By the River, this isn't working!* Her back and leg muscles were sending lightning bolts of pain through her body as she pulled. Soon, they'd give out.

"A little help here!" Tamra called. It grated on her to call for help when she normally could control any kehok, but the alternative was worse, and she had an untrained rider who could be hurt. She only hoped—

Two trainers came running. *Of course they were watching,* Tamra thought. *I should've guessed I'd have an audience for this.* But she couldn't complain, given that they *did* come to help, even though they'd waited for her to humiliate herself before coming to her aid. Truthfully, though, it shouldn't have been necessary. She must be too distracted with her own worries about Shalla and the future to focus properly.

She renewed her attention on the kehok.

Grabbing additional hooks, the two other trainers also latched onto the net. The four of them, inch by inch, dragged the kehok toward the stable.

While they pulled, Tamra pressed her thoughts against his. *Come. Obey.*

She felt his will weaken as they slowly overpowered him.

Keeping the pressure on his mind, they dragged him into an open stall. Tamra clamped the chains to the wall, shackling him. He lay beneath the net, snarling at them, as they slammed the door shut. One of the other trainers locked it.

That should not have been so difficult, Tamra thought again, as the whisper of doubt wormed back into her mind. *Focus, Tamra. You're better than this.* She'd once controlled five kehoks at the same time! Just one shouldn't have even been a challenge. Bending over now, however, she worked to catch her breath. She ached everywhere and knew she'd pushed her body too far. She'd never had so much trouble bringing a kehok into a stable, especially one in chains.

Maybe this was a mistake.

"That is not a racer," one of the other trainers, Osir, proclaimed. He'd been a trainer for a decade longer than Tamra and thought he was at least two decades wiser. He always spoke as if pearls of wisdom were dripping from his bulbous lips. He'd disapproved of Tamra and her methods from the moment they'd met. Tamra wished she could have picked a day when he wasn't working to bring in her new prize.

"He will be," Tamra said.

"No chance. You can tell. He's got the kind of will you can't bend. At best, you break him. But right, you don't like to break your monsters. You've got a 'better way.'" He waved his fingers in the air, as if he thought her "way" was no better than a sleight-of-hand magic trick.

"It works for me," Tamra said through gritted teeth.

"Until it doesn't. Mark my words: you don't have a racer here. You have a killer."

The second trainer, a woman named Zora, nodded firmly. When Tamra had first arrived at the training ground,

Zora had offered to share use of her kehoks. She withdrew her offer after realizing Tamra was *that* trainer and hadn't spoken to her since. Despite running to her aid just now, neither Osir nor Zora qualified as supportive colleagues, which was fine.

I don't need friends, Tamra thought. *I need to win.*

"My new student, Raia," Tamra said, introducing her. "This is Trainer Osir and Trainer Zora. They also have use of this training facility. You won't have much interaction with them, though, because they have their own students." She wanted to add, "Also, they have the souls of roaches," but she refrained. After all, they had just helped her.

Raia bowed her head. "Honored to meet you."

Zora snorted.

Osir slapped a hand down on Raia's shoulder. "Your new trainer won't break kehoks. But she won't hesitate to break you. Watch yourself."

Tamra expected Raia to murmur a polite response. It was what a well-educated rich student would have done. It was also what a poor just-off-the-streets student would have done. But instead, Raia met his eyes and said softly but firmly, "It's why I chose her. I don't break easily."

Tamra didn't even try to hide her smile.

CHAPTER 6

Per Trainer Verlas's orders, Raia spent the night in the stable, which was not at all what she'd been hoping for, after a string of terrified nights spent hidden in sheds, alleys, and abandoned houses. She'd wanted a nice cot in a quiet corner inside a house.

The stable was definitely not that.

She was supposed to work on conquering her fear. Not banishing it. Just dealing with it as a constant that didn't have any power over her. *Easier said than done,* Raia thought. But at least she had a roof over her head and didn't need to worry about being run off by the stable's owner or a city guard, which was an improvement.

And it wasn't as if she had to sleep in a stall. There was an office off the stable that boasted a cot and a washbasin. It even had a cabinet stocked with sausage rolls for her dinner and fruit for her breakfast.

The only flaw was all the monsters on the other side of the wall.

How did I get myself into this?

She was supposed to be on track to becoming an augur, her future assured. The fact that it wasn't a future she wanted was less important than the fact that it would provide her with wealth, security, and comfort—or so her family had repeated ad nauseum. Maybe in a past life, she'd earned her place with the augurs, but she didn't remember that existence, and she wasn't that person anymore. Her parents had never understood that.

What would they do if they could see me now?

She knew the answer to that. *Haul me back in chains as if I'm a kehok. Toss me in a house that might as well be a locked stable and tell me to breed.*

It was better here, even with the horrors that slept only a few feet away. Even if she had no idea how she was ever going to control the one that was supposed to be hers, much less ride him. *I'll learn,* she promised herself.

Lying on the cot, Raia slept fitfully—every time a kehok screamed, she woke convinced her family had found her. She fell back asleep grateful it was just a monster, only waking permanently when dawn poked its way through the dusty windows.

She washed as best she could with the shallow basin of water and dressed in the student rider clothes that Trainer Verlas had left for her: a durable tunic and rough leggings that scraped at her skin. The tunic was scarlet red. To hide the bloodstains?

Don't think like that, she told herself.

She'd chosen this life—the first time she'd chosen her own path—and she wasn't going to panic just because the outfit was ominously colored. She could do this.

That burst of confidence got her out of the office and into the stable . . . and then it abandoned her.

Raia felt as if she were being smothered in screams—horrible, bone-cutting screams that ricocheted through her veins and filled her skull. Inside their stalls, the kehoks raged, smashing against their walls, tugging at their shackles, and squealing as if they were being skewered. For a long moment, she stood just inside the door, her ears too flooded with sound to move as the kehoks bashed against their stall walls and strained against their chains.

All of them except the black lion.

He stood in the center of his stall, the net of heavy chains draped around him, shackled to the wall. He was motionless, but his eyes followed her as she crossed toward his stall door. She stopped several feet shy of it.

"Why aren't you screaming? Not that I want you to. You can stay as silent as you want." She didn't think he could hear her over the others, even if he could have understood her. Yet he was looking at her as if he followed every word.

"What did you do to be reborn like this?" Raia asked. "You're lionlike, so you must have hunted the innocent in your past life. Were you a murderer? An assassin? Did you seek people out to be cruel to them? Did you hunt with words or knives? Your body is metal, so you must have been cold. Unfeeling. A hard man. Did people hate you? Did you hate them? Both?"

She knew she was babbling, but the words wouldn't seem to stop. "Did you know you would come back like this? Did you ever try to change? You know that's what augurs are for—to help you make the right choices and help you lead an honorable life. They could have prevented this from happening to you, if you'd let them, which you obviously didn't. Why not? I mean, I know why my parents don't ask augurs to help them." A waste of gold, they called it. She'd never seen them enter a temple except to pay her fees and check on her progress, and she wasn't permitted to read them herself—it was one of the rules of augur training, no unsolicited readings—even if she'd been skilled enough to see their auras clearly. "I think they're afraid of what the augurs will tell them. I think they know deep inside that they are not any of the things they're supposed to be, and they're scared it will be too hard to fix themselves. Is that what you did? Avoid the augurs because you thought it would be too hard? Or did you simply not care whether you were a good person or not?"

As she talked to the black lion, the other kehoks' screams began to blur into the background. They still made her bones itch and her skin feel raw, but she wasn't as aware of them anymore. She was instead hyperaware of the metallic lion's golden eyes.

Kehoks had beautiful eyes.

She'd heard that before, but she'd never been close enough to see for herself. It wasn't just that their eyes were golden, but the gold seemed to shift as if it were molten metal. The longer she stared, the more she thought the gold was really a mix of colors: reds and yellows and oranges, constantly swirling around black pupils. "It must mean something that your eyes are so beautiful. You must have some good in you."

She hadn't learned much about kehoks in her training, only that they were the worst fate for the worst of souls. The bulk of augur training focused on ordinary souls. Kehoks were a cautionary tale. "I think if my 'fiancé' were to be reborn as a kehok, he wouldn't have your eyes. There's nothing good about him."

It was funny, but the longer she talked to the black lion, the easier it was to stay in the stable. She could almost forget she was surrounded by monsters. At least until the other students began to come inside, and the kehoks burst into rage-filled roars again.

Quickly, Raia ducked into an empty stall.

Peeking out, Raia saw three students: two girls and a boy, all about Raia's age. One of the girls had a shaved head, the boy had a scar on his left arm that looked like a crescent moon, and the other girl towered over Raia by at least two feet. All three of them wore sleeveless tunics that showed off their arm muscles. Looking at them, Raia was aware of how few muscles she had, anywhere. She was also aware that they had blocked the stable's only exit, and that she was effectively cornered inside a stall.

One of the girls whispered something to the boy, and he laughed.

Raia shrank deeper into the stall and wondered if they'd noticed her yet.

"Hey, new girl," the tall girl called between the kehok screams. "Come on out."

Heart thudding, Raia inched forward. She wondered if they planned to hurt her and if she could stop them. *Trainer Verlas will stop them,* she thought. But how would Trainer Verlas know she needed her? Any call for help would be drowned out by the cries of the kehoks. And any screams would be lost beneath theirs.

"Whoa, relax!" the girl with the shaved head said. "You look more scared of us than of the kehoks. Promise we don't bite. At least not as hard as they do."

"It's because I'm tall," the tall girl said knowingly. "You think because I'm tall I have the overwhelming urge to drop heavy objects on smaller people."

"You don't?" the boy asked. "I always assumed you did."

"Of course I do," the tall girl said, "but I resist those urges because I'm civilized. Unlike you. You are literally standing in monster crap."

The boy looked down. He'd stepped in a mound of manure. "Shit."

"Yes," the tall girl agreed.

Watching them, Raia didn't think they seemed threatening. Maybe she didn't need to be afraid of them. Still, experience had taught her caution.

"I'm Silar," the tall girl said. "This is Algana, and he's Jalimo."

Jalimo pointed to his feet. "And these were new boots."

The shaved-head girl, Algana, clicked her tongue. "You should know better than to wear new boots to a stable. What were you going to do when Trainer Osir asked you to muck out stalls?"

"I was going to bribe you into doing it for me," Jalimo said, then turned to Raia. "So what's your name, who's your trainer, and are you a paying student?"

Before Raia could answer, Algana jumped in. "She has to be a paying student. Look at her." To Raia, she said, "Not that there's anything wrong with paying—the trainers need to eat. You just don't look like someone who . . . Well, you don't look . . . Silar, help me out here."

"Oh, no, you stuck your foot in your mouth all by yourself." Silar was grinning. But it wasn't an unfriendly grin. Raia allowed herself to relax minutely.

"My name's Raia, and I'm not a paying student," Raia said.

"Yes!" Jalimo said, punching the air. "Another one of us!

We're all training to be champions. The paying students . . . they're just paying to play being brave. Fierce rivalry between us and them."

Silar rolled her eyes. "No, there isn't."

"We at least look down on them," Jalimo said in a wounded voice.

"And they look down on us," Algana said.

"It's a mutual condescension thing," Jalimo agreed. "But the trainers won't allow an actual rivalry. They said it will distract us from our training. And besides, the kehoks bruise us up plenty. We don't need to fight among ourselves."

"So you *aren't* going to beat me?" Raia burst out, before she thought about her words.

All three of the students stared at her with appalled expressions.

"Like some kind of hazing-the-new-student thing, or establishing of the hierarchy?" Raia tried to explain. It didn't happen inside the training temple, with augurs everywhere to check your aura for any hint of misbehavior, but her parents had always told her it was common elsewhere—they'd stressed that every time they wanted her to appreciate how lucky she was. "I mean, I've heard those things happen. . . ." She felt her face heat up in a blush.

"Definitely not," Algana said. "What kind of messed-up place did you come from that you'd even think that?"

Raia felt her throat go dry. She wasn't going to answer *that*. "I'm sorry." She hadn't meant to insult them. She wondered if she'd ruined any chance she had of becoming friends with them. It would be nice to have new friends. She'd abandoned every one she had when she climbed down that trellis and disappeared into the night. She thought she'd come to grips with the idea of losing everyone she knew, but then she felt tears prick her eyes. She blinked them back and hoped the three other students didn't notice how weak she was.

"Never mind where you came from," Silar said kindly. "You're here now. And all that matters is that the qualifying races start in just a few weeks, and we have to—"

Jalimo pushed past her, deeper into the stable. "What, by the River, is *that*?" He pointed to the black lion, who, out of all the kehoks, was the only one not fighting the shackles that chained him to the floor and walls. Instead, he was staring at them with golden eyes, as if he could dissect them with his gaze. "It looks like it's made of muscle and metal and nothing else. How fast can it run?"

"Never mind how it runs," Algana said, awe in her voice. "Look at its jaws! It could tear you apart in seconds."

"Let me see," Silar said.

"It's the one that Trainer Osir was talking about," Jalimo said. "Must be."

The others crowded next to Jalimo, and as they pressed closer, the black lion exploded, lunging to the limits of his chains, crashing against the door to his stall. All the students shrieked and stumbled backward, except Raia, who stepped in front of his door, as if to protect him from them.

"Trainer Verlas bought him yesterday," Raia said over the roars. "He's my racer."

All three students then switched from staring at the black lion, who continued to rage in his stall, to staring at Raia.

"Your racer," Algana repeated.

"And you're with Trainer Verlas?" Silar said.

Jalimo let out a low whistle.

"Why?" Raia asked. "What's wrong?"

Silar patted her head. "It was nice meeting you, Raia.

We'll all wear mourning gray to your funeral and play the bells to guide your soul on." The other two nodded solemnly.

Raia opened her mouth to ask more questions, but just then the stable door slammed open. "You lot, out!" Trainer Verlas barked at Silar, Algana, and Jalimo. "Your trainers want you. Raia, stay! It's time for your lessons."

Each of the other students clasped her shoulder on their way out, as if saying a final goodbye. Raia gulped and reminded herself she didn't have to banish fear. *I just have to conquer it.*

BRIEFLY, TAMRA WONDERED WHAT NONSENSE THE other students had told Raia, but then dismissed it. *It doesn't matter. I don't have time to worry about gossip.* She had only three weeks to prepare an absolute rookie to race on the black lion.

Luckily, she didn't have to teach her to win. Not for her first race, at least. You were allowed two chances to compete in the qualifiers. Only your top time was used to calculate whether you'd run in the major races or the minor races in the Heart of Becar. So you could consider your first qualifying race part of your training.

By the second, though . . .

Pursing her lips, Tamra studied Raia.

She wasn't likely to achieve much physical change in the three weeks leading up to her first race. But Raia could learn the proper techniques: how to keep her seat, how to handle turns, how to pace herself and her beast so that they'd have the stamina to accelerate in the final straightaway.

First things first, though. Before Raia could even mount a kehok without getting killed, she had to master the basics of controlling one. Tamra shifted her gaze to the black lion.

Not you, she thought. *Not yet.*

Yesterday's attempt to force him into the stable had been too spectacular a failure.

Better to start small. For today, Tamra selected the lion-lizard that her former student Amira had raced. She'd never had any difficulty cowing him. "Behave," she told him as she opened his stall. Attaching a chain rope to his net, she led him out. "Follow."

Keeping her control tight, she led him and Raia onto the training ground. By the time they reached the sands, the kehok was trembling with the effort of trying to resist her, but she didn't even allow him to scream.

Around the circle, the other trainers were working with their students. In the far corner, Trainer Osir cracked a whip at his student's monster. One of Trainer Zora's students was shouting at her kehok and pressing a spear tip against his side. Black blood trickled from a fresh wound, and the kehok screamed his defiance. Tamra ignored them.

"You have one goal," Tamra told Raia. "Get this kehok to cross the training sands in a straight line, without attacking any of the other kehoks or students, and then make him return and lie down in front of you."

"Okay." Raia squared her shoulders and clenched her fists, as if she were about to start a brawl but had no idea how to throw a punch. "How do I do that? Do I use a whip or a spear—"

"Do you see a whip or a spear? No—you will use your will and your voice. On the track, *you* are the only tool you can and should rely on." Tamra pinned her gaze on the kehok as she unhooked the chain. He tensed, aware he was free, ready to run, but she kept her gaze pinned to his. "Walk." Her voice held no hint of compromise, no indication that he had any other option. It was a tone full of expectation: He would obey. He *must* obey.

He did obey.

Haltingly, he walked across the sands, and then with a surer gait, he trotted back.

"Lie down," she ordered.

He dropped onto the sands.

"You try," Tamra told her student.

She saw panic flash in Raia's eyes, but Raia stepped in front of the lion-lizard. He watched her with baleful eyes. "Walk." She pointed across the sands.

Tamra kept the pressure of her mind on the kehok but changed her command: *You will not harm her.* She didn't dictate more than that. Getting him to move would be up to Raia. But Tamra would keep him from mauling her on her first day.

"Walk!" Raia repeated.

The kehok didn't move. Just stared at her. His tongue flicked out and in.

"What am I doing wrong?" she asked Tamra, a hint of panic in her voice.

Tamra crossed her arms and didn't answer. This was something that every rider had to figure out for themselves— their core of confidence. Doubts were rooted in the past, fears were for the future, but kehoks existed only in the present. Raia had to believe the kehok would obey her right here and right now, and to do that, she had to believe she deserved to be obeyed.

Kehok racing, as her own teacher used to tell her, taught you to value yourself.

If it didn't kill you first, Tamra amended.

Raia clenched her fists and glared at the kehok. "You *will* walk."

The lion-lizard began to tremble. He lifted one leg and pressed his paw down, as if he were about to heft himself onto his feet . . . and then he put his leg back down and lowered his head to the ground.

Raia puffed out air, as if she'd been holding her breath. "I can't."

"You escaped your family," Tamra said softly. "You got yourself here. Unharmed. Alone. Your desire to continue is greater than his need to thwart you. He is and will always be a kehok, the lowest of the low. His soul is doomed to be reborn as a monster for all eternity. He is the epitome of hopeless. *You* are a warrior of hope. You will triumph. Make. Him. Walk."

Straightening her shoulders, Raia nodded. Her hands formed fists again, and she widened her stance as if she were preparing to fight. "Obey me! Walk!"

Growling, the lion-lizard began to shake. But he pushed himself up onto his feet. Slowly, jerkily, as if he were trying to resist every step, he weaved his way across the sands. His thick, scale-coated tail dragged behind him, drawing curves his wake.

Tamra wanted to cheer. Instead, she kept her voice calm and even, so as not to break Raia's concentration. "Good. Bring him back."

On the opposite side of the circle of sand, the kehok pivoted. He began to walk back, faster this time, and in more of a straight line. *Excellent! She has potential,* Tamra thought, *which is a vast improvement over—*

CRASH!

From the stables.

The sound of wood and metal shredding.

She heard a kehok scream, but this wasn't one of rage. It was pain. Beside her on the sands, she saw Raia startle and then twist her head to glance toward the stables—

And that moment of lost concentration was all it took.

The lion-lizard thundered toward the girl. Raia flung out her arms. "Stop! No!" But the kehok didn't even slow. Jumping forward, Tamra shoved the girl out of the way and held up her hands, palms out.

"YOU WILL STOP!"

The kehok froze mid-stride. Tamra slapped the chain on him and forced him to a wall, where she clamped the chain to a heavy iron ring. Across the training ground, the two other trainers were doing the same with their kehoks, and then they all ran toward the stable.

Out of the corner of her eye, Tamra saw a flash of gold, sparkling brighter than the sun. Surrounded by an entourage, Lady Evara was mincing her way across the sands from the direction of the ferry dock. Several of her servants held parasols over her head, an action made redundant by the model of a sailboat she wore entwined in her hair, large enough to shield her from any hint of sun.

"Oh, by the River . . ." Tamra muttered.

She couldn't greet her patron now. But she could curse her timing.

Osir reached the stable first and flung the doors open. Before he could even cry out, the black lion burst through and slammed into him, knocking him flat on his back.

"No! Don't!" Tamra cried. Zora and all the students were crying out too, willing the kehok not to kill him. *Do not hurt him!*

The kehok trampled over Osir without stopping to savage him.

As Zora ran to Osir's side, Tamra aimed the force of her voice and the force of her mind at the kehok as he tore across the training grounds. *"You will stop!"*

Halfway across the sands, he faltered but kept running.

Tamra redoubled her efforts. He *would* stop, because she would *not* fail. This was nonnegotiable. She was as relentless as the sun, and he would melt in the heat of her fire. He stumbled in the sands, but then he pulled himself to his feet and pushed forward.

She'd never felt such a strong will in a kehok. Never felt such need.

She lost all sense of everything but where she was in that one moment—the heat of the sun, the wind on her face, the sand beneath her feet, and the kehok straining against her.

She felt the students join her, along with Zora and Osir.

The three trainers, supported by their students, bent their wills toward the black lion. Weighed down beneath them all, he dropped onto the sand like a bird shot from the sky.

At last he lay still.

Tamra grabbed the nearest ankle shackles and ran to his side, fastening them tightly around his paws and chaining them together so the kehok could not stand even if he could muster the will to resist.

She met his golden eyes, expecting to see hate.

Instead she saw sadness.

SEVERAL CHAOTIC MINUTES LATER, TAMRA SLAMMED the bolt shut on the stall door. They'd secured the black lion with triple the number of chains and shackles, and they'd placed him in the strongest stall.

She felt as if she'd wrestled a rhino. She didn't want to think about how Osir felt. Or what he was going to say to her once he quit moaning about his injuries and decided to move from self-pity to blame.

I am to *blame. Again.*

Leaning against the stall door, she surveyed the damage. And the blood.

The venomous jackal-cobra lay in a nearby stall. Its throat had been torn. The black lion had burst through the stall wall into the jackal-cobra's on his way to escape. The jackal-cobra must have blocked him or attacked him, so he'd eliminated the obstacle.

If it had been any creature but a kehok, she'd say a prayer for its soul's swift journey to a favorable rebirth, but there was no point with a kehok's soul. It had only one fate.

Primly lifting her skirts above the blood, Lady Evara picked her way over the threshold into the stable. Her entourage shuffled after her, wordless, their eyes obscured by brilliant blue face paint and lashes dusted with gold flecks.

Seeing the dead jackal-cobra kehok, Lady Evara halted. She pursed her lips. Painted, they formed a purple oval. "You realize the dead kehok was mine."

Tamra winced. *I can't afford to pay her back. She has to know that.* Bowing, she said, "Please accept my apology—"

"Not accepted," she said crisply. "I invested in you, Verlas. Placed my trust in you, and this is how you repay me? You purchase an uncontrollable racer and hire an unsuitable rider. Oh, yes, I saw her little performance out on the sands, and I am not impressed."

"It was her first attempt," Tamra said.

"It should be her last," Lady Evara snapped. "Are you *trying* to make a mockery of me? Truly, I do not know what to think." Spreading open a golden-edged fan, she waved it as if trying to shoo away this disaster.

"The potential is there." Tamra was gritting her jaw so hard that her cheeks began to ache. *If only I didn't need a sponsor, then she'd see mockery.* "All I ask is that you trust my judgment."

Lady Evara snorted, an unrefined sound that seemed at odds with her exquisitely bejeweled self. "'All' you ask is trust?" Closing her fan, she smacked it against her open palm. "My trust is not lightly bestowed, and this is hardly the first time you have disappointed me. And I am not the only one. Must I remind you that your students have abandoned you, save this urchin you have found?"

Tamra met her eyes and wished she felt as confident staring her down as she did confronting a kehok. As firmly as she could, she said, "I can win with this racer and this rider."

"Correction: you *must* win with this racer and this rider. I will be recouping my losses from today's fiasco out of your winnings from your first qualifying race."

Tamra had planned for her share of Raia's winnings to pay for Shalla's tuition. First, second, and third place walked home with gold pieces. She began to calculate the number of races, both in the qualifying round and in the minor races, they'd need to win to pay for both the dead kehok and the augur's bills. And then she realized that Lady Evara had said "*first* qualifying race."

It was rare for a racer and rider to place that high in the rankings in their first race. That's why you were allowed to race the sands twice before you were slotted for either the major or minor races in the capital city, the Heart of Becar. Tamra had hoped to ease Raia and the black lion into the circuit, use the first race to grow familiar with the track, have a decent showing in her second qualifier, and then press her to win in the minors. *We don't have that luxury anymore.* Not if Lady Evara demanded immediate prize money. "You know the first race is traditionally a practice—"

Lady Evara cut her off. "Replacing a kehok is a significant expense. I require the prize money from a *first place* win. If your rider fails to win enough gold to compensate me for my loss, our association is finished. Are we clear?"

Finished? Tamra had no viable backup plan. She had no skills but training kehoks. If she lost her patronage entirely . . . She'd taken a massive blow from the racing commission's fines last year. She couldn't weather another.

In a falsely sweet voice, the kind you'd use to talk to children if you were the sort who hated children, Lady Evara said, "Now, what are the little words we say when someone does you a favor you do not deserve?"

In just as sweet a voice, Tamra said, "Screw you, Lady Evara."

For a brief moment, Lady Evara's expression darkened, but then she plastered over it with a laugh and a smile. "You're a fighter, Trainer Verlas. That's what I've always admired about you. And that's what I am counting on. I am giving you your shot at redemption, and I expect you to give me mine." She leveled a look at Tamra. "Let me be blunt, Trainer Verlas: I expect a grand champion."

Tamra gawked at her. "With a new rider and racer?" Last year, before the accident, Tamra had been on the path to achieving the grand prize. But this year, with a new racer and a new rider, she'd hoped merely to win enough races to pay the augurs—and now the fee for the dead kehok.

That had been an achievable goal.

This was crazy.

"Win, and keep winning. And the gold will keep flowing. But lose, and this is your final season. I have no more patience to spend on you." With that, Lady Evara swept out of the stable.

Tamra was left feeling as if she'd weathered a sandstorm, with glasslike bits of sand flaying her skin. She glanced at the black lion. "You'd better not be a mistake."

He merely stared back at her.

Grabbing a bucket and towels, Tamra began to sop up the blood.

RAIA HELPED TRAINER VERLAS CLEAN THE STABLE, while the others hauled away the dead kehok. Neither of them spoke. When the blood was mopped up, she helped repair the broken stall. Again in silence.

She spent most of the day chasing the same set of thoughts around her head: Her kehok was deadly. All kehoks were, but hers was worse than most. How was she supposed to ride him in a race? And how was she supposed to win? It had taken three grown trainers and a batch of students to subdue the beast. *If I try to ride him, he'll kill me.*

This was a foolish, impossible plan.

By the time the repairs were finished, Raia had convinced herself to quit. But she couldn't say the words. Not with Trainer Verlas so silent.

Growing up in her house, Raia knew how to read silences. There were peaceful ones, where you were content inside the warmth of your own thoughts. There were waiting silences, where you watched time stretch and lengthen. And there were silences like the sky that expects a storm, where the air quivers with unshed lightning—angry silences that you don't dare break. This was one of those, and Raia knew better than to break a quivering quiet.

Tamra spoke first. "You'll stay with me and my daughter tonight."

"I . . ."

"I'm not leaving you here with *him*. Not tonight. Or any other night. It won't be luxurious, but we have enough spare blankets that you can set up a pallet on the kitchen floor. At least you won't have to worry about your kehok breaking through the wall while you're asleep." She glared at the kehok.

Tell her you want to quit, her mind whispered. But Raia couldn't bring herself to say the words. Especially not if speaking up meant she'd lose the offer of a safe place to sleep tonight. She glanced once at the black lion, pinned beneath his chains. She hadn't relished the thought of another night near the monsters, not with the image of what he'd done so stark in her mind, but a night in a real house, safe and warm . . . It was too much temptation. She told herself she was being practical, not cowardly, though she was glad there was no augur around to read her aura right now. *I'll tell her in the morning.*

Leaving the stable, she trailed Trainer Verlas across the sands and toward the city. The sun had begun to set while they were cleaning up from today's catastrophe. It painted the sky with streaks of rust, and it made the Aur River look like liquid gold.

It was only a couple miles before they reached the cluster of houses and shops on the northern shore of the river, the poorer area of Peron. Raia noticed that a lot of the shops were boarded up, and all the homes looked worn-out, as if they'd weathered too many people and too many years. Up close, the white walls were stained from age, and the blue roof tiles were chipped. By doorways, statues honoring the ancestors' vessels were cheap stone carvings, roughly in the shape of herons, turtles, and hippos. *Well-loved,* she corrected, *not worn-out.* Still, she hoped it was safe to be out after dark here. She'd heard rumors of riots in some cities. Even a few deaths.

As they walked between the houses and shops, she watched her trainer brighten when she saw a soft amber glow through some curtained windows. Her pace quickened, and Raia hurried after her.

Raia checked her hands. She'd scrubbed the blood and dirt off of them at the stables. She couldn't do anything about the speckled grime on her tunic. She hoped she was suitable enough to meet her trainer's daughter. She always got nervous meeting new people. She thought of Silar, Algana, and Jalimo, and how she'd felt when she met them—that hadn't been her finest moment, convinced they planned to pummel her.

"Shalla!" Trainer Verlas cried.

Following her inside, Raia saw Trainer Verlas hugging a young girl who was hugging her back just as happily. She looked to be about ten or eleven and reminded Raia of the kind of bird that pecked for bugs on the riverbank—all quick movements and alert eyes. When they broke apart, the girl asked, "Mama, is that blood? Are you hurt?"

"Not mine, and nothing for you to worry about," Trainer Verlas said. "It was a difficult day, but all the trainers and students are fine." Raia noticed she didn't mention the kehoks. "Shalla, I'd like you to meet my newest rider. This is Raia."

Raia heard the words "my newest rider" and froze for an

instant—would she still be that in the morning? Then Raia remembered her manners and bowed her head. "Thank you for allowing me into your home. I hope I'm not an intrusion."

Shalla bowed back before bounding over to drag her farther inside. She shooed Raia into a chair and pushed a plate with a slice of bread into Raia's hands. "Here's what you need to know. My mother's like fresh-baked bread. Crunchy on the outside but soft and sweet on the inside. If she took you on as a rider, then that means you're family, and you're welcome here."

Raia glanced at Trainer Verlas and was surprised to see how much her expression had softened in the presence of her daughter. Her lips were curved in what was almost a smile, and she was looking at Shalla as if the girl had carved the crescent moon.

"I've been wanting a sister for a while," Shalla continued. "Last rider was a boy."

Trainer Verlas protested, "I had more girls than boys with the last batch of paying students, if you want to count them. And there's nothing wrong with boys."

"Generically, no," Shalla said. "I like them fine. But not in my house. Do you have any idea how badly their feet can smell?"

Trainer Verlas laughed. "Yours aren't roses either."

"But they're *my* stinky feet, and I'm used to them." Turning to Raia, she asked, "Do you want fruit on the bread? We have a jar of pomegranate spread. Just to warn you: it's a little sweet."

"Sweet for my sweet," Trainer Verlas sang.

"I made it," Shalla admitted, "and I kind of dumped a lot of sugar in. A *lot* of sugar. You should sleep in my bed tonight. I'll take the floor. You're probably sore from train-ing. Mama doesn't go easy on her riders."

She jumped between topics so quickly that it made Raia's head spin. "I'm fine on the floor, but thank you. And pome-granate sounds nice."

Shalla grabbed a jar and ladled a spoonful onto the slice of bread. She beamed at Raia, and Raia stared back at her.

When Raia was Shalla's age, she was constantly pun-ished for speaking out of turn. Her family didn't believe in children expressing opinions until they were old enough to . . . well, never really. She glanced at Trainer Verlas and thought she had to be an incredible mother for Shalla to be so open and so happy.

She thought about what Shalla had said, about how she was now family. She didn't believe that—your family was your family, whether you wanted them to be or not—but she did feel safer and more welcome here than she had in a very long time, even before she'd felt the need to climb out her bedroom window.

Picking up the bread, Raia took a bite. Sugar exploded in her mouth, so sweet it made her teeth ache—it was much, much too sugary. Shalla was watching her anxiously, as if it were important to her that Raia be as happy as she was.

Raia smiled at her. "It's perfect," she said. Not the bread. That was awful. But Trainer Verlas and her daughter, and the way they'd welcomed her in.

Shalla beamed back at her. "Good. It's important you're happy here."

She seemed so very earnest that Raia couldn't help ask-ing, "Why does it matter to you? You just met me." Cer-tainly her own family hadn't cared for her happiness. Why did this perfect stranger?

"Because you're our only hope." Shalla said it so matter-of-factly, as if it weren't a terrifying statement. "Right, Mama? She needs to win races so Mama can pay the augurs so that we can be together."

The sugar suddenly tasted like sand on Raia's tongue. "You *need* me to win?" It was one thing when she was racing just for herself—a chance at her own freedom—but this . . .

Trainer Verlas sighed. "I wouldn't have put it quite so bluntly, but yes. My daughter is training to be an augur, and I will be using the trainer's share of the prize money to pay for her tuition."

"If we can't pay, we can't be together," Shalla said.

She was looking at Raia with so much hope and trust that Raia felt sick. She thought back to what the other students had said, and the fact that she hadn't seen anyone else training with Trainer Verlas.

I can't be their only hope!

And the fact that Shalla was training to be an augur—it hit too close to home. Her parents wanted her to repay them for the augurs, and now this girl . . . Abruptly, Raia stood, dropping the bread. "This was all a terrible idea. You know I'm too weak to be a rider. You need to find someone who—"

Trainer Verlas cut her off. "I found you. Sit down, Raia, and finish your bread."

Raia didn't sit. This was a mistake. She should have kept going and never visited Gea Market. She could still sneak on board another ferry and make it farther south, far beyond Peron, far beyond all the cities of Becar, until she found a village too remote for her family to ever think of searching there. "I can't. I shouldn't have stopped running—"

"Your family will find you eventually. If you stay and race the sands with me, then when they do find you, you can give them the money we've won from the races—once we win enough, we can pay my debt to Lady Evara, Shalla's to the augurs, and yours to your family." Trainer Verlas smiled encouragingly at her. Her voice was calm, but her hands were clasped so tightly that her knucklebones shone white through her skin. She was trying (and failing, Raia thought) to hide how much this mattered to her. "And then we will be both safe and free."

Raia blinked. Her eyes felt hot. This was all too much. She hadn't wanted to be responsible for anyone else's future. For the first time in a while, she wished one of her teachers were here, so she could ask what the right path was. "How many races do we need to win to be safe and free?"

Trainer Verlas's smile became even more strained.

"Well . . . all of them."

CHAPTER 7

Dar—known to his people as His Highness Prince Dar, the emperor-to-be of the Becar Empire, blessed by the Aur River—thought he would suffocate inside the mourning robes. He was wearing six layers of linen, each in deepening shades of gray to symbolize the dimming of a life, as well as a red silk scarf wrapped around his left arm as a reminder of rebirth. It was just shy of tight enough to cut off circulation.

He'd hoped the discomfort would distract him.

It wasn't working.

He still wanted to bash his bejeweled fist into every snake-smooth courtier and ambassador who expressed his wish to honor his brother's memory. That, however, wasn't done. Emperors-to-be didn't curl their hands into fists. They laid their hands peacefully across their laps, and then nodded at precisely the same incline at every fellow mourner.

They might mourn him, Dar thought. *But they don't miss him.*

Not the way Dar did, where he woke each morning and

remembered anew that Zarin was gone, the memory like a knife in Dar's gut every time. He felt filleted as he went about the ceremony of his day, every nerve exposed and raw.

Everything made him miss his brother.

The taste of a lemon.

The whistle of the wind.

The crash of a platter from the kitchen and then the frantic whispers of the servants.

Years ago, shortly after Zarin had first become emperor, he'd heard a clatter from the kitchen and sprung off his throne to rush to help. Six servants had fainted on the spot at the sight of their new emperor picking up shards of glass from the tiled floor, and three councillors had resigned. Or so Zarin liked to say. Every time he'd told that story, the number of fainting servants and appalled courtiers had increased. Every time a citizen told that story, he or she gushed at the example of their emperor's greateheartedness.

And so when Dar heard a crash, he didn't move. Not because he felt he was above helping, but because that was Zarin's story, and Dar wasn't going to take it from him. *The way I took his throne,* he thought.

This was Zarin's. All of it. The throne. The crown. The linen robes and silk scarves, the exact nods, the precise words, the time spent in the official Hours of Listening, when the great ruler of all Becar silently listened to the advice, complaints, requests, and words of his people for three hours every two weeks without speaking a word. Or scratching an itch. Or sneezing. Or fidgeting in any way.

I don't know how Zarin did it.

Zarin used to complain about the Listening, how the nobles of Becar liked to monopolize it to drone on and on, and how he wished sometimes he could sew his mouth shut so he wouldn't have to exert so much effort clenching his jaw to try not to speak.

Dar had always met his brother in his chambers or in the aviary after the Listening, so that Zarin would have someone to vent to. He'd had so many pent-up words to say, and he needed a safe receptacle to empty them into. *I never minded listening to him.*

He *did* mind listening to these sycophants.

He amused himself the way Zarin had told Dar he did: by imagining what animal the nobles would be reborn as and picturing a hippopotamus or a stork waxing on about flood levels and taxes. Sometimes it even helped. But only a little.

In front of him now was a woman whom Dar was positive would be reborn as a vulture. "Oh, Great Emperor-to-Be." She bowed, a fraction lower than was strictly custom, and Dar wondered if his brother had ever stuffed cotton in his ears to dull their voices. "Accept my humble wishes for peace in your heart and allow me to express my deep sorrow that your brother's reborn soul has not yet been presented for our adoration."

Ouch. That one wasn't even subtle.

Gritting his teeth, Dar inclined his head. The word "yet" hung in the air like rancid perfume. After an emperor died and was reborn, tradition dictated that he be found in his new vessel and granted a life of luxury in the palace, regardless of whether he regained any memories of his past life or not.

Dar had been a child when their parents died—young enough that he had only sketchy memories of them as they were. But he remembered how every day he'd visit a toad in one of the palace ponds that was supposed to have been their father, and how Zarin had insisted they spend one afternoon a week in the aviary with a river hawk that had once been their mother. Two noble rebirths. Both lived lives of comfort and honor, their father hemmed in by garden walls and their mother's wings clipped so she wouldn't try to fly from the palace. Their father had never given any sign that he remembered who he'd been, but their mother often seemed to understand them.

Zarin used to say he hoped he didn't come back as a bird. He wouldn't want his wings clipped, even for the fanciest aviary in the known world, which this was.

If he is a bird, Dar thought, *I hope he's flying free.*

But if he was a bird, Dar also hoped he'd fly home soon. Tradition may have dictated the treatment of a prior emperor, but *law* dictated the treatment of the next one. Namely, Dar couldn't become emperor until his predecessor was found and properly honored.

It was now approaching three months since Zarin's death, with no sign of his new vessel.

"Your Glory-to-Be-Realized—"

Seriously? Is that what she's going to call me?

"—I hope you understand the gravity of our concerns. There is much of importance that is frozen while we wait for your coronation. Construction has been halted on the East Temples, and the tombs of your forefathers have not been tended to. Of particular concern to the Fifth District of Mesoon is the unsigned law regarding fishing regulations . . ."

Dar resisted the urge to slump in his throne and shove his fingers in his ears.

It wasn't that he didn't *care* that construction couldn't continue or laws couldn't be signed. He did care about the problems of his people. It was that there was nothing he could do about it. He already had dozens of augurs combing Becar for any hint of a child, bird, tadpole, or insect with Zarin's soul. He didn't know what else he was supposed to do!

If Zarin were here, he could have asked him.

But of course if Zarin were here, he wouldn't be having this problem. Dar would be back to being the spare brother, the one who was never supposed to become emperor, because Zarin was supposed to *live*, marry, and produce lots and lots of other heirs.

As always when he thought about marrying, Dar's gaze slid to Nori. Across the throne room, Lady Nori of Griault laughed with her head tilted back at a comment Dar couldn't hear. He wished he were with her, laughing with her, instead of stuck on the dais. She was in profile, beside a column, and the sight reminded him of all the nights they'd stood side by side on one of the palace balconies, looking out over the Heart of Becar. They'd been friends since they'd been kids, and Dar clung to the hope that someday they'd be more. *If I ever get up the nerve to tell her how I feel.*

They were distant enough cousins that she was royal without being too-close kin, so a match would make the nobles happy, and she came from an impressive fortune, which would make the royal coffers happy. He didn't care about any of that, though. He just liked her for who she was.

She turned, her eyes meeting his—she must have felt him staring, or another noble had noticed and alerted her. Nori cocked one eyebrow at him and then mouthed the words, *"Pay attention."*

Dar dragged his gaze back to the next supplicant, who was a man he shouldn't have been ignoring, the ambassador from Ranir, the country that squatted on their southern border, beyond the desert. "—difficulty in explaining the situation to my superiors in Ranir," Ambassador Usan was saying. "Our laws have no such condition, and they—we—do not understand why, if you do not possess the authority to renew our treaty, that another cannot be delegated to do so. My superiors are concerned that it is a negotiation tactic, or even a prelude to hostilities. If you could give me some assurance to pass on to them . . ."

Becar had a complex and tenuous relationship with Ranir, due to the king of Ranir's tendency to invade at semi-regular intervals throughout history. During times of peace, Becar typically pretended those incursions hadn't happened, because Ranir was such a valuable trading partner. Listening to the ambassador always gave Dar a headache—Usan could have sought an audience at any other time, but the ambassador deliberately chose the one time Dar was unable to respond. It was obvious that he wanted to emphasize the emperor-to-be's weakness, but Dar thought the ambassador also just enjoyed being annoying. He'd likely be reborn as a housefly.

Dar had heard reports from some of his generals that the Raniran army had been conducting "training exercises" near the border, particularly in areas where the Becaran presence was weakest. But without the authority of the crown, he could not authorize troop movements to secure those areas. *A stupid law*, Dar thought—he agreed with Ambassador Usan, though he obviously couldn't say so out loud, for multiple reasons.

He knew the history behind the law: five generations ago, during the transition period before a coronation, the military, acting of their own accord, had claimed they were defending the Heart of Becar, the capital of the empire, from an invasion. The invasion was a lie, though, and instead the generals ordered their soldiers to capture and kill the royal family, with the intent of installing one of their own as the next emperor. Only one child survived, a young girl who became known as the Empress of Despair, because she never got over the loss of her parents and siblings. She'd made the decree that during the transition period, the military could not authorize any troop movements. Any general who violated the law would be accused of treason and immediately executed. Needless to say, given the cost, the Becaran generals were meticulous about following the law. *Sure, the law made sense then*, Dar thought. *But now?* When the law was made, no one had ever anticipated that a transition period would last so long, and there were no provisions in place for complications arising from such a situation.

It's all a mess, Dar thought, *and the longer it continues, the worse it will get.*

As if on cue, Ambassador Usan was replaced by Lord Mynoc of Leyand, who proceeded to list out all the ways things had already gotten worse: a riot in Seronne, incidents of unrest in Peron, a generations-old market shut down in Androc, news of protests planned outside the palace, complaints from the guild directors from nearly every guild in Becar of shortages, worker grievances over frozen contracts, and financial losses. . . . Becar, in short, was a pot of boiling rice, about to bubble over. "The mess will take decades to clean up," Lord Mynoc said, "if a resolution isn't found soon."

I know, Dar thought. But he could say and do nothing but incline his head in acknowledgment.

At merciful last, the Listening ended, and Dar rose, his knees popping as if he'd aged three decades in the three hours he'd sat there. He thanked his people and the palace nobles for sharing their hearts and minds, using the proper traditional words that he'd memorized, along with the thousand other phrases he'd had to memorize in the past few months, and then he recessed from the throne room.

He was somewhat proud of himself for not running out of there.

He reached his rooms. Two guards were stationed on either side of the door. One bowed, while the other flung the door open. He gave them more sincere nods—he had far more respect for the men and women who protected his life than the ones who swarmed mosquito-like through his court. Only when he was safely inside, alone, did he allow himself to slump his shoulders, rip off the red scarf and three layers of mourning linen, and slam his fist into one of the many pillows that littered his room.

He didn't understand why the palace stewards thought an emperor needed so many pillows. He hadn't needed them when he was an heir. But he did like that they were good for quietly venting every emotion he didn't allow himself to express outside of these rooms.

He raged at the pillows for a quarter of an hour, until he began to feel silly. It wasn't as if the pillows had smothered his brother or contributed to his death in any way. Zarin had sickened and died, the way people do, and it wasn't the fault of anything or anyone. It simply was. Which somehow made it worse.

Dar had no one to blame. No one to hate. Except himself, for being alive while his beloved brother was dead. *It should have been me.* He was the extra one, the friend and the confidant but never the leader. He'd never wanted this, no matter what the people said when they thought he couldn't hear them.

"River take them all," he said.

"Your Excellence?" a guard called through the door. "May we assist you?"

You could stop eavesdropping on me while I'm throwing a private temper tantrum, he thought. But out loud he said, "Thank you, but I'm fine."

Then he had another thought: "Actually, could you send someone to summon Augur Yorbel? I would like to take solace in the wisdom of his counsel." And he wanted another update on the search for his brother.

Just because he hated listening to the nobles didn't mean they weren't right.

YORBEL HAD BEEN EXPECTING ANOTHER SUMMONS TO the palace. For days, he'd kept his official augur robe ready on a hook by his door, and when he heard the slap of sandals on the stone outside his quarters during the afternoon reflection time, he rose from his meditation, dressed, and donned the chain with the pendant that identified him as one of the esteemed augurs of Becar.

He felt like a soldier putting on his armor, but the arrows in the palace were whispered words and the spears were questions he couldn't answer.

The walk to the palace was hot, with the midday sun soaking through his linen robe. His shaved head kept him somewhat cool, at least cooler than the nobles with their coiled braids and myriad ornaments who fanned themselves as they lounged about the gardens. He didn't slow to greet any of them, though he noticed several begin to start toward him. He'd learned from experience that if you walked with purpose, it exponentially increased the odds that you'd reach your destination. Proceed slowly, and people would pounce all over you. So he didn't pause, despite the heat.

In anxious times, people were especially eager to talk to augurs for both guidance and reassurance. *And these are undoubtedly anxious times,* he thought. Just this morning, in a corridor that was usually silent for contemplation, he'd heard two of the younger augurs whispering about Ranir, worrying about whether its king would view Becar as weak—a worldly worry normally outside the scope of a young augur's concerns. He'd heard it all lately: fear of economic collapse, fear of riots, fear of invasion. . . . *I believe we can weather these times, if people continue to honor their better selves.*

Yorbel was greeted at the entrance and escorted into the blissful cool of the palace. In this wing, the walls had been painted a restful blue, with diamond-flecked stars decorating the ceiling. All the palace windows were constructed to allow a breeze in and keep the sun out, and so the cool shadows seemed to whisper with the breath of the wind.

"How fares our emperor-to-be?" he asked his escort, breaking the silence.

His escort, one of the royal guards, looked startled. Yorbel thought he wasn't used to being spoken to by the luminaries he conducted through the palace. Yorbel had never understood that—people were people, no matter their rank. The worthiness of one's soul had very little to do with one's employment or economic status. It was surprising how often people conflated righteousness and wealth. Yorbel had met plenty of rich assholes.

"He fares as well as could be expected, Your Eminence."

"And that is?"

"He mourns his brother. He fulfills his duties. But . . ." The guard hesitated.

"You may speak freely to me," Yorbel said. "I merely see a soul's future. I have no more power than anyone does to influence your destiny. You shape your own fate." He meant the words kindly, even though he knew they sounded pompous. There was a reason he didn't deliver the daily words at the temple—he wasn't as good at talking easily with people as some augurs, even though he tried.

Glancing up and down the corridor, the guard confided, "He wasn't ready to replace his brother. Rumor is he doesn't want to. Rumor is he delays the search for his brother's soul because he doesn't want to take the throne. He doesn't want to admit his brother is dead and gone."

"He has a heart," Yorbel said. "May Becar always have leaders whose souls are as human as their bodies." He'd always liked the boy. Dar had a streak of kindness and compassion that was unusual in one who had grown up surrounded by the backstabbing intrigue of the royal court. Privately, Yorbel suspected his brother, both before and after he was emperor, had protected Dar from the worst of it. Being thrust to the forefront had to have been a shock, even without the grief aspect.

"Yes, but it won't be long before the nobles begin to see his love for his brother as a weakness they can exploit. He needs to be coronated, and fast. Or else"—the guard lowered his voice—"there are rumors that a faction in court wants him declared unfit to rule, on the basis of his delay in finding his brother's soul's new vessel. It's said they've already selected the next empress."

Yorbel placed a hand on the shoulder of the guard. "Then here is a new rumor for you: Emperor-to-Be Dar does not delay. He has dispersed twice the number of augurs as is customary. Late Emperor Zarin's soul has proven elusive. But he will be found, as fast as is possible."

The guard's face lit up in a smile. "That's a good rumor to hear and to share, Your Eminence. Thank you. We—the majority of the palace guard—are fond of Dar. We'd hate to have to kill him."

A door opened, and the emperor-to-be popped his head out. "And I'd hate to be killed. Glad we're all in agreement. Your Eminence, please join me."

Flustered, the guard dropped to his knees and began to sputter apologies.

"You're a good man," Yorbel told him. And added: "Have no fear for your rebirth." He walked past him as the guard began to cry.

Yorbel shut the door behind him.

"Even I know you aren't supposed to tell people their fates like that," the emperor-to-be said. He sounded amused, which was good, since he could have chosen to report Yorbel's indiscretion to the High Council of Augurs.

It was a sensible law, designed to protect augurs: all readings were private, by request only, and for a fee. Otherwise, augurs would be overwhelmed with constant demands. Besides, it was unethical to read someone without their consent. But Yorbel also believed in providing comfort where he could. He had not been given his gifts to hoard them.

"He needed to hear it," Yorbel said, as he took in the state of the emperor-to-be's rooms. Pillows had been shredded and tossed, but every fragile ornament—glass flowers in a priceless vase, the exquisite pitcher that held amber-hued wine—was untouched. From all appearances, it looked as if Dar had thrown a very controlled temper tantrum.

Dar saw him observing the pillows and said, "I was redecorating."

"Of course, Your Greatness."

"Shouldn't that be 'Greatness-to-Be'? Oh, no, wait, don't tell me—you're going to say that greatness has nothing to do with my rank and everything to do with the state of my soul."

Since that was precisely what Yorbel had been about to say, he smiled instead.

"I can tell you, Yorbel, the state of my soul is not good. If one more noble pretends to care about the comfort of my brother's vessel . . . Eh, who am I kidding? I will nod politely because it's what Zarin would have wanted me to do. You know, I never expected the absence of a brother would have more impact on my thoughts and actions than the presence of one." He flopped onto a pillowless couch.

"Dar . . ." Yorbel stopped. He shouldn't be hesitant to speak his thoughts to Dar. He'd known him since Dar was a young boy—he'd been his tutor for a half-dozen years, while perfecting his augur skills, and then his friend after—and Dar clearly hadn't changed how he treated Yorbel since becoming emperor-to-be. Still . . .

"One minute," Dar said. "You're going to say something inappropriate that you don't want every spy in the palace to overhear. I'm fairly certain Ambassador Usan spends his afternoons personally eavesdropping on my conversations, and I *know* the faction from Griault has at least one professional spy in the palace. Let me give them something else to listen to." He hopped up off the couch, strode to the door, and stuck his head outside again. "Your emperor-to-be would like to hear some singing."

"Your Highness?" one of the guards said. "With all due

respect, my husband claims my singing can curdle milk and cause dogs to drop dead in the street."

"Excellent. Then sing very loudly."

Dar shut the door as the two guards outside began to bellow off-pitch one of the traditional Becaran ballads. It was utterly unrecognizable which one.

"Clever," Yorbel said. "You need to know that the search does not go well. Based on the most recent soul reading before his death, the temple predicted that your brother would be reborn as a golden tamarin monkey—there are fewer than three thousand colonies of such creatures in Becar, and we searched them all within the first week. We now have augurs examining every creature of a similar status, but . . ."

"But what if the augur who last read him was wrong," Dar said, finishing his sentence. "Or what if Zarin's soul changed significantly between his last reading and his death?"

"It has happened before." Yorbel hesitated. "The high council worries they'll offend you if they suggest broadening the search. But if your brother's soul isn't found within the next season . . ." He let the sentence dangle.

Dar sighed heavily. "I know. Believe me, I know. Becar needs an emperor, and her loyal subjects won't wait forever. I cannot ask them to. If I cannot produce Zarin's vessel . . . then Becar needs an heir who is not of Zarin's direct line, and therefore not required to find him in order to be crowned."

Yorbel knew what Dar didn't say: in order for another to be crowned, Dar would have to die. Sometimes Yorbel truly hated politics.

"What do you suggest?" Dar asked.

"We have every augur available searching for every conceivable vessel for the late emperor," Yorbel said. "What I propose is that we also search the inconceivable. Send an augur to examine creatures we have not considered." He phrased it as delicately as he could, but he knew Dar would understand what he meant.

Dar took a step backward. "No."

Keeping his face placid, Yorbel said, "I pass no judgment on your beloved brother."

"You think Zarin . . . You think he . . . my brother . . . your emperor . . ." He paced across the room, then paced back, all coiled anger. "I could have you killed for even thinking it. If you weren't my friend . . ."

"But I *am* your friend," Yorbel said.

That stopped Dar.

Yorbel pushed on. "And as your friend, I am telling you: we have to consider everything if we're to save your life. Let me speak to the high council about redirecting a few augurs—"

Dar cut him off. "Absolutely not. Speak of your suspicions to no one, and keep all available augurs searching where they are. If you believe this absurdity is necessary, then *you* do it."

He meant it as a ludicrous suggestion, Yorbel could tell. He, Yorbel, search for a soul's new vessel? That was a task reserved for lower-level augurs. Though Yorbel wasn't one of the high augurs, he was one of the most adept. He was in continuous demand by the aristocrats for readings, which meant a steady revenue stream for the temple. This, in turn, allowed other augurs to offer affordable readings to the working class and near-free readings to the poor. *But matters are desperate if even the palace guards are worried.* Yorbel would do the absurd for the sake of his emperor, both the one who had died and the one who was yet to be crowned. "I will proceed with discretion and will report back."

Dar blinked at him. "Wait—you're going to do it?"

"Yes." There was more he could say, about how he didn't want it to be true, about how he couldn't live with himself if Dar was killed and he hadn't done all he could, about how even augurs didn't know all the secrets of a person's heart.

In a low voice, so soft that Yorbel was barely able to hear it beneath the singing of the guards, Dar whispered, "You truly think it's possible my brother could have been reborn as a kehok?"

"No," Yorbel said firmly. And then added:

"But I think we must be sure."

YORBEL CHOSE THE LONG WAY BACK TO THE TEMPLE AF-ter his meeting with the emperor-to-be. He needed to think. He knew he'd picked the right course of action, but *how* to do it?

In the late-afternoon heat, few people were out. If riots and protests were brewing, the perpetrators were sensible enough to wait until it cooled. Most shopkeepers were tucked back inside their tents and stalls. A monkey was napping in the shade of one building. A young man knelt next to a fountain, washing a pile of tunics. On one street corner, beneath a copper statue of a cat commissioned by a long-dead noble, a beggar child held out a cup, and Yorbel dropped a few coins into it.

"Thank you," the child said, then saw his pendant. "Oh! Master augur! What am I going to—" His cheeks flushed bright red as he remembered he wasn't supposed to ask. "I'm sorry. I can't pay."

"I am not permitted to read auras outside the temple, un-less sanctioned by the high augurs or the emperor," Yorbel said, but he knelt beside the child. "Are you kind to others?"

The boy bobbed his head.

"If you think an ugly thought, do you keep it inside where it can't hurt anyone?"

Another nod.

"If you see someone who needs help, do you try to help them?"

A more tentative nod. His eyes flickered to his cup.

"I said 'try.' You don't need to give up food you need. But if you see someone fall in the street, do you try to help them stand?"

A more eager nod.

"Then that's all you need to do to make sure your next life is better than this one. Cultivate kindness. Never steal anyone's hope." He smiled gently at the boy. "I don't have to read your aura to know you'll be fine."

A tear leaked out of the boy's left eye. He dashed it away with a fist.

"Get yourself something to eat," Yorbel told him, and poured more coins into his cup.

The boy clutched the cup of coins to his chest and then scampered down the street. Hands pushing off his knees, Yorbel stood. He hoped his words helped. He believed every one of them. He just wished he knew how to say it without sounding like he was quoting a rehearsed speech.

"Are you preaching to the poor and downtrodden now?" a light female voice said behind him. "You know the bejeweled crocodiles you typically read will be heartbroken." He turned with a smile on his face—he knew that voice.

"Gissa!" Without hesitation, he threw his arms wide. His old friend . . . and one of the high augurs. He remembered the latter only belatedly, lowered his arms, and bowed. "Your High Eminence."

She laughed and embraced him. "Don't be ridiculous, Yorbel. I've missed you!" She then stepped back and surveyed him. "You have gray hairs in your beard."

He stroked it. "Does it make me look wise?"

"Very wise," she teased. She looked exactly the same as he remembered: pomegranate-round cheeks that always seemed to be smiling, silver braids twisted on the top of her head, and kindly brown eyes. She was the older sister he'd never had, the one who coached him through his studies when he was preparing for the augur tests, the one who teased him when he was acting too serious, the one he would trust with all his worries. Ever since the last emperor died, she'd been stationed in the western cities, helping to soothe the unrest. She'd had special training for unraveling sticky political situations and was frequently sent on missions by the high council. *By the River, how I've missed her!*

"When did you get back?" he asked. Side by side, they began strolling toward the temple. Not too fast, because of the heat. Not too slow, because otherwise they'd be stopped by citizens with questions about their aura. Everyone knew augurs weren't supposed to answer questions outside a formal reading, but everyone thought they'd be the exception. Ever since Emperor Zarin's death, even before the transition period stretched on, the people had been anxious—his death seemed to have rekindled an awareness in Becarans of their own mortality, and the lines at the temple for readings had only grown.

Yorbel wouldn't have minded granting peace of mind to a few anxious citizens, a casual word here or there, like he'd done for the palace guard, except that he couldn't promise it wouldn't devolve into a mad rush for free readings. He knew the local guards wouldn't appreciate it if he accidentally started a new riot in the streets. On the nearest street corner, a greenstone statue of a desert lion seemed to be staring at him reproachfully, as if critical of his thoughts.

"Only this morning," Gissa answered. "I decided to postpone the very exciting task of sorting my travel laundry and instead seek you out. I am hoping you'll dine with me tonight? Fill me in on all that I've missed?"

He wondered briefly how she'd known where to find him. The temple clerks knew about the summons, and all the temple guards saw him leave. It wouldn't have been that difficult to deduce. "I can think of nothing I'd like better, except that I regretfully won't be available." As soon as he had all his affairs in order, he planned to begin his search. An idea occurred to him. "Gissa, since you've returned, I wonder if you'd do me a favor?"

"Did you kill another houseplant? You know there's such a thing as too much love. One of these days you're going to drown a plant so thoroughly that I can't coax it back to life."

"That's not . . ." Well, truthfully, he *had* drowned another plant. It was only that they always looked so parched in the afternoon sun. "Yes, but I have some travel to do in the next few weeks, and I need someone to take over my readings."

"You? Travel? Where?"

Yorbel made a face at her. "I travel sometimes."

Gissa gestured at a palm-tree-lined plaza. "The walk from the palace to the temple does not count as travel. Where are you going, and why?"

He could have told her the truth. She was one of his oldest friends. *Lies stain the soul,* as was often said, especially lies between friends. But this . . .

There was friendship, and then there were politics.

It was better if the two were kept separate.

"The emperor-to-be is displeased with our progress in the search for his brother, and since I am the face he knows best of the augurs . . . I feel a little distance from the capital would be prudent." All he said was technically true, despite the implications.

"The emperor-to-be is a fool to lose faith in you."

He appreciated her loyalty, though he wished he hadn't predicated it with a lie. He reconsidered telling her the truth, but no, he'd promised discretion. He was not so naive as to think all actions were split neatly between right and wrong. You had to balance your intentions with potential consequences. The challenge of navigating that kind of moral ambiguity was precisely why people needed augurs to guide them. "It may be for the best. I haven't walked the sands in far too long. My soul needs this to keep its balance."

"Wise of you to realize that," Gissa said approvingly. "Then, to keep you from stagnation, I will happily do your scheduled readings. And save your plants."

"Thank you, Gissa. You are relieving me of much worry."

It occurred to him that he may need to tell many lies on his proposed journey. He wondered what the state of his soul would be at the end of it.

Better a tarnished soul than a dead friend.

He then buried that very un-augur-like thought deep within.

"How was your meeting with the emperor-to-be?" Gissa asked.

Yorbel knew he shouldn't be surprised, since she'd obviously known where to find him, but still . . . It wasn't as if the meeting itself was common knowledge to anyone but him and the student who had passed along the summons. He could have gone to the palace for any number of other purposes. "You've been back for mere hours, and you already know everything that's going on with everyone. You have a talent, Gissa."

She laughed. "That's the most polite way of saying 'You're nosy' that I've ever heard." Then she sobered. "Truthfully, Yorbel, how is our emperor-to-be?" She was treading closely to asking what they had discussed, which would have been an improper question. Confidentiality after consultation with an augur was customary and important. Also, it was law.

Early on in their existence, augur readings had been public. But people had used their results as an excuse to persecute others, and so the first High Council of Augurs, in their wisdom, had limited readings and imposed strict rules of privacy. *Of course, Gissa knows I can't discuss details of my conversation with Dar,* Yorbel thought. He gave her a true yet vague answer. "He loved his brother dearly and mourns him greatly."

Gissa nodded. "As is appropriate. But he cannot allow his emotions to interfere with his duties. Do you believe he is capable of setting aside his personal pain for the good of Becar?"

He considered his answer carefully. He trusted Gissa, of course, but now that she had been raised to the top tier of augurs, to talk with her was to talk with all the high augurs. And there were some he wasn't overly fond of, despite his respect for them and their integrity. In fact, his disagreement with some of their decisions was what had prevented them from inviting him to become a high augur, or so he had inferred. "I believe he wants to do his duty. But his brother's death was unexpected. He will need time to come to terms with it."

"He may not have time." Gissa was eyeing him more closely than Yorbel was comfortable with, as if she were trying to see what he wasn't saying. He wished the conversation hadn't shifted to politics. "Things are becoming more unsettled in the western cities with the passage of time, not less. As soon as the vessel for his late brother's soul is found, Prince Dar will need to move quickly to restore stability."

"He will be ready," Yorbel said, trying to put as much reassurance into his voice as possible. He hoped she'd believe him, and that she'd convey that to the council.

"Will he? Is he aware of how far the empire could fall before he's crowned? Soon, we will see an escalation of violence, as well as an increase in the threat from beyond our borders—"

"You think it will come to violence?" He knew the courtiers were impatient—the guard had made that clear—but he hadn't known that such concern had spread throughout Becar. Sequestered in the temple most days, Yorbel didn't have a feel for the mood of the bulk of the citizens.

"I do," she said seriously. "In some places, in small doses, it already has. We're lucky it is nearly race season. The races will distract the commoners for a time. But once they end, I fear the worst. He will need to be coronated by the end of the floods and ready to rule, or steps will have to be taken. Do you understand my meaning, Yorbel? The high council will not allow Becar to devolve into riots and war. We serve the greater good."

That was . . . troubling. He thought of all the rumors he'd heard about Gissa's "special training"—rumors he'd always denied, at least out loud. "Gissa, why are you asking these questions? Why did the high council summon you back?" He wasn't certain he wanted to hear the answer.

"In five weeks, when the races end, if the late emperor's vessel has not been found or if Prince Dar is too distraught to accept his responsibilities, *I* will be the one to see the peace is maintained."

"You?" But she was speaking of . . .

"Yes, Yorbel." Her voice was gentle, as if she knew he'd understood what she meant and knew it would upset him. "It is my duty."

"But . . ." There were a thousand things he wanted to say. He looked into her eyes and saw only her resolve—and perhaps a hint of pity. "Only five weeks?"

She looped her arm through his. "Much can happen in five weeks. Let's talk of pleasanter things. Tell me of all I've missed in the temple."

Only five weeks to prevent one friend from being killed . . . and another friend from being his killer. He wondered if his idea to search the kehoks was a waste of time—time that neither Dar nor Gissa had. Maybe he should abandon it as a wild-goose chase and actually chase geese instead. Perhaps the late emperor had simply been missed in one of the initial sweeps. Yorbel was more powerful than most of the augurs tasked with the search. Perhaps if he were to become involved in the main search . . .

But then no one would be checking the kehoks, and that lack of thoroughness could spell disaster.

Wrestling with his thoughts, Yorbel strolled with Gissa, his old friend and the woman known in whispers as the holy assassin, back to the temple.

CHAPTER 8

Standard practice if you had both a new rider and a new racer: train them separately. Drill the basics into each of them first before you expose them to each other. Build up the rider's strength. Accustom the kehok to the feel of obeying commands before you combine the two.

There's no time for standard, Tamra thought.

She was lucky that Raia wouldn't know the difference.

Unlucky that the other trainers would, however. Especially Osir. He wouldn't hesitate to share his opinions loudly and frequently, which could undermine Raia's confidence. Which meant it would be best if they trained elsewhere.

Arriving at the training grounds before dawn light had spread across the sands, Tamra barked at Raia to help her. Together, they hauled one of the racing carts out of its shed. Essentially a cage on wheels, it was used to transport kehoks to the races.

"Back it up to the stables," Tamra grunted. "By the River,

it's heavy." Ugh, her back hurt worse than it usually did, but she couldn't let Raia pull the cart by herself.

Sweating, they dumped it by the stable door. Tamra opened the cage door, then the stable door. Inside, she was pleased to see that her killer hadn't slaughtered any other kehoks in the night. His shackles had held. *A small miracle,* she thought.

"Why couldn't we have used this to get the lion off the ferry?" Raia asked.

"It's reserved for races," Tamra said.

Raia's mouth dropped open. "B-b-but I thought the races didn't start until—"

"No races yet. We need it for practice, so we're borrowing it. Or if you'd like to be technical about it, we're temporarily stealing it while there's no one here to tell us we can't. Happy?"

"Not really." Raia glanced around them as if she expected a city guard to pop out from behind a pile of manure and arrest them. "Are the others going to be angry?"

Tamra considered it. She didn't care if they were, but Raia obviously did. "Honestly, they'll be relieved we aren't training here with them."

"We're not?"

Examining the lion, Tamra held up her hand to Raia. "Love questions. Inquisitive minds are excellent. But I need you to shut up so I can focus."

Raia shut up.

Taking a deep breath, Tamra narrowed her attention on the black lion. "Got another cage for you," she told him. She wasn't taking any chances with partial focus when dealing with him. He could just be biding his time until she loosened his chains.

His eyes flickered toward her. Pinned down tightly, he couldn't move his head. *Oh, sweet Lady.* He hadn't been able to reach food or water all night—a common technique used on kehoks that needed to be broken.

Not common for me, Tamra thought.

If she hadn't been so wrapped up in worrying about Lady Evara's ultimatum last night, she would have noticed he'd been chained too far from the water bucket and fixed it.

She hauled a bucket of water inside the transport cage and then filled the food bin with meat from the shared supplies. She also strapped a barrel of water to the side of the cart for later. The other kehoks began to batter at their stall doors, eager to be fed as well, but she knew the other trainers' students would be tasked with that job. "You'll get yours later," Tamra told them.

She then opened the black lion's cage and loosened his restraints. "Drink. Eat."

The black lion didn't move, or even raise his head. Instead, he began to growl, a low rumble that sounded like distant thunder and grew until she felt it vibrate through the soles of her feet.

"You're hungry and thirsty," she told him. "Stubbornness won't cure that. Move."

She thought he was going to continue to resist, and she'd have her first battle of wills here before the day's training even began. But, dragging his chains, he limped into the cage and began to drink. She closed and locked the door behind him.

"How do we pull—" Raia began to ask.

Tamra gave her a stern look. She then opened the cage with the rhino-croc kehok and guided him to the front of the racing transport. She hooked his chains to the shaft of the cart as if he were a horse hitched to a carriage. Climbing into the driver's seat, she patted the bench beside her. Raia jumped up into the seat next to her.

"Where are the reins?" Raia asked. "Oh. Sorry. No questions. I forgot."

Leaning back and putting her feet up, Tamra flashed her a grin. "No worries. But also—no reins." She tapped her forehead. "Just this."

"But how—"

"You might want to hold on," Tamra advised. To the kehok, she commanded, "Go!"

The rhino-croc charged forward, and the cart lurched away from the stable. Jostled, Raia grabbed on to the bench. Tamra tilted her head back to feel the kiss of dawn, as she aimed the rhino-croc toward the open desert.

They thundered away from the training ground.

RAIA CLUNG TO THE BENCH AS THE CART SLICED through the sand. She'd wrapped a scarf around her face, leaving a slit for her eyes, as protection against the sting of the sand particles kicked up by the kehok's hooves. But she still felt sand on her face. It coated her tongue, filled her nose, and sneaked down her neck beneath her clothes. She felt as if the desert wanted to swallow her.

Aside from the times she'd watched the races, she'd never in her life been this far from the Aur River. Nearly everyone in Becar lived their lives within just a few miles of the river, only leaving the green swath of earth once a year to watch the Becaran Races out on the sands. So she'd only ever witnessed the desert as it looked when it was transformed by hundreds of people erecting viewing stands, pitching tents, and celebrating the turn of another season. In her imagination and memory, the desert was a crowded place.

Now, though, it was empty. Except for the sand. And the sky. Without all the trappings of the races, there was nothing to distract from the expanse of sky that stretched enormous above them. As the sun rose higher above the horizon, it bleached away the blueness, and the sand dunes around them changed from pink to a golden brown.

I never knew.

Legend said the desert was a gift from the sky to the earth. The constellations saw a lush, green world and wanted to shower it with their light, and so they sprinkled bits of stars. Those star bits became specks of sand, and where they fell, nothing grew. So much fell that the creatures feared it would extinguish all of existence. All the birds flapped their wings and all the animals blew to create wind to move the sand into one area. And then the warrior Aur cracked the world in the middle of the sand and created the mighty river. Or something like that.

Raia's father liked to tell that story as a cautionary tale for how even the best intentions can do harm, so why bother trying to be different from who you are? But that was the antithesis of how the augurs taught that story, and Raia was more inclined to believe them.

Because there was definitely something about all the sand that made her feel as if she were looking at a sky full of stars. The desert shimmered so brightly that she squinted from the glare.

At last, Trainer Verlas called to the rhino-croc to halt. He shuddered to a stop, his sides heaving and his tongue hanging out of his mouth. Trainer Verlas vaulted off the bench, unhooked the water barrel, and carried it to the kehok. She pried open the top so the kehok could drink the water inside. He began lapping it up as Trainer Verlas secured shackles around the rhino-croc's legs so he wouldn't be able to run.

Raia climbed down from the bench. She'd been so tense holding on that her muscles were stiff. She felt like a piece of bent metal that needed to be straightened.

"Ready?" Trainer Verlas asked her.

She didn't know what the correct answer would be. Yes? No? For what? Should she ask more questions? She had plenty, starting with: Was it safe to be out here? Sandstorms popped up all the time in the desert. Plus wild kehoks roamed the sands. And desert wraiths lurked beyond the edges of every city.

But Trainer Verlas didn't wait for her to speak. She strode around the back of the cart with a hint of a limp. Raia wondered if it was a race injury and realized she didn't know why Trainer Verlas had quit racing. She'd just assumed it was age, but Raia could recognize hidden pain when she saw it.

She didn't think her trainer would appreciate it if she asked, though. With difficulty, Raia held all her questions inside.

Trainer Verlas unlatched the cage door and swung it open. "I am going to set him free, and you are going to keep him here," she said to Raia.

New, more pressing questions now jumped into her mind. Specifically: *What?*

Yes, she'd called for him to come off the ferry, but he'd wanted to savage her, and there had been a chain net to stop him. *Trust your trainer*, Raia reminded herself. *She wants you to succeed. In fact, she* needs *you to succeed.* Still, there was something she needed to ask.

"How?"

"He'll have two conflicting desires: stay and kill us, or run and be free. You must give him a third option: run with you."

"But . . ." She'd barely escaped his claws when he'd been caged! And he'd proven himself hard to control, even by multiple trainers.

"Banish all stray thoughts," Trainer Verlas said. "All doubts. All memories of the past. All dreams of the future. Exist in the here and now."

Raia nodded. She clenched and unclenched her hands. She felt just as tense as she had clinging to the bench of the cart.

"Control your thoughts and you can control him, without weapons, without special tricks." Trainer Verlas unshackled one of the kehok's legs. He began to shift, his leg muscles taut as if he were ready to run.

Focus, Raia told herself.

"Keep from losing him," Trainer Verlas said. "You lose him, you lose your future."

Raia swallowed and nodded. Without a racer, she couldn't be a rider. If she failed at this, she might as well go back into hiding and to running from her family. *I don't want to run from anyone anymore. I want to run to something.*

"Feel the moment."

Closing her eyes, Raia felt the sand beneath her feet, heard the wind across the dunes, and inhaled the dusty, almost sweet smell that permeated the air.

"Let your need fill you. What is it you want most of all?"

Freedom. And this kehok was the key.

She heard the clink of iron. The low growl of the black

lion. She opened her eyes in time to see him rush out of the cage. His obsidian mane flashed in the morning desert sun.

Without thinking, Raia threw her hands in the air, palms toward the lion. "Stay!"

The lion faltered.

Only for an instant.

And then he was running. Sand flew in his path as he thundered past them toward the east, as if he intended to run straight into the sun's glow.

"Come back!" Raia called.

But he didn't slow. He was a black star streaking across the sandy sky. Unstoppable. She felt small, as if she'd been just another rock beneath his paws.

She felt hands on her shoulders, squeezing hard. "Call him back," Trainer Verlas said in her ear. "Now. Before he's gone too far. Make him hear you. Make him *feel* you."

"Come back!" Raia cried. Ripping the scarf away from her face, she poured every bit of oxygen in her lungs into her shout. She thought of her parents, and the way they'd looked at her when she'd come home in tears after the augur exams. They already knew the news, and they looked at her as if she were muck that had stuck on their shoes. She thought of the man they wanted her to marry, the way his eyes had raked over her. She thought of his greasy fingers when he took her hand to kiss it, the way they caressed her arm, as if testing the thickness of a cut of meat. *I can't go back! Please, lion.*

"Come back now!"

He kept running.

He didn't even slow.

Trainer Verlas's voice boomed across the sands, "You *will* return."

And the lion's stride broke. Raia saw it—his rhythm

hitched, and then he was running back toward them, as fast as he'd run before, with a cloud of sand haloing him.

He ran without stopping into the cage, and Trainer Verlas sprang forward and slammed the door shut. He shook his mane, and it clanged like bits of glass shattering.

"I failed," Raia said.

"It was your first try," Trainer Verlas said. "And he is strong-willed."

"How did you do it? It took all of you before, when he broke out of the stables."

"He caught me by surprise then." Trainer Verlas frowned as if she were angry at herself, as if it were her fault that the black lion had broken out. "Plus, I have more motivation now."

Raia watched the lion pace in his cage. She knew what that felt like—this wasn't the first time she'd tried to run away. When she was first chosen as an augur, she'd made it to the end of the garden before her father hauled her back inside. Six months into her training, she'd tried again, and her family had sent her to live at the temple full-time. She hadn't tried to run from there. She'd realized if she succeeded, she would have to return home. "I couldn't bring him back."

"We'll work on it." Trainer Verlas sank down onto the sand, and Raia saw how strained she looked. Sweat was beaded on her forehead, staining the edges of her scarf.

Raia hurried to the front of the cart, found a canteen, and brought it to her.

Trainer Verlas drank a few swallows. "Been pushing myself lately. Body doesn't obey the way I think it should." She smiled wryly. "It won't listen to my commands, at least not anymore. There's a certain irony in that."

"I did everything you said. I focused on what I want. I

want my freedom so badly that it hurts. I can't want it any more badly than I already do." Raia sank onto the sand next to her. "But it's not enough.

"I'm not enough," she whispered.

"YOU *ARE* ENOUGH," TAMRA SAID BRISKLY. "YOU'RE JUST not ready." No self-pitying nonsense on her watch. It was a waste of the here and now.

Looking out across the desert, Tamra considered the problem. The wind blew across the dunes, swirling the sand as if it were dancing, and Tamra remembered the first time she'd raced the sands, just her and a monster. It had felt . . . like power, like her blood was replaced by wind, like she was as strong as the river, like she was as unstoppable as the sun. She wanted Raia to have a chance to feel that.

Raia was right: she *did* have the fire. Tamra could see it in the way she held herself and hear it in the timbre of her voice, so why wasn't that enough for the kehok? If any of her paid students had displayed half that kind of desire, they would have had their kehoks squatting at their feet like obedient puppies. Maybe it wasn't Raia, then. Maybe it was the lion. Certainly it had taken every ounce within Tamra to draw the lion back—she had surprised him, and that moment of surprise had allowed her to override his will. She'd never met a kehok so difficult to control.

Beside her, Raia was hugging her knees to her chest. She looked, for a moment, like Shalla, and her disappointment felt like another of Tamra's failures. *This is my fault,* Tamra thought. *I promised her the moon.* "We'll find a way to make it work."

"In two weeks?".

"Yes," Tamra said firmly, though she wasn't sure how. "You will be free. I promise."

That seemed to reassure the girl a little.

Feeling as if a weight had settled on her, Tamra glanced at the cage to see the black lion kehok staring at her with his unreadable golden eyes. He was still and silent, alert and watching—which was very un-kehok. A thought occurred to her. "What exactly did you focus on?"

"How badly I want to be free."

And the lion had run.

Huh.

Usually it didn't work like that. Kehoks responded to commands fueled by need, but they typically didn't respond to the underlying need itself. But this kehok wanted his freedom too. He'd broken out of his stall and killed another kehok for that very purpose. . . .

She felt an idea worming inside her. It was a risky, unusual idea that went against much of what she knew about kehoks.

But then again, everything about this situation was risky and definitely went against what she knew.

To win a race, rider and racer had to share a singular purpose. Typically that was imposed on the racer by the rider. What if, though, Raia and the lion could share the *same* purpose? What if instead of trying to stop his bid for freedom, they could make him understand that racing was his way *to* freedom?

It was a complex concept for any kehok to grasp, and she didn't know if it was possible for any kehok to be intelligent enough to understand the ramifications of the reward that awaited the grand champion. But this beast was much more alert and aware than most.

It could work.

Standing, Tamra steadied herself. She limped closer to the cage—her old wound was really throbbing now. The sand shifted around her feet, slowing her. She saw Raia pop up and hurry to her, ready to help, but she shooed her away. In front of the lion, she unwound her scarf and shifted her tunic so that her tattoo showed. "Do you know what this is?" she asked the kehok. "It's a picture of the victory charm. If you race and you win, you win this charm. If you race and you win, you will break the cycle. You will be reborn as human. You won't be a kehok anymore. If you race and you win, you have a second chance. You will have your freedom."

The lion was watching her. She didn't know if he understood any of it.

"Running away from us . . . it won't make you free, because you bring who you are with you. The only way to be free of your fate is to race." She tapped her tattoo. "If you race with Raia, you win this. Your freedom."

"Does he understand?" Raia whispered.

"One way to tell," Tamra said. "You need to ride."

"I'LL DIE!" RAIA SAID. "YOU SAW HOW I FAILED!"

How could Trainer Verlas even think she was ready to ride him? She hadn't even made him stop, let alone come back.

"That's the thing," Trainer Verlas said, approaching the cage. "I don't think you did fail." Padding back and forth within the narrow cage, the lion was watching her. "I think he ran in part because he wanted to, and in part because *you* wanted to. If you run together, you with him, perhaps he'll understand."

"But you can't be sure."

"I'm sure we don't have a better choice."

This was crazy.

"I'll keep him from killing you."

Raia thought of how the others had warned her about Trainer Verlas and said she breaks riders, not racers. She thought of the problems her trainer had already had in controlling the kehok, and she remembered the rumors she'd heard about last year's final championship race. Could she trust her trainer?

Do I have a choice?

Of course she did. You always have a choice. It was just that the other option was terrible.

Raia took a deep breath. There was one question she needed answered before she'd do this. "What happened in the final championship race last year?"

Trainer Verlas halted. It was obvious it was a question she'd heard before and just as obvious it was one she didn't want to answer. But Raia *needed* the answer. It wasn't curiosity or because she wanted to gossip or anything like that.

"My rider lost control."

"Just like that? He'd survived every other race, but in the final one, close to winning everything he wanted—"

"Yes. It was too much. All of it. He wanted too much, and it consumed him."

"You mean—"

"You've heard the rumors. It was just as bad as they say. His kehok killed him before anyone could make it through the track's psychic shield to intervene. But it wasn't rage. It wasn't destruction. It was hunger."

"You're saying his kehok *ate* him?"

"I said 'consume.' I meant it literally."

Raia shuddered. That was a terrible way to die.

"He was still screaming when the kehok began. It didn't wait for him to die." Trainer Verlas's eyes were fixed beyond the cage, beyond the horizon, as if she wasn't seeing any of the desert at all. Her jaw was locked, and Raia was grateful she didn't have the memory that her trainer was reliving. "It was my fault. I should have seen the danger signs—when the race council reviewed his case, they agreed I should have known. Some argued I must have known and had proceeded anyway, because I wanted to win more than I wanted my rider to survive. I was fined for negligence, nearly barred from racing. But the truth is that I didn't see. I wanted to win so badly too that it blinded me—which is almost certainly worse."

Raia licked her lips. They were gritty from the sand. She tasted the dry dust—the desert had its own taste, oddly peppery and a bit like old paper. She felt hyperaware of everything as she stared at Trainer Verlas's face. "What were the danger signs?"

"To race, you must focus on the moment. Your aura must be steady, concentrated on the present. If you lose who you are, if you lose *why* you are doing what you're doing in that moment, then it's over." Trainer Verlas tore her eyes from the horizon and shifted to look at her student.

Raia felt as if the sun were beaming at her, so intense were Trainer Verlas's eyes. She thought she understood what Trainer Verlas was saying—she felt focused right now, as if she were absorbing as well as hearing every word Trainer Verlas said.

"I don't think you will suffer that fate. You know who you are."

Who am I? Raia wanted to ask. "I'm the girl who failed to become an augur."

"That's not it."

"I'm the runaway who's hiding from her family."

"And?"

"I'm a student trying to become a rider, but I don't know if I can. I've failed every task you've given me. I can't even call my kehok back to me. I don't know why you think I'd be ready to ride, except that you want me to so badly that it's blinding you."

Trainer Verlas's eyes bored into hers with such intensity that Raia felt dizzy. "Don't think about failing. Don't think about winning. Just answer me this: What do you want, Raia?"

"To be free." Her voice was barely a whisper.

"Why?"

"Because . . . because I'm afraid he'll hurt me if I marry him."

"And?"

"Isn't that enough? I'll be afraid every day. I won't be happy."

"Because you won't have love? You won't have your own special someone to hold you close at night, to whisper your secrets to, to tell you you're beautiful?"

Raia shook her head. She hadn't even thought of what she did want. She'd been so subsumed by fear of what she didn't. "It's not that I want to marry someone else. I don't want to marry him."

"You didn't want to become an augur either."

"I did!" Eventually. When she saw there was no other choice. When it seemed like the best choice. "But I failed. I disappointed my teachers and my family and—"

"And you felt a shred of relief, because that wasn't the future for you," Trainer Verlas pressed. "You felt a little bit free, because you hadn't chosen the augurs. They chose you, based on a past life you don't remember. And when you failed, you set yourself free. Life isn't just about who you were—it's about who you choose to be."

"I didn't want to fail! I worked hard, but I just didn't have the talent—"

"It wasn't you."

"It wasn't me," Raia agreed. She'd never had the natural strength they expected her to have. Her instinct with auras was weak, and she'd never been able to hone it properly, the way the others did. She'd struggled, asking question after question about things her teachers believed should have been obvious, trying to understand why she couldn't do what they asked of her, and it only became worse as she advanced through the levels. It had been a kind of relief to fail. But her family hadn't felt that way.

"Why did you come to me?" Trainer Verlas asked.

"Because you're the best," Raia said promptly. *And because I thought you might take me. You're desperate. Like me.*

"Why racing?"

Because I need the prize money. Because I have no other skills. Because it's said anyone can become a racer. Because I have no other options. But she didn't think those were the reasons Trainer Verlas wanted to hear. She opened her mouth to say something about the excitement of the races, the thrill of the crowd, the hunger for the prize. None of those words came out. Instead, she found herself saying, "Because I want something that's mine. All my life, I've never gotten to choose. I didn't pick my family. I didn't want to become an augur. I never agreed to marry."

She couldn't read Trainer Verlas's expression. She had

no idea if this was the right answer or not. But Raia couldn't seem to stop talking: "It's not like I've dreamed of becoming a rider. I chose this because it was the best out of my terrible options. But . . . I chose it. Myself. And that matters. Doesn't it? It *should* matter."

Pushing off her knees, Trainer Verlas stood. "Yes, it should." She limped to the cage. "Help me saddle him. You're going to ride him, and I'm going to keep him from killing you."

Raia jumped to her feet. "Wait—was that the right answer?"

"There isn't a right answer. Anyone who says there is is lying."

Free from his shackles, the lion lunged at Trainer Verlas as she approached the cage door. But she held up one hand, and he slunk backward. Raia hadn't heard her say a word.

"Why did you stop racing?" Raia asked. She clearly still had control over kehoks. Raia wasn't sure she'd seen any rider who was so comfortable with them.

"Injury to the leg. Can't stay in the saddle for long enough to complete the race. No more questions now." Trainer Verlas opened the cage door. "Bring me the saddle."

Raia scurried to the supplies by the front of the cart. She'd seen the saddle there. Hefting it out, she carried it to the cage.

The lion was lying at Trainer Verlas's feet.

"Place it on his back," Trainer Verlas instructed.

Cautiously, Raia entered the cage. She lowered the saddle onto the lion. He lunged forward with a roar, and she screamed and slammed against the back of the cage with her arms over her face.

Then she heard a whimper.

He was lying down, cringing, while Trainer Verlas fastened the saddle onto him.

"I don't know if I'm ready," Raia said. She'd reacted without thinking. What if she cowered like that while she was on him? Riders were supposed to be in command, and she was barely in command of herself.

"Of course you're not. But it's okay, because there's no such thing as ready," Trainer Verlas said. "There's only the moment and what you do with it." She pointed to straps on the saddle as well as to a lump of leather at the front. "You tie yourself in here. You hold here."

At least it was a training saddle. A race saddle had no straps.

She didn't find that overly reassuring.

Raia tiptoed toward the lion. It watched her. He was far more massive than an ordinary lion. It would be like mounting a horse. A very dangerous horse. Gingerly, she touched the saddle.

He shuddered.

"Can you really keep him from killing me?" Raia asked.

"This time," Trainer Verlas promised. "I can't interfere in an official race. But it's only us today, and we're nowhere near a track. All you need to do is hang on."

"But if I'm just cargo right now, why do this?" It felt as if she was endangering herself for nothing. Shouldn't she learn to control him first, and then work up to riding him? Then she realized she was questioning her teacher again—exactly the kind of behavior the augurs had always scolded her for. They'd told her she'd succeed if only she'd apply herself to her lessons instead of questioning them. She *had* applied herself, but she'd also questioned, in large part because the lessons didn't seem to work for her. What if the same was true here? "I'm sorry. I just don't want to fail again."

"You can't fail," Trainer Verlas said. "All you need to do is feel whatever you feel as you ride, and then you'll know whether you found the right answer or not."

Raia climbed onto the saddle, and the kehok shuddered again beneath her. She could feel his shaking up through her thighs. Her trainer helped her secure the straps. She wrapped her hands around the saddle grip. Her heart felt as though it was thumping so fast that the beats blurred into one another.

"Go," Trainer Verlas said. "Run."

The lion shot out of the cage. Raia screamed as the wind slammed into her. She hunched over the saddle as it shook beneath her. And then the lion was running across the sands.

Wind streamed into her, stealing the scarf from around her head, yanking her hair backward. She was within a cloud of tan, as the lion kicked up sand as he ran. The sun beat on her back. And she realized she was no longer screaming.

This . . . this was amazing!

The lion ran across the sands, and she felt as if she were within the wind, part of it, sweeping across the dunes. His gait was even, gliding over the desert, but he was running so fast that the sand around her was blurred.

Riding the lion, she felt free.

And she finally understood what Trainer Verlas was saying: *I chose this.* That was her reason. It didn't matter if it was anyone else's. It was hers, and that was enough.

I am enough.

CHAPTER 9

Everything changed after Raia rode the lion.

Before dawn the next day, Tamra and Raia were back at the training grounds, dragging out the cart, hooking up the rhino-croc, and driving out into the sands with the black lion kehok. This time, Raia was the one to fasten the saddle, with Tamra holding the black lion steady.

"You'll keep me alive again, won't you?" Raia asked.

"Of course," Tamra promised. And true to her word, she kept her focus on the kehok—at least for the first few days. Slowly, she withdrew her control, though she stayed ready and alert, as she watched Raia and the black lion run across the sands. *She can do this,* Tamra thought. *She has the fire. She only needed for her kehok to feel her burn.*

On the third day, Tamra and Raia removed the chain net and harness. His speed doubled, and Raia rode with an enormous, giddy smile.

On the fifth day, after they'd run so far they were spots on the horizon and then returned, Raia slid off the lion and announced, "I'm ready. Teach me how to race him on my own."

"You already know."

Raia stifled a sigh, but Tamra still heard it. "You've been saying from the beginning—I have the fire inside, but I—"

"I haven't commanded the black lion during your rides since your third day."

That silenced Raia.

Tamra smiled.

From there, the lessons accelerated. Seven days before the first qualifying race, Tamra introduced the challenge of running with other kehoks. She controlled the rhino-croc, forcing it to run alongside the black lion. At first, the black lion was distracted, trying to attack the other monster. But then he seemed to realize that only slowed him down, and he began to ignore the other racer.

So Tamra made the rhino-croc crash into them, cutting them off.

This time, the black lion did attack, and it took Tamra imposing her will on top of Raia's to separate the black lion from the rhino-croc. Blood was spattered on the sand as the two monsters circled, growling at each other.

"Stop for a rest?" Tamra offered. Soon, they'd need to take shelter from the searing heat anyway. Her tunic felt saturated with sweat.

"No." Raia mounted the black lion again.

With a rush of pride, Tamra tightened her grip on the rhino-croc's mind. She performed the same move, cutting them off, and this time the black lion tossed him back and kept running.

The next day, Tamra added the lion-lizard to the exercise. She ran both kehoks close to the black lion, trying to mimic the claustrophobic feel of running with twenty other racers and their riders inside the racetrack.

Raia was able to get the lion to leave them in the dust.

Five days before the first qualifying race, Tamra stopped Raia as she went to haul out the transport cart. "You'll run on the track today."

It was time to see how well she ran against other racers.

Raia didn't question that. Instead, she ran for the saddle and into the stable to prepare the black lion, while Tamra limped to the racetrack. All the time out on the sands had aggravated her old injury, as much as she tried to hide it.

She leaned against the gate to the starting stalls and gazed across the familiar oval of sand. It was churned up by the other racers whom the other trainers had been running through here, day after day.

"You're going to try the track today?" Osir asked from behind her.

"She's ready," Tamra said.

"After one week? On that monster? Doubt that."

"Then watch," Tamra said. "You'll see."

She said it with a confidence she didn't feel. It was one thing to race across the open sands. It was another to experience the claustrophobic intensity of the track, knowing your trainer couldn't help you, knowing it was just you and a monster who wanted to rip you apart. Still, the girl had come a long way in a short amount of time.

And they really didn't have a choice.

"It helped to not have the distraction of other students," Tamra said.

"Tell yourself that. Green rider and an unbroken killer?" Osir snorted. "My riders have been learning how to function within a group, to take the curves in the track, to handle a crowd. Mark my words: yours will spook. And as long as she's within the track's shield, you can't help her. None of us can."

"I know all this."

"It doesn't seem like it."

"She has the control."

Osir lowered his voice. "Place a wager?"

"I don't bet on my riders." Tamra pushed away from the gate and began to walk back to the stable. Raia would need help bringing the black lion to the starting stall—she wouldn't know where to go, and he might resist the change from the open desert.

"Because you know she'll lose!" Osir called after her.

Over her shoulder, she flashed him a smile that showed none of her doubt. "Because I know she'll win. It's not sporting to bet on a sure thing."

INSIDE THE STABLE, RAIA TALKED TO THE BLACK LION AS she saddled him. "Today we're not going out into the desert to train. We're going to run around a racetrack. So I need you not to eat me."

She never knew how much he understood, but it made her feel better to talk.

"You know we're a team. We want the same thing. Are you going to work with me today?" She shouldn't phrase it as a question. More firmly, she said, "We're going to work together. You and me."

Yanking on a strap, she tightened the saddle. He growled, low. "Sorry, but it has to be tight," she told him. Otherwise she'd go flying off, which he'd probably like, but she wasn't keen to try.

He glared at her, but he couldn't do anything about it.

He no longer wore the iron chain net—it would slow him down too much in a race—but he wasn't loose either. His head was muzzled, and his legs were shackled. Regardless of the progress they'd made, she wasn't releasing him until Trainer Verlas told her it was time. *Just because I've ridden him doesn't mean I'm not still afraid of him.* She was fully aware of what he could do.

She heard footsteps enter the stable.

The other kehoks screamed.

"Oh, shut up." It was Jalimo, one of the other students.

Rising up on her toes, Raia peeked over the stall door and saw two of the three students she'd met before—Jalimo and Algana. She hadn't had a chance to talk with them since she'd arrived, and she still hadn't met any of the other students who trained here or any of the paying students. She'd always been here and on her way out into the desert before they arrived, and back well after they left. Her throat suddenly dry, she said tentatively, "Hi."

"Hey, you're not dead!" Jalimo said. He elbowed Algana. "She's not dead."

Algana beamed at her. "Raia! We heard a race cart was out, and we thought . . . well, that is . . ."

Jalimo jumped in helpfully. "What she means to say is: we thought you were dead and your trainer took a cart to dispose of your body. Lots of sand. Jackals. You know."

"That is *not* what I meant to say," Algana said.

"It wasn't?"

"Well, it was, but then I thought better of it. She obviously wasn't dead because the cart kept coming back and going out again." Algana picked up a saddle and slung it onto the back of a rhino-like kehok with cheetah markings on her side.

"Right," Jalimo said, clearly having not put those facts together. "Anyway, I thought those carts were just for getting to races," he continued as he began to prepare another kehok, a lizard with powerful elephant-like legs.

Raia felt her face warm, and she hoped they couldn't tell. "We, um, borrowed one?"

"You should have trained here with us!" Algana said. "What were you doing out in the desert anyway? My trainer says it's dangerous to give the kehoks a taste of freedom. They'll spend the whole race trying to break out of the track." She quickly added, "Not that I'm criticizing your trainer!"

"She is," Jalimo said.

"A little bit," Algana admitted. "But we were worried about you."

"You were?" Raia hadn't thought they'd give her a moment's thought beyond their one conversation. She hadn't thought about them at all, and now she felt bad about that. She'd been so focused on running faster and faster with the black lion. That was one of the best things about riding: not thinking about anything else.

Okay—she didn't feel *that* bad.

Silar entered the stable, ducking through the doorway—she wasn't quite tall enough that she needed to duck. It was most likely habit. "Yeah, they gossip about you all the time. Hi, Raia, good to see you again."

"Friendly, worried gossip!" Algana yelped.

"Nothing bad," Jalimo said. "Just that you'd probably been gored by your kehok, left while you bled out, and then dumped in the dunes for the buzzards to find and destroy any evidence."

"But it was friendly because we didn't *want* that to happen," Algana said, with a hopeful don't-be-angry-at-me smile.

"And if it had, we wanted you to be reborn as something nice. Like a butterfly, at least."

Raia laughed.

Silar went directly to another stall, one with a kehok that looked like a dog made of silver metal. "Trainer Osir said we'll be racing one another."

Raia's laugh died. When Trainer Verlas said she'd be on the racetrack, Raia had assumed it would be solo—a few laps to get the feel of the track. She didn't think she'd be racing with other riders. At least not immediately. *I shouldn't have assumed.* "He did?"

"Said we have to be ready for anything on the track," Silar said. "And that you would . . . keep us on our toes." Raia doubted those were the words he'd used. And she wondered if Trainer Osir had other motivation. *He's made it obvious he doesn't approve of how Trainer Verlas handles her riders and racers. He probably wants me to fail.*

She wondered if Trainer Verlas realized that, and decided the answer was yes.

She wasn't sure if that made her feel better or worse.

Jalimo looked worried enough for the both of them. "Just to be clear, do we need to worry about your kehok trying to gut our kehoks?"

Probably, Raia thought. "I won't let him?" She tried to sound confident, but her voice curled up at the end as if in question. She winced and wanted to ask: *Can we still be friends if I almost kill you?*

"Great!" Jalimo said, as if the uncertainty wasn't obvious in her voice.

Raia turned to the black lion and whispered, "You won't let me down, will you?"

He growled.

She reminded herself she needed to be confident, like Trainer Verlas. She wondered if Trainer Verlas had ever doubted herself with a kehok. There must have been a first time she tried to ride one. Raia knew she'd had accidents—the limp that sometimes worsened was from a race. Surely, she'd had some doubts at some point?

The students quit talking when their trainers came in. Raia was relieved to hear she wasn't the only one who needed assistance in safely coaxing her kehok out of the stable. She kept the shackles on him for the trip to the starting stalls on the track. The openings looked ominous, like mouths ready to chew them up and spit them out.

"He hasn't run on a track ever," Raia said anxiously. She was hoping Trainer Verlas would say she could take a lap without any of the other riders and racers. Truth be told, she was hoping her teacher would tell her to bring the lion back to the stable and forget this folly.

"Run him as if you were on the desert sands," Trainer Verlas advised instead. "Treat the turns as if they're sand dunes. Use them to build power. Let him loose on the straightaways."

"It will all be new to him."

"You're coddling him."

"I just don't want him to kill my friends."

"Then don't let him." Trainer Verlas acted as if it were easy.

The first time she ran with the rhino-croc it hadn't gone well. In fact, the first time she'd tried anything new it hadn't gone well. She didn't see why this would be any different.

"It's going to be a disaster," Raia warned.

Trainer Verlas stopped, which meant Raia stopped, which meant the kehok had to stop. He pawed the sandy ground and snorted at them through the muzzle. "Raia. Quit it. You have to be in the moment."

Raia hung her head. "I know." She didn't know why she was feeling so nervous when everything had been going so great out on the dunes. *Maybe because it* has *been going great. I don't want to go back to messing up.*

Of course, worrying about messing up was the exact thing that could mess her up. But recognizing the paradox didn't make it any easier to dismiss.

They resumed walking toward the stalls, and Trainer Verlas ordered the black lion into his. Jalimo and Silar were on either side of her, with Algana beyond Silar. There was room for up to twenty in the starting stalls, but only the four of them were racing today. Other students were drifting toward the stands, attracted by the prospect of a practice race.

"Riders up," Trainer Verlas ordered.

It was different mounting a kehok in the stall than out on the sands. She mimicked the others, climbing a ladder and then lowering herself into the saddle. She strapped herself in. Beneath her, the black lion's mane bristled, clinking together like glass.

"We're just going to run," Raia told him. "No different than out on the sands." Louder, to Trainer Verlas, she asked, "You'll be there, won't you? To keep this from being a catastrophe?" *It will be fine,* she thought, trying to will herself to believe it. Still, she wanted the reassurance that this wasn't as dangerous as it seemed. Surely, she'd have a safety net for this first time in the track.

"Race conditions, remember?" Trainer Verlas pointed to the air above the racetrack, where the psychic shield shimmered like heat over the sand. "No trainer can interfere."

She smiled in what was probably meant to be a comforting way. "We'll be near, though, in case of emergency. Of course, if the worst happens, it most likely will occur too fast for us to make it through the shield."

That . . . was not comforting.

"You can do this," Trainer Verlas said with finality, and then she stomped back toward the stands, where the other trainers and about a dozen paying students were all waiting and watching.

"*That's* your trainer's idea of a pep talk?" Jalimo said, staring after Trainer Verlas. "'We'll help you, but by then you'll already be dead'? Very helpful."

She'd been thinking the same thing, but she felt as if she should defend Trainer Verlas. "Well, what does your trainer say to you?"

From the stands, Trainer Osir cupped his hands around his mouth and bellowed, "Show them no option! Show them no mercy! Ride them hard!"

Raia raised her eyebrows at Jalimo.

"He more shouts than peps," Algana admitted.

They all focused on the track ahead. It was a narrow straightaway into a curve. Like running through a canyon. *I can do this,* Raia thought.

And then: *I wish I was out on the sands.*

"Ready?" Trainer Osir bellowed.

No, Raia thought. She immediately corrected that: *Yes. We can do this.* "Run. That's all we have to do," she whispered to the lion. "You know how. Run like there's no one around. Run like we're on the open sand."

"Prepare!" Trainer Osir shouted. Then: "Race!"

And then Trainer Verlas hit the lever that unlatched the gates simultaneously. The gates slammed open, and all four kehoks leaped forward. Raia clung to the saddle. "Run!" she cried. "Run!"

Out of the corner of her eye, she saw Algana hit the backside of her cheetah-rhino with a spiked whip. "Faster or death!" she cried.

The others echoed her: "Faster or death!"

Raia's focus snapped. She didn't want—

She felt it the moment her concentration broke, and knew with absolute certainty what would happen next: *Blood.* He'd attack the others. Claws. Teeth. Jaws ripping at their legs—she saw it in her imagination in a fast burst of images before she clamped it down. "Run!" she screamed at the lion. "Please, just run!"

And to her shock, he did.

He powered past the other kehoks, leaving them in clouds of sand kicked up by his hind paws. She heard the cheers behind her as she took the lead, and she leaned forward into the wind, rising up a few inches in the saddle, the way she did out on the sands.

They neared the first turn, and she tried to think of it like a dune, like her trainer had said, and take the curve—

But the black lion didn't turn.

He ran straight toward the wall of the track.

"No! Turn! Please, turn!"

Raia felt his weight shift. *Oh no, he's going to—*

He jumped, sailing into the air.

The racetrack walls were built high, so that no kehok could escape into the crowd, but they weren't high enough for the black lion. His stomach scraped along the top, and he landed hard on the other side. Raia was knocked forward into his mane. Her forehead hit the obsidian, and pain blossomed, obliterating all other thought.

She didn't lose consciousness, though. She kept clinging to the saddle as the black lion ran across the sands, away from the racetrack and toward the open emptiness.

TAMRA WATCHED THE BLACK LION CLEAR THE WALL and run, with Raia on his back, into the desert. She wanted to shut her eyes and unsee it.

Around her, all the students were shouting. They'd never seen a kehok leave the track. It was common for them to attack their rider or the other racers. Sometimes they refused to run. Often they tried to attack the audience. They *never* fled. It had caught everyone off guard, Tamra included, and no one had reacted fast enough to stop it, even once they'd removed the shield.

At least I've given them something new to gossip about, she thought.

"Mount a rescue," Osir ordered. He began to bark at the other trainers.

Tamra held up her hand.

He quieted.

"She'll come back," Tamra said, eyes fixed on the desert.

"You're betting a lot on a student who couldn't control her mount enough to stay in the race!" Osir said. "If we move fast, we *might* be able to reach her before her kehok quits running and decides to kill her."

Tamra repeated, "She'll come back. Wait."

"She's not a paying student, right?" Zora said anxiously beside her. "Where's she from? Does she have family who will inquire about her?"

Tamra pressed her lips into a line and told herself that Zora was only looking out for the welfare of them all. If Raia had family who would press charges, they could all be brought before the race council for endangerment of a student. "She's an orphan, she says." Just because she later admitted it was a lie didn't mean Tamra couldn't say it.

"Good," Zora said.

The other three students had finished the race and were jogging toward the three trainers. In the lead was the girl with the shaved head—Tamra had never bothered to learn her name. "We're going after her, aren't we? Why isn't anyone going after her?"

"Raia knows how to race the sands," Tamra said. "She's safest if we keep our distance. Pursue her, and she'll have a harder time coming back." The lion would run faster or, worse, turn on her if he sensed them chasing after him. Her odds were better if she were on her own.

I should have realized she wasn't ready, Tamra thought.

Deep inside, Raia was still running away.

Damn her family to the depths of the River.

Tamra stayed in the stands, waiting, while the others continued to whisper around her. She ignored all further attempts to argue with her, and instead kept her eyes trained on the sands. Raia and the black lion were no longer visible.

The sun crept across the sky.

She didn't move, even though sweat stuck her tunic to her back, even though the wind blew sand in her eyes. She kept her eyes and her will focused on the desert, as if she could summon them back—she knew at this range it was impossible, but she maintained her vigil.

By sundown, Raia hadn't returned.

Tamra did not allow herself to doubt or worry. Raia *would* come back. She was stronger than her fear. *I could not have judged her so badly. I will not lose faith. I believe in her.*

That was what she said each time another student or trainer came to question Tamra:

"I believe in her."

By nightfall, the others were gone, and it was only Tamra, watching the darkening desert. *Shalla will be home.* She'd be fixing herself supper and wondering where her mother and Raia were. She'd set two extra plates at the table. *I can't go home without Raia.* What would she say to her daughter? That she waited for a while and then gave up? What kind of message would that send? Giving up on Raia meant giving up on everything: winning the races, paying the augurs, protecting Shalla's future, and being a good mother.

I should have gone after her.

It was far too late now. The time to do that was in the first few minutes. By now, the wind would have obscured all tracks. If she wasn't back by dawn, Tamra would have to search for her. For her body.

If she didn't return . . .

She will, Tamra thought. She stared at the desert, a black sea beneath the stars, and commanded it: *Bring her back.*

She thought she saw a flicker of movement.

Stepping onto the bleachers, Tamra peered out toward the darkness, as if squinting would somehow make it brighter. She must have imagined it. Now she saw nothing except the shift of shadows that was wind blowing across the sands.

Except were the shadows thicker in one spot?

She stared at it, willing it to resolve into shapes. *Come back.*

And then she saw them: Raia on the black lion, stumbling across the sands, back toward the training ground. They were a hundred yards out when they both fell and didn't move.

Tamra ran to the shed, yanked out the transport cart,

and then ran to the stable and hooked up the rhino-croc. She drove it out onto the sands. Her eyes scanned the darkness, looking for where she'd seen them fall.

She spotted them: motionless mounds between the waves of sand. "Faster!" she commanded the rhino-croc. He thundered over the dunes, the only sound beyond the wind.

Reaching them, Tamra jumped off the bench. She ran to Raia.

Raia pried her eyes open. "I'm sorry. He wanted to run. And I guess . . . so did I."

"I know." Tamra helped Raia stand and hobbled with her over to the cart. She pressed a canteen of water into her hands, and Raia drank greedily. Carrying a second canteen, Tamra then limped back to the black lion. She opened it and poured the water onto his tongue.

He pulled his tongue, wet, back into his mouth.

"Come on," she told him. "Into the cage. There's food and water for you."

All fight sapped out of him, the black lion hauled himself forward and flopped into the cage.

Inside, he ate and drank as Tamra drove the cart back toward the training grounds. Raia didn't speak. She just drank from the canteen and looked up at the stars.

"It must have been a beautiful night for a run," Tamra said conversationally.

Raia smiled, albeit weakly. "It was." Then her smile faded. "I think . . . we might need a little more practice before the real races."

"That might be a good idea," Tamra agreed.

CHAPTER 10

Clothed like an ordinary traveler, his augur pendant tucked beneath his shirt, Yorbel boarded a westbound ferry. He hadn't realized he'd become accustomed to the berth that people gave augurs until he was mashed between a dozen unwashed laborers on the ferry platform. He tried to breathe only through his mouth.

The river air tasted sour this close to the city's docks. The fishermen were loading their boats with bait—barrels of fish heads and dead crabs. But as the sails puffed with breeze, the ferry sailed farther from the capital, and the air began to smell sweeter. Lilies grew thick by the banks on either side, and Yorbel saw farmers already at work in their fields, ankle-deep in watery soil, hurrying to harvest before the yearly floods began. He had almost been one of those farmers. Both his parents had been, until sickness claimed them, and as the firstborn, he would have inherited their strip of land, not far from the city, if the augurs hadn't spotted him when he was eight years old and seen the purity of his soul.

His most vivid memory of that day was of the sky. It had been a brilliant blue. He'd been out in the fields with his parents, most likely watching a dragonfly instead of helping with the planting, and an augur had strode across the rows, crushing the sprouts.

He remembered his father had yelled, but he didn't remember the words. What he remembered was how the augur had loomed over him, and he'd looked up and seen the expanse of blue surrounding him. So much blue that the man was left in shadows, and Yorbel couldn't see his face. But he remembered the augur had spoken kindly and held out his hand. He'd given his parents gold for the crushed plants, and then he'd taken Yorbel with him.

His mother had cried blue tears—at least that's what his memory said, though he didn't see how that could be true. Tears were clear. The augur had told him they were happy tears, because his parents knew it meant that in his past life he'd earned this honor, but Yorbel hadn't been sure. He hadn't been certain of much those early days. He liked the temple and his lessons, but he missed his home and his parents. He wasn't allowed to run free in the afternoons the way his parents had let him, while they rested in the shade of the palm trees. On the other hand, he was allowed to sleep later than dawn if he wished, and to eat as much as he wanted at meals. He'd never tasted such food: oranges so ripe that juice dribbled down your chin, meat so sweet that you'd think it was dessert, and rice that popped on your tongue with spices that made you dream about distant lands.

Odd the things one remembers, Yorbel thought. The taste of citrus. The blueness of the sky. Yet he couldn't remember the sound of his mother's voice or the name of the augur who had changed his life. The little things that made him who he was, the choices that shaped his aura, sometimes seemed so arbitrary. He couldn't remember the day he'd been told his parents had died, when he became a ward of the temple—but he did remember waking one morning and realizing he'd cried in his sleep. His tears had tasted salty, and he'd wiped them away before his teachers saw.

Who can say what shapes a person?

And who could say what shaped an emperor? That was why Yorbel had to search among the kehoks. He believed that the emperor had been a good man. He trusted those who had read his aura, even though he personally had never done so. *But the sight of the blue sky, a taste of an orange . . . a moment can change a life.* Who knew what moments the emperor had experienced before his death? There were things that could darken one's soul in the space of a heartbeat. Decisions that could doom you.

True, it was unlikely for an emperor to suffer such a sudden fall from grace.

But it wasn't impossible.

A life can change in a moment.

So can a fate.

He hoped Dar would forgive him for his thoroughness and that he would be proven wrong when one of the other augurs found the late emperor's vessel among the many innocent beasts or birds. He hoped he'd be able to return to the palace, confess his failure, and beg forgiveness for his lack of faith in the purity of the late emperor's soul.

And he hoped it would all happen before time ran out.

He thought of Gissa, ready to do her duty. He hadn't asked her if she'd ever performed such a service before.

Cowardly of me. But he hadn't wanted to know. He preferred to believe her secret title was honorary, an homage to tradition rather than a reflection of action.

It won't be necessary for her to act. Either I or another augur will find the vessel.

He wrapped that certainty around him like a cloak on a cold desert night.

On the south side of the Aur River, bells began to ring. It started as a few high notes that mixed with the calls of the brilliantly colored birds that flew beside the ferry, fishing in its wake. The bellringers then added another melody, low, that echoed the first bells. Soon, there were several melodies, dancing together, echoing and blending. Yorbel let the loveliness of the music wash over him, calming him. It was then he realized he needed calming.

It had been so long since he'd felt nervous that he'd nearly forgotten the sensation. His days were routine. His future was assured and his fate certain. But today was different. *I don't know how today will end. And, River forgive me, I'm excited to find out.*

It was almost embarrassing, especially given all that was at stake for Dar and Gissa, but he was excited to have an adventure.

He hadn't felt this way since he was a boy. He was glad that none of the other ferry passengers could see his thoughts or read his aura at that moment.

This is a serious task, he scolded himself.

But he allowed himself a smile as the ferry docked, and the ferryman shouted the name of Yorbel's stop. "Excuse me," he murmured as he weaved his way across the crowded platform and stepped off the boat.

Ahead of him was Seronne Market.

He had a plan: There were hundreds of kehok training grounds. Far too many to search. But he didn't have to check every kehok. He only had to look for those with new souls. And any new kehoks would either currently be in or have recently passed through one of the kehok auctions.

If he could either examine those kehoks (if they were yet unsold) or compile a list of who owned them (if they had been sold), then that would make for a thorough search. It was still a daunting task. *But a doable one,* he thought. There were dozens of markets along the Aur River, but that was still better than searching hundreds of stables.

He strode into the market and was instantly assailed by smells and sounds and colors. The temples were austere gray and white, quiet places for contemplation and study. This . . . was not. He rarely left the grounds, and when he did, it was usually to the palace. This was distinctly different. He felt as if he'd fallen into a vat of marbles and been shaken around.

A woman danced with red scarves in front of him, while a monkey scampered behind her. A man carting a basket of fish pushed past him. A man shoved a tray of perfumes in front of him, demanding he smell, love, and buy. Another man, carrying a woman on his shoulders, walked by—she was juggling oranges. All around there were musicians: drummers, flutists, singers. He paused to buy a bag of roasted pecans, an indulgence, but the smell was irresistible. He ate them, tasting the salt and sweet on his tongue, as he found his way to the kehok auction.

All the music could not entirely drown out the human-like screams, and the closer he drew, the less he could taste the pecans. He slipped the unfinished bag into one of his pockets. This was where his work would begin.

Carefully, he began to widen his thoughts. It felt a bit

like listening to all the musicians and seeing all the brilliantly painted buildings at once, except he wasn't listening with his ears and he wasn't looking with his eyes. He began to see blurred colors flickering within the people around him.

If he concentrated on one person, he could see their aura: flecks of gold or streaks of black, a dusting of rust, and if he were to calm his mind, those colors would take form. Soon he was seeing the people overlaid with the images of what they would become, if they continued on their current path: a woman who bore the shimmering outline of a rabbit, a man who melded into the ghostlike shape of a boar, one who carried a cricket within him, another who would be reborn as human.

It made Yorbel's head ache to see the world this way, overlaid with future ramifications of all the people's past choices. Most augurs didn't possess the strength to see so much at once. They required the quiet concentration of the temple and a one-on-one consultation. But there was a reason Yorbel had been selected at age eight for training.

But as strong as he was, as he approached the cages, his steps faltered.

The aura of the kehoks was unmistakable: layered with shadows, streaked with red, and sliced with angry, blinding-white lightning bolts. Confronted with such angry ugliness, he couldn't breathe for a moment. He'd never seen one this close up before. It was nauseating, the way the colors bashed and swirled. *So this is what a doomed soul looks like. I think I'm going to be sick.*

He felt a hand land heavily on his shoulder. "You all right?" a man asked.

Yorbel blinked at him, and for a moment could see only the soothing gray of a balanced soul. He forced himself to concentrate on the silhouette of the man until it resolved into a bearded man with a tuft of gray hair around his ears, a bulbous nose, and a wide mouth. "It's been a while since I've been to a market."

The man chuckled. "You had that look. Can I point you in the right direction? That way"—he gestured to the left—"you'll find some of the best pastries in all of Becar. My wife bakes them, so I have to say that, but it happens to be true."

"Tell me, please, where can I find the recordkeeper for the kehok auction?"

"Ah, you'll want Overseer Irin. She keeps tabs on this section of Seronne." The man pointed her out—a tall woman in a red robe who strode between the cages. She carried a leather-bound book tucked under one elbow and had the imperious look of someone in charge. *I should have spotted her myself,* Yorbel thought.

"Thank you," he said to the man. He wanted to repay him with words of comfort about his aura, but he remembered that he was here as an ordinary traveler. "I'll be happy to buy from your wife, once my business is complete." The man smiled at that, and moved on to his own business.

Yorbel trailed behind the red-robed woman, trying to catch up with her, but she was crossing the market at a fast clip. He was breathing heavily by the time he got within a few cages of her—a life in the temple hadn't prepared him for a day of exertion. She'd paused to examine three stacked cages, making notes in her book.

The seller, a shorter woman with scars on her arms, watched the overseer anxiously and then heaved an obvious sigh of relief when Irin tore a piece of paper from her book and handed it to her.

As the seller scurried away, the recordkeeper lingered

by the triple-stacked cages as she updated her book, which gave Yorbel a chance to catch up to her. Before Yorbel could introduce himself, though, she spoke. "You've been stalking me. Poorly."

"Apologies, Overseer Irin," Yorbel said with a slight bow. "I did not intend to alarm you, but I'd like to take a look at your records."

She raised both eyebrows. "No."

"It's important."

"To you, perhaps."

"To the family who hired me." Yorbel reached into his tunic and displayed the augur's pendant, then tucked it back in. He was proud of himself for the discreet phrasing. He'd given the matter careful thought on the journey to the market. Lots of families hired augurs for various reasons.

"Oh. One of those." Overseer Irin did not seem impressed or even surprised. He wasn't sure what reaction he expected, but it seemed he wasn't the first augur to come to this kehok auction. He'd planned a more elaborate lie, but maybe it wouldn't be necessary. "Revenge or mercy?" She sounded bored.

"Excuse me?"

"Look, there are only two reasons a family hires an augur to search for a kehok: either its former self was one of their loved ones, and they wish to show off the so-called greatness of their own souls by forgiving him. Or its former self wronged one of their loved ones, and they wish to exact their revenge. Which is it?"

Neither choice was exactly it, but Yorbel was relieved that Overseer Irin hadn't immediately guessed his true purpose. That meant he wouldn't have to hide his identity as closely as he'd feared.

It was an interesting yet simple ethical dilemma: deceiving people blemished his aura, but the harm he'd cause by revealing his true purpose would cause far worse damage. Shading the truth harmed no one but himself and made that the obvious choice.

Didn't it?

It was important that people didn't realize he was looking for the late emperor's soul. He might not be connected to the daily concerns beyond the temple, but even he knew it would be bad if people lost faith in the augurs' ability to read a soul's future. And the augurs having misread the emperor's soul would be a disaster.

And we thought we were seeing riots now . . .

"Suppose it doesn't matter. Their gold is just as good either way." Overseer Irin held out her hand, palm up, and waited.

Belatedly, he realized she expected him to pay her.

He had no idea what the standard bribe of a kehok auction official was, but he knew how much gold he carried and how many markets he had to visit. He laid a gold quarterpiece in her hand and wondered how badly bribery scarred his soul and hers.

She didn't budge.

He added a second gold quarterpiece.

She closed her hand, and she passed him the book.

"I'm taking a break," she informed him. "If you don't know how to read, that's your problem." She then strode off, away from the kehoks and toward the enticing aromas of market food.

She should not have required a bribe, and he shouldn't have acquiesced. But the alternative . . . *It is remarkable what a person can justify.* First deception, then bribery. He had devoted a lifetime to the study of ethical behavior, but had never had the opportunity to test it in himself. It was shocking how easy it was to feel moral while committing acts he'd previously labeled immoral. And how easy it was to feel smugly self-righteous while doing so.

He wrestled with his guilt for a moment, and then he leafed through the book, deciphering her scrawled hand-writing.

By the time Overseer Irin returned, he'd found the information he needed: this market had two new-soul kehoks and six whose auras had not yet been checked. Luckily, none had been sold. He jotted down the names of their sellers and cage numbers in his own notebook, and he returned the records to her.

He then consulted his list and walked with more purpose through the rows of cages until he found it: a massive crocodile with thick, powerful legs. *He'd make a great racer,* Yorbel thought. He didn't know much about the races, beyond what all spectators knew, but it was obvious this one had impressive leg muscles.

Yorbel spread his feet in a wide stance and settled his breath. Peering into a creature's past life was more challenging than viewing the current state of its soul. It required a higher level of concentration and the ability to sort through irrelevancies—

"You wanna buy?" A woman's voice cut through his thoughts.

"Just looking," he replied.

"If you're just looking, then keep moving. Others want to look and buy."

He spared her a glance. She looked as deadly as one of the kehoks, with daggers strapped to her muscled arms and ankles, as well as a sword dangling from her waist. "I may want to buy, after I look. A minute to contemplate, if you please."

She fell silent.

He focused on the kehok. The aura was the usual swirl of gray, red, and white streaks. Layer by layer, he picked that apart, looking for the shape underneath the shadows. Even though the new vessel retained no memories of its own life, the soul remembered. Its imprint was there, so long as he could sort through the present and future enough to see the past—

"Fast runner, this one," the seller said. "See those hind legs? Sign of a winner."

"Do you mind?" he said icily.

"You trying to win a staring contest? Fancy yourself a rider? Pardon me for saying so, but you don't look like one."

"One moment, and I will answer all your questions."

The seller quit talking.

He focused again on the kehok. Gently, he sifted through the shadows until he saw the shape: a human with evil threaded through her soul, who had done terrible things, who had—

He pulled his mind back from the maw of darkness.

It didn't matter what this kehok had done as a woman. She hadn't been the late emperor.

Yorbel left the seller without answering a single one of her questions.

BY THE TIME HE HAD COMPLETED TESTING ALL EIGHT kehoks in Seronne Market, the sun had eaten the day. The sellers were tossing thick black sheets over the kehoks' cages, shielding them from the night. Other vendors were closing their stalls.

Of the eight, five were not new souls. The other three had been, respectively, a murderous woman, a traitorous man, and a former child whose soul was so twisted that it had made Yorbel physically ill to view. He'd vomited behind a barrel.

Viewing all eight in one day had left him drained. It was more than he'd ever tried to see at one time, far more tiring than reading auras of ordinary people.

He made his way to the bakery that the kind man had told him about and purchased a bag of sausage-and-onion rolls. He'd planned to visit two markets a day, but he'd be lucky if he reached the second before all the inns closed for the night. He wouldn't be able to view their kehoks until morning.

At this pace . . .

He didn't want to think about what that meant. Or about how much he'd be slowed if any of the kehoks with new souls had been sold, which they likely had been. He'd been lucky here, in that all the new or untested kehoks were still at the auction, but that wasn't going to be true everywhere he went.

I'll work as hard as I can, as fast as I can, he promised himself. He could do no better than his best. But telling himself that didn't help. He was beginning to feel an urgency he hadn't felt before. This wasn't so much an adventure as a race. And that held a certain irony, seeing how kehok-racing season would be starting soon. Because then the countdown would begin.

Two weeks. Can I visit them all that quickly?

For Dar's sake—for the empire's sake—he hoped so.

He caught the final ferry toward the next town with a market large enough for an auction, Strak. It was as crowded and odiferous as the morning ferry, but this time he was so weary and frankly odiferous himself after spending the entire day in the muck by the kehok cages that he didn't notice. He let the sound of the evening bells sweep over him and tried deliberately not to see any of the auras of the fellow passengers.

Landing near Strak Market, he disembarked, paid an innkeeper for a room, slept until his head quit aching, and then repeated the day. This time he was not as lucky: Strak Market had only three new-soul kehoks, but two had been sold. He obtained the buyers' addresses and visited two of the three training grounds before he ran out of daylight.

He finished his visits the next morning, continuing with the same lie he'd told Overseer Irin in Seronne Market. The only surprise was how easily the lie was accepted.

Except it wasn't a surprise. People wanted closure. So hiring an augur to find the shame of your family was, apparently, far more common than Yorbel ever imagined. Though it pained him each time he told the lie, no one questioned it.

Midday, he took the ferry to Esmot Market. He decided to wear his augur robes and display his pendant, since the explanation for his presence had proved so plausible. He paused to speak with the recordkeeper when he heard a disturbance between the cages—raised human voices, not kehok screams.

The recordkeeper, a squat, sweaty man whose name Yorbel had already forgotten, heaved a sigh. "Third time this week. Can't even keep the troublemakers out. 'Cause it's everybody these days." He waddled toward the shouting, which was starting to set off the kehoks.

Yorbel followed, smoothing his robes and straightening his shoulders. He felt almost excited. At last, here was an action he could take that wasn't morally problematic!

One of the sellers was red-faced and spitting as he shouted

at a customer. He jabbed a beefy finger into the customer's shoulder. "Don't care about your sob story! We all got problems! Blame it on the pretend emperor!"

Before Yorbel could reach him, the customer grabbed the seller's finger and twisted it back. "Hands off, you greedy, twisted kehok lover!"

With a roar, the seller launched himself at the customer, and they hit the ground, landing at Yorbel's feet. Seeing him, the seller's eyes went wide. The customer twisted to see what had distracted the seller, and then he scrambled back up.

"Is this the best way to resolve your problems?" Yorbel asked in his best teacher voice.

"Uh, um, no, Your Holiness," the customer said.

"Resolve your differences in a civilized, empathic way," Yorbel instructed. "Kindness will benefit you both in the end." He then turned to the recordkeeper. "We have unfinished business, sir."

As the customer and seller began haltingly to come to an agreement, Yorbel stepped aside with the recordkeeper. He managed to keep from crowing in satisfaction. For the first time in days, he felt more like himself.

"Wish I could keep one of you around all the time," the recordkeeper said. "People have trouble remembering their best selves in times like these. No offense meant, but wish you augurs would hurry up and find that River-drowned vessel."

Ignoring the recordkeeper's comment, Yorbel concluded his business, learning the names of the trainers who owned the kehoks with new souls. Even after visiting them, he couldn't stop thinking about the fight he'd witnessed—the combatants had blamed Dar.

If the government stasis didn't end soon, would they all

blame Dar? Was Gissa right? Was Becar so fragile that it couldn't weather a little waiting? *Maybe it is,* he thought. Maybe stability and peace were flimsy things that had to be nurtured and protected.

Now he kept his ears open as he visited market after market. He overheard hundreds of such anxious conversations: The poor were suffering while the government was suspended. Halted construction projects meant hundreds of out-of-work construction workers. Unsigned trade agreements meant shortages of spices, textiles, and other goods. It was one thing to hear it in the abstract; it was another to see the fear and worry on the faces of men, women, and children. They needed the late emperor's vessel to be found as badly as Dar did. Yorbel helped whenever he could, soothing tempers and spreading serenity.

A week later, after visiting multiple markets, training grounds, and racetracks, he'd examined so many condemned souls that he felt as if he would never be clean. He felt stained within and without, to the point of worrying about the state of his own aura. He understood better why the council encouraged augurs to keep their distance from kehoks—they feared the spread of the monsters' depravity. And they hated what the kehoks represented: their collective failure to save every soul in Becar.

The longer Yorbel searched, the more unlikely he thought it was that the late emperor could have been reborn as a kehok. These souls were so shriveled and damaged. If the late emperor had a propensity for this kind of pure evil, then one of the high augurs would have detected it. The corruption he was seeing among these monsters was so absolute that Yorbel knew he'd been naive to think it could happen in a moment.

I'm wasting my time. He should be with the other augurs,

scouring the nests and burrows of more pure creatures, instead of wading through the dregs of society while Becar crumbled around him.

But he'd committed himself to this task, and he couldn't return to Dar and tell him he was probably wrong but that he hadn't thoroughly confirmed it. He had to be absolutely sure.

Others will search those purer creatures. This task is mine and mine alone.

BY THE TIME YORBEL REACHED GEA MARKET, IT WAS TWO days before the first of the qualifying races, and the kehok auction was abuzz with gossip, predictions, and excitement. It was also nearly empty of kehoks. Most had been sold to trainers with wannabe riders.

Worse, Gea Market had no version of Overseer Irin. Their recordkeeper was collecting bets on the qualifying rounds—he didn't care about tracking the past lives of the kehoks. He cared about which racers were fit and ready for the first set of races. Everyone seemed to be gambling this year, and the whiff of desperation around the season made Yorbel feel sick.

"Apologies, Your Glorious Holiness," the recordkeeper told him, as he accepted yet another bet from a woman who looked as if she couldn't afford even enough for her own dinner. "Can't help you." He then smiled slimily at the poor woman as he marked her down for five gold pieces.

Yorbel left him and resorted to interviewing the sellers directly. It was both tedious and time-consuming, and by the end of the day, he had a low opinion of kehok sellers. Without any direct profit, they were singularly uninterested in helping him.

Getting fed up, he approached one more seller, a man with arm muscles so massive he could have arm-wrestled a kehok and stood a fair chance of winning. Glaring at everyone, he was standing in front of two caged kehoks, one coated in slime and the other in spikes.

Yorbel felt a headache squeeze his skull. Sending his mind across the two kehoks, he could tell immediately that neither were new souls. He considered moving on without talking with the muscled man, but duty propelled him. "Sir, I'm searching for a kehok bearing a new soul."

"Don't have one," the man grunted, without even looking at him.

"Yes, I know," Yorbel said testily. "Have you sold one within the past three months?"

"Maybe. Don't know. You people charge so much for aura readings that I didn't have a chance to have my catch properly tested."

"Then you did have one that was potentially new? Would you mind sharing with me the name of the owner who purchased it?"

"Are you going to buy one of my kehoks?" The muscled man shifted his weight, like an elephant leaning to his side. He finally looked at Yorbel.

"I'm not. All I need is information."

"If you're not buying, I'm not giving out."

Oh, for River's sake. The sun was nearly down. The market would be closing soon. He didn't want to spend another second here. "Fine. If your information leads me to a kehok I want to purchase, I'll pay you a twenty percent finder's fee. Charge it to the Augur Temple in the Heart of Becar." He yanked out his medallion so the seller could see it.

The man inspected it. "Been a long time."

Yorbel stuffed his pendant back into his tunic. "Excuse me?"

"Augurs buying kehoks. Used to be they'd buy them for the emperor. Last two emperors didn't like the races much, but in the old days, they say the Becaran emperor had the fastest kehoks on either side of the Aur. You buying kehoks for the emperor-to-be? Is he reopening the royal stable?"

"Of course n—"

That actually was not a terrible idea.

Because if he did find the late emperor's vessel, then it was a decent way to get the former emperor back into the palace without raising suspicion. And if he didn't . . . he could purchase a random kehok to justify why he'd spent his travels visiting markets.

Of course, if I'm wrong and I don't find the late emperor's soul within a kehok, then I'll be the proud owner of a smelly monster.

On the other hand, I've come this far . . .

"Of course, I can't divulge that information right now. But I can say that the emperor-to-be loves the Becaran Races and has an interest in restarting the royal stable," Yorbel said. "I'm on the lookout for the perfect racer."

Another lie. Or a possible future truth?

"Now, tell me who purchased your new kehok, for if it's as strong as you seem to be implying, I wish to purchase it from them."

The seller nodded. "Tamra Verlas, on behalf of Lady Evara."

CHAPTER 11

Three days before the first race, Tamra packed extra clothes for Shalla and went with her to the augur temple. Carrying Shalla's pack slung over one shoulder, she held her daughter's hand. "It will only be a few days, until the race ends."

"I know, Mama. You worry too much."

"I worry extra so you don't have to." She squeezed Shalla's hand as if she were joking, though she one hundred percent was not. When Shalla was little, Tamra used to bring her everywhere: to the auction, to racing lessons, to the races themselves. Even after the augurs, she'd been allowed to bring her when she had to leave overnight. But now that Shalla's training had intensified, she couldn't skip multiple days of lessons. She'd fall behind, and that wasn't acceptable by those who made the rules.

The augurs would take good care of her.

That wasn't a worry.

The worry was they wouldn't want to give her back.

With all that pressure, her heart raced faster as they approached the temple. Every time she came here, it reminded her of all the things in life she couldn't control. Her hand gripped Shalla's tighter, and her palms began to sweat.

Set into a rocky hillside, the augur temple of Peron was built to appear impressive and intimidating. And it succeeded wildly. Built of blue stone and edged in gold, it gleamed in the sun. Multiple cupolas with golden points looked as if they were about to etch words on the sky. Many gleaming white archways echoed the curves of the surrounding hills. Through the arches, you could see both the hills and the desert beyond, stretching into the distance. It made it seem as if the temple contained the world.

At the gate, Shalla hugged and kissed her. Tamra held on for a few seconds longer than Shalla wanted, and Shalla squirmed out of her grasp with a laugh. "Silly Mama."

"Yes, I am." Tamra tried to think of something silly to say, to make that wonderful laugh even louder, but in the shadow of the grand cupolas and arches, she could come up with nothing but serious thoughts.

Finding strength, she said, "Don't get too comfortable here. You'll be back in your own bed as soon as the races end."

Shalla whispered conspiratorially, "I can't get comfortable. Their pillows smell like duck."

Tamra smiled. She knew the augurs and their trainees had only the finest—goose-down pillows, silk bedding, pastries at every meal, and hot bathing pools—so Shalla was saying that only to make her feel better. But she liked that Shalla had said it. "Be good, be smart, and be strong."

"My teachers always say 'be nice.'"

"Sometimes being good, smart, and strong means being

nice. But sometimes it doesn't. You be who you are, and don't let anyone change you in ways you don't want to change."

"I like that. Did you just make it up?"

"Probably not," Tamra admitted. "I think I stole it from someone wise."

"You're wise," Shalla said.

Tamra couldn't help smiling. "As wise as an elephant?"

"Wiser," Shalla said solemnly. "You'd notice if a bird sat on you."

Laughing, Tamra hugged her again, and then released her. She gave Shalla her pack after making sure all the clasps were secure. In the cupolas, the bells began to ring, and Shalla hurried to join the other students on the opposite side of the gate.

Tamra saw several of them look back at her. She knew they were destined for this, that their past lives had molded them to be self-sacrificing, noble, and above all, good. But she couldn't help imagining she saw longing in their eyes. They varied in age, from eight to eighteen, and all wore the matching tunics that marked them as augur students. All of them, boys and girls, had either braided hair, like Shalla, or shorn heads, and their faces were scrubbed clean of any hint of dirt or grime. She wondered how many of them were wards of the temple and how many missed their families. And she wondered how many didn't want to be augurs and how many wished they weren't stuck within these walls. Before Raia, she would have said the answer was none. These children were honored above all others, and rightly so. It was foolish to waste time imagining injustice when all the sadness and regret were in her own head. Unless it wasn't foolish. Unless some of them wished their lives were different.

Lingering by the gate, she watched Shalla talking and laughing with a few of the girls and boys as they filed into the temple. Each of them grew silent and serious as they crossed the threshold, though. As Shalla crossed, she shot a glance back, and Tamra saw her hand twitch in a tiny wave.

Tamra waved back, and then Shalla was gone through the arch.

It hurt just as much as it did the very first time she'd watched her walk into that temple.

Squaring her shoulders, she marched away from the students' gate and toward the visitors' entrance to the temple. She gave her name to the guard and waited with the other temple visitors. Nearly all the others were here for readings from the augurs, and they displayed a variety of nerves: from laughing like shrill birds, to wringing their hands, to shifting from foot to foot, to standing motionless as they stared at the temple. The petitioners ranged from young to old, poor to rich, alone to in hyena-like packs.

She ignored them all.

At last, the guard called her name, and she was escorted inside.

Lit by torches, the visitors' entrance to the temple was covered in murals that depicted every bird, fish, and animal in Becar. The colors shone more brilliant than in real life— the feathers of the birds were brighter than on any real bird, the flash of the animals' eyes shinier than any real animal's eyes. Even the black seemed blacker, and the white seemed whiter. By the time she reached the receiving room, Tamra's eyes were watering from all the flickering colors. It was a relief to step into the cool gray of Augur Clari's office.

Augur Clari, one of the many teachers at the temple, was a strikingly beautiful woman with black-and-white-streaked hair that seemed more due to choice than age, as if she'd instructed her hair on how to age elegantly. Her skin was smooth, as if the sun had never dared burn it, and her eyes were perpetually calm.

Tamra hated her, of course.

Not because of her beauty, but because she was the one who had identified Shalla's talent. And because she never failed to act as if she alone knew what was best for Shalla, without any consideration of what Shalla—and certainly not what Tamra—wanted.

The worst part was that most people would say Augur Clari was right.

Even Tamra, if she were forced to admit it.

"Ah, Mother of Shalla." Augur Clari graced her with a smile.

Tamra also hated that Augur Clari never used her name, even though she knew it, though she supposed she'd been called much worse things. As titles went, it was one she wanted. Bowing slightly, Tamra replied, "Augur Clari, thank you for seeing me."

"I see all of you," Augur Clari said serenely. "And I see you are concerned. Surely, it's not with regard to Shalla. We are very pleased with her progress. She performed excellently on her exams and is proving to be a credit to the temple. And to you, of course."

Tamra tried not to grit her teeth at the thought of the temple taking credit for Shalla's brilliance. All the credit belonged to Shalla alone. She was the one who worked hard. She tried her best every day. Any victory was hers. But Tamra knew she was being irrational. The augur was only trying to be nice.

Augurs were very skilled at "nice."

"I come with two requests," Tamra said, forcing her voice to sound even and polite. "The first is for Shalla to reside in the temple for the next two days. I have been training a new rider and racer and will need to be away from home for their first race."

"Of course!" This time Augur Clari's smile seemed more genuine. "Shalla is always welcome to stay with us. Her teachers will be well-pleased to have the extra study time. I am delighted that you see the wisdom of not interrupting her studies."

"Would you let me interrupt her studies?" Tamra asked, before she could stop herself.

"No, we would not allow it. But I am pleased to not have to convince you of that."

Tamra winced. She'd had plenty of arguments in this very room over the years about how many days and how late Shalla would remain in the temple. They rarely went Tamra's way. In fact, she wasn't sure she'd ever won an argument with an augur.

"You mentioned a second request?" Augur Clari prompted.

"I would like to ask to defer the next tuition payment until after this season's races are complete. As I said, I have a new rider and racer and—"

"I'm afraid that won't be possible."

"Why not?" She didn't ask often, not even when they were so tight on money that she'd skipped meals, and she wasn't asking to skip payment. "You don't need the money." The augurs of Becar were said to be wealthier than the emperor himself. "The temple—"

"The temple has rules. If we violate them for one, we must violate them for all."

Tamra felt her hands curl into fists and forced herself to relax them. She had to stay calm and speak steadily—raging at the augurs never worked. "I am not asking to miss a payment, merely to wait a few weeks—"

Augur Clari held up a hand. "Mother of Shalla, you must allow me to express my concern."

It took enormous self-restraint for Tamra to resist saying: *Must I?*

"Ever since your"—she hesitated, as if unsure how to put it delicately—"tragic change of fortunes at last year's races, you have had difficulty meeting your payments. We note that you changed your living situation and are concerned that Shalla is not living in conditions that are optimal for her focus. To put it bluntly, she worries about you, worries whether you'll continue to have a roof over your head, and worries whether you will have enough food on your table, and that constant anxiety is both a drain on her and a distraction from her studies. Augurs-in-training cannot afford to be distracted. They are too vital to the stability of Becar. Shalla in particular shows wonderful potential. We would hate to see that potential limited by—"

"Bullshit."

Augur Clari blinked. "Pardon me? That kind of language is—"

"Accurate. You've wanted to take Shalla away from me since the day you met her. You'd take all the children away if you could. You're just looking for an excuse."

Augur Clari's expression grew icy. Tamra wasn't even sure how she did it, since her face didn't appear to move, but suddenly her eyes seemed colder. "I do not need an 'excuse' to be concerned about the welfare of my students. It is nonsensical to allow a talented student such as Shalla to suffer nightly when she could be living in luxury."

It was plain that Augur Clari believed every word she was saying. She believed she was acting in Shalla's best interest, as well as on behalf of all Becar. "My daughter doesn't suffer—"

"At the temple, children are given all they need. Far more than their birth parents can give them. We provide the best of everything. Food. Housing. Education. Intellectual stimulation and well-curated companionship. Your daughter would grow up with her peers, surrounded by the best of everything. She will want for nothing."

"Except for love."

"If you loved her, you'd see this is the best thing for her. Your insistence on keeping her is selfish. You aren't thinking of her or her future—"

"I think *only* of her!"

"Then please, Mother of Shalla, do the right thing. Give Shalla to the temple. Give her her future. Give her a chance at greatness!"

"She is a child! And she belongs with her mother!" Tamra realized she was shouting, but she couldn't seem to stop. She'd heard this speech before, though never this directly. It made her feel as if her veins were choked with fear and her throat was thick with anger. It made her feel as if she were a kehok, raging against an iron net.

Augur Clari, though she had raised her voice, remained the picture of serenity. Hands folded on her desk, she regarded Tamra as if she were a misbehaving dog. She radiated disapproval, but no other actual emotion. "Your next payment will be due upon your return in two days. If you fail to meet this highly reasonable extended deadline, then steps will be taken to transfer responsibility for Shalla's welfare to the augur temple, for her own good. I am certain that when you reflect on this, you will see the wisdom—"

"You'll have your payment," Tamra snapped. "And I will have my daughter back."

She then stalked out of the temple. Halfway across the city, her rage melted into tears. By the time she reached her training grounds, her tears had hardened back into rage.

They will never steal my daughter. Ever.

BACK AT THE STABLE, TAMRA AND THE OTHER TRAINERS loaded their kehoks into the racing transport carts. The black lion growled when he saw others being loaded into cages like his, and Raia laughed at him. "Don't worry," she said fondly. "They aren't going into our desert."

Tamra rolled her eyes. "Don't befriend the monster."

"Too late," Raia chirped. She scampered around the cart, securing all the latches, making sure the rhino-croc was hooked up properly. By now, she knew it all better than Tamra did, so Tamra was happy to let her do the work. Standing back, Tamra studied her—three weeks hadn't made Raia stronger on the outside, but maybe she shone a bit brighter on the inside. *She can do this,* Tamra thought, and was surprised at her lack of surprise at that thought.

Out of the corner of her eye, Tamra saw Osir come up beside her. "You're really bringing that pair to the qualifiers? You know what happened last time they ran on a track. You were lucky to get her back! How has anything changed in the past few days?"

Out in the desert, she and Raia had sketched a track

in the sand, an oval, and practiced running it—rather than across the dunes—nonstop for the past few days. They hadn't had any fresh disasters. Of course, everything could be different on an official racetrack with other riders and racers all around her and with spectators cheering from the stands. Tamra knew that firsthand. But she wasn't going to say all that.

"What changed is he came back—she brought him back. And he's the fastest and strongest I've ever trained." In his cage, the black lion paced to the limits of his chains. He growled at the lizard with elephant legs being loaded into the next cart. "He can win races."

Osir snorted. "Sure he can. If he can run in an oval, not merely a straight line."

"Why don't you worry about your own racers."

"Because if I don't worry about your kehok, it seems no one will," he said with pointed finality.

He drifted away before Tamra could reply, which was fine since she didn't plan on saying anything pleasant. She oversaw the packing of supplies: saddles, nets, chains, enough food for the racer and enough for the kehok pulling the carts, as well as tents, bedding, and cookware. They'd camp by the racetrack, beyond the city of Peron.

For the hundredth time, she wished she could have brought Shalla.

After Raia strapped the water supply to a shelf on the side of the cart, Tamra announced, "We're ready."

"Do you really think so?" Raia asked.

Tamra knew she wasn't asking about the supplies. "It doesn't matter what I think." From here on, it mattered only what Raia thought—at least until she finished the race. Then

Tamra could critique her performance all she wanted. Unless, of course, Raia lost, and Lady Evara followed through on her threat to withdraw her support. Regardless, for now, it was all about how Raia felt.

Raia was studying the black lion kehok, who was still pacing inside his cage, his tail swatting the bars. Occasionally, he snapped his jaws in the direction of one of the other racers. "What if he wants to run off the track again?"

"Do *you* want to run off again?"

She shook her head definitively. "Did that already."

"Then that's all that matters. Your need has to overwhelm his need. That's how you control him." Tamra felt as though she'd said that a thousand times. She hoped it had sunk in.

"I thought you said it's best if his need is my need?"

"That's how you ended up running toward the horizon."

Raia looked deep in thought for a moment, then said, "I think I'll travel with him. Explain one more time what we're doing and why."

"You can't reason with kehoks," Tamra cautioned. She knew they'd won his cooperation by dangling the word "freedom" in front of him, but he understood it only as a bare concept. He wasn't capable of understanding the multiple-race schedule of the Becaran Races. "They're smart, but not that smart. They're fueled by rage and loathing for themselves and the universe. Don't make the mistake of thinking he understands you, much less likes you." As unusual as this kehok was, it was dangerous to start believing he was anything but a monster. *That's how people get hurt.*

But Raia was already moving to the cage and letting herself inside. She settled, sensibly, in one corner, out of reach of his claws. Tamra felt the other trainers and riders staring at them and knew they were judging her.

"Another of your special training exercises?" Osir called.

She made a rude gesture at him as she climbed onto the bench. "Go," she instructed the rhino-croc. He lurched forward, beginning their journey to their first race.

CHAPTER 12

The day after she'd said goodbye to her mother, Shalla scrubbed her cheeks and pinned her braided hair back tight against her scalp. Their teachers liked all students to be clean, especially when meeting citizens. She hummed to herself, checked her tunic for any stray stains, and then lowered herself to the center of the floor and crossed her legs to wait.

This was a room for waiting: a smooth black floor, a blue glass ceiling, and eight tiled walls. She began with the first tile, a large bronze star. This was where you always began. She then let her eyes trace the pattern, following the swirling lines from star to star.

By the time she'd completed three walls, her mind felt nicely calm, the way it was supposed to, not all swirly like it had felt when she'd rushed out of the house. Mama had wanted extra time to say goodbye because she was leaving for a race. She'd be gone for two nights, and Shalla was to stay with the augurs in the temple for extra training.

Shalla didn't like to let Mama see, because she didn't want to worry her, but she hated staying at the temple. It wasn't that she disliked the place—everything about it was beautiful and clean and smooth as ancient stone. And she had plenty of friends here. The students who were wards of the temple had been so glad that she was staying for a little while, and she was happy to spend more time with them. Plus, she liked her studies and understood how important it was that she excel.

But it wasn't the same as being home.

At home, no one was grading her.

At home, she didn't have to win anyone's approval.

At home, no one judged her. Mama just loved her, no matter what she said or did, and that made it restful, even if the food wasn't as good or the beds weren't as comfortable. Being there made her feel comfortable on the inside.

In her soul.

I feel like I belong, instead of always trying to belong.

Her teachers would have said that was ridiculous. She belonged here, with others like her, whose past lives mirrored hers. *But they aren't like me—at least, they don't have a mama as nice as mine.*

Shalla grinned at the thought of Mama's reaction to being called "nice." "Nice is for people without ambition," Mama liked to say. "I'd rather you be strong."

Mama was nice *and* strong, and Shalla was happy that she'd found another rider who seemed to recognize that. Shalla was proficient enough at reading auras to tell that Raia was a good fit with their little family. *No bumpy edges,* Shalla thought.

That's what auras looked like to her: shapes. More advanced students saw colors and patterns, but she saw layers of shapes. Or at least she could when she concentrated properly.

The door to the waiting room opened, and one of her teachers, Augur Clari, entered. Shalla looked at her with her second sight and saw a blur—it was impossible to read the aura of a highly skilled augur. As a side effect of their power, they were always shielded, kind of like a racetrack. Shalla thought it made them very calming to look at.

"Apprentice Shalla, I come with questions."

"Then I will offer answers," Shalla replied immediately, using the traditional response.

"And if you cannot offer answers?"

"Then I will posit questions that will lead you to the path of peace."

Augur Clari nodded her head approvingly. "You have told us that your mother, Trainer Verlas, has taken on a new student by the name of Raia."

"Yes, they are on their way to their first race." By now, Mama and Raia would have already left. Shalla wished she could have gone with them. She knew if she'd told Mama that, Mama would have fought for her to be allowed to go, but she also knew the augurs would say no. There was too much for her to learn. *Besides, I don't want to be behind in my lessons.* She had a duty to Becar—and, as her teachers said, to her destiny.

A slight frown. "Did I ask that?"

Shalla lowered her head. "You did not." She should have realized that Augur Clari already knew. Mama had been planning on talking with her before she left for the race.

"Focus yourself, child."

Shalla looked again at the gold star and traced the swirls with her eyes. Augur Clari waited motionlessly as she completed the first wall, then spoke again. "Where did your mother meet this student?"

"Gea Market."

"Very good. And can you please describe this Raia?"

"She has no bumpy edges," Shalla said. "Some shimmering lines. Overlapping ovals but they are full of holes." The holes, she knew from her studies, were from fear. The lines were choices not yet committed to. But the ovals indicated she was on the right path. A truly balanced soul would be all circles, with no sharp or rough edges.

Augur Clari graced her with a slight smile. "Tell me her appearance when not seen with the inner sight."

"Oh! She's medium height, as tall as the middle of our kitchen cabinet." Shalla didn't know her exact height, but she could picture her, standing in their kitchen. "Black hair that she wears in three braids that she ties together. Her skin is more olive than mine, and she's prettier when she smiles. Like she's so surprised that she's smiling, so she smiles even more."

"Can you guess her age?"

"She's seventeen. She told me so."

"What else did she tell you, about where she's from and why she's here?"

Shalla wondered why Augur Clari was asking so many questions about Raia. She wanted to ask her own questions, but that would lead to a lecture. It wasn't her place to question, unless it was to request a clarification of a lesson. "She wants to live in the present and future. I respected that."

"Very well." Augur Clari turned to leave, her robes sweeping like a whisper against the black stone floor.

"Augur Clari, I come with questions," Shalla tried. "Why do you ask about Raia? She's a good student, a good housemate, and a good friend."

For an instant, Shalla thought she'd overstepped and Augur Clari was going to scold her instead of answering. But then Augur Clari said, "Because it appears she has not been a good daughter."

She opened the door, and Shalla saw there were three people clustered nearby, as if they'd been listening in on their conversation. Using the serenity of the waiting room to boost her inner sight, she studied them: a man and a woman, whose auras looked like triangles intersecting. And a third man, younger and handsome, whose aura looked like crossed arrows so sharp that Shalla recoiled.

Why were these people with ugly souls in the temple? Why had Augur Clari brought them here, to listen to Shalla? And why did they want to know about Raia?

As these questions popped into her mind, her calm shattered, and she lost her sense of their auras. Augur Clari shut the door as the strangers began to badger her with questions about where to find Mama's training grounds, where the races were, and where they lived.

Surely, Augur Clari won't give them any more answers, Shalla thought. Her teacher must be able to see their auras. She was skilled enough to naturally read auras, whether she was calm or not. *She wouldn't put Raia in any danger. Or Mama.*

Shalla wished she weren't confined to the temple until Mama returned. She very much wanted to talk to her. And warn her.

MILES AWAY, TAMRA BREATHED IN THE SMELL OF THE racetrack: the thick scents of kehoks, human sweat, beer, roasted pigeon, all mixed with the sweet smells of citrus and jasmine. She'd been told the warring scents were enough to make the faint of heart dizzy, but to her, it smelled like coming home.

Already there were a half-dozen racers and riders on the track, getting a feel for the sand, snarling at one another. Tamra didn't intend to take Raia and the lion there yet. They'd be better off at the camp, where they could grow accustomed to being in a new location together. The races would start in the morning—Raia had been scheduled for the third heat, while her friends from their training grounds were slotted in heats two, four, and five.

Tamra eyed the competition as they rode by: the usual mix of lizardlike kehoks, plus a jackal, a few felines, and one massive snake. The riders looked young. *Every year, they look younger.* And nervous. A few were talking to each other, but most were coaxing their kehoks onto the sand. All the monsters wore muzzles and shackles, a requirement before the races. The officials didn't want any fighting between the racers ahead of time.

She found their campsite. Since she came from one of the lesser training grounds, it wasn't an ideal spot—too close to the latrines for any real privacy and without any shade. But riders couldn't expect luxury at the qualifiers. As you progressed through the races, the tracks and the accommodations became nicer, until the finals, when racers were housed in glorious stables and riders had a plush campsite with a view of the palace. She'd even gotten a glimpse of the emperor himself once, or the late emperor to be more accurate, in the Heart of Becar.

Leaving Raia in the cage to continue whatever ridiculous conversation she was having with her monster, Tamra pitched the tent. She then filled the canteens with fresh water from the tanks. As she was hauling them back to their site, she heard a voice she vaguely recognized.

"Found another fool to maul?"

She turned, thinking it was one of the trainers she'd clashed with in a prior season, but to her surprise, it wasn't. "Fetran. You're looking well." Her student, one of the two who had gotten hurt. And now the pipsqueak was sneering at her.

"All Becar is going to know your training methods are for shit when I, after suffering injuries caused by your negligence, come back and win with the guidance of a new trainer."

It was the longest speech she'd ever heard Fetran make. She wondered who wrote it for him. "Good luck with that," she told him neutrally. "I don't wish you ill."

"You've already done me ill," he snarled.

"You lost control of your racer on a shielded track," she pointed out. "You do realize that to win a race, you need to succeed at what caused you to fail."

"Now that I'm free of you, I will!" He then pivoted and stalked off. "Just watch me win! I'm in the third race with your new fool, and I'll be placing first!"

Tamra rolled her eyes. She wanted to point out that he hadn't ever been tied to her. In fact, his parents had paid her to teach him, as they were probably paying his new trainer. She hoped the little idiot didn't die in the race. While that would teach him a valuable lesson, he most likely wouldn't remember it in his next life.

Returning to her campsite, she said to Raia and the black lion, "I'd like you two to do me a favor in the race. See them?" She pointed to Fetran and his mount, a large green-scaled lizard with thick horns on its head. "They'll be running in your heat. Whatever else happens, please make sure you run faster than them."

RAIA PREPARED HER BED NEXT TO THE BLACK LION'S cage—outside it, of course, because she wasn't an idiot—but she didn't want to sleep inside the tent. She wanted the lion to be able to see her and know she hadn't left him alone.

Watching her, Trainer Verlas shook her head. "After this race is over, we're going to have a long talk about not projecting your own thoughts and emotions onto a simplistic killing machine."

"He's not simplistic," Raia said, checking for rocks under her bedding. "He understands me."

"Just don't forget he'll kill you if he can."

"He and I had a long discussion about that. It was a one-sided conversation, but I think he agreed with me. He knows if he kills me, you'll kill him." She thought he'd understood much more than that, but she knew she wasn't going to convince Trainer Verlas. She'd have more luck convincing her the sky was purple. Even despite all the progress they'd made out on the sands, Trainer Verlas still seemed to believe the kehok couldn't understand more than the basic idea of *racing equals freedom*.

"Very true—if he kills you, he dies." Shooting one more glare at the black lion, Trainer Verlas let herself into the tent. "He's useless to me if he won't take a rider, and you're the only one I've got." The tent flap flopped shut behind her.

Climbing into her bedroll, Raia looked up at the stars. Only a few were visible. Most of the sky was a matte gray, lightened by the torches that lit the racetrack and the nearby city. "We're racing tomorrow," she said out loud.

She let the words roll around in her mind, trying to get used to them. She knew there were other riders here who had dreamed of this moment for years. They'd imagined themselves as riders when they were little kids, playing at it with horses and goats and whatever else would let them ride. But she never had—she'd never had any choice in her future. Her parents had always told her what to do, who to be, and who she would become. The first act that she'd taken on her own, in the augur temple, had been to fail.

I'm not going to fail this time.

She held that thought close to her as she slept, and she dreamed about running fast. She woke to sounds all around her—the laughter, cheers, and shouts of other riders and their trainers, the screams of kehoks being brought out of their cages and prepared for the race. Sitting up, she saw Trainer Verlas was already awake and alert.

Seeing her, Trainer Verlas tossed her a canteen. "Rinse out your mouth, use the latrine, do what you need to do, but try not to think too much."

It was good advice.

Hard to follow, but good.

Raia cleaned herself, dressed, and tried not to stare at the other riders who all looked so much more confident and experienced than she felt. *Of course they're more confident. I bet all of them have run around a track at least once without jumping out of it.* All around her, the other riders were chattering excitedly, as if this was a festival, while they prepared their mounts. But Raia was in anything but a festive mood.

"Hey, Raia, smile!" Jalimo called.

Making a fist, Silar bopped him lightly on the head. "She's focusing, idiot."

"Ow." He rubbed his scalp as if she'd pounded him. "I

was just trying to say she should enjoy herself. It's not every day you get to dare death."

"That is literally what we do every day," Silar said. She waved at Raia. "Good luck out there. Hope you make it through!"

"Yeah, we can hope for that, since we're not racing against you," Jalimo said.

"Good luck!" Raia called to them. "Hope you make it through too!"

She couldn't decide if it was better to have friends who were rooting for her, or worse because there were people to disappoint. But there wasn't time for an endless spiral of self-doubt—Trainer Verlas made sure of that. She barked orders, and Raia hurried to feed the black lion, saddle him, and prepare to walk him to the track.

"You'll lead him without any chains from here to the track and wait until the race officials are ready before you proceed to your starting gate," Trainer Verlas said. "It's showboating, but it also serves as an essential first step. Anyone who cannot control their kehok during the pre-race period is immediately disqualified. I won't be allowed to help you. I'll be with the other trainers in the stands."

"I can do this," Raia said, though she wasn't certain if she was talking to Trainer Verlas, the black lion, or herself. But she felt it was true, for one of the first times in her life. Perhaps the only other time she remembered was when she'd cheered herself on as she climbed out the window of her family's house and fled into the unknown.

"Once the race starts, all you need to do is run," Trainer Verlas reminded her. "Stay in the moment. The future will follow as it will."

Raia nodded.

She was beginning to understand why so few people even tried monster racing. *Constant terror* is *a bit of a distraction,* she thought. But if she couldn't dispel her fear, she could use it, like Trainer Verlas kept telling her.

Across the camp, Raia heard a commotion: cheers and shouts as other riders and spectators flocked to cluster around a new arrival. Standing on her tiptoes, she tried to see who the fuss was about, but Trainer Verlas poked her in the shoulder. "Just a hotshot rider. Every season has them. Ignore him. You won't gain anything by comparing yourself to anyone else."

Turning her back on the popular rider and his fans, Raia saddled the black lion. Trainer Verlas checked all the buckles and straps, and then Raia rechecked them.

Beyond the campsites, from the stands by the racetrack, she heard even louder cheering. Her heart felt as if it were beating in her throat. She swallowed hard. The first heat was underway.

"Ready?" Trainer Verlas asked.

"Can I say no?" Raia asked.

"I'm going to assume you're joking."

"I'm joking," Raia said quickly. *I'm not.* She took a deep breath in, and she began to remove the chains and shackles.

Trainer Verlas laid a hand on her shoulder. "Let me. You mount."

Raia climbed into the saddle while Trainer Verlas moved around the black lion, unhooking the chains and removing the shackles. She was murmuring to the lion, but Raia couldn't hear what she was saying. *Probably threatening him,* Raia thought.

She felt the black lion tense beneath her—he knew that the chains were released. "Steady," she whispered in his ear.

He flicked his ear back at her.

He'd heard her.

She just didn't know if he cared.

"Walk," she commanded.

For one excruciating instant, he did not move, and she thought her racing dreams were over before they began. But then he strode forward. She kept her eyes fixed ahead of her. She knew Trainer Verlas was somewhere nearby, watching. She knew others were probably watching too, but she kept her focus narrowed on just her lion and where she needed him to go.

Bearing her, the lion walked regally out of the campsite and toward the racetrack. The route was hemmed in by walls, but they were no higher than the walls at the practice track. She knew he could jump them if he wanted to.

Don't think about that, she warned herself.

Beneath her, the lion began to growl, a low rumble that vibrated through her thighs. "Walk forward," she told him. "One, two, three, four. One, two, three, four . . ." He walked in rhythm with her counting, so she kept it up.

Logically, she knew the walk from the campsite to the racetrack wasn't far. But it felt like miles. All around them were shouts and screams from the other riders and racers. She counted louder, trying to keep her lion focused as they waited for the first two races to finish.

Other riders on their racers began to fill the holding area around her. She heard excited whispers and tried to ignore them. As the second heat finished, she heard Silar's name called: second place! She felt a burst of happiness for her friend and leaned forward to whisper to the lion, "We're next."

"You want some advice?" the rider next to her offered.

Startled that anyone was speaking to her, Raia shot him a look.

And then stared at the rider.

He was, in a word, beautiful. High cheekbones, black eyes with thick lashes, perfect bronze skin. He wore red sleeveless leather, showcasing his muscles, and his hands were folded casually on the standard rider's whip. He was riding a kehok that looked like a silver spider.

It took Raia a moment before she realized that he was the one the others were whispering about. He didn't seem to notice, either because he was oblivious or because he was used to it. She guessed the latter. "Sure," she said belatedly. "Advice would be great."

"Don't run."

"What?"

He flashed a smile at her, showing off his perfect teeth. "It would be a shame to see a girl as pretty as you damaged out there."

Okay, he was now far less beautiful.

"I'll be fine."

"It's your first race, isn't it? Pity it's against me." Leaning closer, he added, "Someone should have told you you're not going to win."

Motionless beneath him, his kehok watched her with liquid-gold spider eyes.

"You're trying to get into my head and shake my confidence. It won't work." She had already doubted herself far more effectively than this stranger ever could, and she wasn't letting any of it stop her.

His eyes widened as if in genuine surprise. "It's fact, not opinion. I'm Rider Gette."

As if she was supposed to recognize his name.

"Nice to meet you, Gette. I'm Raia, and I'm going to win."

She nudged the lion ahead so she couldn't hear his response.

At last, the track officials scurried out and began beckoning the riders, shouting at them to get to their starting gates. Raia and the lion walked forward with all the other competitors onto the racetrack. In the stands, the spectators cheered.

Raia had a moment of panic—she didn't know which gate was hers. But then she saw Trainer Verlas in the stands. She was holding up eight fingers.

Gate eight.

She guided the lion into the gate and was relieved when he didn't fight her.

"All we have to do is run," Raia said. "Just this moment. Just this race. Stay on the track. Cross the finish line. Be faster than everyone else." Reaching forward, she stroked the cool surface of his mane. It felt as smooth as glass beneath her fingers. "We are faster than all of them. I know we are." She'd run with her lion across the desert so fast that she'd felt as if they were flying. She knew he could be fast out in the desert. He just had to be fast now, in this moment. They both needed to drown out the distractions and just look forward. And then the future would follow.

PRESSED AGAINST THE FRONT OF THE STANDS BY SEV-eral layers of other trainers and assistant trainers, Tamra studied the racers as they entered the track. The winged lizard—he'd be fast but hard to control. The rhino-like kehok—dependable but slow. The cheetah-hyena—quick in short bursts. It would need a rider who knew how to pace it, and its rider was a kid who looked like an overeager jack-rabbit. *They'll run out of speed before the last lap,* Tamra judged. Certainly the petulant child Fetran wasn't a threat. So far, Raia's only real competition was a blue lizard. Its rider was older and calm, and she guided her kehok into the starting gate without any theatrics. *We can outrun them, though.* Then she studied Raia and the black lion.

Maybe.

The key wasn't whether he could be fast; it was whether he would run fast here and now, when it mattered. *That* was what a rider needed to do: unleash her monster's speed at exactly the right moment.

And Raia hadn't learned how to do that yet.

She hadn't had time to learn much of anything.

Still, it was possible. The lion had the raw speed, and Raia had the determination.

Around her, all the spectators surged to their feet as the final rider and racer took to the track. She recognized him instantly:

Gette of Carteka, the winner of last year's Becaran Races.

He looked as she remembered: clean-shaven and handsome in the highly manicured way of a man who knows exactly how handsome he is. He was riding a silver spider kehok and wearing sleeveless riding armor that showed off his lack of scars.

Shit.

We aren't going to win.

If they didn't place first, they wouldn't win enough gold. She wouldn't be able to repay Lady Evara for the slain kehok and still have enough left over for the augur's latest demands. . . .

But it was too late for more training or even a pep talk.

She closed her eyes and took a deep breath. *The future will be what it will be.* She'd told Raia not to think about the future, but it was Tamra's job to worry.

And I won't let our dreams end before they begin.

Pushing back from the front of the stands, Tamra scanned the audience, looking not for a familiar face but for a familiar type—and she saw him. Short, squat, with a clipboard that he was scrawling on as fast as his little fingers could write, the bookie was busily taking bets from a crowd that shoved and maneuvered to reach him. She usually avoided such people.

Elbowing aside several people, Tamra pushed her way to the bookie.

"Name," he said.

"Trainer Tamra Verlas."

He glanced up. She felt the looks of a few around her— her name came with a wealth of rumors and gossip and opinions. "*You* want to bet? But . . . you have a rider in this race. . . ."

She heard whispers around her—it was well-known in the circuit that Trainer Tamra Verlas *never* bet on her own racer. She refused to listen to them. *I do what I must.* "Odds?"

The bookie erased the shock from his expression. All business, he barked, "New racer. New rider . . . thirty to one."

She nodded. She expected as much. Raia was untried. "Two gold on a trifecta: the silver spider first, the blue lizard second, the black lion third."

He blinked. Two gold was a lot for a qualifying race. And to bet on a trifecta in a qualifying round was nearly un-heard of—the racers and riders were untested. Even more, to bet against your own rider . . . It was considered bad form at best. Stupid at worst. Racing was such a mental game, and if a rider knew her own trainer was betting against her placing first . . . *I'm not betting she'll lose,* Tamra consoled herself. *I'm betting she'll place third.*

I'm betting she'll win us what we need to keep going.

If she was right, she could come home with enough winnings to appease both Lady Evara and Augur Clari, at least until the next race. . . . "Odds?"

He licked his lips. "Two hundred fifty-seven to one. Only exact placement pays."

Tamra dropped the two gold pieces into his hand, and he quickly tucked them into one of his pouches and jotted down her bet on the clipboard. Others pressed around him to place their bets. She wiped her now-sweating hands on her pants. She'd done what she always swore she wouldn't do. Then again, she swore she'd keep Shalla out of the clutches of the augurs.

One of those was *much* more pressing.

She felt Osir's eyes on her, judging her, a smug smile on his face. She avoided meeting his gaze. Let him think whatever he wants. She told herself she didn't care what his opinion was. What mattered was Shalla and Raia.

Pushing back to the front of the stands, Tamra looked out again at the starting gates. Raia was gazing around her with a caught-gazelle kind of expression. *Third,* Tamra thought. *All she has to do is finish third.*

"Ready," Tamra whispered, as the race official shouted, "Ready!"

"Prepare," she whispered, as the race official shouted, "Prepare!"

"Race!" she shouted, as the race official and every trainer and spectator in the stands shouted, "Race!" A second official pushed the lever that released the starting gate doors.

All twenty doors flung open, and the kehoks poured out, the silver spider in the lead.

Sand was thrown into the air, and Tamra tasted it. She heard the shouts and screams and cheers all blended into a single roar, and she was cheering too. And crying. Because this felt like home.

WIND SLAMMED INTO RAIA'S FACE. SAND FLEW AROUND them. And she heard thunder. It rumbled through her, shaking her bones and permeating her every thought.

In the desert, when she rode the black lion, there was silence. Here, twenty kehoks pounded around the track—the sound extinguished the roar of the wind and the cheers of the crowd. Gette on his spider had pulled ahead of the pack.

"Run!" she urged the black lion. *Run!*

Around her, the other riders were screaming at their kehoks, forcing them faster, faster. She saw them out of the corner of her eyes: bits of nightmares so very close around her. She felt the heat from their bodies as they ran. The smell of their sweat clogged the back of her throat.

She wanted to escape them. She couldn't help it. Every inch of her wanted out of here.

As the other kehoks jostled against the black lion, slamming into Raia's legs, she only felt it more strongly. *Out, out, out,* her blood thrummed. And the black lion faltered.

In that moment, the other racers shoved past them.

The black lion stopped in the middle of the track.

Sand settled around them. The thunder receded as the racers rounded the corner. "Oh, no, no, no! You have to run!" Raia shouted at the black lion.

He pawed the dirt and eyed the walls.

The walls were much taller on this track than the practice track, and they were crowned with stands full of people. She met Trainer Verlas's eyes. *I'm disappointing her. I'm failing!*

She couldn't fail. There was too much to lose. . . . *Don't think about the future. Think about now!* "You want out of this race?" Raia shouted at her kehok. "Then win it! The only way out is *through*!"

His muscles were quivering.

She leaned forward to make certain the black lion could hear her. "You don't want to run with them? Good. So don't. Run beyond them!" The open sands were beyond the pack of racers.

He heard her.

Slamming the dirt beneath his paws, he began to run. Faster. She leaned against his mane and clung to him, her eyes straight ahead at the pack of racers. "Run *through* them!"

Low to the ground, he shot forward. She heard the wind in her ears, displaced by the thunder of the other racers' hooves. Ahead was a cloud of sand, and she urged him faster. She closed her eyes as they met the cloud and plunged inside. All around her she heard the screams, smelled the sweat, but she kept pushing him faster, faster.

Out of the corner of her eye, she saw a lizard snap at them, lunging with its jaws, and the black lion veered to the side, bashing against another kehok, then running on. Raia kept her body scrunched as small as possible, shielded by his metal mane. Head down, she focused only on the sand before them.

They passed another racer, then another, and then another. The pack of kehoks smashed together behind them as they rounded the next turn of the track.

Four more ahead of them.

She could see the finish line, the flags waving above it, red against the blue sky, murky through the cloud of sand. They passed another racer. And then another.

Ahead there were only two left: a silver spider and a blue lizard.

"You're faster," Raia told the black lion. "Show them you're faster!"

His muscles strained as he pushed faster. And in that instant, Raia felt what Trainer Verlas had been telling her about over and over: the moment. She felt as if every inch of her skin was aware—of the lion beneath her, the clothes against her skin, the sand pelting her cheeks. She saw every color at once, heard every noise. In those precious seconds, there was nothing but the race. She and the black lion were flying across the sands, part of the wind, part of the world. And she knew they could not lose. . . .

Until the silver spider crossed the finish line first, followed by the blue lizard. And the black lion, with Raia—destroyed, distraught, disgraced—thundered across the finish line in third place.

OFFICIALS SWARMED THE RACETRACK AND AROUND the kehoks. Assistant handlers leaped onto the sands and raced to their assigned racers. Shackles were attached, chains looped around the monsters while the kehoks fought, fueled by the exhilaration of the race and their desire to kill.

It was chaos, but a controlled kind of chaos—race officials always ensured that the kehoks were stabled as quickly as possible, to minimize any chance of accidents.

On the black lion, Raia saw it all swirl around them. The lion's sides were heaving, but he wasn't fighting her like the others were their riders. *We lost.* She felt numb. If they hadn't stopped, if she hadn't lost focus . . .

A rider knocked into her shoulder, hard. She nearly slipped off the saddle, and then a hand caught her elbow. She pulled herself back up and looked over into Gette's smiling face.

"Told you I'd win. Better quit while you're not dead. You're not thirsty enough for this."

He winked at her, released her elbow, and let himself be swallowed by the adoring crowd. A second later, Trainer Verlas was beside her.

"Get off and help me chain him," Trainer Verlas ordered.

Raia blinked at her. "I don't want to quit."

"Good. I didn't think you did."

"I felt it," Raia told her. "At the end. No future, no past, exactly like you said. But it was too late. *I* was too late."

Trainer Verlas nodded and held out a hand to help her slide down. "Focus on your lion now. Keep him calm. Keep *yourself* calm. The aftermath of a race can be even more dangerous than the race itself, especially once the racers are exposed to the emotions of the crowd." She slapped the hook of a chain onto the lion's collar. "Muzzle him."

Obediently, Raia slipped the chain muzzle over the lion's face. He didn't fight her. "You ran well," she told him. "It's not your fault. I failed you."

"You'll do better next time," Trainer Verlas said briskly.

Raia shook her head. "There isn't going to be a next time, remember? I want to race again, but we can't. This was it. We had to win. You told me so yourself. Lady Evara—"

"You placed third," Tamra said. "That's good enough for your first race."

"But Lady Evara said—"

"She said I had to repay her for the slain kehok with our winnings. And third was enough for that." Tamra shook a pouch clipped to her belt, which Raia looked at with surprise. "Let's discuss what went wrong, and what you're going to do next time." Together, they led the lion across the fields toward the campsite.

Raia didn't know what to feel. Confusion. Relief. How would the winnings from third place at a qualifying round possibly be enough to satisfy Lady Evara? And the augurs for Shalla? And her parents? "But how . . ."

"You weren't going to win that race. You will win the next—you can still qualify for the major races if you win your second qualifying race. It's best of two that determines placement. But to have that chance, I had to do it." Trainer Verlas took a deep breath, then confessed, "I bet against the present so we can have a future."

Raia realized that Trainer Verlas was looking at her anxiously, as if she were worried. Trainer Verlas so rarely looked worried. It was a strange expression on her face: the crinkle in her forehead, the extra-hard grip on the kehok's chains. She'd heard that trainers didn't bet on their riders, at least the good ones didn't, the ones who trained champions. "You placed a bet? *Against* me?"

The lion made a lilting kind of sound, a query at the end of his growl.

Maybe I should be offended. But I wasn't going to win that race—it was my first. She did the right thing. Raia met the lion's golden eyes. She knew she was imagining it, but she thought he looked as worried as Trainer Verlas. *Worried about me?* The thought almost made her smile. "It's okay.

This is good," she said to both the lion and Trainer Verlas. "It means we'll get another chance."

She knew it wasn't possible, but he seemed as if he understood. While all the other kehoks fought their riders and racers as they were shoved back into their cages, the lion walked docilely inside his cage and lay down, paws crossed in front of him. She climbed into the cage with him and sat in the corner. "And next time, we'll outrun them."

He growled as if in agreement.

CHAPTER 13

After Raia climbed into the cage with her racer, Tamra hitched the rhino-croc kehok to the transport cart. She was aware she was smiling, which probably looked alarming to anyone close enough to see, but she didn't care. *That could have been a disaster, and it wasn't!* She'd happily celebrate a non-disaster.

"Well run," Osir said from behind her.

"Thank you," Tamra said.

"Except for that hesitation. You know, I could work with her on that."

"She's my rider. Poach elsewhere." She swung herself up onto the bench and flashed her smile at him. He was scowling at her, as if he were deeply insulted. She noticed, though, that he didn't deny it.

"My riders raced well too!"

"Congratulations." She rode past him, pulling the cart with her racer and rider behind her. A few of the other students and trainers waved at her, acknowledging her once again, the way they used to before last year's disaster. Sitting up straighter, she commanded the rhino-croc to trot faster, prouder.

By the entrance to the campsite, she saw the wounded being patched up by the track doctors. She met the eyes of her former student Fetran, who had failed to finish and was having his shoulder bandaged. He looked miserable.

Demonstrating her professionalism, she did not say anything snide. But she gloated privately as they headed home.

Seeing no need to rush, Tamra enjoyed the journey. At the peak of the heat, they rested at a watering hole, and continued on in the pink dusk. They reached the stable just as the first stars were scattered across the sky.

She loaded the rhino-croc into his stall while Raia maneuvered the black lion out of the cage. Together, they secured the locks and double-checked all the chains. "Can I give him extra feed?" Raia asked.

"Absolutely. He earned it." Tamra was already thinking about what kind of pastry treat she could buy for Raia and Shalla tonight. She was looking forward to telling Shalla all about the race and hearing about whatever she'd learned in her studies during their absence. "I'll stow the cart."

Leaving Raia in the stable, Tamra hauled the cart back to the shed. She noted that the other trainers and their students had already returned and left—they must have rushed back from the racetrack after their own mix of victories and disappointments. But Tamra didn't regret the slow return. All of them needed the reprieve. Already she was planning out the next training sequence—they'd have a week before the next race to squeeze in as much training as possible. Next race, now that Raia had a taste for it, they were going to win first.

She heard a noise behind her. "That was quick. Did you clean the saddle?"

"I apologize for the intrusion," a man said.

Tamra spun around, and then hissed as pain spasmed up her leg. In the doorway to the shed, a stranger in plain gray robes blocked the light from the torches outside. He was bald with a beard, and his eyes were a soft gray. He reminded her, oddly, of a just-washed blanket. Everything about him was crisp and soft at the same time, and he was a calming kind of good-looking. "Can I help you?"

He inclined his head in a slight bow. "Perhaps. I am Augur Yorbel." Reaching into his robes, he drew out a pendant. It glittered in the torchlight. "Are you Trainer Tamra Verlas?"

Her breath caught in her throat. "Shalla! What's happened? Is she all right?"

He looked perplexed.

"My daughter! That's why you're here—" She broke off, studying him. "That's not why you're here? You're not one of my daughter's teachers from the Peron temple?"

"I am not," he said apologetically. "I am—"

She heard shouting from outside, in the direction of the stables. It sounded like an argument, which was not a great idea around the kehoks—it riled them up, and she needed the black lion to rest. Whatever this augur wanted, so long as it wasn't about Shalla, he'd have to wait. Stalking past him, she headed outside. "Excuse me."

He trailed after her.

She saw two strangers in front of the stable, while Raia cowered in the doorway. The pair of strangers, a man and a woman, were shouting at Raia.

"Are they with you?" she asked the augur.

"No, they are not. In fact, they—"

Tamra picked up her pace, ignoring the twinge in her leg. She shoved past the couple to stand in front of her rider, facing her and blocking them. Raia's cheeks were damp, and her eyes were darting from right to left as if she were a cornered creature. Tamra laid her hands on both of Raia's shoulders, forcing her to look at her rather than at the man and woman. "Did you finish cleaning the saddle?"

Mutely, she shook her head.

"You need to finish your tasks before you can socialize." She turned Raia one hundred eighty degrees and gave her a slight shove into the stable. She then pivoted to face the strangers with her hands on her hips. "You're trespassing on the North Bank Peron Training Grounds. If you'd care to come back during training hours, someone would be happy to give you a tour of the facility and answer all your questions."

It didn't take much intuition to know that these were the parents Raia had been running from. The man and the woman looked vaguely like her, except they were much more pissed off.

"We are not here for a tour," Raia's father snapped. "We are here to speak with our *daughter*. Privately." He took a step forward that would have been intimidating if Tamra hadn't spent the bulk of her life around monsters who exemplified the word.

She raked him up and down with her eyes. "She isn't your daughter here. She's my rider." From the looks of him, she judged he'd never thrown a punch at anyone he thought would fight back. Tamra had done plenty of fighting in her time, though she hadn't gotten herself into that kind of situation in a decade or so. Tamra's back ached at the thought of this turning into a brawl. She wished Raia's parents had waited to descend until morning, when she'd be fresher. But there was no way she would let this man get the drop on her, tired or not. "Now that the race season has begun, I need her fully focused on her training and race preparation, not distracted by personal issues."

"You're talking nonsense," Raia's father sputtered. "Raia is no racer!"

"The kehoks are called 'racers,' and the jockeys are called 'riders,'" Tamra corrected primly. "Raia is a talented rider who shows enormous potential. She has successfully completed her first race and must prepare for her second."

Raia's father's eyes bulged, and her mother's mouth flopped open. "Our Raia?" she squeaked. "You must be mistaken. Our Raia would never associate with such . . . activities." She said the word as if Raia were rolling around naked in manure.

"No offense taken."

They gaped at her. Tamra had encountered people with this attitude before, who thought riders and trainers were sullied by their association with kehoks. Those same people would pay fistfuls of coins for the shaded seats in the stands during the races and drop large sums in bets on their favorite beasts. She didn't bother to defend the profession. Hypocrites like these two would never understand. "'Your' Raia has made her choice. Feel free to cheer for her from the stands."

Crossing her arms, she hoped that Raia hadn't lied about her age. If she were younger than sixteen, she wouldn't have the right to race without her family's permission.

"See here," her father said. "We are her family! We have the right to—"

"The right to benefit from her fame and fortune?" Tamra finished for him.

"Excuse me?"

"You don't, by law," Tamra said. "All her winnings are hers, since she is of age. However, she has told me she wishes to come to an arrangement with you, to compensate you for certain costs you may have incurred. . . . Bah, screw that. She owes you nothing. You're her *parents*. You're supposed to support her, not profit off her." She put her hands on her hips. "Sorry excuse for parents, blaming her for what she couldn't control, and then selling her off."

"We would never!" Raia's mother cried, her hand over her heart as if Tamra's words had shocked her into palpitations. "We only ever thought of her happiness!"

Tamra resisted rolling her eyes. As earnest as they seemed, she didn't buy it. She'd seen the look in Raia's eyes when she talked about her parents and fiancé. "Really? And you didn't come here to pressure her into a marriage she doesn't want?"

"We know what's best for her!" Raia's father blustered.

"That's all we ever wanted," Raia's mother said, right on the heels of her father, "what's best for her. We want her to be happy, with her future secured."

Now Tamra did roll her eyes. "And did you ever ask her what she wanted?"

"She's a child!" Raia's father said. "She doesn't understand the world. She refuses to see things the way they are!"

Tamra snorted. "How much?"

Both parents stared at her.

"How much will she have to give you for you to leave her alone?" Tamra spoke slowly and clearly, so there was no chance they'd misunderstand. If Raia wanted to buy her freedom, then Tamra would do her best to see that it didn't cost her too dearly—and that she never had to talk to these people again if she didn't want to.

Raia's father stepped toward her. "This is absurd—"

Tamra held up one hand. "Diplomacy is not my strong suit. Do you know what is?" She shifted her focus to the kehoks inside the stable. *Scream*, she silently ordered them.

From within the stable, screams rose to claw the darkening sky.

Silence.

The screams cut off.

"Your daughter ran away from you because you're monsters," Tamra informed them. "And came *here*. You can understand, then, how she must feel about you. So how about we sit down and settle this? I'll be the one looking out for Raia's best interests, and you two can pretend you are."

Raia's parents gawked at her.

She smiled at them, accentuating her scar. "Let's talk."

INSIDE HER RACER'S STALL, RAIA WHISPERED TO THE black lion, "I'm a coward."

He regarded her with his golden eyes, and she imagined he was telling her she wasn't. You couldn't be a coward and ride a kehok.

"But I am," Raia insisted. "I'm letting Trainer Verlas fight my fight. I should be out there, standing up for myself, not in here with you."

He shuffled toward her, then hit the shackles and let out a whimper.

"Oh, did I chain you too tight?" Raia inched toward him. "Stay calm while I fix it. Behave." She focused on him and tried to ignore the voices of her parents and Trainer Verlas beyond the door to the stable.

He lay down like a housecat and stretched his paws forward so she could reach the clamp. She loosened it, giving him several more inches of slack in his chains.

"Better?" she asked.

He licked his paw, around where the shackle had rubbed against his fur. He no longer wore the chain net and hadn't for a while. Just the shackles that chained him inside the stall, which seemed much more humane.

"You aren't so bad," she told him.

He gave her a look that seemed to say, *Yes, I am.*

She laughed, but the laugh broke and she felt tears on her cheeks. "You just want to run free. Like I do." Tentatively, she reached toward him and touched his mane. He didn't flinch. She stroked the metallic spikes. They were cool and smooth beneath her fingers. "Let me get you more water."

She stepped out of his stall and halted. "Celin!"

Her—Raia's mind recoiled at calling him her "fiancé"—*he* stood before her, filling the stable. He always seemed over-large to her, even though she knew he was no larger than her father. He loomed when he stood, and his broad shoulders dominated the corridor between stalls. She knew she was supposed to think he was handsome—certainly there had to be something about him that had enticed his prior wife. Or maybe her family had liked his fortune too. A nice purse to go with nice hair, nice cheekbones, and an easy smile. He was smiling at her now, as if he could charm her.

"You're here!" she yelped, and then wanted to smack herself for saying something so obvious and so unhelpful. What she should say was *Get out* or *Leave me alone.* Or she should scream and hope that Trainer Verlas came running.

He held out his hands, palms toward her. "Don't be alarmed, Raia."

She backed up against the stall door. "Why are you here?"

"For you." He took a step toward her. "I'm here to offer you your dream future. I'm here to save you!"

She inched along the door, until her toes touched the hay of the lion's stall. *Save me? I don't need saving!* "I found my own future, thanks. You didn't have to come all this way—"

"Your parents told me you were deliriously happy at our engagement. Those were their exact words, 'deliriously happy,' because after the augurs dismissed you, you had no future, and I represent a new future!"

Raia's mouth felt dry, and her palms were slick with sweat. "I'm sorry this isn't what you want to hear, but I don't want to marry you." In fact, she'd climbed out a window and fled into the night to avoid marrying him. *You'd think he'd get the hint.*

"You say that, but I hear your fear talking."

Yes, you do. That was absolutely right. She was so full of fear that she felt her muscles shaking. She inched sideways into the stall with her lion. "Of course I'm afraid! I ran, and you chased. If you cared at all about my happiness, you would have let me go."

"Raia, my dear, sweet Raia." His voice was patient, soothing, as if she were a skittish wild animal. "You've heard hateful rumors about me, spread by hateful people, who want me to be miserable. And that's why you weren't thinking clearly when you fled!"

"You don't know what I was thinking." Her fear was turning into anger now. He had no right to call her "my" anything. She wished she could command him as if he were a kehok. She'd make him run into the desert and never return. *Leave me alone!* she thought.

"Your parents do! They know you better than anyone, and they were worried—"

"They don't know me at all," Raia said. "And neither do you."

"Ah, but I do." He sounded almost apologetic. Reaching into his tunic, he pulled out a wad of paper. "Here is the record of your birth. Your parents splurged for an augur reading, you know. According to this, you were a goat in a prior life. That accounts for your stubbornness."

She shivered. Where had he gotten that?

"And here is the record of your admittance into the temple for training, the report from the augurs who originally identified you. Your parents bequeathed me all your records and the reports from your regular readings, along with the bills they paid for your training."

Raia began to shake. It was suddenly hard to suck in air. All of that . . . it was private. It was supposed to be sealed by her parents, to remain in their possession until their deaths. "You shouldn't have that."

"Your parents have handed full responsibility for you over to me." Celin was smiling again, and it wasn't anything she could have called charming. In fact, it made her want to scream, if only she could get enough air into her lungs. He pulled out another paper. "Your parents and I are all concerned for your happiness."

She stared at the paper, a formal declaration that she was unfit to make decisions about her future. They'd used her augur readings, combined with her failure at training and the fact that she'd run away, to declare her incapable of rational decisions.

By her parents' decree, Celin was now her guardian.

In effect, if these papers were legal, he owned her. She

was shaking so hard now that she felt like vomiting. Of all the possible scenarios, she'd never imagined that her parents would take things this far, or that they'd find a man willing to assist them.

This can't be happening, she thought. She tried to see if the papers had an official augur stamp, but Celin was already tucking them back into his pocket. If she challenged it . . . But that would require gold she didn't have.

Behind her, the black lion began to growl.

"You see, for your own good, you're mine," Celin said. "And once we're married, I will help you understand that." He flashed another charming-yet-terrifying smile.

"I don't want—"

All of a sudden, the kehoks screamed.

Raia spun around. *Why*—

And then the sound cut off.

The black lion was standing, silent, quivering. She quickly examined him, careful to keep her distance from his claws and teeth. "What happened? Are you all right?"

Lunging forward into the stall, Celin grabbed her arm. "Raia, come out of there. You're not safe."

"Let go of me!" Forgetting the kehok, she pulled away from Celin and stumbled back against the black lion. She felt his hot breath against her neck and froze. He wasn't muzzled, and his chains were loose.

Celin froze too. "Just move slowly. A step toward me."

Facing the black lion, Raia said, "You won't hurt me." She put as much force of will as she could into it, which wasn't easy while her insides were screaming in panic. She knew she was too close to him and she couldn't trust herself to focus properly with Celin here, filling her with so much fear. She glanced back at him.

"Of course I won't hurt you," Celin said soothingly. "So long as you listen to me, I will keep you safe and happy." He took a step forward. He was still reaching his hand toward her. He filled the only exit from the stall. "Stay calm. Deep breath."

She obeyed, taking a deep breath, settling her thoughts. But not for his sake.

As she steadied herself, she slipped into her inner sight, as she'd been trained. She'd never been able to see the future or past of a soul, but she could manage a few wavering shapes that revealed its present state. She thought she saw Celin's aura: spiked, layered with shadows. "Tell me what happened to your last wife," Raia said.

He opened his mouth to speak.

"If you lie, I'll know. I may have failed to become an augur, but I have been trained. I'll see in your aura if you try to lie." She wasn't certain that was true, but he didn't know that.

"It's illegal to read someone without their consent." Celin frowned at her.

The aura wavered. It was difficult to stay focused when her heart was fluttering in her chest. "It's illegal to declare someone incompetent when they're not too. What happened to your wife?"

He shrugged, as if it were of no consequence. "I wanted what was best for her, but she didn't listen."

True. "And what happened?"

"She tried to run from me, despite all I had given to her, despite all I wanted for her. She was not in her right mind."

"You killed her."

He didn't answer.

But that was answer enough. He wasn't even trying to

hide how warped he was, how badly he wanted to own her, how he wanted to control her. With the papers he had, he must have felt it was his right.

"Raia, I swear I will never hurt you. Just let me take care of you. I will see to your happiness in every way imaginable. You will want for nothing."

Except her freedom. He and her parents had conspired against her, declaring her incompetent, binding her to him without her consent. Condemning her. All the while, thinking they were doing what was right. Like she was certain Celin had believed when he killed his last wife. *He'll hurt me, if I let him.*

Then she heard in her head, as clearly as her own thoughts, a gravelly male voice she'd never heard before: *I will not let him.*

The black lion lunged forward. In the loosened chains, he could reach the stall door. He swiped with his massive paw, and his claws tore Celin's throat.

Celin's eyes widened, as if he were surprised that anyone would dare hurt him. He was a man who hurt others; no one had ever dared touch him.

He was dead before his body hit the ground.

CHAPTER 14

When Raia screamed, Tamra slammed open the stable door and rushed inside. She scanned the stable: body, kehoks, Raia. . . . Raia was huddled against the wall, far from any kehok and far from the body. A quiet part of her mind whispered: *Body?*

But a louder part shouted: *Raia is safe!*

Tamra pivoted to face her kehok. He was still chained, shackled inside his stall, but his muzzle was spattered with blood. It looked like wet blackness on his metal face. Lunging forward, she swung the stall door shut and locked it.

The lion did not move. He only stared at her with his beautiful eyes.

And then, only then, did she look down at the body.

Tamra had seen blood before. And death. But that didn't make it any easier. She didn't recognize him, which helped. She hadn't bothered to learn the names of all the students who worked with Osir and Zora, but she knew by sight who belonged in the kehok stables and who didn't. He wasn't anyone who should have been in here with Raia.

He could have been handsome, if he wasn't dead. But his empty open eyes and gaping mouth—as if he continued to be surprised he'd died—robbed him of any beauty he'd once had. His clothes were expensive layered silks, hemmed with gold embroidery.

A dead rich man in the stable.

And her kehok had killed him.

His throat had been torn. It was a clump of red, and the stain was spreading down his silk tunic and pooling on the sand-strewn stable floor. Beside Tamra, Raia's parents were wailing.

It didn't take much to figure out who he was. The fiancé, the one Raia had run from because of his dead wife. He must have come with the parents and snuck into the stables to corner Raia while Tamra was distracted. While the parents keened over the dead fiancé, Tamra knelt next to Raia. "Are you all right?"

Raia shook her head hard.

Tamra clarified. "Are you hurt?"

Another shake of the head.

Good. In fact, that was the only good thing about any of this.

Across the stable, Raia's mother had dropped to her knees, carefully beyond the edge of the pool of blood, and was wailing loudly enough to match the kehoks. Raia's father was shouting, "How could this have happened? Who is responsible? Someone must pay for this . . . this . . . abomination!" And the augur was witnessing it all, silently.

"Shit," Tamra muttered.

She felt old as she pushed on her knees to stand. All

her muscles still ached from the ride, and even her bones felt tired. The shrieks of the other kehoks mingled with the screaming of Raia's parents until they all bounced around inside of Tamra's skull.

"Quiet," she ordered, and projected her will like a blanket, smothering the kehoks.

All the kehoks quieted at once, leaving only Raia's parents making noise—which seemed telling.

Out of the corner of her eye, she saw the augur's attention shift to her. She supposed that was because she'd silenced all of them—that little parlor trick always drew notice. *I guess hiding the body isn't an option.* She knew a very nice desert just beyond the tracks with hot winds and sands and wraiths that would happily flay the flesh from a corpse until it was unrecognizable. But there were far too many witnesses.

Also, that wouldn't be good for my soul.

But that was a secondary issue. When it came right down to it, no matter what the augurs preached, she didn't much care what happened to her in her next life, so long as everyone she cared about in this life was safe. And now they decidedly weren't.

Without the screaming of the kehoks to drown them out, Raia's parents were shouting even louder. Raia's mother was howling, "This is murder! Murder! It's the murder of my baby's future! The murder of all her dreams!" while her father was shouting that the city guards must be called, someone was responsible, and justice must be served.

"Oh, shut up," Tamra told them. "Your wailing isn't helping anyone."

Belatedly, she realized this might be insensitive. For all she knew, they'd truly cared about this overdressed corpse and their pain was real. On the other hand, they'd come here to threaten and coerce her rider—not to mention the fact that this man should never have been inside the stable in the first place—and that lost them any sympathy she might have had.

Plus, they haven't even checked to make sure their daughter is okay!

Now that she'd caught their attention, they aimed their anger at Tamra. She heard the words "irresponsible" and "unforgiveable" before it degenerated into curse words spat at her. She filled her lungs, intending to yell them into silence, when the augur stepped forward with his hands raised.

"Please," the augur said.

His simple word quieted Raia's parents. Tamra was impressed despite herself—even without being able to read auras, she could feel his holiness. It permeated his voice, his demeanor, his very being. That inherent purity was why augurs were so essential to Becar. It was said one augur could stop an army or soothe a mob, and feeling his serenity fill the stable, she could believe it. *He's much better at this than Augur Clari,* Tamra thought.

"Most Holy One." Raia's father bowed. "You must help us seek justice for this good man, viciously slain! The kehok must be destroyed, and his trainer punished!"

Tamra felt her heart sink. That could happen. This wasn't a death on the tracks, where accidents were expected. This was a civilian inside a stable. If the augur believed the cause was negligence . . . A second charge of negligence would destroy her. *And take Raia and Shalla down with me.*

"Is there no hope for the boy?" the augur asked.

Tamra glanced at the widening pool of red. "Um, no." Definitely no. She added, "I am deeply sorry for the *accident* that occurred here today." She emphasized the word "accident."

The augur hurried past them, crossing to Raia, and Tamra and Raia's parents backed out of his way. He bent down beside Raia. "Are you hurt, child?"

Now *that* was what an augur should do: be kind to those in distress. Of course, Tamra hadn't seen many augurs who acted that way. She thought of Augur Clari once more, so certain of her superiority. But this augur didn't seem to care that the hem of his robes was dipped in blood, or that Raia's parents were muttering behind him about how they'd been wronged and what reparations should be made for this calamity.

"Can you tell me what happened?" the augur asked in a gentle voice.

Raia lifted her tear-streaked face, and Tamra wanted to gather her in her arms and soothe her, like she did Shalla after a nightmare. Except this nightmare was real.

"He s-scared me," Raia whispered. "I—I backed away. Into the stall. And he came toward me. And my racer—the lion kehok—he tried to protect me. It happened so fast. I didn't—"

Raia's mother gasped. "Oh, Raia, is this . . . is it *your* fault? You *made* that monster attack him? River protect you from your fate, for we cannot!"

"I didn't!" Raia cried.

Tamra stepped in front of her parents. "You said yourself she couldn't be a rider, and now you think she has enough control over a kehok to command him to kill? You can't have it both ways."

"She admitted it!" Raia's father blustered. "He tried to protect her."

Tamra snorted. "She's mistaken. Kehoks don't protect people. They slaughter them." She gestured at the body on the ground. "If anyone is stupid enough to get close to a ke-hok they can't control, then the results are their fault. Any child knows that."

"That monster should have been secured!" Raia's mother cried. "Muzzled! I've been to races. I've seen how they're supposed to be chained. It's negligence—"

"He's in a stall, shackled to the wall," Tamra said. "He can't be muzzled or he can't eat or drink. If this man chose to enter that stall, then it was his own fault."

"He was following her! She must have baited him, enticed him to follow her." Raia's father jabbed a finger toward Raia. "Call the city guard! Have her arrested for murder! She intentionally lured him into the stall, knowing what would occur. She caused this, despite all we have done for her, all we've wanted for her! She is an ungrateful, manipulative, vile—" He kept going, hurling insult after insult.

Tamra hated a whole slew of people—those who had doubted her, mocked her, ignored her, rejected her—but she'd never instantly hated anyone as badly as she did Raia's parents. What kind of parents spoke with such contempt for their own child? Raia was their daughter! They should be defending her! Worried about her! Any emotion but this . . . loathing.

The wonder wasn't that Raia had run. The wonder was that she hadn't run sooner. The fact that her spirit hadn't been crushed by them was a miracle.

"I don't have to be an augur to know how you'll be reborn," Tamra told them. And then she remembered the very real augur who was in the stable behind her, with Raia.

It didn't matter what these monstrous people said about her or Raia. But it *did* matter what the augur said and did. The city guard would take any word he spoke as proven truth.

"She feared these people," Tamra said to him. "You can clearly see why. As to the cause of death, this man followed her into a stall with no regard for safety. You can't thrust your hand into the fire and then blame the flame if you're burned."

"The law states—" the augur began.

"Look at him!" Tamra said, pointing at the lion. "He's chained inside his stall! Every reasonable precaution was taken." As Tamra gestured toward the kehok, she noticed the shackle around his neck was looser than usual. *Oh, by the River . . .*

She moved to shield the stall from view, but the augur was already standing, looking at the kehok. She couldn't read his expression, but he looked as if he'd been frozen.

"Gracious One . . ." Raia's mother said.

"Honorable One . . ." her father echoed.

But the augur didn't seem as if he was listening anymore.

YORBEL KNEW HE WAS ONE OF BECAR'S MOST SKILLED augurs. He didn't need peace or silence to read the auras of those around him, which was one of the reasons he'd believed it made sense for him to be the one to search the kehok auctions. If he wished, he could slip into his second sight as easily as putting on a robe. Sometimes he slipped into it even when he didn't wish it, which was not a fact he cared to share with the high augurs, though of course they themselves were impossible to read. But an unshielded soul was like an open book.

He'd read the man and woman already: their souls were pierced with so much anger and hate that it tore holes in the fabric of their essences. The trainer had pegged it right. While it was unlikely they were corrupt enough to be reborn as kehoks, it was very likely they'd be reborn as an insect so low that it would take many iterations of rebirth before their souls would be able to pull themselves out of the muck and return as any respectable creature.

He'd read the girl who huddled in the corner as well. She looked like a candle's flame that was battered by wind, flickering, close to being extinguished by the shadowy fear that lurked around her. And the trainer had a core like a rock, with shadows that licked at its exterior but couldn't touch its center. The dead man had no soul to read. Yorbel knew that before he even asked if he could be saved. He'd refused to allow himself to read the kehoks—their auras would drown out any sense of the here and now. He knew he wouldn't be able to function if he let them inside his head, and he needed clear thoughts for this situation.

A man had been killed by a kehok.

It was a common occurrence in the wild. It even happened often enough on the racetrack. Riders lost control. Every season a few were lost. Sometimes bystanders. It was the primary reason he never attended the Becaran Races. He had no interest in witnessing death as entertainment.

This, though, was different. A death in a stable. As loath as he was to admit such corrupt souls were in the right, the man and woman were correct that there should have been enough safety precautions in place as to make this kind of accident impossible. It was negligence on the part of the kehok's trainer, perhaps reflecting on the stable as well.

It also pointed to a kehok who was unsuited to the races. It was irresponsible to keep a kehok that killed so quickly and easily—such a kehok would surely cause more death on a track. The required action was clear. He had to report it to the city guards, have the training facility penalized, the trainer charged and stripped of her license, and the kehok eliminated before it caused any more disasters.

But then the trainer had said, *Look at him!*

And Yorbel had looked without thinking to shut his inner sight.

Staring at the metallic black lion, he felt as if the air had turned hot enough to choke him. He gripped the wall, suddenly dizzy. Unlike the other kehoks he'd seen on his journey, this one had two layers of auras.

First was the layer he expected: the decayed horror of a kehok's broken soul. But it was flimsy, as transparent as a silk scarf. It seemed to flutter loosely around the kehok, like a tunic that didn't fit.

Beneath the scarf-like layer, though, was a more solid shape. It was coiled at first, hard to see, as if it were hiding beneath the shadows. A less skilled augur would have missed it entirely. An augur who didn't know what to look for would have ignored it. But Yorbel was neither of those things, and so he peered at it, shutting out the distractions, the yammering of the girl's parents, the pleading of the trainer, and the quiet sobbing of the girl.

As he separated the tangle of shadows—like pushing aside a cobweb—he caught sight of the soul beneath the soul, and one thing became instantly clear.

I know this soul.

The longer he stared, the more certain he was. He saw the shape of the man this monster used to be. The late emperor Zarin. *I was right.*

He wished with every fiber of his being that he wasn't.

He drew in a breath.

Behind him, the trainer was insisting, "There's no need to call the city guard! This was an accident at a kehok training facility."

"You want to hide what happened here—" the father began, about to launch into another rant, as if volume could hide the shadows he held within. The fear, both his own and theirs, inside the stable was so thick that Yorbel could taste it, sharp as copper on his tongue.

The trainer cut the man off. "I'm hiding nothing! Call the carriers for the body and the mourners to perform the rites. We already have an augur here to lead them, if he's willing. Are you willing?" That last was directed at him.

Yorbel was finding it difficult to think. He'd never been one to like making decisions under pressure. He preferred to consider all angles, weigh all options, and then make a calm, measured decision. He did *not* feel in any state of mind to make any kind of calm, measured judgment on anything, even if she'd asked him what he wanted for lunch or whether he liked the color blue. "I do like blue," he said out loud.

"What?" the trainer said.

Get control of yourself, he told himself firmly. *You're a highly educated, well-trained expert in death, resurrection, and the care of souls.*

And even more important: *Dar trusts me to bring his brother home.*

"I am an augur from the Heart of Becar," Yorbel said in his most official tone. "I will handle this matter. Come, let us find a place we can speak to one another beyond the touch of death, and I will tell you how we will proceed."

He hoped he sounded as if he knew what he was doing, because he was acutely aware he had no idea.

CHAPTER 15

Tamra led them across the sands to the visitors' waiting room, the nicest area in the training facility and also the farthest from the stable. The "nicest" room still had cracks in the walls, stained cushions on the chairs, and a dead plant in a pot. It had died on Tamra's week to water it three months ago, and no one had cared enough to chuck it out.

With her arm around Raia's shoulders, Tamra guided her rider to a chair on the opposite side of the room, where she wouldn't have to sit close to her parents. Into her ear, she murmured, "Tell me you didn't loosen the chains deliberately."

Raia's eyes widened. "It's my fault. I *did* loosen them."

Tamra's grip on her shoulders tightened. *No one knows that. It may still be okay.* "Before or after you knew your personal nightmare had joined you in the stables?"

"Before. I swear. I didn't mean for this to happen!"

The last bit was loud enough for the others to hear. Tamra winced. "I know you didn't," she said firmly. She nudged

Raia to lower herself into the chair. The girl was shaking, and her skin felt clammy to the touch. If those horrible excuses for parents started yelling again, Tamra thought Raia might burst into tears or faint. "I'll be right here with you."

Sure enough, as soon as they shoved their way into the room and plopped their butts into seats, Raia's parents started in again. "Pure One, you must understand. Our daughter does not accept how the world works. She doesn't understand that we must all follow the paths laid out for us—"

The augur held up his hand. His voice was smooth, as if gentling a horse. "The truth will come out. In cases of violent death, an augur is asked to read the souls of the witnesses, to aid with determining their guilt or to identify the level of comfort they will need."

Beside her, at the word "guilt," Raia grabbed Tamra's hand and squeezed it. Tamra squeezed back. This was the first bit of good news. If the augur read her, he'd see Raia's innocence. Or at least she hoped he would. If Raia doubted her own innocence . . . Could guilt stain a soul if you weren't truly guilty?

"Then you should be able to read that *she*—" Raia's mother pointed at Raia, her hand trembling. "She—she—We did everything for her! Sacrificed everything! Gave up our own dreams, our own future, to secure hers, and she . . . she destroyed the life we worked so hard to give her." She buried her face in her hands, and her shoulders heaved as if she were crying. When she lifted her tear-streaked face, Tamra saw she wasn't faking it. She truly believed everything she was saying. Maybe they honestly didn't know how terrible they were. Not everyone was willing to submit to the kind of regular augur readings that would have made them aware.

"Your choices don't give you the right to control her future," Tamra said.

"That's exactly what gives us the right!" Raia's father boomed. "We're her parents! Without our choices, she wouldn't exist. It's our job to guide her toward the best possible path, and it's her duty to walk that path! You would understand if you had children, instead of spending your days with monsters."

Raia jumped in. "She's a better parent than you'll ever be! She'd never try to declare her own daughter incompetent and sign her rights away!"

Tamra felt as if her vision blurred red. "They did what?"

"He—he had papers saying he had been named my guardian. He and my parents—they planned to force me to marry him by claiming I wasn't rational enough to make my own decisions." She was shaking, her shoulders tight and eyes fixed on the floor, but her voice was steady and clear.

Tamra curled her hands into fists and rose. She kept her voice measured and low. "Augur—what's your name?"

"Yorbel," he supplied. She heard curiosity in his voice and wondered what he was reading in her aura. She hoped she got extra points for not pummeling Raia's parents.

"Augur Yorbel, I would like to formally submit my request to adopt this girl, Raia"—she realized she didn't know Raia's last name, so she skipped over it—"as my daughter, on the grounds that her birth parents are spiritually stunted and incapable of guiding their daughter on the path of righteousness." She thought she got most of the traditional words correct, or at least close enough. She also hoped Shalla meant what she said about wanting a sister. "And to invalidate any agreements between her biological parents and the deceased."

Raia's parents were sputtering. "You can't—!" "She's *our* daughter!" "We know what's best for her!" "All we wanted—"

Ignoring them, Tamra said to Yorbel, "Everyone deserves a family that loves and respects them." If Tamra had had that . . . Well, she knew how important it was.

Beside her, Raia said, "Trainer Verlas, you really want *me*—"

"This is nonsense!" Raia's father blustered. "And a distraction! Celin of Seronne lies dead, and this woman is trying to shift attention from her own culpability."

Augur Yorbel held up his hand again. "You have a point. The dead man must be addressed before anything else." He inclined his head toward Tamra. "Your request will be filed after the current matter is resolved. First, though, I must speak with the owner of the kehok. Am I correct that this is Lady Evara of Peron?"

Tamra bit back everything she wanted to say to Raia's parents. She was so angry that she felt as if she were vibrating. To have a child as smart and driven as Raia and to treat her like this. . . .

"Trainer Verlas?"

"Yes—you are correct."

"Summon her here, please."

She hadn't been able to think of what could have made this worse, but now she knew. Tamra also knew that tone of voice—she'd used it often enough with students and kehoks alike. It was a "don't argue with me" voice, and since it was coming from an augur who held her future in his hands, as well as Raia's and Shalla's, she was absolutely going to obey.

She exited the room and hurried to the cabinet where they kept the messenger wights. Sliding one of the drawers open, she lifted out the wight. It twitched at her touch.

This wight looked like a crumpled paper bird. She stroked it until its wings unfolded. She didn't know what exactly the wights were—it was said they were bits of excess soul that were shed when someone or something was reborn. They weren't precisely alive or dead, and they had no feelings, thoughts, or memories of their own. But they were ideal for delivering messages. You could imprint them with a simple message and destination. "Lady Evara of Peron," Tamra instructed it. She hesitated for a moment. She didn't want to use the word "emergency," but she also didn't want Lady Evara to ignore the message. She settled on: "Augur requests your presence at the training grounds."

She released the wight and watched as it wobbled into the air. Other facilities could afford fresher wights that didn't look as if they'd disintegrate in a stiff breeze, but they were stuck with these.

After watching the wight flutter its way toward the river, Tamra went back inside. Augur Yorbel was seated cross-legged in the center of the room, his hands on his knees as if he were meditating. Raia's parents were clasping each other's hands, sitting silently by the cold firepit. Raia was also silent, curled up in the chair with her arms wrapped around her knees. Not wanting to break the quiet, Tamra crossed to her and put her arm around her.

No one spoke for a long while.

Tamra wondered what Augur Yorbel had said to quiet them. She'd never had this much luck with her students. She studied him as they waited.

He didn't look overly impressive. Older. Or more accurately, her age. His head was shaved bald, but his beard had flecks of white and gray checkering the black. His skin looked soft, as if the sun had never scorched it or even touched it much, and his face was thin and long. She wouldn't call him handsome in a classic way, but he was peaceful to look at, especially in his meditation pose. His breathing was soothingly even, and his back was as straight as a palm tree—not stiff, just straight, as if he never thought about his posture but achieved it naturally. She'd seen Shalla spend hours trying to perfect her posture for meditation, yet this man made it look easy. He looked, in short, like what she'd imagined an augur would be like when she was a child—until she met real augurs up close and they shattered that image. He looked like a good man . . . *who has the power to destroy my life with only a few words.*

She'd had very few lucky breaks in her life. Lady Evara was one, even though she came with strings. Shalla. Now Raia. The rest, all the good and all the bad, she'd done herself. But it all added up to knowing that too much hope was a dangerous thing right now.

She heard a clattering outside from the sands. Standing, she saw Lady Evara, with her entourage hurrying behind her, rushing from the stable toward the waiting room. She winced and retreated. Maybe she should have been more specific in the message about *where* to come.

Lady Evara burst into the room. "Why is there a dead man in my stable?"

Raia's parents jumped up, both talking at the same time, pointing at Raia and at Tamra, saying it was a crime and reparations were owed and this was negligence on the part of the trainer and malice on the part of their daughter—everything they'd spewed before but multiplied, as if they'd been using the silence to think up every argument they could.

As they talked, Augur Yorbel unfolded his legs and

slowly and gracefully stood. He clasped his hands in front of him and waited until Raia's parents took a breath.

"Lady Evara." He bowed. "I wish to purchase your kehok."

Everyone stared at him.

What? Tamra thought.

Then: *He can't! I need that kehok! Raia needs it!*

"Well, that's delightful," Lady Evara said, "but there's still a dead man in my stable."

"Once our business is resolved, I will call the carriers and mourners, and I will personally explain this accident to the city guard so that there is no risk of confusion."

Tamra jumped in. "Yes, it *was* an accident. The man ventured into a kehok stall without the knowledge or permission of any trainer."

Lady Evara snorted. "That's not an accident. That's idiocy."

Tamra suppressed a smile—she should have known Lady Evara would take her side, even without hearing all the facts. She wouldn't want to lose the gold of having a kehok destroyed, or risk a blow to her reputation. "Agreed, Gracious One," Tamra said.

But what did he mean about purchasing the kehok? That was nearly as alarming as the thought of the city guard and racing commission becoming involved. She could win but still lose here.

"I tell you, it was no accident!" Raia's father blustered. "This was negligence"—he poked a finger toward Tamra—"and malice." He then poked his finger toward Raia.

His wife nodded emphatically and added, "We'll testify to it, if we must, though it breaks our hearts. It is the duty of a parent, and a true Becaran, to put what is right above what is easy."

Fixing her piercing eyes on Raia's parents, Lady Evara said, "This could have occurred with any kehok in any facility. On behalf of those in my employ, I deny any allegations of negligence or malice. You will withdraw those foolish claims and swear never to repeat them."

Raia's parents looked offended. Her mother said, "A man has died! We will not compromise our moral principles."

Raia uncurled herself in her chair. "They will if you pay them." Her voice wavered, but she sat up straight, and Tamra felt a burst of pride. She most likely had little experience in standing up to her parents, at least successfully, judging from what Tamra knew of her life with them.

As her parents began to object to this view of their character, Augur Yorbel stopped them. "You seem to have forgotten that I read souls."

Raia's father fluffed himself up like a peacock. "Outside the temple, it is forbidden—"

Chiming in, her mother said, "You cannot read auras without consent!"

"Silence, both of you!" Lady Evara barked. "If you behave very, very well while the augur and I do our negotiation, then you may be appropriately bribed for your silence at its conclusion. Alternatively, you can continue to irritate me, and I will see to it that your reputations and livelihoods are destroyed. Am I clear?"

Raia's parents gaped at her.

That, Tamra thought, *was amazing.*

Augur Yorbel frowned. "I am uncomfortable with the ethical ramifications of the word 'bribe' . . ."

Without missing a beat, Lady Evara corrected her wording. "You will be consoled with monetary comforts in recompense for your pain and suffering."

Both Raia's father and mother sat down promptly, stiffly, and silently, and Tamra revised several of the insulting things she'd believed about Lady Evara in the past.

Raia was even more elated—she looked as if she wanted to cheer. She contained herself, though, which Tamra thought was wise. This was now between Lady Evara and Augur Yorbel, and if the track bookie were here, Tamra knew whom she'd bet on. *But is a win for Lady Evara a win for us?*

"You mentioned the purchase of my prize kehok," Lady Evara said, "and I am afraid that's not a simple request. The Becaran Races are my passion, and the black lion and his rider have shown significant potential with their performance in their first qualifying race."

Augur Yorbel inclined his head, as if acknowledging Lady Evara's passion. "As you may know, the emperors of Becar have a long tradition of participating in the famed Becaran Races with kehoks of their own. It was only in recent generations that this tradition was broken and the royal stables disbanded. The new emperor-to-be has tasked me with restarting a stable, in his name, beginning with the finest, fiercest racer I can find."

Lady Evara smiled, and Tamra couldn't help but think of the jackals that lurked on the edges of the city—her smile was like their expression when they scented prey. "You are purchasing for the emperor-to-be. With his funds. To bring him his very own racer. How wonderful." Even Raia's parents had leaned forward in their seats, as if scenting gold in the air. Tamra recoiled from all of them.

It was all coming apart. Even if they stayed out of jail and weren't banned from the track, how could their future be anything but ruined if the augur bought the lion? Tamra felt a tightness in the base of her stomach, as if her body wanted to revolt. She wished there was a breeze in the waiting room. The air felt thick and still, with a sour scent. As if their conversation was curdling the very air.

Affecting a sigh, Lady Evara continued, "But I am afraid even that noble purpose does not affect my reticence. This kehok, with its superlative trainer and promising young rider, has a chance at bringing me to the grand champion's ring, a long-held dream of mine. Ah, to see the Heart of Becar again at the peak of the races! To be at the center of it all! The thrill of it! The joy! You are asking not only to purchase a kehok, but also to purchase a dream."

That . . . seemed a bit much. But she didn't really care about Lady Evara's dream of grand parties and overflowing praise. Even without them, her patron would be rich and comfortable and no worse for wear. But for Tamra, Shalla, and Raia, this was their future. Tamra had to bite the inside of her cheek to keep from speaking up.

She had to bite hard enough that she bled, so she wouldn't scream.

"Two thousand gold pieces," Augur Yorbel said.

Raia's mother made a little whimpering noise.

Tamra felt her jaw drop. That was an extraordinary amount for an opening bid. Hadn't this man ever haggled before? And how could Lady Evara refuse? Tamra could already feel Shalla being pulled from her life by the augurs.

"Far too low," Lady Evara said. "For me to even consider an offer—"

And then Raia jumped in, before Tamra or anyone could stop her. "I have to come too."

Everyone turned and stared at the girl.

Lady Evara, who hadn't so much as glanced at Raia yet, pierced her with her uncomfortable gaze. Tamra saw Raia squirm, as if she wanted to slip out of the chair, out the window, and out into the desert.

Knowing protocol had already been violated with this interference in their negotiation, Tamra spoke up, nothing left to lose at this point. "A racer needs a rider and a trainer. You buy the kehok, then you must also employ us." Even as she said them, though, she wished she could take back the words. Because the reality of what she'd just demanded hit her: she couldn't go to the Heart of Becar with a kehok and an augur, miles and miles away from Shalla!

And yet, Raia needed this, and Tamra did too. It would mean separating from Shalla for now, but if they won, it would ensure they could have a future together. "The races have already begun, and there isn't time for the kehok to become accustomed to a new trainer and rider."

She expected Lady Evara to be angry at the interruption, but instead she was smiling even more broadly. "What a splendid idea!" Lady Evara cheered. "You can't simply purchase a kehok and expect to be competitive in the race. Hire Trainer Verlas, Rider Raia, and me as the emperor-to-be's personal consultant. Plus three thousand gold pieces, and I will be appeased."

"Our daughter owes us a percentage of her winnings!" Raia's mother chimed in.

"Fifty pieces for your silence now," Lady Evara said without even glancing at them, "and five percent of her winnings, after my cut."

Tamra quickly added, "And if she wins grand champion, you set her free."

"Fine," Raia's father said. "But if she fails to pay, we

spread word of the murder and cover-up that happened here. You don't want that kind of gossip when you're in the Heart of Becar."

Augur Yorbel looked somewhat panicked, Tamra thought. She wondered if he'd ever had to negotiate, seeing how all his needs were seen to by the temple. She almost felt sorry for him.

"Agreed," he said. "We will leave for the Heart of Becar in the morning. Until then, we will honor the life of . . ." He trailed off, clearly unsure of the man's name.

"Celin of Seronne," Raia supplied. "He was known for killing his prior wife and escaping justice by blaming his servants."

"Ugly gossip," Raia's father said, but his face paled just a bit.

"I saw his aura, and it was corrupted," Raia said. Then she ducked her head and added, "Or what I could read of it."

"Which shows once again how dishonorable—"

Augur Yorbel stopped them before they argued again. "We will honor the passage of a life, for all life is holy, and we will pray for his redemption—and our own."

"Splendid!" Lady Evara clapped her hands. "Deeply sorry for your loss. I must pack!" She hurried out of the shabby waiting room. Watching through the window, Tamra saw Lady Evara climb into her chariot. Pulled by four strong men, she thundered away toward her palace.

Raia's parents accompanied Augur Yorbel to summon the carriers to handle the body, and Tamra and Raia were left alone. "That didn't go as I'd expected," Raia said tentatively.

"Strangely, I think it went better."

Raia smiled.

"And I meant what I said," Tamra told her. "You can be my second daughter, if you wish, as soon as we can arrange it." Before anything else, though, she had to explain to Shalla why she had to leave again for even longer.

TAMRA HURRIED ACROSS THE SANDS AS THE MOURNING bells began to ring.

In response to Augur Yorbel's summons, the carriers had arrived quickly, and she'd left after they'd wrapped the body in linens. Escorted by bells, they would carry Celin to the Silent Cliffs, where his body would be stacked with others within the dark and lifeless caves. Under the blessing of the stars, his name would be carved on the stone entrance to the caves, and the official mourners would sing the rites to guide his spirit to its new vessel. *Probably to his new life as a river snail,* she thought. *Or a leech.* Or perhaps, somewhere out in the desert, a brand-new kehok had popped into existence, fully grown and hungry to kill.

She knew she should be thinking kinder thoughts, for the sake of her own soul, but screw that. He'd frightened Raia in life and turned their lives upside down in death. She wasn't inclined to think charitably about him.

Maybe he'll be a slug, the kind that's caught on a rock in the heat of the day, then withers and is reborn as a trout. That was a pleasant thing to imagine as she hurried toward the temple.

She buried those thoughts deep as she approached the temple. Giving her name to the guard at the visitor's entrance, she asked to speak with Augur Clari. She hoped it wasn't too late for visitors to be admitted and was relieved when she was led to the augur's office.

Inside, Tamra dropped a bag of gold pieces, a portion of

her winnings from betting on Raia's race, on Augur Clari's desk. "Tuition."

Augur Clari glanced up. "I am surprised. But you could have left your payment with the bursar. Instead you asked to see me in person? There's more you wish to say?"

"I . . . I need to go to the Heart of Becar for the rest of the race season."

The augur's lips pinched together, and Tamra couldn't tell if she was pleased or annoyed. She felt as if she were being judged and was failing.

"You know Shalla cannot accompany you," Augur Clari said.

"I know." The law was clear. Shalla's training could not be interrupted. "Will you . . . Can you . . ." The words burned in Tamra's throat as she tried to speak.

"She always has a home here, I've told you that," Augur Clari said in a kind voice. "And if you do not return, she will continue to be cared for."

Tamra reeled back as if she'd been slapped. "I will return!"

Augur Clari smiled soothingly. "Of course you will."

Tamra squeezed her hands into fists, digging her nails into the flesh of her palms, as she willed herself to control her emotions. "With your permission, I'd like to take Shalla home tonight, so I can explain."

Standing, Augur Clari swept to the doorway, her robes brushing against the stone floor. "Have the student Shalla prepare herself," she told the temple guard. "Her mother is here to take her home for the night." The guard disappeared down the hall, and Augur Clari turned back to Tamra with her hands clasped in front of her. "I know you think ill of us, but we truly want only what is best for your daughter. I hope someday you understand that. We are not your enemy. The sooner you understand that, the more peace your soul will feel."

Tamra bit back her usual response: *What's best for her is to be with someone who loves her.* But how could she say that when she was leaving? By the time she got back, Shalla could have grown another quarter inch, learned countless more things, had a thousand more thoughts and moments that Tamra wouldn't share. . . . Instead, she bottled that all up as she thanked Augur Clari, then returned to wait outside, back by the gate, for Shalla to appear.

Only a few minutes later, Tamra saw her walking sedately at first and then breaking into a huge grin when she saw her mother. She practically flew out of the gate and into Tamra's arms. "Did Raia win?"

Of course that was her first question. She couldn't have known everything that had happened after the race. "Third. But it was enough to pay for tuition. All is well."

"Knew she'd be fast!" Shalla crowed. Looping her arm through Tamra's, she half walked, half skipped away from the temple. Tamra let herself be tugged along through the lantern-lit streets. "Is she at our house?"

"She'll be there by the time we are. She had some things to finish up first. Shalla, my sweet star . . ." She couldn't find the words to tell her, not just yet. Instead, she let Shalla chatter about her day and all her lessons while they walked home. They paused at a bakery just about to close, and Tamra bought a bag of sweets, which Shalla guessed were to celebrate the race. "Have one."

"Now?" Shalla said. "Before bed?"

"Okay, fine, have two."

Shalla laughed but didn't argue, popping one of the sugary sweets into her mouth.

As they drew closer to their house, Tamra knew she was running out of time. She'd planned to tell Shalla at the start of the walk, so she'd have time to react before seeing anyone else. She also wasn't convinced that she'd stay unemotional, and she didn't want Raia to see that and blame herself for this mess. "Shalla . . ."

"Can you just tell me whatever awful thing you have to tell me?" Shalla asked. "You've been acting melodramatically tortured the entire way home."

Tamra smiled in spite of herself. "I'm that obvious?"

"Really obvious. Did someone"—she lowered her voice—"die?"

"Yes, but we didn't like him so it's okay."

"Mama! That's terrible!" She tucked the sweet into her cheek, making it bulge. "You know that's not a nice thing to say, and Augur Clari says—"

"I need to leave," Tamra blurted out. "For the racing season. You'll need to stay at the temple while I'm gone. But I promise at the end of the season, I'll be back, and everything will be better."

Shalla tried not to cry—Tamra could see her trying so hard—but in the end, she sobbed against Tamra's shoulder, just outside their front door, while Raia watched through the window.

THE NEXT MORNING, RAIA DID HER BEST TO AVOID cartwheeling with joy on the road to the training grounds. She knew how hard it had been for Trainer Verlas to say goodbye to her daughter, but Raia felt stuffed full with hope and light and also Shalla's ludicrously sugary jam.

Her mood crashed, though, as soon as she saw her parents at the dock. Several travel cases were stacked next to them. Clearly, they intended to join them on the trip to the Heart of Becar. Slowing, she felt as if her brain were stuttering to a halt.

Seeing them, Trainer Verlas ordered Raia, "Get the kehok ready."

Grateful to her trainer for understanding she didn't want to talk to her parents, or frankly ever see them again, Raia hurried to the stable, hoping they hadn't seen her. Inside, she skirted the stained floor—the worst of the blood had been scrubbed away by the carriers, but nothing could erase the deepened shade of gray stone around where Celin had fallen.

As she opened the stall door, she heard a sound behind her and tensed.

"Hey," Jalimo said.

She breathed out. It was just Algana, Jalimo, and Silar entering the stable, not her parents. "Hi. You, um . . ." Raia didn't know how to ask if they knew what had happened, but from the way they were staring at the stain, she didn't have to.

"Is that where . . ." Algana trailed off.

"Yes," Raia answered.

"He was your fiancé?" Silar asked.

"My parents wanted him to be." Raia thought of the night she'd climbed out her window to escape how badly they wanted him to be. So convinced they knew what was best for her, they hadn't been willing to listen to what she wanted. "He walked into the kehok's stall, and . . . It all happened so fast."

"Are you traumatized forever?" Algana asked. "Is that why you're leaving?" Jalimo elbowed her. "What? It's a legitimate question. Okay, maybe I could have phrased it more sensitively. I'm working on that."

"I'm not . . . I mean, I am, but . . ." She wasn't sure what she was supposed to say and what she wasn't.

But she was spared from coming up with an answer by Silar, who yanked her close and enveloped her in a hug. To Raia's surprise, the other two crowded around, wrapping their arms around her too, sandwiching her between them.

She hadn't realized they were on hugging terms, but . . . this was nice. "Um, thanks?"

Releasing her, Silar said, "Listen, if you want to talk . . ."

"Thanks, but I just want to forget it ever happened."

"You know, we're here for you, even if we'll technically be a lot of miles away and you don't actually know us all that well when you think about it," Algana said.

Silar rolled her eyes. "What she's trying to say is: Riders have to stick together."

"Except on the track," Jalimo amended. "Then I'm just trying to win."

Algana and Silar laughed, and Raia tentatively joined in. One of the kehoks screamed, hating the sound of their laughter.

Raia's laugh died as she looked again at the faded bloodstain on the stable floor.

"Want us to help you with your kehok?" Jalimo offered. He unhooked a barbed stick from his belt.

But Raia stopped him with a shake of her head. That wasn't the way Trainer Verlas liked her to handle her kehok, though she wasn't sure how to say that without insulting Jalimo and his trainer.

"You know, it's okay to let down your guard sometimes and trust that people just want to help," he said.

Not today, it isn't. Until she was safely on that ferry without her parents . . .

She had a sudden, wonderful idea. "Actually, there is something you could help me with. Could you . . . talk to my parents?"

"What? I don't do parents," Jalimo said, backing away as if she'd suggested he cuddle a kehok. "I mean, I'm not good with them. They hate me."

Silar nodded. "That's true."

"It doesn't actually matter what you say to them. I just need them distracted for long enough that we can leave without them." Raia was sure that Trainer Verlas wouldn't let them on the ferry, but she couldn't risk the chance of Augur Yorbel overruling her. It would be better if they simply missed the departure.

Jalimo brightened. "Ah! That I can do! How about we tell them there's an emergency and they're needed immediately on the other side of the sands? What kind of emergency would distract them?" He rubbed his hands together as if gleefully imagining the possibilities.

"And not alarm anyone else," Silar added. "An emergency is a terrible idea. How about we offer a free tour of the training track?"

"Or we ask for their help in finding a bag of lost gold," Jalimo said.

Algana rolled her eyes at him. "They aren't four-year-olds who want a treasure hunt."

He ignored her. "We say it was winnings from the last race, belonging to some rich guy, and there's a reward for whoever finds it. It's plausible!"

Raia grinned. "Anything. So long as they miss my departure." She felt like hugging all of them again. Somehow, miraculously, she'd made friends here, even though it hadn't been long. She wished briefly that she were staying, that she could have spent more time with them. She wished she could put into words how grateful she was for their helping her now.

"We've got this," Jalimo told her.

"Safe journeys," Silar said. "May you travel with the ease of a heron."

"And we'll see you soon!" Algana said. "After the qualifiers are over. Maybe we'll all race together in the Heart of Becar."

"Sounds wonderful," Raia said, and meant it.

Jalimo tugged Silar and Algana out of the stable, and they chattered to one another, elaborating on his lie, expanding it, making it more plausible. . . .

As their voices faded, Raia turned back to the kehok. He hadn't made a noise or a move since she'd opened the stall door.

"Ready?" she asked him, almost back to the way she'd felt when she'd woken up this morning, as if the sun had risen just to greet her.

He retreated, pressing against the wall.

Raia realized no one had come and explained to him what had happened. She moved closer in slow, unthreatening steps. "You aren't being punished. We're going on a boat to the Heart of Becar, to race for the emperor-to-be."

Behind her, she heard someone enter the stable, but this time her attention was focused on the kehok—she was too close to him to risk losing focus, no matter who had come in.

A soft, sad voice said, "He won't understand you. He's a kehok." It was Augur Yorbel. "Alone for so long . . . without reminders of his past life . . . he cannot be anything but a kehok."

She wished she could have a moment, just her and the kehok, to do what Trainer Verlas had asked her to do, but she couldn't ask an augur to leave. She kept her concentration on the kehok. "Come on. We're going to the boat. You and me. I'll be with you."

"He's never been to the capital, and he can't know what an emperor is. All memory is lost when one is reborn. Even if he once knew . . . To him, he's only existed for a few months."

She couldn't tell Augur Yorbel to leave, but she *could* ignore him. Raia stared into the liquid-gold eyes of her kehok and kept talking to him. "The emperor-to-be wants us to race for him, in the Heart of Becar. We're going to run more races, and we're going to win. But you need to come with me, if we're ever going to meet the emperor." She didn't expect him to understand every word, but she thought he would grasp the need of it. "Come with me."

The black lion stepped forward.

Raia slid a chain over his face, muzzling him, and then moved to unlock the shackles from the wall. At some point, chains had been tightened around him, constricting his legs. If she could keep him calm, this wouldn't be any different than taking him to the starting gates of the racetrack.

He walked beside her out of the stall. Seeing Augur Yorbel in the stable doorway, he stopped and made a noise that was halfway between a growl and a whimper. Raia hadn't heard him make that noise before. She didn't know what it meant. "You might want to keep your distance," she advised the augur.

Augur Yorbel backed away, out of the stable and then

out of sight beyond the door. She guided the kehok out and down toward the dock. The kehok came with her easily, as if he were a tame dog, and she wondered if he was beginning to trust her. She didn't think her focus had improved so much, especially as frayed as it was right now. But he gave her zero trouble as he walked toward the cage on the dock and then inside it without any resistance. *He wants to come,* she thought. *Maybe he does understand?*

"Nicely done," Trainer Verlas said.

Raia wanted to say it wasn't her doing, but the trainer had moved on to preparing the cage to be loaded onto the ferry. Raia glanced around and saw her parents' travel cases, but her parents were nowhere in sight. "Were Algana, Jalimo, and Silar here?"

"Yes. You may not be surprised to hear it, but they just went off with your parents." Trainer Verlas sounded amused. "I've let the ferryman know there's no need to wait."

Raia grinned. *It's nice to have friends.*

When the ferry arrived, they loaded the crate, and Raia, Tamra, and Augur Yorbel boarded. Lady Evara was already on board, along with three of her servants—they must have boarded at any earlier stop.

As they prepared to set sail, Raia noticed the kehok staring unblinkingly at the augur. *Maybe because he's new?* she thought. But the kehok showed no interest in the ferryman, who was scurrying all around preparing the boat. She was unable to consider it further, though, because it was time to leave.

The ferryman and his helpers pushed off from the dock. In the distance, across the sands, Raia saw multiple figures: her parents and her friends. Her three friends were waving enthusiastically, while her parents jogged toward the ferry—too far away to reach them.

Smiling, Raia waved back as the sails filled with wind.

If her parents shouted for them to stop, she didn't hear.

Standing between her trainer and the black lion, Raia turned her back on the training grounds, on her friends and her parents, and faced her future.

THE HEART OF BECAR

The High Council of Augurs filed into a black-walled room. Each one of the eight men and women paused at the threshold until the others who had already entered said in unison, "You are known to us." It was an ancient ritual, performed at every council meeting for the past five hundred years.

Before reaching the windowless room, each high augur first had to walk in darkness through a labyrinth of stone walls at the heart of the temple. Legend said that those walls were coated in a poison so ancient that both its ingredients and its antidote had been lost to history. Legend also said that five hundred years ago, the makers of the labyrinth had been murdered to keep its secrets and reborn as jackals whose descendants guarded the entrance to the labyrinth to this day.

Regardless of the legend, it was fact that the multiple layers of stone walls between the room and the world made it impossible for spies to hear what was discussed. And it was fact that all the high augurs avoided the guard dogs at the entrance, and none of them touched the labyrinth walls, out of a healthy mix of respect for tradition as well as paranoia.

Inside the room, each of the eight high augurs claimed their seat, stone thrones carved with the images of the birds, animals, and people their predecessors had become in their next lives.

The eldest and the head of the council, High Augur Etar, sat in a throne carved with the images of men and women.

High Augur Niasa occupied a throne with herons and a river dolphin.

High Augur Teron, a butterfly and a turtle.

High Augur Gasadon, a crocodile, a cricket, and a man.

High Augurs Utra, Siarm, and Nolak, all on thrones with birds and fishes.

The eighth and newest high augur, High Augur Gissa sat on a black obsidian throne with no carvings. By tradition, the vessels of the holy assassin were kept a secret, even—or especially—from his or her successors.

A ninth throne sat empty. It was carved with the image of a kehok.

High Augur Etar began the meeting.

There were no pleasantries. Only this:

"When must he die?"

One by one, the high augurs stood and reported.

"There's violence in the eastern cities."

"Revolts in several of the quarries. The overseers have controlled them, but they are increasing in frequency and destructiveness."

"Ships were sunk at the docks of Carteka."

High Augur Utra, who was in charge of external affairs, leaned forward, and the others fell silent. "Credible reports have come out of Ranir. King Hamra of Ranir has begun mobilizing troops in earnest. There is little doubt in my mind that he is planning a full-scale invasion. I estimate he will be ready by the end of the flood season. If our military is not deployed to repel such a force, it could spell the end of the empire."

High Augur Teron exhaled a heavy puff of air. "The laws must be changed—"

"And cannot be until an emperor sits on the throne," High Augur Etar said. "Even then, overturning centuries of tradition will not be a simple task. There will be resistance, and rightly so. The sacredness of our laws is what protects civilization itself."

"The mood of the people is tense," High Augur Niasa said. "It will explode, and we will have large-scale riots in our cities. With that kind of internal chaos, the empire is indeed ripe for invasion."

"And even if Ranir had no interest in conquering Becar by the end of this flood season, we are exposing ourselves to an economic crisis that will weaken Becar for decades—they could simply bide their time and invade later," High Augur Teron said.

All the high augurs, except for Gissa, began talking at once, expounding on how the crisis would worsen the longer the problem persisted.

High Augur Etar held up his hands. "This is known. We have only one question before us: *When* must he die? It is a terrible thing to take even an emperor-to-be from our people. It will end a dynasty most see as eternal. We must be certain the time we pick is right. His death must do more good than harm. Given the news from Ranir, can we still afford to wait until the end of the races?"

"We *must* wait until the end of the races," High Augur Siarm insisted. "You know the mood of the people during race season—it is their festival and their joy. If we take that from them, it will spark the very reaction we hope to prevent."

There were nods from around the room.

"Then nothing has changed?" High Augur Etar asked.

The only response was a heavy silence.

High Augur Gissa rose. "One thing has changed. A small thing. But we can't protect the empire if we ignore the small things. My sources have told me that an augur I know—a dedicated, holy man—is returning from his travels with a kehok for the emperor-to-be, as well as a rider, a trainer, and a race consultant. It is believed that the emperor-to-be has an interest in sponsoring a racer, and he has ordered the reestablishment of the royal stables, beginning with this one. If this is true, the emperor-to-be will undoubtedly recruit more, bringing a variety of kehoks in close proximity to the palace, under the scrutiny of a well-trained, highly skilled augur."

More silence.

"This may not be a small thing," High Augur Teron said.

"Since the augur in question is my friend, I will speak with him. He does not lie, and he certainly will not to me." This was fact. Gissa did not allow emotion to color her voice. She knew she was best suited to learn what Augur Yorbel knew and also the most likely to influence his future behavior. "Perhaps he can be persuaded that this is not an endeavor appropriate for augurs. To be near such vile creatures is a threat to one's soul, and Becar cannot afford the corruption of one of its most precious lights, especially in times such as these."

"And if you do not like what you hear? Or if he will not listen to reason?" High Augur Etar asked her.

Gissa did not hesitate. She knew her duty. "Then I will kill my friend, with sadness in my heart but strength in my hand."

"And those who accompany him?"

"If they are innocent, they live," Gissa said. "However, if they do not have the best interests of our beloved Becar at heart, then they die with him."

"So be it," High Augur Etar said.

The others echoed him, and the council ended.

INSIDE THE PALACE, IN A SUITE WITH A VIEW OF THE AUR River, Ambassador Usan of Ranir decided he despised sand. It wormed its way in everywhere, making even the finest silks feel gritty when the wind blew, which seemed to be all the blasted time. When he'd first arrived in Becar, he had found it mildly irritating. But now, he reflected, he loathed it.

Home was across the desert, on the shores of the Callifan Sea, where the breeze was crisp with salt and you could eat a slice of warm bread without having to chew grains of sand. He hated the bread here, and he hated the insistence of Becaran chefs on putting onions in everything.

But most of all he hated the people and their dewy-eyed insistence that all animals and birds were long-lost relations and thus should be honored. He hated the smug augurs, who treated the Becarans like goats to be herded and fed garbage until they were stuffed with self-righteousness.

The sooner his king could conquer this sand-blasted country, the sooner Usan could go home. He merely had to withstand its irritations a little longer. The country had almost reached its boiling point—even the augurs were having trouble keeping their herds soothed. Usan had done his part to stoke the fires, fueled by the unprecedented access to King Hamra of Ranir's treasury, with careful whispers in important ears and judicious bribes in the appropriate pockets. His work was nearly done.

It won't be long now, Usan thought. Everything was in place, and soon, very soon, he'd be able to return home, triumphant.

Humming to himself, he exited his suite, nodded politely to the guards, and progressed to the Court of Statues, where the elite liked to amuse themselves with petty gossip. He graced several courtiers with friendly smiles before inserting himself into a conversation near a platter of honey-drenched pastries.

It was there he realized all his careful plans were on the verge of falling apart. A noble with a high-pitched voice was talking about those barbaric races and how there were rumors that the emperor-to-be was contemplating reopening the royal stables. Word had come to him from his contacts who worked the river that an augur, a highly respected one, was soon arriving with a recently purchased kehok that would be Prince Dar's prize racer.

"An augur is bringing one of the desert abominations to the palace?" Usan asked, as if this were of only mild interest to him. His mind raced through all potential consequences. "How unusual."

"Indeed! The royal stables have been closed for decades," the noble said. "I do not understand what could have prompted Prince Dar to prioritize restarting the royal racing program during such a time of need."

"Perhaps that's exactly why—it's a time of need, and the people need hope," said another noble, a woman with a bit of honey smeared on her cheek that blurred her carefully applied makeup. She shoved another pastry into her mouth after her statement.

The others nodded in agreement.

"When is this 'prize kehok' due to arrive?" Usan asked. He hid his alarm under a veneer of casual charm, smiling at a server who delivered a flute of amethyst-colored liquid. He'd given up trying to identify the various fruity drinks Becarans liked to serve. All of them tasted sickly sweet to him. He sipped this one and schooled his face to hide a grimace.

"Imminently!" the first noble said, warming to the topic. "Prince Dar can't expect to solve any of Becar's problems with this distraction. Surely the people won't forget his failures merely because he chooses to participate in the races!"

"It is a clever move," the woman said around the pastry she had stuffed in her cheek in order to speak. "He'll win over the populace if his racer performs well."

The man snorted. "Foolishness."

"Popular foolishness," the woman corrected.

Potential disaster, Usan thought, downing the rest of his unpleasant drink and discarding the glass.

The woman with the pastry was correct. The mood of a nation was a fickle, variable thing. A freshly placated populace wouldn't riot as quickly or as expansively as he needed them to. It was his job to ensure that the Becarans ran out of patience with their darling emperor-to-be on a very specific schedule, so that when the time was right, the city would explode. Then, before a new emperor could be selected and crowned, King Hamra of Ranir would sweep into the city to restore peace and order. This new stunt by Prince Dar could jeopardize that dream.

He scanned the Court of Statues until his gaze landed on one of its most important members: Lady Nori. She was gracefully weaving between other nobles, gifting them with a smile or a light laugh. Young and beautiful, she was a natural jewel in a river full of artificial ones. It was no wonder Prince Dar was reputed to favor her. Everyone did.

Usan angled his path through the crowd to intersect hers, watching her without seeming to. She was truly skilled at the art of delighting everyone while favoring no one. If he were advising Prince Dar, he would tell him to secure her allegiance as quickly and permanently as possible—she would be a valuable asset to a new emperor. But since he was, by definition, on the opposite side, he was not rooting for the couple to, well, couple.

"Ah, Lady Nori, a pleasure to see you," he said. He smoothed his expression into one of gentle surprise at their encounter. It didn't much matter if she saw through that—the appearance of casual conversation was all he needed.

She inclined her lovely head. "Ambassador Usan. You look well."

"I am sunburned in places that haven't even seen the sun, and when I look in the mirror, I see a parched skeleton." He liberated a flute of mango wine from the tray of a nearby server. "I fear I will never not be thirsty again. How do you Becarans do it?"

Lady Nori laughed, a sound that reminded him of bubbles. "Didn't you know? We were all sand beetles in our past lives. The desert is in our blood."

"I half believe that." He took a sip of the treacly wine. Must these people sweeten everything? "I also half believe the rumors circulating about Prince Dar and his new kehok.

I'm not quite sure what to think of it. Playing with toys while his people suffer."

Her smile dropped. "Prince Dar thinks only of his people."

"Of course."

"It's an ingenious attempt to boost morale. He will be a spectacular emperor!"

From her reaction, it was clear that the noblewoman returned the emperor-to-be's affections, though he couldn't gauge whether either had confessed to that. *Ugh, spare me the defensive indignation of a young woman whose lover has been insulted.*

"I only meant that he should devote some attention to what is going on in his own palace, rather than focusing on activities beyond it." Leaning closer, he said in a voice barely louder than a breath, "I have heard rumors of discontent among his own guards."

Her eyes widened.

Yes, that was all he needed to do. Plant doubt. Turn the Becarans on one another.

"Warn your prince," Usan said.

She clasped his hand, her expression every bit as concerned as he'd hoped it would be. "Thank you. I will."

He hated so many things about Becar, but this was one thing he loved: its people were so easily manipulated. Raising his glass, Usan toasted the lovely, innocent, and gullible Lady Nori before he drifted back into the crowd, looking for other opportunities to serve his king.

CHAPTER 17

Tamra had visited the Heart of Becar, the glorious capital of the Becaran Empire, countless times over the years. *Still takes my breath away,* she thought as they sailed beneath an archway made of two stone figures crossing swords. Ahead was the city: white spires with gold domes, palm trees along the streets, and colorful markets near the docks. And of course the statues.

The statues of the emperor's city lined the river and dominated the city squares. Made of stone, bronze, wood, clay, and glass, they'd been carved by artisans over many generations. Many were hundreds of years old, and a few were reputed to be a thousand. They depicted every creature that had ever walked, swum, crawled, or flown in Becar—every type of vessel that a human soul could be reborn as. *Except kehoks,* Tamra thought.

Beside her, Raia was gawking at everything.

Tamra grinned at her. "Wait until you see the palace."

"The Heart of Becar is a marvel," Augur Yorbel agreed. "It is said that three hundred years ago—"

Lady Evara interrupted. "Yes, lovely. Spare us the history lesson, and tell me: Are the royal stables and training ground ready? I know Trainer Verlas will want to start immediately."

Augur Yorbel looked uncomfortable, as he usually did whenever Lady Evara issued one of her demands. So far on this trip, she'd insisted on private sleeping quarters on the riverboat, as well as ripe mangoes at every meal and buckets of fresh flowers to cover the scent of kehok. She'd also brought a glass bowl with three koi fish in it that she insisted one of her three servants carry near her at all times, because she said she found it soothing when traveling.

Rich people are strange, Tamra thought.

In this case, though, Lady Evara was correct. Tamra did want to resume training with Raia and the black lion as quickly as possible. It was mere days until the next round of races.

"I've sent messenger wights, and we will be met at the royal dock with a transport," Augur Yorbel said. "But you will understand if the facilities require more time to be restored to their former glory."

"Sadly, I am not a particularly understanding person," Lady Evara said. "If you wish the emperor-to-be's return to the Becaran Races to be triumphant, we must be supplied with all we need to make our debut on the national stage a success."

"Um, yes, well, of course." He looked rattled, and Tamra almost felt sorry for him. She wondered if he was underselling the royal training ground, or overselling it. Exactly how neglected was it? She'd been on plenty of less-than-luxurious tracks. Odd that the emperor wouldn't prepare the stables *before* recruiting a racer. She wondered if all this was some spur-of-the-moment whim, like Lady Evara's fishbowl.

He turned to Tamra and asked, "What do you need?"

"Supply of raw meat and fresh water for the kehok, a stall he can't break, and a track. And no audience until we're ready." She felt Lady Evara glaring at her for not asking for more, but that was truly all she needed. They'd be at the royal stables for only a couple weeks, just until the major and minor races started and all racers converged on the Heart of Becar. They'd be required to stay at the official race camp-site then, a few miles beyond the city. "We can sleep in the stables."

Lady Evara sniffed. "You cannot. Quiet quarters are a must for a well-rested rider, as well as private baths, funds for new racing clothes, and a chef dedicated to our needs. I will draw up a list." She flounced away from them, into the silken tent that had been erected for her at the back of the boat. Her three servants followed, one still carrying the fishbowl.

Augur Yorbel was watching her leave as if she was more alarming than a kehok, and Tamra decided she did indeed feel sorry for him. "Raia, can you check on the kehok? The new sights might be alarming him." She waited until Raia scurried across the deck to the cage before saying in a low voice, "You have no idea what you're doing, do you?"

He jumped as if startled, then looked sheepish. "It's ob-vious?"

"Frankly, yes."

"I am out of my depth. Ask me to read a soul, ask me

to *save* a soul, and I can do it! I have trained for that. But ask me to restart a racing program at the highest level on the most public stage . . . Well, I am wondering what I've gotten myself into."

She laughed, liking that he was so honest about it. "How did you get stuck with this?"

He hesitated. "I volunteered."

"That was your first mistake."

"I've made a few." He sighed mournfully, as if he were cataloguing every single mistake he'd ever made.

"You're the first augur I've ever met to admit he's ever made any," Tamra said. Certainly you'd never catch Augur Clari saying anything as vulnerable as that. She guarded her infallibility as if it were a precious jewel. "Us ordinary people are in over our heads on a daily basis. You get used to it."

"Then will you be my guide?" He sounded so innocent, with a hint of pathetic, that it was charming, and Tamra couldn't help smiling. She wondered if he'd ever spent much time out of the temple. *Poor sheltered augur,* she thought, and found herself actually believing it. "Tell me what's needed, and I will see you get it."

"Just the basics for me. And whatever will placate Lady Evara. You *don't* want her making your life miserable."

He shot a look at the silken tent.

"She's testing you right now, to see how far she can push her demands. Like a toddler. My advice? Listen to everything she says, and then do what you think is best, regardless of whatever she demands. Really, that's the only way to handle the wealthy."

He smiled, and it transformed his whole face, changing him from an unapproachable augur to a man with warmth and humor. "You're the first 'ordinary person' I've met to ever give life advice to an augur, instead of the other way around." Then, more seriously: "Thank you."

"You're welcome. I—"

From the tent, Lady Evara called, "Augur Yorbel? We have matters to discuss!"

He sighed; then his face smoothed back into a pleasant, professional demeanor. Bowing slightly to Tamra, he crossed the deck. She watched him.

As soon as he'd left, Raia returned. "That was so sweet."

Tamra frowned at her. "What?"

"He admires you."

"Don't be ridiculous," Tamra said. "He was asking for advice."

Raia was grinning. "I think it's romantic."

Tamra wavered between annoyance and amusement. She certainly hoped that Augur Yorbel wasn't having romantic thoughts about her. She had no time in her life for such foolishness, especially in race season. "I don't need romance in my life right now. I have something more important: a purpose. And so do you." She pointed at the statue of a crocodile on the side of the river. It was carved of pink stone, polished so it shone. "Concentrate on that statue. Learn its curves, its shadows. Your mind must be strong and focused if you're to win the next race. For the rest of the journey, I want you to pick objects we pass and let them fill your thoughts. See if you can ignore the wonders of the Heart."

"Fine, but you *shouldn't* ignore your own heart."

"Focus!"

"Okay, okay." Quietly, Raia said, "But love is important too." Then, with more determination, "And I won't lose again."

Tamra shook her head. "Just when I think you almost understand, you say something ridiculous. It can't be about winning or losing. It's always just about the moment. What you want in that moment can silence the failures of the past and the pressures of the future." She paused before adding, "And yes, love is of course important, but love isn't only giddy new romance. My life is full of love. Now, focus on that crocodile."

"You'll see, Trainer Verlas—this is a fresh start. The augur choosing us . . . We have a second chance!" Raia sounded so certain.

Tamra pointed firmly at the statue, and Raia finally studied the crocodile.

As she did, Tamra kept thinking about this unlikely hope. *I've had so many chances. A lifetime of them.* She'd been given a way out of her childhood with kehok races. After she'd been injured too badly to continue racing, she'd been given a way out of despair and a new future with the birth of her daughter. And now this new chance to secure a future for herself and her daughter . . . and possibly a second daughter.

I don't know that I deserve yet another chance.

She'd failed her rider last year. She'd failed her students last month. And in doing so, she'd failed both herself and Shalla. *But Raia* does *deserve this.* Tamra watched as her rider began to breathe slower and more evenly as she narrowed her focus on a single, stationary object. As they sailed past the crocodile statue, Tamra directed her toward the next target: a colossal tiger, sheathed in gold.

She continued to lead Raia through the exercise until they reached the royal docks, which were a sight in and of themselves: every post carved into the shape of a man or woman, dancers and soldiers and farmers and fishermen. "Good job," she said.

Raia beamed.

Stepping off the boat first, Augur Yorbel took the lead, presenting documentation and talking in a low voice to the dockmaster, who bowed and then welcomed them to the Heart of Becar.

Lady Evara and her entourage disembarked next, as soon as a plank was laid between the boat and the dock. They boarded waiting chariots. Following, Tamra, with Raia, helped load the kehok in his cage onto a cart. An expensive-looking red sheet was draped over the cage. *So the citizens won't have to see such a hideous creature in their beautiful city*, Tamra thought. *Or so they won't see a reminder of what could happen to them if they aren't careful with their souls.* Either way, she didn't object.

She climbed into the seat of the cart, next to Raia, who'd already hopped up beside the driver—a silent woman in a royal city guard uniform. Raia was bouncing in her seat like an overexcited puppy. As they drove toward the palace, Tamra tried to absorb some of Raia's enthusiasm. *Maybe I don't deserve this second chance, but I am going to make the most of it.*

Raia twisted around, trying to see everything, so many times that Tamra thought she was going to topple out of the cart. Certainly, there were glorious sights in every direction: a tower sheathed in gold, a statue of a heron sculpted out of glass, a mosaic detailing an ancient emperor's victory repelling an invasion . . . but Tamra noticed the people. Namely, that there were too many of them, mostly workers who should have been off at construction sites or quarries. She expected the farmers—historically, the Becaran Races began as a way to distract farmers who couldn't work while their fields were saturated during flood season—but this many workers loitering in the streets was unusual.

All these men and women out of work, purposeless and some of them penniless, had to be causing more trouble than usual. She thought she spotted some soldiers from the Becaran army patrolling with the guards. It was a good thing they'd have the races to distract them.

That was, according to legend, the reason the Becaran Races began. After the great warrior Aur split the desert and created his mighty river, the people flocked to its banks. Discovering the land was fertile, they rejoiced. But the great crocodile Ferlar, who inhabits all the rivers of the world—a description Tamra had questioned the first time she'd heard the tale and been told he was "so large he needed all the rivers"—heard their celebration and hated it. In response, he flicked his massive tail, causing the fields to flood. Despondent, the early Becarans began to squabble and then war among themselves. To cheer up his people, the warrior Aur plucked a couple kehoks out of the desert and forced them to run as fast as they could. And thus, every year when Ferlar flicks his tail and floods the farmlands, the Becaran people hold their races to distract themselves from the tragedies they can't control.

Except for the part with the enormous crocodile, Tamra thought that was a plausible explanation. For at least a thousand years, the races had been giving people something to cheer for, and Tamra had the feeling that this year Becarans needed to cheer more than ever. *Turnout is going to be massive,* she thought.

She hoped Raia wouldn't be distracted by the size of the audience. She was glad Raia had done the extra focusing exercises on the trip here—that would help. As they drove through the city, Tamra silently crafted her training schedule.

Soon, they saw the palace, and Raia gasped so loudly that Tamra laughed. Composed of several sprawling buildings, the palace was painted every color imaginable: vast murals of river scenes, beside massive thirty-foot-tall portraits of every emperor and empress who had ever ruled.

They circled around it, driving behind and beyond. Still on the palace grounds, the royal kehok stables were through three archways and beyond a high-walled garden, tucked out of sight. After a surprised-looking set of guards yanked open a black gate, they rode inside, and Tamra saw that Yorbel had not exaggerated. She climbed off the cart, wincing as her leg ached, and joined Lady Evara in surveying their new home.

As Yorbel had said, the royal kehok stables had not been maintained.

That's the polite way to put it, Tamra thought.

Lady Evara, however, had no interest in putting it politely. "I have housed rats in better accommodations than these." She had her hands on her hips, her voluminous hat was askew, and her cheeks were flushed.

"Technically, kehoks are lower than rats," Tamra said. She supposed there were some people who could even want to be reborn as rats, especially given a worse alternative.

Lady Evara fixed Tamra with a glare and then pivoted to face Augur Yorbel, who was inching backward as if he wanted to be elsewhere. "This does not begin to fit the requirements I detailed to you. I question whether the emperor-to-be is serious about this endeavor."

"He's more serious than you know," Augur Yorbel said. "If you will excuse me, I will see what can be done to rectify this situation." He bowed twice before exiting quickly, out through the black gate, toward the palace.

Lady Evara glowered at his retreating back, at the weed-choked practice track, and at the dilapidated stables. "I don't even comprehend how anything so close to the palace was allowed to fall into such a state of disrepair. This is absolutely unacceptable."

Raia, who had gone inside the stable to explore, poked her head out. "It's not so bad."

"Your rider is too cheerful," Lady Evara informed Tamra.

"She's young," Tamra said. "It'll fade."

"True." Then Lady Evara lowered her voice, so only Tamra could hear. "Tell me the truth: Can you do this? Can you shape that girl and her monster into champions? Because this is an opportunity for all of us. Yes, for me as well. You needn't look so surprised."

Tamra knew why she needed this, but Lady Evara? She hadn't questioned it when Lady Evara had insisted on coming, but now that they were here, she thought it was an odd choice. Lady Evara could have bargained for more gold from the emperor-to-be's bottomless coffers, rather than tying herself to the risk of the races. She could have stayed in the comfort of her own palace, with all her luxuries around her. "Why do you want a champion so badly?"

Lady Evara waved an arm at the palace spires that rose above them. "For fame! For glory! For personal reasons that I have no intention of sharing with you." She laughed airily, as if none of this meant anything to her and it was all a grand joke.

"Fine. Yes, we can win."

"What do you need to make it happen? Tell me, and I will secure it for you."

It was so similar to Augur Yorbel's offer that Tamra thought Lady Evara must have overheard their conversation on the boat. She wondered if the lady had thought of Tamra and Yorbel's interaction the same way Raia had, and then firmly told herself to stop it with the ridiculous thoughts. "That's a far cry from offering only two hundred gold pieces to buy a racer." She would have asked what changed, but she knew the answer. An invitation to the Heart of Becar. Proximity to the emperor-to-be. A chance at greater glory. An opportunity to escape the dreaded "boredom" that Lady Evara so feared. Tamra wondered if Lady Evara had ever cared about anything but her own pleasure and amusement. "I told you and Augur Yorbel what I need already."

"Augur Yorbel . . . bears watching."

"Excuse me?" That was not the response she expected. "Why?"

"He's lying to us."

Absurd, Tamra thought. *He's not the kind of person who can lie.* He was exactly what he seemed—a sheltered-from-the-world, out-of-his-depth augur. A good man. She trusted her judgment on that. She'd met enough bad people in her life to feel confident in her ability to recognize liars and cheats. And yet, Lady Evara was so assured in her declaration. "About what?"

"I don't know, which is what bothers me. Can I count on you to be my ally here? Our goals are aligned, after all. Vigilance is required."

This was the strangest conversation she'd ever had with Lady Evara. Her sponsor had *never* talked to Tamra as if she were someone she trusted. The fact that she was doing so now was even more bizarre than the idea that Augur

Yorbel might not be who he seemed. But Lady Evara wasn't wrong—they did have a common purpose, and as long as that was true, it couldn't hurt to work together.

"Sure. We're allies."

"Splendid!" Lady Evara beamed at her. She then began shouting at her three ever-present servants to clean up this place so that it was fit for her to see. Obeying, they dispersed, presumably to find cleaning cloths, water, and soap.

Or to find a new, less demanding employer.

Tamra joined Raia inside the stable, ducking under an array of cobwebs.

It had once been a grand stable, a few decades ago. Much of the woodwork was intact. In the dim light that filtered through the windows, Tamra could see paintings on the walls: depications of famous races with beautifully intricate sketches of kehoks and even more exquisite renderings of past emperors watching from their stands. Each stall was re-inforced with metal, now bearing rust stains. She tested one door. "Still sturdy."

"It's like a forgotten secret," Raia said happily.

It was odd, Tamra thought, that when the emperor-to-be sent an augur to restart his kehok racing program, he hadn't also ordered cleaners and carpenters to fix up the stable. "Rich people don't always think about the details it takes to do things," she said, mostly thinking out loud. "They just expect them done." Belatedly, she remembered that Raia came from wealth.

But Raia was nodding as if Tamra had said something wise. "I'm sure an emperor-to-be is the worst. Just make a pronouncement and don't think about the consequences. You want a pineapple; you get a pineapple. Never mind that they aren't in season, and it requires a dozen people to travel to where they are growing, bargain with the farmers, and then journey back."

"Exactly. I bet it was a whim he had. He probably forgot all about it as soon as he sent Augur Yorbel off to buy some kehoks." Or maybe Lady Evara was right, and something was truly off here. What if he didn't know about Augur Yorbel's plan at all? Maybe the whole idea was the augur's. It would explain why the stable wasn't ready for them, and why no one official had come to greet them beyond simple transport here. But that made no sense. Why would Augur Yorbel want them here? He didn't seem to care—or even know—anything about racers and the races.

"He might have a new whim every day," Raia said, warming to the idea. "Start a zoo. Build a university. Collect bells. Or birds. Or musical instruments."

Maybe, Tamra thought. But did any of that matter? She had a job to do. *Whatever's going on between the augur and the emperor-to-be, it's not my business.* "Let's get the kehok loaded into a stall, and let Augur Yorbel worry about emperors and their whims. Our concern is only the next race."

CHAPTER 18

Yorbel wondered if the emperor-to-be would have him executed for bringing such news. Certainly, others had met such a fate for far less throughout Becaran history. He fidgeted as he waited in the corridor for a guard to escort him in. He told himself that he had nothing to fear. Dar was reasonable and, more important, his friend. *Friends don't execute friends.*

Stay calm, he told himself. *Professional. Kind.*

He hadn't sent a messenger wight to Dar, or to anyone in the palace. The only one he'd sent was to the temple, for assistance in arranging transport for himself, the kehok, and the others to the old royal stables. In that message, he'd explained that he'd been asked to recruit kehoks to reestablish the royal stables, so that the emperor-to-be could sponsor racers in this season's Becaran Races. It was not precisely a lie.

To Dar, he'd tell the full truth, of course.

And he would pay whatever cost he must. His soul was already paying for the falsehoods and deception that it had taken to come this far. Soon, though, that would be over, once the truth was out, and he could begin to make amends.

"His Excellence will see you now," a guard informed him, and then opened the door.

Cautiously, Yorbel stepped inside, as if Dar would strike him down on sight. But Dar was at his desk signing papers. "One moment."

Yorbel stood silently. He waited, and then he wondered aloud, "Why spend the time signing? Your signature carries no weight until you are coronated."

"But once I am, there will be no delay for those who are in need." Dar signed three more papers, and then stood up and faced Yorbel. "My brother *will* be found. The high council has informed me that they have doubled the number of augurs searching. And now that you have returned from your fruitless search, you can join them."

There was a stiffness and formality to him that Yorbel had never seen. *He's afraid of what I'm here to say,* Yorbel realized. *And I'm about to make his fears come true. I'm sorry, Dar.* "Can you ask your guards to sing?"

His face crumpled.

"I'm sorry."

He sank back into the chair as if his legs failed to hold him anymore.

"Ask them to sing," Yorbel begged. "Please." His friend deserved the dignity of receiving the news in private, before the rest of the empire learned of it.

Dar shook his head. "Can't stand their harmonies." Then he mouthed: *Be careful.*

Either he didn't trust his guards anymore, or he'd overused the singing-guard trick and knew it would alert the spies that something important was being discussed. Or both.

Yorbel chose his words carefully. "I believe the people will be thrilled when they learn you are reopening the royal kehok stables and sponsoring a racer in this year's race. It is a wonderful way to connect with the people and show them you wish to be their emperor."

"Neither my brother nor my father involved themselves in the races. You don't think a break with tradition will upset people?"

If he were merely asking about the races, the answer would be no—it was Dar's father who had broken with tradition. But he wasn't asking about that. Yorbel considered how to respond. If the people found out the late emperor had been reborn as a kehok, there would be outrage, sorrow, denial, fear, all of it. Yorbel hadn't devoted much time to worrying about the ramifications beyond saving his friend's life. "Some will be upset, yes."

There would be backlash against the augurs, of course, for failing to read the emperor properly—the augurs would be blamed for not alerting people that a monster was ruling the empire. And for not saving his soul before it was too late. Also, a pall would be cast over Dar, and people would question the state of his soul.

But the truth must come out, Yorbel thought.

It would shake people's faith in augurs for a little while, but not forever. Once the truth was known, the people could begin the process of healing. The empire could move forward. Dar could be coronated, and whatever unrest Gissa worried about would end. The important thing was that the vessel had been found! The empire could weather this if it meant saving Dar's life, couldn't it?

"We must be careful how we announce the news to people," Yorbel cautioned.

Dar nodded. His face twisted, as if he wanted to cry or rage but knew he dared not do either, and Yorbel wished he could say or do anything that would help. He was acutely aware he had caused this pain by bringing this news.

"It would be best to wait until we're certain of the correct course of action," Dar said.

"Indeed." Yorbel hesitated, trying to formulate his next question. "The royal stables are in a state of disrepair. Perhaps you would like to visit them and meet the racer that I have procured on your behalf?"

"Yes!" The word came out like an explosion, and then Dar contained himself. Yorbel felt a burst of both pride and aching sympathy for this boy who was being forced to grow up so fast. "Yes, that is an excellent idea. As it happens, I am between duties now." He shot a look at the stack of unsigned papers that remained. "Please lead the way."

RAIA COAXED THE BLACK LION INTO A STALL AND bolted the door after him. It seemed sturdy enough, and Tamra had pronounced it suitable—whichever emperor had commissioned it had poured plenty of gold into its original construction.

Beneath all the cobwebs and sand, the stable was still beautiful. Lady Evara's servants were scurrying all over the grounds outside, cleaning the viewing area first, where Lady Evara might wish to sit, as well as the exterior of the stable, exposing the murals.

Guess I should make myself useful.

She darted out and helped herself to a bucket of soapy water and a sponge. Across the track, she saw Trainer Verlas with Lady Evara, greeting a contingent of guards. She hoped they'd come to help clean. Regardless, she knew Trainer Verlas would handle it.

She started with her kehok's stall door, wiping it down while staying out of reach of his claws and jaws. He paced inside. Now that they'd arrived, he seemed to be growing more and more restless. "You want to be running," Raia guessed. "Me too."

Soon, she was sure, Trainer Verlas would have them out on the track. She wouldn't want to waste much time—she wasn't the type who cared about the aesthetics of a place. Lady Evara could keep neatening and prettifying as much as she wanted, but Raia knew her trainer's patience for that would wear out quickly, which was good.

"We have to win next time," Raia said.

The lion snarled, but he didn't seem to be paying attention to her. She found a sink near one of the adjacent stalls— the fanciest sink she'd ever seen, with multiple faucets and a wide basin of black stone. She carried a bucket over to it and, after the pipes finally started spewing clean water, filled it and then lugged it back over to where the kehok could reach it.

Outside the stables, she heard a commotion, and without thinking, she ducked into the adjacent stall. As soon as she was hidden, it occurred to her that she didn't need to hide. She was *supposed* to be here. This was her racer.

Then she heard Augur Yorbel say, "Your Greatness, it would be safest to view the kehok while he is secure in his stall."

That can't be . . . She peeked between the slats and saw the doors open. Sunlight flooded inside, silhouetting about a half-dozen guards who marched together into the stable.

In between them was a taller figure, a man. But he was too shielded by guards for Raia to see his face.

She stayed hidden.

Filthy from the journey here and from scrubbing the filth from the stalls, Raia did not want the emperor-to-be of the Becar Empire to see her this way. Or at all.

Inside the adjacent stall, her kehok began to rage. Screaming, he fought his shackles and threw his body against the walls, as hard as his bindings would allow.

Steady, she thought at him. *Calm down!*

Beyond the stall, she heard Trainer Verlas boom, "Silence!"

The lion whimpered but continued to struggle quietly. Raia shifted so she could see him, drawn back into one corner. He looked as if he were in pain. She wished she dared go to him.

One of the guards asked, "What is agitating him?"

Another replied, "It's a monster. They're always like this."

"Your Greatness," Trainer Verlas said to the emperor-to-be, "it's most likely your soldiers. No doubt their swords remind him of when he was captured. It's a common reaction in kehoks."

Lady Evara hurried to say, "I promise that his rider has complete control over him on the track. Let her demonstrate! Where is that girl?"

Raia knew that was her cue to expose herself, but she hesitated. She wasn't certain she could control him when he felt so cornered, and she didn't want to fail in front of the emperor-to-be of all Becar!

In that moment of hesitation, the emperor-to-be spoke. "I will view him alone."

"Your Excellence . . ." a guard protested.

"He is secure, as you can see," Prince Dar said. "And there is no threat here. Guard the door. Outside."

Reluctantly, the guards shuffled out of the stable.

"Alone, I said."

Raia saw her trainer, the augur, and Lady Evara bow and exit.

She'd missed her chance to come out. Now it was too late. She was hiding in the presence of the emperor-to-be. There was no way this could be construed innocently. His guards would immediately think she was a threat. *I'll be arrested. Accused of being a spy or an assassin from Ranir . . .* Motionless, she watched through the slats.

The emperor-to-be approached the kehok's stall. He knelt, which put him eye level with her, and she had a clear view—which meant that if he turned his head, he'd see her too. She didn't dare move.

He was young, not much older than she was, with a thin face, as if he wasn't eating enough, and deep circles under his eyes, as if he wasn't sleeping enough. He wore intricate gold necklaces tight around his neck, and his hair was braided and pinned with diamonds and rubies. But his face looked so ordinary, framed by all that wealth. And so very sad.

"Tell me it isn't true," he whispered.

She almost flinched, but he wasn't talking to her. He hadn't even glanced her way. All his attention was focused on the black lion.

The lion was still whimpering, but he wasn't fighting anymore. He was merely looking at the emperor-to-be with his golden eyes, which Raia thought also looked sad.

"Zarin, this can't be you," Prince Dar whispered.

Suddenly, Raia felt as if there wasn't enough air to breathe. *What did he call him?* She had to have misheard.

"Please, Zarin. Do you remember me? Do you know who you were?"

No, she hadn't misheard. Zarin. The late emperor.

Even in all her running and hiding, she'd heard people gossip about how his soul's new vessel hadn't been found, about how they thought the new emperor-to-be was delaying the augurs because he didn't want to be coronated, about how they were losing gold every day because there was no new emperor yet, about how they feared an attack by Ranir when they were at their most vulnerable . . . She'd heard them blaming the emperor-to-be and saying the augurs should work faster and look harder.

It didn't make sense.

And yet it did.

This was why Augur Yorbel had come to their stable, why he had bargained so badly to buy a kehok, why the palace hadn't seemed ready for them when they arrived.

"You were *good*," Prince Dar said. "You were good to me. How could this—You didn't deserve this. Did you? How could you have hidden such darkness from me? How did I not know? I knew you!"

His voice was barely louder than a breath. He sounded as if he were breaking in two. She knew how it felt to be betrayed by the people who were supposed to love you, to discover they weren't who you thought they were. She remembered the day she'd been ejected from the temple and how she'd felt when her parents had raged at her failures. This had to hurt even worse. She at least had caught hints of who her parents were before that moment.

It sounded as if he'd had no idea.

"It could be a mistake," he said. "Yorbel could have read you wrong. You can't be him."

Raia wasn't skilled enough to read a kehok's aura. She didn't know what the augur had seen, but surely he wouldn't go through all this if he wasn't certain. It was too important for mistakes.

Prince Dar seemed to agree with her unspoken thought. "Of course, Yorbel is never wrong. But how could this have happened? How could the augurs who read you when you were alive not have seen—" He cut himself off as his voice broke.

He curled a fist and bit into the side. She knew the look on his face—he was trying desperately to hold himself together so the men and women outside wouldn't guess at his emotions. She wished she dared to comfort him. Just one word . . .

But she said nothing.

At last, Prince Dar pushed off his knees to stand. He smoothed the silk beneath his golden necklaces. He stilled his face. Only a second later, the stable door opened. "Your Excellence?" a guard asked. "Is all well?"

"This kehok will make a fine racer," the emperor-to-be said, in an entirely different voice. He sounded pleased, even jovial, and Raia felt as if she were hearing herself, the voice she'd used when she told the other trainees at the temple that of course she was fine, everything was fine, when everything was falling apart.

She stayed hidden as he left the stable and the door closed behind him.

She didn't move for a long time.

CHAPTER 19

Raia kept cleaning, because it was better than feeling as if she were choking on the terrible knowledge she now had. Her arms were shaking as she scrubbed, and she felt as if she were chattering from the cold, except the air was syrupy and hot inside the stable. Sweat pooled under her arms, at the nape of her neck, beneath her hair, but her mind was consumed by only one thought:

Do I stay silent, or do I tell?

She knew it was a dangerous secret. If people knew the late emperor had been reborn as a kehok . . .

No, not just a kehok. My kehok.

Again, Raia felt the old urge to run, as far away and as fast as she could. But where could she go? This was a lot bigger than just running from her parents.

Once people knew the truth, they would immediately look for who to blame. The augurs, of course. And anyone who had been close to the kehok.

This was the kind of secret that cost lives.

But it was also the kind of secret that felt too heavy to carry alone. She couldn't do it. It shouldn't even be her burden!

She heard the stable door open and jumped, ready to duck out of sight once more, but it was just Trainer Verlas, followed by Lady Evara and Augur Yorbel. Lady Evara was gushing. "He seemed so pleased! Didn't he seem pleased? Rider girl, there you are! Where have you been? The emperor-to-be ordered the immediate rejuvenation of the stables and training track. He'll be adding other racers, riders, and trainers to his stable if this all works out, so you'd best stop cleaning and focus on your training. We have to make sure that we are the jewel of his fleet, so to speak."

Raia felt as if her throat were glued shut.

"Smile, girl! This is what success smells like!" Lady Evara spun through the stable, her hands out as if she were spraying invisible sparkles in all directions. "Well, maybe not quite as dusty . . . but we're on the big stage now, and we are going to make the most of it! Tamra, my dear—"

Trainer Verlas cut her off. "Immediate training. Got it."

Raia put down the sponge and washed her shaking hands in the sink.

She almost managed a smile for Trainer Verlas. "I'm ready."

Trainer Verlas narrowed her eyes. "You don't look ready. Do you feel well?"

"Yes, I—"

Augur Yorbel staggered backward. "By the River, you were here! You were here, the entire time. What did you hear? What do you know?"

Just like that, the decision was ripped from her.

Raia wished she could hide again. Or vanish into a hole.

She should have run. But where? How? She was miles and miles from anyplace she knew, with only the clothes on her back. And there was no way they were going to let her out of here now.

Always the lioness ready to defend her cubs, Trainer Verlas inserted herself between Augur Yorbel and Raia. Her hands were jammed on her hips. "What is my rider supposed to know?"

Lady Evara checked outside the door and then shut it firmly. "I told you all wasn't what it seemed. Never doubt my instincts." She'd instantly snapped from effervescent to all business, which made Raia wonder how much of her flighty aristocrat manner was just an act. Her eyes were narrowed, and her gaze flitted back and forth, as if she were checking every corner of the stable. But this wasn't the time to wonder about her.

Augur Yorbel looked as if he wanted to faint, and it occurred to Raia that he was just as surprised and upset about all of this as she was. If the augurs had known the late emperor was reborn as a kehok, he would have been found a lot sooner, Raia realized. Instead, it was only one augur who had come searching for her lion. It was Augur Yorbel's secret too.

"It's all a lie, isn't it?" Raia said. "About wanting us to race?"

"A necessary lie," Augur Yorbel said. "My soul will pay the cost of it."

"Yeah, that's nice for your soul," Trainer Verlas said. "Explanation, please. We came here to race, and we need to race. You can't change the terms—"

Lady Evara laid a hand on Trainer Verlas's arm. "Hush.

Let the man speak." To Augur Yorbel, she said, "You brought us here under false pretenses. Pray tell me why so I can react with the appropriate level of outrage. Or panic."

Augur Yorbel didn't speak. His eyes kept flickering between them and the kehok, and he looked so lost and trapped that Raia spoke instead.

"The kehok is, or was, the late emperor Zarin," Raia said. It was amazing that such a terrible secret took only a sentence to say. She hadn't known that a few words could turn the world upside down, but these words . . . they changed everything.

There was a heavy, terrible silence, pregnant with everything not yet said. Raia thought it felt like the desert before a thunderstorm. She thought about the conversation she'd overheard, if there was anything else they needed to know, but that one kernel of truth was all that mattered.

"Is this true?" Lady Evara asked.

"Yes," Augur Yorbel said.

YES.

With that word, Tamra felt as if the sun had been extinguished. She tasted bile in the back of her throat and wanted to vomit.

The late emperor, a kehok? *Our kehok?*

It was inconceivable.

Such a thing should never have happened. The emperor . . . he was supposed to be beyond reproach, nearly a deity. More holy than any augur. Akin to the stars. To think he could have a soul as tarnished as the worst depraved soul . . .

"This can't be," she whispered.

"Well, this is far worse than anything I could have

imagined," Lady Evara said in a clipped voice. She was clutching her hands together, the only indication that she was surprised by this news, though she had to be.

Augur Yorbel nodded unhappily. "It was a last resort, searching for his soul among the kehoks. There was no indication that he would be reborn as anything lesser, much less . . . this. In fact, every prediction was certain he'd be back as a tamarin, or higher. I had hoped my search would fail." He turned to study the black lion, who was crouched in a corner of his stall. "I think, in a way, it has."

All of them looked at the lion.

He doesn't look like anything special, Tamra thought. Standard kehok: a beast that could never exist in nature. She remembered the seller in the market had said it was his first turn as a kehok. That he'd been recently reborn. Certainly, he was the most intelligent kehok she'd ever trained, but that didn't mean . . .

"This can't be possible," she insisted again.

"Move past that," Lady Evara said impatiently. "I must know what happens next."

"If it were any other vessel, there would be a public announcement," the augur said. "Celebrations. A verification ceremony, and then a coronation. The vessel would live the remainder of its life in luxury in the palace."

"If you reveal the vessel is a kehok, there will be riots," Lady Evara said. "Or even civil war, as the high houses of Becar question the suitability of anyone in the family line of the late emperor Zarin." She said this clinically, as if discussing an interesting bit of trivia.

Augur Yorbel looked horrified, as if those options hadn't occurred to him. Tamra hadn't begun to think about how other people would react, but Lady Evara was right. It would be chaos. *Even deadly chaos,* Tamra thought. Already the mood of the country was on edge. This could be the thing that pushed it over. There would be violence for certain.

"You could have just bought the kehok," Tamra said. "You put all our lives in danger by bringing us here." She knew they'd insisted on coming, but they hadn't known all the information—he had. And he should have refused to accept their terms. She shouldn't be involved in this mess. And Raia . . . Tamra looked at the girl, who was on the verge of tears. She didn't deserve to face whatever storm this would unleash.

"A true point," Lady Evara said. "Glad you've caught up to the conversation. Augur Yorbel, you have endangered us all. We are tainted by association with this terrible secret."

"No one will blame you for not realizing what no one could have suspected," Augur Yorbel said. "I will do everything in my power to see you are not—"

Lady Evara cut him off. "You won't have the power to help us once this secret comes out. The blame will fall heaviest on the augurs. Especially the augur who discovered this horror. You will be in no position to defend us because you will be consumed with defending yourself. So here is what we will do: You will find a new rider and trainer, for however long His Greatness-to-Be intends to continue this charade. You will compensate us for the inconvenience of the journey here. And we will return home, disavow all knowledge of your motives, and lie low until the chaos passes."

That was the most sensible option.

Except there was Shalla, currently training at the temple, to consider.

"How bad will it be for the augurs?"

"Did you not hear me say 'riots'?" Lady Evara snapped.

"The people will feel the augurs failed them. They will feel betrayed. And frightened. Think about it: thousands of people base their life choices on augur readings. They rely on augurs for guidance and depend on them to steer them in the right direction. But if an augur can misread such an important personage as the emperor himself, who is to say which readings are correct and which are flawed? They will fear for their own future lives. And they will seek to punish any augur they can for creating that fear.

"I think the seriousness of this cannot be underestimated," Lady Evara continued. "Do you agree, Augur Yorbel? You must have some inkling of the truth of my words, else you would not have brought us here under the cloak of all those soul-corrupting lies you told."

Augur Yorbel hung his head. "The emperor-to-be must decide how to tell the truth."

"He can't tell the truth if it's going to cause riots!" Tamra shouted. "Just pretend you never found the vessel. We'll pretend we don't know. Treat him like any kehok and run our races. Then, no chaos, no fear, no betrayal, no riots." *And Raia and Shalla will both be safe.*

"An emperor *must* be crowned," Augur Yorbel said. "The truth must come out. It is out of our hands. Ultimately, it will be Dar who decides what to do."

Tamra noticed he called the emperor-to-be by his first name.

Lady Evara clearly noticed as well. "He'll listen to you. Advise him to keep this a secret. At the very least, that will buy us time to put some distance between us and this mess."

That was a sound plan. Perhaps if she reached home before the news broke, she could grab Shalla and run. If there was enough chaos, the augurs would have no ability to chase her. She and Shalla could escape, invent new names, and start a new life. Raia could, of course, come with them. They'd be a family of three, somewhere far, far away.

"Yes, keep it a secret, at least until we're gone," Tamra said. "Let me get home to my daughter. She needs me. And Raia—she's suffered enough."

She noticed that Raia was staring at her. Or not at her, but at her tattoo. Surprisingly, she looked more thoughtful than scared now, any sign of tears gone. *Does she understand how serious this is?* Tamra wondered. *Of course she must.* All of Becar was going to go up in flames once word got out.

Augur Yorbel buried his face in his hands. "There is no good answer. People will suffer, and I cannot prevent it. Keep the secret, and the emperor-to-be cannot be crowned . . . and chaos. Expose it, and shake the faith of thousands."

"And chaos," Tamra echoed.

Lady Evara checked outside the door again, then said, "Very much not our problem. Unless you make it ours. *That* much is within your power. Let us go into hiding before the river floods, so to speak, and you will at least save three innocent souls."

Four, counting Shalla, Tamra thought.

Out of the corner of her eye, she saw Raia had crossed the stable and opened the door to the black lion's stall, to view the chained beast within. She wondered what the girl was thinking. It had to be upsetting to know the creature she had been riding, been controlling, was once an emperor. She hoped Raia understood that none of this was her fault. Neither of them could have guessed whose soul this kehok contained.

Staring into the kehok's stall, Raia spoke. "Or you could save him."

"Sorry?" Lady Evara said. "Tamra, tell your rider not to talk nonsense."

"He could win and be reborn." Raia turned and pointed at Tamra's tattoo of the victory charm, the one that enabled the winning kehok to be reborn as human.

There was a breath of silence as Raia's words floated in the air.

Sweet River, Tamra thought. *She's right.*

If Raia and the black lion were the grand champions, then the augurs would use the victory charm—he'd be killed and then reborn as human, a perfectly respectable vessel for a late emperor. He could be found easily as a newborn human baby, then, and all riots and chaos would be averted.

Lady Evara's eyes widened. "It's an incredible risk. He could lose. Or the secret could come out before the final race. My plan is far more practical."

Tamra touched her tattoo. It would solve . . . well, everything. If the kehok were reborn as a human and then found, Prince Dar could be crowned. The augurs would be blameless. Shalla would be safe.

Everyone would have everything they wanted.

"You know, when I said I wanted a grand champion, that was to motivate you!" Lady Evara said. "Before this news, if you'd failed, it would merely impact my treasury. But the situation has changed. The risk is too great. Win with a first-time racer and rider?"

Crossing to stand beside Raia, Tamra looked at the black lion. He snarled, biting at the shackles that bound him. He was every bit as strong as she'd thought when she first purchased him, and Raia had proved she had the determination, if she could harness it for the races. The first qualifier had shown there was definitely the potential. . . .

"Can you convince the emperor-to-be to keep this secret until the end of the races?"

"I believe I can," Augur Yorbel said. "Can you truly win?"

Tamra looked at Raia. All would depend on her. That was a heavy weight to put on her shoulders. *But she won't be carrying it alone.* "Yes. We can."

CHAPTER 20

It was late when Yorbel at last reached the sanctuary of his room in the augur temple. He shed his outer robe, hung his pendant on a hook, and then flopped onto his cot.

"Ow."

The cot was too stiff to fall onto like that. But he kept lying there anyway, because he never wanted to move again. He felt like a rug that had been washed and beaten, yet was still very, very dirty.

It was not that the day had been physically exhausting— *I'd rather have scaled a mountain or crossed the desert,* he thought, *if I didn't think either would kill me*—but it had been draining in every other way possible. Mentally, emotionally, and—most important—spiritually.

After the kehok's rider had learned the truth and they'd all agreed to withhold it, Yorbel had spent a full hour being coached by Lady Evara, a morally questionable socialite, on how to be morally questionable. She'd grilled him not only on what he'd say if anyone asked him about the kehok, but

also how he'd say it. Apparently the "how" was as important as the "what" when one lied, and he had to pay special
attention to eliminating any twitch that would betray his
guilt.

It had been an unsettling hour, to say the least.

Afterward, he felt as if his insides were coated in filth
that he didn't think would ever clean off. Plus, he and his
clothes smelled faintly of kehok and stable.

As soon as he had enough energy, he was going to drag
himself to the baths and soak in water that smelled like nothing but sandalwood and lavender, and then he was going to
sleep uninterrupted until the dawn bell and not venture outside the temple for days. He just wanted—

A knock sounded on his door.

"By the River," he muttered.

Peeling himself up off the cot, he lurched over to the
door and opened it. He intended to tell whoever it was that
he was indisposed, and unless the temple was burning down
around his ears—

It was Gissa.

She was holding a plant and smiling at him. "I heard you
were home."

"Gissa!" He'd thought there was no one he wanted
to see. *I was wrong.* Seeing her was better than a soak in
sandalwood-scented water. Looking at her, knowing that if
everything went as planned, he was going to spare her from
her terrible task, helped more than he would have thought
possible.

"May I come in?"

"Of course!" He backed away from the door so she
could enter. She set the plant on his table and checked the
leaves. "You fixed it."

"Water it once a week. *Just* once a week." She sat on the edge of his cot and then wrinkled her nose. "You may want to consider watering yourself more often."

"I've been traveling."

"With at least one fragrant companion, or so I've heard."

He sank down onto the cot next to her. He wanted so badly to tell her what he'd found—she should know that she would not have to kill Dar and sully her soul. She could remain pure and still serve the temple and Becar. But he'd made promises.

She had to suffer only until the end of the race season, and then all would be well. *Provided everything goes according to plan,* he thought. They were placing a lot of hope in the hands of a young girl. Of course, the rider wasn't alone—she had her trainer. He'd seen the core strength in Tamra Verlas, and he trusted that.

"Hello, Yorbel? You look as if you're listening to bells playing miles away."

"Sorry. I am overtired. Yes, you heard correctly—I purchased a kehok to start the emperor-to-be's racing program."

"Why, by the sands, would you do such a thing? You didn't mention the emperor-to-be setting you on this task when I talked to you before you left."

Ahh, that was true. "It was my own initiative," he admitted. Also true. "I thought it would be a pleasant distraction for the emperor-to-be. He has been consumed by worries that he's powerless to alleviate."

"So you bought him a pet monster? Why not a puppy? Or a kitten?"

"The people seem to enjoy the races," Yorbel said. "I thought it would give Dar a connection to the people. Frankly, I only wanted to help."

Gissa laughed. "You are . . . you are who we all should be. *Good*."

He almost winced. Good people did not deceive their closest friends, especially when the truth could lift a worry from her shoulders. But he thought of Dar and instead said, "Tell me what I've missed here. How fares everyone in the temple? How are you? Have you enjoyed being home?"

"Oh, no, you aren't changing the subject so easily! You're the one who went out and had adventures. Tell me about this kehok you found. I admit I have never seen one up close."

"Most are repugnant—slime, tentacles, jaws, a melding of animals that shouldn't be associated with one another. In contrast, the beast I purchased for Dar is oddly beautiful, like a statue of a lion made of metal. But because of that, it is even more disturbing, as you look at it and know it shouldn't exist in the world." It was horrifying that the late emperor had become a creature that felt so *wrong* when you looked at it. That should never have been his fate. He should have been reborn as a being that was part of the natural order and granted peace in his next life for the good he'd done as emperor. His glory should have been remembered in murals and statues and pillars proclaiming his achievements.

Gissa patted his arm. "You must be relieved to be home and done with that." She stood as if preparing to leave. "You look exhausted, and I'm afraid I've burdened you further with my curiosity." She didn't cross to the door, though.

"Talking with you is never a burden." He meant that. Simply being with a friend already made him feel lighter. "It's only that this was a difficult day. I am not suited to the tasks I have assumed, though I suppose one could argue I have only myself to blame."

She laughed again. It was nice to hear her laugh, so free

and uncomplicated by all he knew and wished he didn't know. "At least you didn't try to read the kehok. Imagine how you'd feel if you sank your mind into that filth. Dirt can be washed off." Peering at him, she frowned. She sat down again, closer to him, and placed her hands over his. "Oh, no, you *did* read the monster. Yorbel, you shouldn't have. What did you see? Unburden it to me. Perhaps that will restore some measure of lightness to your own soul."

"I saw so much darkness."

"And?"

He wanted to tell her all and spill the filth from his own heart. She was right—if he could unburden himself of even a bit of it, he would lighten his load. But that would be unfair to Gissa to ask her to carry his secrets and guilt and pain, especially since she'd have to keep it from the other high augurs. He couldn't ask that of her. Once this was over and she was free, then she could know all. Instead, he spoke the lie he'd practice with Lady Evara, and felt himself shrivel inside. "This kehok has been through many lives as a monster. His humanity was a distant shadow. He must have lived and died as a man many decades ago. I could not see clearly what horrors he committed that doomed him to his fate, and for that I am grateful. All I know is the pain he caused eats at his soul even now, driving him forward."

"An ancient monster is its own particular kind of horror."

"He felt and caused much torment," Yorbel agreed.

"You must regret looking so deep into the well of depravity," Gissa said. "Can I assume you will not go plunging your soul into any more kehoks? If the emperor-to-be acquired one such beast, he'll want more. You won't be reading all their souls too, will you?"

Yorbel was able to answer this vehemently and honestly. "Absolutely not! I have done all the kehok reading I ever intend to do in my lifetime. There is nothing that could persuade me to stare into that brand of oblivion again." He didn't intend to even go near the stables until this was all over. His part in this was done.

Gissa smiled. "Good. I'm glad I don't have to worry about you, then. Stay safe within these walls, Yorbel. You are exactly the sort of augur Becar needs in difficult times."

Her sweet vote of confidence felt like an arrow striking his heart. Rising, he walked her to the door and thanked her again for saving his plant and taking on his responsibilities while he was absent. "I believe it will be a long while before I travel again, even outside of this room."

"I'm very happy to hear that." Rising up on her tiptoes, she lightly kissed his cheek. "We all missed you and are happy you're home."

He closed the door behind her and leaned forward, pressing his forehead against the smooth wood. *If we win the races, then Gissa's soul will be safe.*

And if we don't win . . . If they started to lose, if the plan began to unravel, if the secret leaked, if anything at all went wrong . . . *then I will tell her—and all the high augurs—the truth.*

IT'S A LOT OF PRESSURE TO PUT ON A KID, TAMRA thought.

Arms crossed, she watched from beside the track as Raia guided the black lion through the turns. The lion built speed on the straightaway. He had so much strength and power in his muscles that he seemed to be reaching out and yanking the earth beneath him, then throwing it behind him. But as he neared the turn, he slowed, only slightly. Any other observer might have missed it, but not Tamra.

She knew it was fear—Raia's fear, about all this—that was slowing him. "Dig into the turns!" Tamra called. "Embrace them!" The turns could be an asset if you approached them the right away. The lion needed to throw himself into them as if they were a pole they could swing around, but he couldn't, or wouldn't, do it if his rider held him back. "Use them to power you forward! You *want* the turns! Turns are your friend!"

Leaning forward, Raia and the kehok raced toward the next turn. This time, they didn't slow—and the lion lost his grip. His hindquarters whipped out, and Raia screamed as she and the lion skidded sideways and slammed into the wall of the track.

Beside Tamra, Lady Evara gasped.

"She's fine," Tamra said, and vaulted over the track wall. She landed in the sands and winced. *Shouldn't have done that,* she thought. She half strode and half limped across the track to where Raia was checking over the lion for any injuries.

"He's not fragile," Tamra snapped. "And neither are you."

"What am I doing wrong?" Raia asked.

"You see the turn, and you hold back—you see it as another obstacle to victory, instead of seeing it as a tool you can use. A lot of kehoks lose speed on the turns. If you can *gain* speed, you'll leave them choking on your sand."

"But if we don't slow—"

"He has to dig in *harder* on the turns. Plant his paws and push off. Think of a swimmer reaching the end of a pool— how does she switch directions?"

Raia's eyes widened as she understood. "She bends her knees, twists, and pushes."

"Exactly what you need to do." Placing her hands on Raia's shoulders, she turned her to face the track. Across the sands, Lady Evara was cooling herself with a gilded paper fan. "See the turns as walls you can use. *Want* the turns, because they're where you can gain the advantage."

Raia smiled. "Got it."

She mounted her racer again and guided him back onto the track. Tamra backed up to the wall and ducked through the gate rather than trying to hop over it. "Do it again! Now!"

Raia and the kehok shot forward.

Yes! Tamra thought as they approached the curve. The kehok wasn't slowing. He was running low to the ground, keeping his body steady while his legs pumped—

And then a clatter behind her echoed across the track.

The lion faltered. His head snapped toward the source of the noise, as Raia too glanced across the sands. Reaching the turn, they took it at a mere quarter of the speed as before.

Tamra spun around, glaring, to see who had broken her rider's concentration. Two men had entered through the black gate and were greeting Lady Evara in the stands. "By the River . . ." She recognized them. Everyone who knew anything about the Becaran Races knew them. "No, no, absolutely not." *I do not have time for this bullshit.*

The younger man, who was unmistakably Gette of Carteka, the winner of last year's Becaran Races, was bowing to Lady Evara, lifting her hand, and kissing the back of it—the same Gette who had beaten Raia in her first qualifier. Beside him was his trainer, Artlar. They'd caused the commotion, leading a slew of their servants into the stable grounds, whom Artlar proceeded to order to unload crates and trunks from a gilded cart. Artlar was a seasoned trainer: a decade older than Tamra with a claim to training multiple grand champions over the years. He'd never ridden in the races himself, but he was still famous across all of Becar. He was tall, well-muscled, with a thick beard that covered a web of scars from his early training days—it had been many years since Artlar had suffered any injury from a kehok.

Tamra marched toward them. She tried to erase the memories that spilled into her mind: the final championship race, as her rider lay dead in the sands, the blood of other riders and racers pooling around him, as this rider ran his racer through them. Its hooves had pummeled the soft bodies. Blood had splashed with each strike of its hooves, and the rider had not slowed. He had slammed through the finish and then exalted in his win.

She hadn't wanted pity, either during or after the race. But what he'd done was worse.

He had run through their bodies. He hadn't known they were already dead. If they hadn't been, he would have been reviled and fined, just as Tamra had been, but since they were, he received not even a slap on the wrist as he was awarded his prize. Later, when asked—she'd heard the reports of his boasting—he said the weak deserved to fall.

She wanted to wipe that smarmy smile off his face.

She gained control of herself by the time she reached the stands. As the Lady with the Sword as her witness, she wasn't going to smile at these bastards, but she *was* going to resist the urge to spit in their faces. "You've interrupted our practice." It came out like a snarl.

"Your rider has some trouble taking that racer through the turns," Artlar said, with a nod toward Raia. His voice was friendly, even jolly, and loud without trying to be loud, as if he'd never learned how to lower his voice so it didn't boom. "Not to worry. Gette will have him at top speed."

"Raia is his rider," Tamra snapped. "I shouldn't need to tell you how important it is that she is the only one who rides him, especially this close to the next race. The tighter their bond, the stronger the control."

"Which is why we have no time to waste." Artlar smacked Tamra's shoulder as if they were buddies. *He is not my buddy,* Tamra thought. He then turned to his protege. "Gette, fetch your gear! I want you to take that monstrosity for a spin before his muscles cool off and tighten. Let's see what we're working with here."

With her hands on her hips, Tamra blocked Gette. "You aren't working with our kehok."

Artlar glanced at Lady Evara. "Deeply sorry you weren't informed, but yes, we are. Special request from the emperor-to-be. He wants the finest to train his fastest."

Tamra shot a look at Lady Evara. She had a fixed smile plastered on her lips. *She's furious,* Tamra thought. And that made her think that Artlar was telling the truth.

Aur's balls. This can't be happening. We've worked for this! We earned this! If the black lion were to race, then Raia should be his rider. Out on the track, Raia was working on the turn, pretending their practice hadn't been interrupted. She was performing the maneuver beautifully, with no idea that it was pointless.

This was going to crush her.

Glaring at Artlar, Tamra felt her hands curl into fists, and Lady Evara gave a slight shake of her head as if to say, *Don't.* This wasn't a battle she could win with words or fists. Not if the emperor-to-be had invited them here.

It made a terrible kind of sense. Prince Dar wanted his

brother's vessel to win. Who better than the men who had won last year? Traditionally, the winning rider would be gifted with a life of luxury and, if he didn't wish to retire, first pick of any kehok he wanted for next year's Becaran Races. But a summons from the emperor-to-be . . . Who'd say no to that?

And neither of us can stop them, Tamra thought.

She stood, feeling helpless and hating feeling that way, as Gette pushed past her with a smug smile on his lips. His trainer, Artlar, proceeded to oversee the unpacking of their equipment. She watched them open a black wardrobe filled with leather armorlike uniforms. Gette pulled a tunic over his head and strapped on calf guards. Then one of their servants began unloading a variety of whips ranging from leather straps to whips with spiked balls at the end. She didn't doubt Gette intended to use them on the kehok, unaware he'd be whipping the late emperor.

"The emperor-to-be won't approve of that style of training," Tamra warned him. But would Prince Dar ever know? He was in his palace and would want to keep his distance to avoid raising any suspicion. She felt a terrible helpless anger curling in her stomach—it was cousin to the way she'd felt during that final race last season.

"The emperor-to-be wants results," Artlar said. Then he winked at her. "Just watch as we deliver them." He then vaulted over the track wall without wincing and strode across the sands, toward where Raia and the kehok were practicing. He had a weighted club belted to his waist.

Lady Evara leaned closer to Tamra and said in a soft voice, "Will it damage my soul if I hope the kehok eviscerates them?"

Tamra said just as softly, "If it does damage one's soul, then you and I will be reborn as the same type of beast."

A ghost of a smile flitted over Lady Evara's face. "There must be a way we can protest this. Changing a racer's rider this close to a race is madness. I am here as a race consultant. The emperor-to-be should listen to me."

Tamra felt a flare of hope. Lady Evara was persuasive. If she could talk to Prince Dar, then maybe he'd change his mind and restore their racer. "You think you can get an audience?" It would need to happen quickly. Every minute Artlar and Gette were here was a minute less of training that Raia—

"Truthfully? No. I have yet to convince even the head servant to grant us rooms in the palace. Apparently, my position in Peron does not translate as well as I'd hoped in the Heart of Becar, and the court at large is unaware we are in the emperor-to-be's favor. I am an outsider here."

"Maybe Augur Yorbel . . ."

"If he ever returns."

She was right. Augur Yorbel had given no indication that he'd return. He'd acted as if once he persuaded the emperor-to-be to keep the secret that his task was done. His last goodbye had felt final, which disappointed Tamra rather more than it should have.

"Though," Lady Evara added, "perhaps I *could* send a messenger wight to his temple, saying we require Augur Yorbel's advice. If we could convince him to see reason, then he could arrange a meeting with Prince Dar. It's worth a try, at least." She squeezed out of the viewing seats and hurried toward the gate.

Across the track, Tamra saw Raia step in front of the kehok, blocking him from Artlar. "Uh-oh." This was *not* the time for Raia to learn to be brave, not if these men were telling the truth. You did *not* go against the emperor-to-be's express wishes. As much as Tamra wanted to kick these men off the training grounds, she was well aware that she didn't have the power here.

Hurrying across the sands, Tamra saw Raia was shaking. Behind her, the lion was growling—his metal mane was spiked vertically around his snarled face. *Calm,* she projected at the kehok.

"Raia, this is Trainer Artlar," Tamra said as she reached them. "His rider, Gette, won the Becaran Races last year, and the emperor-to-be apparently requested they—"

Artlar cut her off with a broad, fake smile. "You've been very brave, little girl. I saw you place third in your very first race—that's excellent! You should feel proud of yourself. I'm sure you have a bright future in racing ahead of you."

Raia glanced from him to Tamra and back. "Um, thank you?" She glanced across the track at Gette, who was pulling on heavy red leather gloves. "He didn't mention he was the grand champion."

"He's a modest boy," Artlar said.

"I hadn't noticed that," Raia murmured. "Why is he on our training track?"

"Because the emperor-to-be has commanded it, and it's not for you to question. If you'll step aside, we'll take it from here." He moved closer to the kehok, his shadow falling across the lion so that only the lion's golden eyes were visible in the patch of darkness.

"He's unsettled," Raia warned him. She was shifting from foot to foot, as agitated as the kehok. "You should step back. He doesn't like to be cornered."

"Helpful information." Artlar lunged past her, so fast

and large that the kehok was pinned against the wall, and slammed the weighted club into the side of the lion's face. "The key is to *keep* him unsettled. Off-balance, so that you are always the one in control."

"Stop! You're scaring him!" Raia yelped.

"Trainer Verlas, haven't you taught your rider yet that these monsters are *not* like other creatures? You can't expect them to have the same emotions. You certainly can't pity them. That's when accidents happen, when you believe you have a bond with a creature. Such thinking can lead to tragedies."

Tamra knew he was talking about last year's tragedy, but she refused to be baited. Last year had been a miscalculation. She'd let herself become blinded by her thirst to win. "A kehok who fears his rider races against him, not with him."

"Foolishness, born of softness."

"If you knew me," Tamra said, "you'd know there's nothing soft about me." There had to be a way to stop this. If this kehok ran the races, then Raia had to be the one to ride him, because both Raia and Tamra needed the prize money to secure their futures. Without this opportunity, everything they'd accomplished up to this point was just so much sand.

He snorted. "I know all I need to know about you. And right now I know you're delaying our work. Gette, this kehok is ready for you!" Again, he slammed the club into the side of the kehok's face.

The lion fixed his eyes on Raia.

Tamra saw that Raia's eyes were wet. *No crying in front of assholes.* She grabbed Raia's hand and pulled her back with her toward the stands. Lady Evara had vanished, hopefully to send a wight to the temple. "Believing you have control when a kehok is afraid is narrow thinking," Tamra lectured.

"The fastest speeds don't come from fear. They come from need." She didn't know whether she was talking to Artlar, Raia, or herself. Plenty of riders used fear as their primary motivator.

In her day, though, she'd beaten every one of them.

But it's not my day anymore.

She should have expected this to happen, once they'd learned what, or who, this kehok was. Of course the emperor-to-be wouldn't want to take any risks with a damaged trainer and an untested rider. This kehok *had* to win for Emperor Zarin to be reborn. Could she blame him?

"I can't believe you're allowing this," Raia said. "That 'champion' has no right. He's messing with *my* racer!"

"I'll find a way to—" She stopped. "Wait, repeat that."

"He's with my racer?"

Ordinary kehoks didn't form any kind of attachment. But this was no ordinary kehok, a fact she was positive the emperor-to-be had not shared with Artlar and Gette. And Raia had spent the past several weeks bonding with the black lion in a way that shouldn't have been possible. Maybe the lion wouldn't be so easy for them to control.

Maybe Gette would fail.

"Raia, listen to me carefully," Tamra said, speaking softly so her voice wouldn't carry across the sands. "We can't interfere with them—Prince Dar himself invited them here. You have to resist the urge to control the lion in any way. But you *can* remind him he's yours."

"He knows—"

"Look at him and say, 'You're my racer, and I'm your rider.'"

Pivoting, Raia didn't hesitate. "You're my racer, and I'm your rider!"

The lion let out a roar, and then subsided with a whimper when Gette struck him in the flank with a spiked club. "Trainer Verlas, control your student!" Artlar called.

Tamra flashed a fake smile at Artlar and Gette. "Apologies! Excitable youth. I promise we'll be an audience from now on." She plopped herself into Lady Evara's fancy cushioned chair and propped her feet up on the track wall.

"What now?" Raia whispered.

"Sit with me and watch. Do nothing else." Tamra patted the chair next to her. She was sweating more than she should be, but it was important to look confident and unconcerned in front of Artlar and Gette. Small victories were still victories.

Reluctantly, Raia sank into the chair.

"Do you want to take bets on how long they'll last?" She kept her voice light, as if she were certain they'd fail and didn't have a worry in the world.

"You . . . don't think they can do it?" Raia asked.

"He's your racer. Not theirs." *Please, Lady, let me be right.* If this kehok was truly different than the others, more intelligent, more . . . She hesitated in thinking the word "loyal." No matter his lineage, he was still a kehok.

"But he's a kehok," Raia said, as if echoing her thoughts. "He's special, yes, but he doesn't remember who he—"

Tamra cut her off before she said anything she shouldn't. "He remembers we promised him his freedom. That's what he races for. Freedom. He won't race out of fear. Not your kehok." *I hope,* she thought.

Raia blinked at her, and then slowly, tentatively, she began to smile.

Despite all their bluster about being ready, it took Gette and Artlar the better part of an hour before they had the track set up with all their tools and other supplies: several different saddles, an array of whips and weapons, hurdles and hoops for the kehok to jump over and through as it learned obedience. As they prepared, the trainer and rider each took turns coming over to the kehok at seemingly random intervals to terrorize him—hurting him while he was chained to the wall to prove their dominance.

It was difficult not to interfere. But if this was to play out the way she hoped it would, then she had to let them fail entirely on their own. She took calming breaths to try to keep herself lounging in the chair, rather than leaping onto the sands.

"Trainer Verlas, I can't stand this." Raia shot to her feet. "Not with a rider like Gette."

Tamra put her hand on Raia's wrist. "You *must* stand this," she hissed. "You might win this battle, but you'd lose the war."

She heard a gate open and glanced back to see Lady Evara had returned, with Augur Yorbel. He looked decidedly unhappy to be here. Nudging Raia, Tamra vacated the chairs. She didn't say a word as they swept past her, but Lady Evara's gaze lingered on her, questioning.

Tamra nodded. *This will work,* she thought. *I've never been wrong about a kehok.*

Her thoughts flashed back to last year's final race, and she firmly pushed the memory away. She was *rarely* wrong about a kehok.

Adjusting her massive hat—a tower of flowers—Lady Evara took her seat, graciously offering the seat next to her to Augur Yorbel. Tamra couldn't hear what they were saying to each other. She leaned against the track wall with Raia beside her. Across the sands, she saw Artlar had noticed the arrivals.

"The Great Artlar has an audience now," Tamra said softly. "He'll begin."

She was right.

Only a few minutes after Lady Evara and Augur Yorbel arrived, Artlar unchained the kehok from the wall, while Gette whipped him in the face with one of the spiked whips.

The kehok yelped.

Tamra saw Augur Yorbel start up out of the chair, but Lady Evara held him back, no doubt telling him that the new trainer and rider had been requested by the emperor-to-be.

Lady Evara caught Tamra's eyes as Augur Yorbel settled back down, and Lady Evara winked at her. It was as clear as if she'd spoken: *Let the bastards hang themselves.*

Tamra wasn't certain when she and Lady Evara became partners in all this, and she wasn't sure how she felt about that, but it was nice to have her on her side. Tamra certainly wouldn't want to be her enemy.

On the sands, the trainer and rider had affixed a saddle onto the kehok. Tamra recognized the type: it had spikes beneath it, so that with every shift of the rider's weight, the kehok would receive a jolt of pain, to encourage him to obey the rider's slightest movement. It was a vicious saddle. She'd never let any of her students use one.

It wasn't because she was soft—it was because tools can fail. Fear can backfire. The one thing that wouldn't fail you was a belief in yourself, a solid determination that tied you to the moment.

Gette mounted the lion.

Tamra held her breath. This was it.

Stepping back, the trainer barked an order. Gette wielded a short whip with spikes all along the barrel. He swung it in a circle, building up speed, as he guided the kehok toward the starting line.

The lion turned his head, looking directly at Raia.

"What do I do?" Raia whispered.

Artlar had noticed the kehok's behavior. He jabbed a finger toward Tamra and Raia, and shouted, "No interference!"

"Understood!" Tamra called back. "This is all you!" To Raia, she advised, "Say nothing. Do nothing. Keep calm." She hoped she was making the right decision here. She was certain this would work. Mostly certain.

Ninety percent certain.

Eighty-five . . .

And I thought I wasn't a gambler.

Beside her, Raia was squeezing the edge of the track wall so hard that Tamra thought she'd break it. "They're hurting him! I can't do nothing!"

"Then try trusting your kehok."

Raia gawked at her. "You always say never trust a kehok."

"I know I say that. And it's true, if you're trusting them to be something they're not. But you should trust your kehok to be what he is." She thought of how he'd run off the track the first time he and Raia had raced together. "Remember what you said to him when we first met? You said, 'The only way you'll win races is if I'm your rider.'"

Raia nodded.

"Trust him to remember too."

On the track, Artlar shouted, "Go!"

The lion took off fast, as fast as he'd ever run for Raia. Shouting, Gette whipped him, and the lion ran harder, faster, barreling toward the turn without slowing.

In that instant, Tamra doubted everything she'd believed and said. She'd been wrong. He was going to run for them. He wasn't—

And then the kehok veered sharply left, to the wall where Gette and Artlar had set up the array of weapons. He smashed full speed into the stand, and weapons flew off the wall, clattering to the ground and flying up to hit his rider.

Gette flew backward off the lion, crashing hard onto his back on the racetrack.

"Stop!" Artlar commanded.

But the lion didn't pay any attention to Artlar's order or to the downed rider. Instead, he pivoted and ran straight at the trainer. Artlar readied his club, and the kehok leaped toward him and then sailed over his head toward the stable.

The lion ran through the door, disappearing inside.

Groaning, Gette got to his feet. He was bleeding from his forehead.

He finally had his first scar.

Lady Evara was laughing.

"Raia, do you think you could show these gentlemen how it's done?" Tamra asked calmly. She felt like melting into a puddle of relief, but she didn't allow that to show.

"Yes, Trainer Verlas." She sprinted to the stables.

A moment later, the lion padded out of the stable. Raia had removed the saddle, as well as every single one of his chains and shackles, and was riding him bareback toward the track with no restraints and no weapons. Tamra nearly yelped—she'd just meant for Raia to ride him. Removing every chain was taking a large risk.

On the other hand, she was making a *very* clear statement.

Raia rode the lion in a slow, stately circle around the

track, demonstrating her control. The lion's eyes and her eyes were fixed on Artlar and Gette, who stood frozen in the spot where Gette had fallen.

Very politely and very softly, Raia said to Gette, "Such a shame to see a boy as pretty as you damaged. Someone should have told you you're not going to win. You're just not thirsty enough."

As Raia rode the kehok back into the stable, Tamra thought she'd burst with pride. "Augur Yorbel, could you please inform the emperor-to-be that his prize racer will only run for one rider?"

"I will tell him," Augur Yorbel said with a sigh.

"Thank you," Tamra said, and then she smiled at both Artlar and Gette, a wolflike smile that stretched her scar.

This kehok may be a nightmare, but he's our *nightmare.*

CHAPTER 21

"All right, move it out!"

As Trainer Verlas barked at the various servants and guards, Raia scurried to check that everything was secure inside the cage: the kehok's shackles were clamped to the iron bars, they had a supply of food loaded into the cart, her riding clothes were packed into a trunk. At last, she climbed into the cage with her kehok.

This is it, Raia thought.

Her last chance to qualify for the major races.

If they'd stayed in Peron, they'd have traveled to whatever race was nearest—qualifying races were held on tracks up and down the Aur River. But since they were already in the Heart of Becar, she'd be racing her second (and last) qualifier on the same track that would be used for the finals, only a few miles from the palace, beyond the edge of the city.

On the journey to the royal stables, the black lion had been hidden beneath a shroud of red velvet, but now he traveled exposed, laden with chains within an iron cage. Riding with him, Raia felt as uncomfortable as he was. She was wearing a royal uniform, at the insistence of Lady Evara, and she hated it. The gold embellishment around the collar pricked at her neck, and the red leather felt stiff. She wished she could wear her old practice clothes. She also wished they could travel under the velvet. She felt as if she was in a parade.

She sort of was.

All the streets on the way out of the city were lined with people, cheering, heckling, and just plain gawking at the emperor-to-be's entry in the Becaran Races.

"Everyone seems to have an opinion on whether or not we should win," Raia said to the lion. "Of course, Trainer Verlas would say all that matters is our opinion on that." She tried a tentative smile and wave at the crowd, and was rewarded with raucous cheers and ribbons tossed into the air.

Riding in her chariot alongside the cage, Lady Evara called, "Isn't this fantastic? You're famous!" She blew kisses at the crowd and then urged the horses pulling her chariot to trot faster.

It all made Raia feel sick to her stomach. She'd heard that the emperor-to-be himself would be at the race, even though it was only a qualifier. Given that, attendance was expected to exceed that of all prior years—or so Lady Evara had gleefully reported. Raia had already been invited to a slew of parties in the houses of the wealthy.

Thankfully, Trainer Verlas had declined on her behalf, saying she had to focus. *I think if I attended a party, I'd vomit on the host's shoes.*

She wished they'd just arrive already.

It got worse the closer they drew to the racetrack.

Just beyond the city, the racetrack was marked with a line of flags. Raia tried to focus on them instead of the thickening crowd. She tried to steady her breathing. She felt as jumpy as a frog startled by every ripple in the water. She didn't know how she was going to shut out all the eyes that would be on her—especially knowing that Prince Dar would be one of the ones watching.

She felt even worse when she saw the crowd by the archway that marked the entrance to the racing grounds. Clustered so densely that she couldn't even see the sand, they were cheering for all the racers arriving.

"Splendid," Lady Evara said. "A proper welcome. You don't look pleased."

"I just want to race."

Raising her voice, Lady Evara called to the crowd, "Hear that? She just wants to race! What do you think of that?"

Everyone cheered.

Lady Evara beamed at her. "Beautifully done."

Trainer Verlas called from the front of the cart. "Let her be, Lady Evara. Not everyone loves a circus. Raia, you're not their performing monkey. You can play along or ignore them. Your choice."

Trying to block out the crowd, Raia endured the rest of the journey out to the riders' camp, a quarter mile from the racetrack. Spectators weren't allowed in the camp, but that didn't make the atmosphere any calmer—riders, trainers, and track officials swarmed everywhere.

Climbing out of the cart, she looked around. The camp here was much fancier than at the track near Peron: a tent for each rider and trainer, with water pumped from the river for bathing, and an enormous, magnificent stable for the kehoks, with a view of the palace. Trainer Verlas had said they'd be here only for the day, but once the qualification races finished up and all the riders and racers converged on the capital, they would move back to this camp for the remaining races—the main races were scheduled in such quick succession that it wouldn't make sense to travel back and forth to the royal stables. *Guess I'd better get used to it*, Raia thought.

She didn't think that was going to happen anytime soon. *How did I end up here?*

She thought of Celin and her parents, and told herself this was better than the alternative. No question there. She wondered where her parents had gone after she'd left them at the training grounds and hoped they hadn't blamed Silar, Jalimo, and Algana.

She snapped out of these thoughts when Trainer Verlas started barking instructions at her. Raia changed into her riding gear surrounded by dozens of other riders doing the same. "You're slated for heat six," Trainer Verlas told her. "Heat three is currently on the track. Keep the kehok's chains on."

As soon as she was dressed, she led the kehok to the holding area. Gripping his chains, she tried to focus on keeping him calm. Around her, other riders and their trainers were coaxing their monsters into position behind the stands.

A kehok built like a bear lunged at another that looked like a giant river crab. The crab snapped its claws at the bear's neck, and their riders and trainers jumped forward, shouting at the racers and hitting them with spiked clubs until they retreated. Beside her, the lion growled, a low rumble that Raia felt travel through the chains and into her arms.

Look at me, she ordered him. *Just at me.*

The lion swung his head toward her, and she stared into his golden eyes.

From the spectator stands, Raia heard screams. She

blocked them out, keeping her focus just on her kehok. She stroked his metal cheek. They had to win this race. So much was depending on it, and she'd yet to prove they could win any race.

Behind her, she heard someone say, "Oh, sweet Lady, is he dead?"

"By the River, I knew he wasn't—" Trainer Verlas gripped the lion's chains. "Keep your kehok steady. And don't look."

Raia didn't mean to look, but the rider next to her screamed as his kehok reared onto its hind legs and clawed at the air. The rider dangled from the chain for a half second, until his trainer and two others leaped onto its waist and pulled the beast down by force of muscle and will.

Beyond them, Raia saw the body being carried on a stretcher. The boy's head was turned to the side, and she caught a glimpse of his empty eyes as the race officials passed by the holding area. Below his chin was a mangled mass of red that her brain couldn't interpret.

"I told you not to look," Trainer Verlas snapped.

"Did I know him?"

"Fetran. You raced your first qualifier against him." Trainer Verlas scowled at the black lion, though he hadn't moved beyond watching the procession of officials. "He used to be my student. Could've told them he wasn't ready for this. In fact, I did."

Raia wasn't sure she was ready for this anymore either. A boy had died! Just a few minutes ago, on the track she was about to race on.

"Stop it," Trainer Verlas said. "You aren't like him. Don't let it get in your head."

A voice boomed across the holding area. "Riders up!"

Raia tried to steady her breathing once more as she led

the lion across the camp and to the racetrack. Beside her, he growled, resisting each step, and she was having trouble focusing with all the shouts and cheers around her. Somehow, she made it, and loaded him into the stall at the start of the race.

"You're faster than any of them," Trainer Verlas told her. "All you have to do is run."

And win, Raia thought. Glancing up at the stands, she saw the royal booth. Unmistakable, it was raised on pillars and draped in flags. Prince Dar was already there, on a black throne, flanked by nobles and guards. She couldn't see his face from here, which made it worse. He looked more like a statue than a person. She wondered if he'd seen the death in the previous race. He must have. She imagined what he'd say if it had been her with her throat torn—

"Raia? *Raia*." Trainer Verlas clasped her arm. "You can do this. Just run."

But Trainer Verlas was wrong. She couldn't do this. She'd been fooling herself. How could she race with the emperor-to-be watching, knowing if she failed . . . She'd just seen how badly a rider could fail.

She wanted to ask Trainer Verlas how she had kept racing knowing what could happen. But there was no time—the trainers were all backing away, beyond the psychic shield so there would be no interference with the racers, and the cheers were growing so loud that Raia felt as if they were clogging her skull. Distantly, she heard the race announcer call, "Ready!"

She wasn't! She needed a few more seconds to pull her focus into—

"Prepare!"

I can't do this. It's too much! She felt as if her skin were going to burst and all her fear would pour out of her like smoke, leaving her a shell of nothingness. Beneath her, the lion was growling, shifting his weight as if he wanted to batter the walls.

"Race!"

The stall gates were flung open, and her kehok surged forward with the others.

"*Run!*" she urged.

She tried to focus on the sand, but this time it felt off. She was too aware of the other racers, of the cheering in the stands. She couldn't shed the feel of the emperor-to-be's eyes on her back, judging her as she headed for the first turn.

She felt the lion pull back as they hit the turn, like they used to do. As they rounded the turn, several of the other kehoks jostled in front of them, and Raia and the lion slipped back in the pack.

We are faster than this, she thought.

As they ran toward the second turn, Raia felt something shift inside her. She suddenly stopped thinking about the crowd, the emperor-to-be, and why she had to win. She breathed in the scent of the track, the sweat, the stink of the kehoks. She felt the wind in her face, throwing sand in her face. It stung her eyes. She tasted it on her tongue.

"Own the turn," she whispered.

Leaning forward, she urged him faster. His paws dug deeper and harder into the sand, and he ran lower. As they approached the turn, she felt herself straining for it, wanting it.

And she felt exactly what Trainer Verlas had been trying to tell her—they claimed the curve for their own, pushing off it like a swimmer in a pool and gaining speed. They shoved past the kehoks ahead of them until there was only one in front: a monster with a hawk's head and a beetle's body.

Raia fixed her eyes beyond the other kehok, focusing instead on the finish line.

Only the race. Only the moment. Only the finish line.

They ran, pulling ahead of the hawk-beetle, by one stride, then two. The cheers were like the wind in her ears. They flowed around her. All she felt was the rhythm of the lion's stride. She raised her gaze up above the finish line, and she saw them: her parents, wedged between the other spectators. For the barest instant, her focus faltered.

The lion's paws strained toward the finish line—and then, with an inhuman burst of speed, the hawk-beetle shot past her.

Raia and the lion crossed second.

Slowing, she felt as if the world were crashing down around her. She felt the sweat on her skin. Heard the cries of the crowd like a hammer. Leaning forward, she lay against the cold, smooth metal of the lion's mane.

We lost.

SECOND.

Tamra breathed in, tasted the mix of sweat and kehok stench, and tried to wrap her mind around the standings that were posted on the flags raised above the tracks. *We lost.*

We can't come back from this. Not if we want to be grand champion. After this, Raia and the lion would be placed in the minors, with no chance at running for the charm.

Lady Evara fluttered her fan. "What does this mean? How could this happen?"

"It happens," Tamra said, keeping her voice steady. She

could *not* let Raia see how bad this was. It would shake her confidence, and then . . . There was no "and then." This was it.

"Is it over? Is that it?" Lady Evara asked. "We lost, and that's it? There should be a rematch! Or what if she wins another race? Can she run in another qualifying race? We can bribe someone to erase her first race results, say that this was her first . . ."

Maybe I was wrong, Tamra thought. *Maybe we don't have what it takes.* Maybe she should have let Gette race the black lion, fled back to Peron, and . . . She didn't know what. There wasn't a backup plan.

She twisted to look up at the royal box, but Prince Dar was too far away for her to see his face. She had no doubt that he'd schooled it into an empty expression—as royal-born, he'd know how to hide his emotions.

She wondered if Augur Yorbel had watched the race and what he was feeling.

"She ran well," Tamra said. A slow start, but she'd compensated for it, taking the turns exactly as they'd practiced. She'd had enough speed in the final leg, but then that other kehok, the one shaped like a beetle with a hawk's head . . . It had spurted forward as if burned. She didn't think the creature had had that much left in reserve. Certainly its rider hadn't looked like the kind who held back enough for a last push—he'd stormed full-speed out of his gate. She frowned, her face a mask of concentration as she replayed the race in her mind.

"It shouldn't have happened that way."

The more she thought about it, the more convinced she was. That kind of rider with that kind of technique . . . he shouldn't have had the strength for such a final burst of speed.

She noticed a commotion near the finish line. Judges were on the sands, arguing with one another. The crowd near them was beginning to push and shove.

"Ooh, a scandal!" Lady Evara said, delight in her voice.

A second later, Tamra realized what she meant: a new flag was being raised and the old results flag was being lowered. Raia and the lion were first.

"The hawk-beetle kehok cheated," Tamra guessed. She'd been right—the rider hadn't given his racer the extra push. The extra push must have come from his trainer, who, Tamra saw, was down on the sands, near the finish line, arguing with the judges.

He must have found a way to position himself within the psychic shield. Tamra felt as if she could breathe again. Her knees felt wobbly as she plopped down onto a bench.

"That was so exciting!" Lady Evara said.

"One word for it," Tamra agreed. *Lucky* was a better word.

Standing, she looked for her rider. Raia had already disappeared into the stable. Tamra wasn't sure she'd seen the change in results.

"I feel breathless," Lady Evara said. "What happens next?"

"We go back to the royal stable, and prepare for the next race." The first major race. If they could win enough major races, then they'd race in the final championship race. If . . . If . . . If . . .

This was too close. We can't let it get this close again.

They'd had one lucky break. She was certain the River wouldn't grant them another.

It hadn't granted that foolish child Fetran another.

Lady Evara was eyeing her with a piercing look, and

Tamra was reminded yet again that she was much more calculating than she acted. "Do you have ideas for ensuring the next race is less exciting? We have yet to have a solid win. It would be lovely to feel confident about our chances as we head into the majors. There are still a lot of races between us and the final championship race, and I don't think my nerves can take this much excitement."

Tamra wasn't concerned about Lady Evara's nerves, though—she was worried about what today's race was going to do for Raia's confidence. The longer she went thinking she'd lost, the more damage would be done. "I'll work with her."

"We need strategies, dear Tamra," Lady Evara said. Her tone was light as always, but her expression was dead serious. "There are trainers, as we've seen today, who would do *anything* to win."

Narrowing her eyes, she studied Lady Evara, hoping she wasn't saying what Tamra thought she was saying, and especially hoping she wasn't saying it here in the midst of the stands, where anyone could overhear. "Those who attempt to cheat at the races are disqualified."

"Only if they're caught." Then, a second later, Lady Evara tilted back her head and let loose as cascading laugh, as if to say of course she was only joking.

Tamra knew she should laugh along, but the best she could manage was a glare. "Don't," she warned. "We will win this, fair and square."

"Very well," Lady Evara agreed. "But remember: all of Becar needs you to succeed."

"Believe me, I know." Tamra pushed her way through the crowd, ignoring all the other trainers and people congratulating her, and tried to get Lady Evara's words out of her head. That kind of pressure could break a rider—or a trainer.

RAIA DIDN'T CRUMBLE UNTIL SHE WAS SAFELY ALONE, back in the royal stable, away from all the eyes and words. If one more person said congratulations and talked about how lucky she was that the cheater had been caught . . .

I wasn't lucky. I lost.

Her concentration had been poor at the start of the race and had slipped at the end. She'd deserved to lose. It was only because her racer was as fast as he was that they'd come in second.

Sliding down onto the floor, her back against the wall, Raia sat outside the lion's stall. She listened to him chew his food and wondered what he thought about the race. She didn't know how much he understood about why they had to win. He knew that winning meant freedom, she was certain of that.

She heard the stable door creak open and was certain it was Trainer Verlas, returning for another pep talk—she'd been the one to break the good news to Raia, followed by a dissection of Raia's performance and a reminder that she needed to focus on the race, not be distracted by all the pressure, et cetera. Raia knew Trainer Verlas was right, and she knew she should stand and look ready to face the next challenge, but it was hard to summon up the energy. "Just resting a minute," Raia said. "It's been a long day."

"Indeed it has."

Raia knew that voice. She scrambled to her feet. Nearly falling over, she bowed. "Your Excellence! I'm sorry. I didn't expect you to come here!"

The emperor-to-be winced. He was dressed in a royal guard's uniform, instead of silks with gold necklaces. "You aren't supposed to recognize me. I'm here incognito."

"Oh!" She bowed again. "I'm so sorry! Forgive me, Your . . ." She trailed off. She'd had plenty of etiquette training, between her parents' insistence on proper manners and the augur's emphasis on control at all times. *None of it covered this, though!*

He was frowning at his uniform. "This should have worked. It fooled everyone I passed, and some of those people have known me since I was teething. Most people don't even know what I look like—they see the silks and stop there."

"It was your voice," Raia said.

"Have we met?" he asked.

"Um . . ." She wasn't sure if it was better to explain that she recognized his voice because she'd eavesdropped on him. "You sound royal?"

He sighed. "It's all the lessons. My tutors were firm about proper diction."

"They'd be proud," Raia said. "You pronounce things perfectly." She felt her cheeks heat. *Why did I say that?* It was an inane thing to say. *Complimenting his pronunciation?* "I, um, assume you're here to see . . . him." She almost said "your brother" but stopped herself in time. She began to scoot sideways, like a scuttling crab, toward the door.

"You are Raia, his rider, aren't you? I came to talk with you."

That's terrifying, she thought. She wished she could say no and flee, leaving him to Trainer Verlas. She had no idea what to say to royalty! Lowering her head, she said, "I'm honored, Your Excellence." It came out okay, which was a relief.

"Augur Yorbel has told me you are aware of the situation."

"Yes." She wasn't sure if she should say more. "I'm sorry."

"Me too." He sighed heavily.

Peeking up, she saw he'd drifted to the side of the stall and was looking at the black lion. The lion didn't stop eating. "I will work harder and win the next race," Raia said.

"I came to tell you I thought you ran brilliantly," Prince Dar said. "After seeing you race, I believe you can do this."

She narrowed her eyes. "Did Trainer Verlas tell you to cheer me up?"

He looked startled. "It was my own idea to come."

"Sorry." Of course her trainer couldn't order an emperor, or even an emperor-to-be, to do anything. She felt like slinking inside one of the stalls and hiding until he left, except there was no way to do that when he was staring right at her. And he was staring, as if he were studying every aspect of her soul. She wanted to squirm but held herself still.

"You remind me of me," he said suddenly.

She thought that was unlikely.

"Both of us are in over our heads."

That could be true, she thought. She'd never thought she'd have anything in common with an emperor. In fact, she hadn't thought much about royalty before at all.

"I was never supposed to be emperor," he said. "I was the spare. Zarin was supposed to rule for decades. He would have married in a few years, had heirs, and one of them would be stuck with being emperor or empress."

She thought about saying sorry again, but he didn't seem to need a response. He was staring at the kehok.

"I don't understand how this could have happened. He

shouldn't have died. And he shouldn't have been reborn as . . . this. He was a good man. A great brother. All I want to do is set things right, and if you can win the races . . . It won't fix everything. But it will help." He was talking openly about the secret, but then he must have felt secure that they were alone in the stable.

Raia dared move a little closer, to see into the stall beside him. "What was he like?" She tried to imagine her lion as a human. She thought he'd be determined. And strong. And angry.

"He protected me," he said simply. "The court is a piranha tank, and he let me stay out of it. Whenever people tried to draw me into their political machinations—dropping hints that they hoped I'd pass to him, feigning friendship in hopes of creating an alliance—he'd find a reason to send me elsewhere, a task that needed doing, a site that he needed me to visit. Every time he could, he made time for me. He used to love stargazing—you wouldn't think that of an emperor, but he'd memorized all the constellations by the time he was ten, and he liked to climb up onto the dome above his bedroom and look at the stars. I never had any interest in them, but I'd climb up there with him, and he'd spend hours trying to teach me which star was which. I used to pretend I was incapable of remembering any of them, just to mess with him. Just so he'd spend more time with me, pointing out the stars. Does that sound like the kind of man who deserved to be punished like this?"

She knew from her augur lessons that the universe was never wrong. But she wasn't going to say that to him. "We'll win, and he'll have a second chance. The charm will set things right."

A thought occurred to her.

"I . . . only had a few years of augur training, so there's probably a very good reason why this couldn't be possible, but . . ." Raia licked her lips, unsure if she should say her thought out loud. She'd already started though, and the emperor-to-be was staring at her. "If there's a charm that can make a kehok be reborn as a human . . . is there any chance there could also be a charm that could make a human be reborn as a kehok? I mean, a human who didn't deserve it?"

Prince Dar stared at her. "I don't know. I never considered . . . But it *does* stand to reason. Yes, I suppose it could be possible. . . ." A smile lit his face. "I think I want to kiss you."

Startled, she took a step back.

"Oh! No, I didn't mean . . . Don't be alarmed. My heart belongs to another."

Raia felt herself blush. She hadn't really thought . . . Well, she had thought for a moment, but of course it was absurd. He was a prince, and she was only a rider.

Only a rider. The thought nearly made her smile. For the first time, she hadn't thought of herself as a failed augur, a disappointment to her parents, or a runaway.

"I need to talk to Augur Yorbel. Yes, he'd know if that was possible." He didn't try to kiss her, but he did wrap her in a hug. He smelled of sandalwood and lavender. She hadn't been hugged often and never by an emperor-to-be. It was . . . nice. Releasing her, he beamed at her, and the joy in his face was like dawn after a cold, dark night. "You've saved me today, and you will save my brother in the races."

He then sprinted out of the stable.

Raia stood without moving. The hint of sandalwood and lavender still hung in the air. She breathed it in, and felt better than she had in days.

DAR CLIMBED ONTO THE GOLD DOME ABOVE HIS bedroom—a thing he hadn't done since Zarin had died. He remembered which tiles were loose and where to lie with the best view of Zarin's favorite constellations: the Jackal, the Wheel, and the Lady with the Sword.

"Lady, tell me: Am I clinging to false hope?"

In the hour since he had sneaked down to the stable, he hadn't been able to stop thinking about the words of the kehok rider. A charm to turn a human to a kehok. He'd never heard of such a thing, and he'd studied plenty of old legends. But if it was possible . . .

He heard a clattering from below him and didn't move.

Puffing, Yorbel hauled himself onto the roof. He hiked up his robes with one hand, and he climbed painstakingly slowly with the other.

"It's not *that* steep," Dar said.

"Apparently I'm *that* old," Yorbel said.

Dar snorted.

"May I ask why you requested my presence here, Your Excellence?" Yorbel sounded a touch exasperated, which was amusing since the augur was normally unflappably calm. He lowered himself to sit beside Dar.

"Spies can't hear us. Plus, great view." Leaning back, Dar pointed at a trio of stars. "Look, the ears and nose of the Jackal. Always rises in flood season."

"Very nice."

"You're in a foul mood tonight, Yorbel."

"And you're in a surprisingly good mood. Your racer nearly lost."

True. "But she didn't." He'd seen the way she'd pulled herself out of a slow start. He'd also seen the hiccup near the end, but the fact that she could overcome a bad beginning spoke well. A lot of riders would have folded after that. And the way she attacked those turns!

"Spared by a technicality."

"You watched the race?" He'd thought that Yorbel had washed his hands of the whole business after he reported on the poor performance of the supposedly top-notch trainer and rider that Dar had called in. He'd delivered that news with the air of a man who had had enough, and Dar had been content to let him return to his cocoon of a temple.

"From a distance."

"You should have joined us. Lady Nori would have been happy to see you." He'd been lucky enough to have her with him in the stands, even if he hadn't been able to explain to her why he'd cared about winning so badly.

Yorbel was silent for a moment. "I hadn't planned to watch it at all. But I couldn't stop thinking about her. *It.* The race, I mean. Sneaked out of the temple like I was a recalcitrant schoolboy."

Dar laughed at that image. It felt good to laugh. He hadn't done enough of that lately. He wondered who the "her" was. *The rider?* That was the "her" he couldn't get out of his head. She'd given him hope, in a way no one else had. He thought hope had died with his brother. "Yorbel . . . the victory charm used on the winning kehok. How was it created?"

"Only the high augurs are privy to that secret," Yorbel said, "if it hasn't been lost to history. The victory charm was made many centuries ago."

"And there is only the one? Because it was such a difficult process?"

"Very arduous. The sacrifices to the souls of the augurs who created it . . . As students, we used to speculate on it, and we were always told that the truth of it defied imagining."

"Do you know of any other charms that we ever made? To influence how a soul is reborn?" Even though he knew the dome was safe, Dar kept his voice low.

"You are talking sacrilege, Dar," Yorbel said, equally quietly. "The fate of a soul is sacred. To interfere . . . Hush, and never speak of this again."

"I don't wish to do it," Dar said. "I want to know if it could have been done. If it has been done. To Zarin."

"Impossible."

"Why? The victory charm exists."

"As I told you, the cost—"

"Emperors have enemies," Dar said. "Becar itself has enemies. Some who might be willing to pay any price to see the empire fall, to see my family fail." He thought of Ranir to the south, who had been nipping at their borders for centuries, and of Khemia to the west, who had had their own political unrest recently. Any of their neighbors would be happy to consume the Becaran Empire, if it were to weaken. Plus there were closer-to-home enemies, rival houses who would sacrifice much to see their own lineage on the throne. He could conceive of at least a half-dozen suspects without even trying, and there were undoubtedly more enemies he was unaware of. It was, frankly, exhausting.

"No augur would consent to make such a charm," Yorbel said. "It wouldn't matter what someone was willing to pay. We know the value of our souls."

"But it *could* be done," Dar said. "The knowledge exists."

"I don't know if it does or doesn't."

"But it might," he pressed.

Yorbel looked as if he'd tasted a poisonous leaf. "It might. I could make inquiries, discreetly, of course. There is one member of the council who is like a sister to me, High Augur Gissa. I have known her for many years and would trust her with my life."

"Would you trust her with mine?" Dar asked.

He expected Yorbel to say yes, of course. But the augur was silent, which told Dar all he needed to know. Whoever this Gissa was, her loyalty didn't extend beyond the temple, perhaps not even beyond her friends.

"If anyone were to know that I, or anyone close to me, was interested in a charm like this, they might suspect the truth about Zarin's vessel," Dar said. "And if the truth comes out . . . No. Winning the victory charm is still the best plan. It's enough for me to know that it's possible for such a charm to exist, for Zarin to still have been the man I thought he was." That was a very comforting thought.

"Then yes—I believe it is possible," Yorbel said in his always-reassuring voice; then he hesitated. "But if it is and you are correct . . . then it means your brother had a very powerful enemy."

Which means that I do too, Dar thought.

And that was a much less comforting thought.

AFTER RECEIVING A SUMMONS FROM THE PALACE, LADY Evara chose her hat with care: not the hat with the triple-masted ship, not the hat with the live hibiscus growing from the rim, not the hat with a cradle for her bowl of koi fish, but yes to the hat with the diamond the size of her fist.

She used to think of such hats as fashion, but now she saw them as her disguise.

A hat like this said: I have wealth. I am one of you. I belong.

And it was a lie.

She'd spent the last of her gold ensuring no one suspected she was a fraud.

She'd hit on the plan of owning a grand champion kehok when she first discovered her inheritance was . . . inaccessible. Her parents, before their deaths, had written a quaint little clause into their will. In order to inherit their wealth, their daughter had to be "worthy." In other words, an augur had to read her soul and determine her soul was unblemished by human faults.

Even after death, they wanted to make sure she felt their disapproval.

She'd spent the first six months trying to make herself good enough, but the standard they'd set was impossibly high. Her soul was, like most, blemished. Her parents' had been too, of course, but that didn't matter for the legality of the will. So Lady Evara was stuck, unable to access the fortune that should have been hers and unwilling to tell anyone *why* she couldn't access that fortune without suffering censure and ostracization.

Ever since their deaths, she'd been pretending she was good enough to live in her home, to wear her silk clothes, to call herself "Lady Evara." Meanwhile, her funds had been dwindling.

Along came Trainer Tamra Verlas, and Lady Evara had been certain she had a winner, a way to wealth that didn't rely on her parents' whims and an augur's judgment. When that went up in flames, Lady Evara was able to look both eccentric and generous by spending a minimal amount to support her—all the while hoping Tamra would become desperate enough to do something mad and crazy and wonderful, like train a needy rider and a barely controlled kehok, which was exactly what had happened.

She had to admit she hadn't predicted the latest development.

But it was all to the good, at least if she could keep it from falling to pieces. If she could be seen as aiding Tamra and the rider girl, and if this emperor-to-be was in fact legitimized, the reward could be more than she'd dreamed. As a bonus, she'd also be helping a single mother and an unloved runaway, which was a delicious rebuttal to her late parents' belief that she wasn't a worthy person.

It was a positive sign that she'd been summoned to speak with Prince Dar. She hoped the diamond hat would project the right image—that he needed her more than she needed him, which was abundantly not true. She had spent the last of her gold on the three servants who had traveled to the Heart of Becar with her. Once they'd reached the capital, she'd quietly and discreetly let them go after only a day, with promises of good references to ensure their silence on her financial situation—because, even though they didn't know the exact cause of her ruin, they did know she couldn't have kept them on. So far, no one had noticed. But that wouldn't last forever.

Checking the mirror one final time, Lady Evara allowed herself to be led into the palace. Only years of practice enabled her to avoid gawking at the wonders inside:

A waterfall that cascaded down a fifty-foot copper wall.

Pillars intricately carved to look as if they were lace.

Statues so lifelike they were indistinguishable from the courtiers who milled among them. And courtiers who were themselves works of art, their faces painted to resemble animals and their clothes merely a display case for elaborate jewel-encrusted necklaces, bracelets, and anklets. She felt positively drab beside them, and Lady Evara *never* felt drab.

By the time she reached the emperor-to-be's sitting room, she wished she had chosen to wear all her hats at once. *That* would have made an impression, though perhaps not the one she wanted to make.

Do not let them intimidate you, she told herself firmly. *You have value.*

She didn't believe that, of course, not when evidence said otherwise. But it helped to think it.

The guards announced her, and she swept inside. "Your Excellence—" she began.

Lounging on his throne, the emperor-to-be held up one hand. He addressed a ragtag collection of musicians who looked as though they'd been scooped up off the street. A few were drummers, with homemade-looking drums made from spare pots, and the rest were carrying various horns. "I'm looking for musicians who can rally the people in celebration. Give me your most rousing music!"

As the musicians launched into the worst cacophony she'd ever heard, the emperor-to-be beamed wider and wider. He gestured for Lady Evara to join him.

She longed to jam her fingers in her ear, but she settled for wincing every time one of the horn musicians squeaked a note that should have been impossible for the human ear to hear. The emperor-to-be beckoned her closer.

"What do you think of the music?" he shouted.

"It's very . . . enthusiastic," she shouted back.

He beckoned her closer, and she climbed up onto the dais so she was standing in front of the emperor-to-be. She immediately knelt so she couldn't tower over him—it was the obvious response to such an awkward situation.

He leaned closer. She expected him to comment again on the music, but instead he said, "I have an enemy, and I believe it may be someone in the palace, specifically an aristocrat or diplomat with access to a deep treasury, which unfortunately does not narrow the list of suspects as much as I would like. I need someone with no current alliances to anyone in the Heart of Becar to lure my enemy into revealing him- or herself, and I believe you are the perfect person for that job."

She blinked at him, but she had not survived as long as she had, fooling the rest of the aristocracy into believing she still belonged with them, without learning how to react quickly. "I am your loyal subject."

"Excellent. As my adviser to my new racing team, I will require you to report to me frequently on their progress. See to it that you are seen coming and going by as many as possible. If my enemy has any brains at all, they'll try to use you. I want you to report any attempts to bribe or subvert."

"You want me to be your spy." This was a delightful turn of events. A chance to help the emperor-to-be, to be useful to the empire itself. Her parents certainly never expected her to have an opportunity like this. "Out of curiosity, what makes you think *I* can be trusted?"

"Because you have already proven I can trust you," he said simply.

Oh, of course, she thought. She *had* been keeping the secret of the late emperor's vessel. She hadn't thought of that as a show of loyalty to the emperor-to-be as much as a necessity to avoid catastrophe, but she supposed it could work as both. "I will do my best, Your Excellence."

"My coffers will be open to you, as necessary."

Well, that was excellent news. She wondered what qualified as "necessary."

As the horrendous horn music began to die down, the emperor-to-be abruptly shifted the conversation. "What kind of gift do you think would please my kehok rider? I wish to show both my thanks and encouragement as she prepares for the next races."

Lady Evara realized the subject change was due to the fact they could be overheard as the music lessened, but he still sounded genuine. "I believe she would like a gift that expresses your belief in her ability to win. A small token. Anything large, and she would feel it as additional pressure."

"Good advice. A pin perhaps, that she can wear on her riding armor?"

"A perfect idea." A pin would show everyone that Raia had the emperor-to-be's confidence, without seeming like a courtship gift. Unless it was a courtship gift? She eyed the emperor-to-be and then dismissed the thought. She knew the court rumors about him and Lady Nori. Everyone expected him to propose once he was crowned. "Would Your Excellence like me to assist in choosing one?"

"Indeed, I would be grateful." He raised his voice to a guard behind her. "Could you please escort Lady Evara to the royal jeweler? She will arrange a commission for my rider, on my behalf."

Very pleased with this interesting opportunity, Lady Evara bowed again to the emperor-to-be and followed the palace guard, making sure to smile at as many aristocrats as she could as she flounced by. *Playing spy is going to be fun.*

And lucrative.

And even better, it was a lovely chance to prove her family wrong. She belonged among the jewels of the empire, and no one was going to take this life from her—even, or especially, the dead.

CHAPTER 22

Tamra oversaw the move from the royal stable to the official racetrack campground. She ignored Lady Evara's complaints about the primitiveness of the quarters compared to the palace where she was certain the emperor-to-be would see they were treated with exquisite meals and luxurious beds. When her griping finally got to be too much, Tamra told her, "It's better for Raia and me to be here. But you should stay in the palace, as our liaison to our sponsor."

Lady Evara had loved that idea so much that she'd double-kissed Tamra's cheeks, and then left Tamra blessedly alone to finish settling in; she had sent Raia to the stable to check over the kehok while she unloaded their supplies into the tent.

Stretching sheets over the cot, Tamra thought about Shalla. She hoped she was happy, that the augurs were being kind to her, that she didn't miss home too much, that she wasn't worrying about anything. Tamra had been sending her little messages via wight—just notes describing things she'd seen in the capital, telling her that training was going well, saying she loved her and was proud of her no matter what—but Shalla hadn't written back. Tamra wondered if the augurs were preventing Shalla from responding. She didn't even know if they were delivering her notes. *It would be just like them not to,* she thought. *They'd say it was interfering with her studies.* She considered whether or not she could ask Augur Yorbel to intervene, insist that Shalla be allowed to see her notes and write back to them. Maybe she'd ask the next time she saw him.

The tent flap ruffled behind her as Raia poked her head in. "Trainer Verlas?"

She finished smoothing the sheet. "Has he been fed? Fresh water?"

"Yes, but . . . are you sure he'll be safe?"

"You worry more than a mother hen," Tamra said. "The kehoks are locked up to keep *us* safe from *them*. The monsters aren't in any danger. You'll see him in the morning."

"It's just . . . I don't like the latch on the stall. It didn't seem secure enough."

Everything here was top-notch, rigorously maintained and inspected before every racing season, but still she approved of Raia's concern. "How about I double-check? Would that make you feel better?"

Raia brightened, reminding Tamra of Shalla after she chased a nightmare away. "Yes, please. Thank you, Trainer Verlas."

Tamra noticed Raia was fiddling nervously with the pin Lady Evara had given her on behalf of the emperor-to-be. Affixed to her rider's uniform, the pin was an exquisite bronze lion, and Tamra wasn't certain if it was meant to be a mark of the prince's favor or a warning against failure. She said nothing about it, though.

It's natural she's tense, Tamra thought. She was carrying the weight of an empire on her back. Tamra remembered how anxious she'd felt during her own racing seasons—*and I was only carrying the weight of my own ambition.* "Get some sleep if you can. I'll be back soon."

She pushed open the tent flap and stepped out into the night. Fires were lit in pits beside some tents, and trainers and racers were still scurrying around, preparing for tomorrow's races. Still other tents were closed up tight, their inhabitants already asleep. Above, the stars were mostly blotted out by the smoke from the fires, but she could still see the three stars that formed the sword of the Lady.

Shalla, are you looking up at the stars too?

Tamra breathed in the mix of cooking meat, smoke, and kehok stench, but under it all was the sweet, dry taste of the desert blowing in from beyond the campground. Even though she was so far from home, the familiar scents and sounds and sights of the camp made her feel as if everything were right with the world.

One of the two stable guards at the door recognized her, and she was grateful he didn't call her the "cursed trainer"—at least not to her face. They waved her through, and she entered.

She was the only one in the stable, aside from the four guards stationed inside. Two were posted by the door and another set at the opposite end. They were there to make sure she didn't meddle with any kehok but her own.

It was rare, but there had been instances of sabotage in the past. The racing commission dealt with such cases firmly.

The stable was vast, with a high ceiling. Used annually, it was far cleaner than the royal stable had been, even if it lacked the opulent murals and carvings. This was a more utilitarian space: stall after stall, with basins for water, storage for food, and even an emergency area for any hurt riders or racers. *Still impressive, though,* she thought. It was built to store hundreds.

Their kehok was twenty-third down on the left.

Approaching the stall, Tamra projected the order: *Calm.* "It's only me."

The lion was uneasy, pacing back and forth, rattling the shackles. He hadn't touched his dinner. He must have picked up on Raia's nerves.

"You're racing tomorrow," she scolded. "You need to sleep tonight."

He made a low growl in the back of his throat, and she wasn't sure if that was agreement or a get-out-of-my-face growl. Tamra checked the latch and lock. "Huh."

Raia was right.

The lock was intact and secure, but the latch itself was missing three of its screws. A solid hit, and the whole mechanism would fall off the door, lock intact but useless. "Guess she's not just paranoid."

It was easy to see how no one had noticed—the screws were tucked underneath the latch. If she hadn't been examining it, she wouldn't have seen it either. Raia must have noticed that it felt loose, even though it appeared locked. *Poor workmanship,* Tamra thought. Someone had been careless, or saving money.

It wasn't a major problem. The kehok was still shackled within his stall—the external lock was an extra precaution in case some trainer or rider forgot to secure the shackles.

She should be able to find spare screws in one of the many maintenance sheds around the race grounds.

Heading for the stable door, she asked one of the guards, "Do you know where I can find a screwdriver and some spare screws? A few are missing on our stall's latch. Incidentally, you might want to check the other latches, in case the same idiot skimped on those." She'd check herself, but she knew the guards would protest her being so close to other racers.

"Yes, ma'am," the guard said. "Maintenance shed—"

CRASH.

Tamra spun around.

Three kehoks had wrenched themselves out of their shackles and battered down their stall doors, breaking through what were undoubtedly faulty latches. Yelling, the guards drew weapons and ran toward them. The three kehoks—a bloodred bull, a praying mantis with thick gorilla arms, and a spikey monstrosity—were focused on battering a single stall door.

The black lion's.

She knew the lion was secure within his stall, which meant he couldn't fight back. They'd savage him. Kill him. The latch snapped, and Tamra yelled, *"Stop!"*

Running after the guards, she shouted again, "Stop!" She put every inch of will behind that command and shoved it at the three kehoks just as the guards reached them.

The kehoks froze.

A bit of her mind that wasn't consumed with rage whispered, *This can't be a coincidence.* Three kehoks with loose shackles, targeting one without? They should have gone for the guards, or attacked each other. Or tried a closer stall. But they had targeted the lion.

My *kehok.*

No one hurts my kehok.

Tamra flung herself between the kehoks and the guards. "Back to your stalls!"

The three attacking kehoks flinched away from her, stumbling over their hooves and paws. She spread her arms wide. Out of the corner of her eye, she saw the guards staring at her, their weapons ready but hesitating to strike at the racers—it was worth their jobs if they damaged any racers unnecessarily.

"Back!" she commanded. She felt fury surging through her, and she directed every drop of it at them. "Get back!"

Cowed, all three scuttled backward.

"Into your stalls!"

Heads down, they scooted backward. They retreated into their stalls while she continued to bear pressure on their minds. She was implacable, pinning them inside their stalls as if they were bugs pinned under her thumb.

To the guards, she ordered, "Shackle them."

The guards obeyed, rushing into the stalls and securing the shackles while she held the three kehoks down with the strength of her mind. When all three were secure, they shut the doors, and she turned back to the black lion.

He was unharmed, thank the Lady.

One of the guards ventured, "That was incredible, Trainer . . ."

"Verlas," another guard said. "That's Trainer Verlas."

"You held three kehoks at once! Three that weren't even your racers!"

All the guards started gushing at once.

Tamra just felt tired. She held up a hand. "Screws and a screwdriver? So we can fix the latches and ensure this doesn't happen again?" She eyed the latches of the other stalls. "And you should check *all* the latches."

"Yes, ma'am." One of the guards scurried out of the stable in search of tools, while the others began checking the latches on the stalls. She propped up the door of the lion's stall. The kehoks had broken through the weakened latch, but it was fixable. It was almost as if—

"Excuse me, who owns the three kehoks who escaped?" she asked.

The guard checked the labels beside the stalls. "All three are owned by Trainer Limra."

Tamra wasn't familiar with the name, but it was suspicious that all three who attacked were owned by the same trainer. "Is there a shield on the kehok stable?"

"No, ma'am, only the racetrack."

She nodded. So this Trainer Limra *could* have directed all three of his or her kehoks to attack hers, if he or she knew that the latches were faulty. Tamra didn't have any proof, of course. But it was an unsettling suspicion. "I'll be keeping my kehok by my tent for the duration of the races."

"We are deeply sorry this incident occurred," one of the guards said. "The latches will be fixed, and the incident will be reported to the race council. You can trust that—"

"I'll sleep easier if he's near me," Tamra said. "But thank you for your quick reactions." At least the guards tried to protect her lion. With three kehoks targeting him, if she hadn't been here, he'd have most likely been killed regardless, but at least they'd tried. She unhooked the lion's shackles, kept her mind fixed on him so he'd behave, and led him out of the stable.

He walked placidly beside her, like a tame pet.

She kept a lid on her simmering fury, trying not to think too hard about the suspicion that this was a deliberate attempt at sabotage. Or call it what it really was: attempted murder.

"Raia?" she called to the tent. "Come help me set up the cage."

Raia popped out of the tent, saw the lion, and immediately took his chains, cooing to him while Tamra swung open the cage door. The lion walked in without any resistance, curled up, and lay down in the center of the cage.

"I'll guard him," Tamra said. "You sleep."

"Guard him? But . . ."

"Sleep, Raia. He's safe now."

RAIA WOKE, CONVINCED HER LION WAS IN DANGER, and burst out of the tent.

"If you don't go back to sleep," Trainer Verlas said, "I will tie you to your cot." She was seated by a campfire, placidly sewing up a rip in her tunic. She barely glanced at Raia. Most of the camp was quiet, with a few lit fires nearby and the clatter of wagon wheels in the distance.

"Sorry," Raia mumbled. She reassured herself that her kehok was still in his cage, and then she ducked back in and tried to fall asleep. She woke again. And again. Each time, the kehok was safely in his cage, pacing as if he were trying to guard her, rather than the other way around. Each time, Trainer Verlas sent her back inside as if she were an unruly toddler.

When dawn came, she gave up on sleep and tossed her blankets off. Her mouth felt full of cobwebs, and her eyelids felt stiff. Her leg muscles ached, which could have been from riding so much lately or from sleeping terribly. This time, she wasn't going to be sent back.

Outside, Trainer Verlas had a mug of mint tea in her hand. She thrust it into Raia's hands. "You talk in your sleep."

At least that meant she'd slept more than she'd thought she had. "I'm sorry. Did I say anything embarrassing?"

"Only every deep, dark secret you've ever had." Trainer Verlas flashed her a rare smile. "You called for your lion a few times. But nothing coherent. He's fine, by the way."

At least that was a relief, on both counts.

"You're slated to run in the third major race of today. Get yourself some breakfast, and try not to let the crowds freak you out. Or the word 'major.' It's just a race. No more or less important than any other."

Which was to say, Raia translated, vitally important.

"Thanks for the tea." She checked on her kehok again. He'd quit pacing and was sitting motionless, watching dawn spread across the bustling camp. It was beginning to fill as riders and racers poured in from up and down the Aur River, converging for the main races.

She ducked into the washroom, sponged herself down, and dressed before seeking out the communal breakfast, served by the race organizers. She was halfway to a pyramid of pastries when she heard a familiar voice:

"You made the majors!"

Raia turned to see Jalimo jogging up to her. He was followed by Algana. Catching up, Algana panted, "We saw the standings and were so happy for you. Shocked too. Because, well, you kind of forgot to turn when we ran together."

"Good to see you," Raia said. "Where's Silar?" For

a moment, she flashed to an image of the dead boy's face, Fetran. *Not Silar.*

"Why? Did I stick my foot in my mouth again?" Algana said. "I did, didn't I. Silar is usually the one to point that out."

Jalimo pointed at the fruit table, where Silar was peeling a mango. She waved when she saw Raia looking at her. Raia waved back. "How were your qualifiers?"

"Pretty excellent," Jalimo said. "At least for them. Silar is racing against you. Algana's in the fifth major race today. And I'm in the minors."

"There's no shame in the minors." Algana patted his shoulder.

Drifting over to join them, Silar bit into her mango and wiped a bit of juice from her cheek. "Think of the benefits, Jalimo: there's more time to relax when everyone knows you've already lost." She winked at Raia as Jalimo sputtered.

"I'm racing you?" Raia asked Silar. She liked it better when her competitors were nameless strangers. *Fetran,* she thought again. She wished she didn't know his name. What if that happened to Silar or Algana or Jalimo? *Or me?*

Algana jumped in. "She'd appreciate it if you ran straight off the track again."

Silar elbowed her. "No, I wish you all the best in our race. May you soar swift as an eagle across the finish line."

Raia looked at her for a moment. Silar held her pious expression.

And then they both burst out laughing. Jalimo and Algana joined in. "You just . . . hopped over the wall . . ." Jalimo said, laughing. He mimed the action of the lion.

Raia finished, "And kept running. Straight into the desert."

Catching her breath, Silar said, "Seriously, I do want you to do well."

"Me too," Raia said. And she meant it. "So long as you come in second, and I'm first." She smiled, because she meant that too.

A hand landed on her shoulder, and Raia twisted to see Gette smiling at all of them. "First or second, what does it matter? Raia here will win on a technicality anyway. It's her style." He laughed, but none of them joined in. "I'm Rider Gette. A pleasure to meet more of my fellow competitors."

"Whoa," Jalimo said.

"He's Jalimo," Algana said quickly. "I'm Algana. And she's Silar. You know Raia?"

"Old race buddies," Gette said. To Raia, he said, "You'll be happy to hear you won't be facing me in any of the initial races. Fate has spared you. Our schedules don't coincide. But I'll be rooting for you. So I can beat you and your lion again in a later race." He patted her shoulder and then drifted off. A flock of other riders clumped around him, asking for his advice, his opinion, or just his attention.

Raia and her friends stared after him.

"Changed my mind," Silar said. "You have to win our race. So you can kick his ass later."

"RIDERS UP!"

The race official's voice trumpeted across the holding area, and Raia mounted her lion. She felt oddly calm. The chaos—the screams of the kehoks, the cheers from the spectators in the stands—was blending together into a blanket of sound that wrapped around her. She breathed in. And out.

Urging her kehok forward, she rode him to the starting stall.

Silar was two stalls down, on her silver dog kehok. As she eased her monster in, it bucked. Raia opened her mouth to cry out as Silar was thrown backward, caught herself on the wall of the stall, and steadied her beast.

The lion let out a growl. Leaning forward, Raia stroked his mane. "She's got this. Concentrate on us. Silar will be fine." She knew she was talking more to herself than to the kehok. Her friend seemed to have control of her kehok now.

"Ready!" the race official called.

Raia focused on the track beyond the starting gate. She breathed in, tasted the sand that already filled the air, the stench of the kehoks, the sweetness of the garlands of jasmine that decorated the spectator stands.

"Prepare!"

She didn't look at the stands. She knew Trainer Verlas was there. Most likely Prince Dar. She didn't want to know if her parents were there as well. Or Gette, watching and hoping she'd fail. Or hoping she'd win so he could beat her later, as promised.

"Race!"

The stall gates were flung open, and the kehoks surged forward.

Raia felt the wind hit her face. Sand flew into the air. Leaning forward onto the lion's mane, she saw only the track in front of her. His paws ate into it.

He rammed his shoulder against a red lizard kehok, and the reptile snapped at him. Her lion dodged, claiming the inside line. He raced past a long-legged kehok with a rider who was whipping him nonstop. Ahead was Silar's silver dog, slowing to take the turn.

Her kehok sped up. Pushing against the turn, they flew past Silar.

Behind her, Raia heard a commotion: kehok screams, shouts, but it faded into the blanket of sound. She heard only the lion's paws on the sand, her breath heavy and fast, and the whistle of the wind. She felt as if she were flying across the desert, alone with her lion.

Ahead was the finish line, marked with black paint on the sand. Race officials flanked it. Beyond she saw the spectators, cheering and screaming, and she let the sight of them flow into her.

Faster, she thought.

And the lion ran faster.

He burst across the finish line. First. Definitively first. No technicality this time.

Raia pumped her fists into the air and turned as the race officials descended on her to chain her kehok. She expected to see Silar on her silver dog barreling across the finish line after her, in second, but instead she saw a crab kehok, a giraffe with a wolf's head, a scaled rhino . . . "Silar. Where is she?" she asked the closest race official. "She rode a silver dog kehok."

"Two racers are down," the race official said. "Accident on the track. Congrats on your win." He moved on to the next kehok.

Raia slid off the lion's back as Trainer Verlas appeared, taking the lion's chains. She was talking, but Raia didn't hear. She walked toward the track, feeling numb. Her own heartbeat felt louder than the roars of the crowd. She should have asked how bad an accident. Broken bones. Just a fall.

Silar's fine, she told herself. *She has to be.*

The medics jogged toward the finish line, carrying a stretcher between them, and Raia broke into a run. She stumbled on a divot in the torn-up track, but caught herself and ran to the side of the stretcher.

Silar lay on it, her face twisted in pain.

"You're alive!" Raia said. She almost wept.

"Can't feel my legs," Silar whimpered. "Why can't I feel my legs?"

"You'll be all right," Raia said, reaching for her hand. Their fingers touched, but the medics didn't slow. They brushed past Raia, hurrying Silar to the healer's tent.

Raia stood alone on the track as people swirled around her, congratulating her, urging her to move along and make way for the next race. She looked up at the stands and saw Prince Dar looking down at her, with a beautiful silk-clad woman beside him. He raised his hand at Raia and smiled in approval.

Turning away, Raia wanted to vomit.

CHAPTER 23

A t dawn, before the next day's races began, Trainer Limra, a squat woman who sweated profusely, approached Tamra to apologize and rant about the unsafe locks—she swore she'd triple-checked the shackles on her kehoks the prior day.

"Luckily, all the kehoks survived," Tamra said, even though it hadn't been luck. She eyed the other trainer, watching her reaction. By now, the stable guards would have finished their reports to the committee, and a formal investigation would have been opened. If she were being uncharitable, Tamra would have suspected that Limra was apologizing *because* an investigation had been opened. "Accidents happen."

"Yes, they do!" Limra said enthusiastically.

I am uncharitable. "If you'll excuse me, I have to prep my rider for today's races."

"Of course," Limra said, heaving a sigh of relief. She'd probably expected Tamra to rage at her like a lot of trainers would have, but Tamra had no interest in expending the energy. Whether it truly had been an accident, the black lion was safe now. Another night had come and gone without any problems, and Tamra had even allowed herself to catch some sleep. Then Limra added, "I knew *you* would understand, after what happened at last year's finals."

Tamra bristled. "Oh? Have we met before?"

"Our riders raced together last year. As you said, accidents happen." She then hurried off toward the stable.

Watching her waddle away, Tamra swore under her breath. *As if we didn't have enough problems.* She would bet large sums of gold that Limra's rider had died in that race, at the teeth of Tamra's kehok.

At least the racing commission would see to it that Trainer Limra wouldn't get another chance to sabotage any more stalls. Whether she was found guilty or not, she'd be watched closely for the rest of the season.

And I'll be watching too.

Because Trainer Limra might not be the only one with a grievance.

Not wanting to worry her, Tamra didn't say a word about it to Raia. She helped her dress in her riding uniform, helped her secure the kehok saddle, and then kept an eye on her as she guided the lion to the starting gate.

Raia was unusually quiet too. But she didn't seem distracted. In fact, the opposite. She seemed determined.

"Everything all right?" Tamra asked.

"Should it be?"

Tamra considered that for a moment. "No. But are you ready to race?"

"Yes."

She said it with such surety that Tamra didn't doubt her. Checking over the saddle one last time, Tamra turned away. Raia's voice stopped her: "Silar might not ever walk again."

Tamra ran through names in her head, trying to connect the name Silar to a face. Ah, yes, one of the other riders from their training ground—one of the three who always palled around together and seemed to have adopted Raia into their little group.

"I'm running for her," Raia said. "Because she won't ever have this again."

Tamra considered and discarded a dozen different responses—platitudes about her friend, wisdom about the arbitrary whims of fate, advice on how to work through the pain Raia felt. Instead, she simply said, "Good. Run for Silar. And for all of us."

The race official called, *"Riders up!"*

Joining the others, Raia and the lion proceeded to the starting gates.

Tamra felt the stares as she climbed into the viewing box beside the racetrack. Word of yesterday's kehok "incident" in the stable had spread, combined with reports of the lion's win in their first major race, making her and Raia a significant point of interest. Tamra wondered if any of the spectators suspected the incident wasn't an accident—she doubted it. From the snippets of conversation she overheard, most were discussing the fact that she'd controlled three kehoks and stopped it from becoming a catastrophe. She didn't linger long enough to be able to tell if they were impressed or appalled, and she didn't care which it was, so long as there weren't any more attacks on her racer. What was more important, and satisfying, was that the odds on Raia and the lion had improved.

As the racers positioned themselves in their starting

gates, Lady Evara sidled through the crowd to join Tamra. "I heard you had some excitement yesterday, in addition to our protégé's first major win."

Tamra didn't take her eyes off Raia. "I need you to ask Prince Dar for guards for the kehok. Trustworthy ones. The racing commission won't supply extra guards for privately held kehoks, and I won't hold the lion in the public stalls."

"Sounds like a necessary expense," Lady Evara said. "Consider it done."

"Good," Tamra grunted.

On the track, the race officials shouted:

"Ready!"

"Prepare!"

"Race!"

The kehoks shot out of the starting gate.

Raia and the lion burst into the lead.

She ran with a fire and passion that was beyond anything Tamra had seen her use. "At last," Tamra murmured. Somehow, while she'd been worrying about attacks and sabotage, Raia had discovered something it often took riders years to discover: how to convert pain into power, and powerlessness into strength. "She's going to win again."

"How can you tell?" Lady Evara asked. "She's not even at the turn!"

"She'll win."

"I'm placing another bet."

BY NIGHTFALL, THE REQUESTED GUARDS WERE WAITING for them at the camp, along with Augur Yorbel, to Tamra's surprise. He bowed to Raia. "Congratulations on your win today."

"He ran fast," Raia said modestly. "I just let him do what we both wanted to do."

He waited while Tamra helped Raia secure the lion in his cage, and then she shooed Raia into the tent to bathe, eat, and sleep.

"So I'm fairly certain it was attempted murder," Tamra said without preamble.

Yorbel startled. "You mean . . ."

"I've no proof, but thank you for the guards."

"The emperor-to-be has enemies," Yorbel said, considering it.

"So do I, apparently." She told him about the trainer Limra. "I could, of course, just be paranoid. It would be an enormous risk to plan such a thing—the race commission will investigate, and if they find her guilty, she'll be barred from racing for life. I can't see how the risk would be worth the revenge, if her only motive was last year's race."

"She could have been hired by the emperor-to-be's enemies, chosen because of her history with you."

"Gold plus revenge?" Tamra nodded. It was plausible. "In that case, I'm doubly thankful for the loan of the guards." The four soldiers from the palace had taken up position on each corner of the kehok cage. It was ostentatious, but hopefully, everyone would assume that the emperor-to-be was just overzealous about his return to racing and extra anxious after the incident in the stable. She doubted anyone would suspect the truth.

With a groan, she lowered herself onto the bench next their firepit. The fire was embers, so she tossed a log onto it. Flames shot up, and the fire ate at the edge of the bark.

Yorbel sat next to her. "My augur friends do not understand my obsession with this year's races. Sometimes I don't either. I cannot help but wonder if this is the best path."

"She won again," Tamra pointed out. "If she keeps this up, she'll be in the championship race."

He sighed. "I thought my involvement in this would be over by now."

"I asked for guards," Tamra said. "I didn't ask for you."

He laughed. "That was blunt. I know you didn't. Dar requested I accompany the guards. He wants my assessment of the situation."

"And your assessment is you don't like lying to your friends, and you worry about whether this will work?" she guessed.

He stared into the flames, as if the tiny sparks of fire held the key to unanswered questions. "I have devoted my life to the study of ethics. Read countless volumes on morality and the betterment of the soul. Engaged in discussions with the wisest minds. Spent hours in contemplation. Only to face reality and be unsure if I have made the correct choices. Again and again, I find myself in situations where there are no good choices. How does one live a moral life and still live in reality?"

"You know, I never thought I'd be in a position of counseling an augur on morality, but here goes: You're doing the best you can with the crappy dice you rolled. Sure, when the options are choose right from wrong, there's an obvious way to act. But when the choices are just 'better' or 'worse'?" She patted his knee. "You're doing fine."

He met her eyes, and a faint smile touched his lips. "Shockingly, that makes me feel better."

"Frankly, I don't worry about the state of my soul," Tamra said. "I worry about whether the ones I love are safe and happy. What happens to me after I'm dead . . . I won't remember who I was or anything in this life, so what does it matter?"

"You would give my colleagues fits if you said that to them," Yorbel said.

Tamra massaged her neck. She'd been tense all day, and her muscles were aching as punishment. "You're not having fits."

"Inside I am screaming," he said in a flat, calm voice.

She laughed. "Inside we all are."

He laughed too, then said, "I have no idea why I'm laughing. That's horrible."

"Because it's better than crying." She thought of Shalla and hoped she was well and happy and not worrying about her mother. "You know, I used to think all augurs were inhuman, after they took my daughter. Or separate from human, at least. Augur Clari is constantly trying to convince me to abandon Shalla, to catch me in a missed payment and yank her away from me permanently."

"I grew up in a temple," Yorbel said. "The augurs were kind to me."

Tamra snorted. "Did they love you?"

"I believe they did, in their way."

"Unconditionally?"

"I . . ."

"Or would they have kicked you out if you'd failed their lessons?" She nodded at the tent behind them. "Raia was in augur training, enrolled at the temple. Like all the others, she was forced to train at the temple, no choice in her future. And then, after she'd accepted her fate, they determined she wasn't right for it. They spit her out, taking her choice away a second time. Seems to me that's the opposite of unconditional love."

He didn't argue with her on that. But he did say, "The empire needs augurs."

"Does it?" Tamra dared. It wasn't a question she'd ever voiced out loud, much less one she ever expected to say to an actual augur. She'd seen the way the augurs reminded people of their better selves—without them, it was said, the empire would dissolve into chaos. Would it really, though? "Does it truly benefit people to know what their soul will become? What does it matter? Shouldn't they just be good people because they love their family and they care about the people around them? People should be good because it's right, not because an augur tells them it's what they should do."

He was silent.

"It's not as if we carry our memories into our new life, at least not reliably," Tamra said. "So I'll be a fish. Or a bird. Or a cricket. Or whatever. Does it matter, so long as I've done the best I can?"

"You truly feel this way?"

He sounded stunned, as if no one had ever questioned the entire purpose of his life's work before, which she supposed was most likely the case. She wondered if she should apologize.

But why should I apologize when it's what I believe?

"I used to believe I had to do something extraordinary to make my life worthwhile," Tamra said. "Now I only want Shalla, and more recently Raia, to have a chance at happy lives."

"But your next life . . ."

"Death erases all we are and all we were. So the past and the future? They don't matter as much as what you do in the moment. In every moment." She grinned at him. "It's okay if you don't agree. I'm not the one who spent hours in contemplation of ancient ethics texts."

"You are, I'm told, the one who can control multiple kehoks at once," Yorbel said. "I heard the rumors on the way in. It's an unusual talent."

She shrugged. It was a useless talent for a rider—you could race only one kehok at a time—but pretty handy for a trainer when there were multiple kehoks acting up. "It's just being stubborn."

"I believe it's linked to your whole philosophy of life," Yorbel said seriously. "You are somehow able to let go of the past and future and focus on the present. You don't merely pay lip service to the idea of making the most of each moment. You inhabit the moment fully, and the kehoks respond to that. Amazing."

She laughed. "I haven't been called 'amazing' in a very long time. And certainly never by an augur. Either this is a sign that I'm doing things very right . . . or you're doing things very wrong."

"Very right," he insisted.

Certainly, there were two things she knew she'd done right.

One of them was many miles away, but the other was right here, asleep in a tent near her beloved monster.

YORBEL RETURNED TO THE TEMPLE WITH NO CLEAR idea of what he thought or felt about anything anymore. *The sky could be green, the sands purple, and the river red, for all I can tell,* he thought. *And that's fine. Everything's fine. Better than fine.* Because at last he knew why he kept being drawn back to the races, why he was able to so easily swallow the lies that entailed, why he was inexplicably happy despite all the fear and worry he should be feeling:

Tamra.

She was amazing.

He hummed to himself as he walked through the familiar stone corridors. Nodding to augurs as he passed, he climbed the stairs to his room. He was still smiling as he opened his door.

Gissa was seated by his desk. She'd turned the chair to face the door and was sitting calmly, patiently, with her hands folded in her lap.

He let out a "Gahhh!" before his brain caught up with his scream and cut it off. "Gissa! You surprised me. How long have you . . . Have you been waiting long?" Also, why was she here? Why not wait until he was in his room and then knock, as was customary? "Is everything all right?"

"You tell me." Gissa rose, circled around him, and shut the door.

Yorbel instinctively backed away, though he wasn't sure why. This was Gissa, one of his oldest friends. Still, she looked as if she was about to lecture him like his second-year teacher, whose approach to reading auras was to yell at you until everything blurred red.

"You said you were finished with all that kehok business, that you'd be staying in the temple, yet every time I look for you, you're out again. I'm here because I'm concerned about you, Yorbel."

He chuckled. "I don't need a mother hen, Gissa. I'm a grown man." She saw him as too hopeless to keep a plant alive, much less take care of himself. Pointing to the plant on his windowsill, he said, "See? Not dead yet."

"You are darkening your soul."

He sank down onto his cot, feeling as if the air had been sucked out of him. He knew it wasn't possible for Gissa to read him, any more than it was possible for him to read her. Gissa, though, was looking at him as if she could see every shadow that stained his soul, and it unnerved him.

"You know beyond Becar," she said, "at the mouth of the Aur River, where it opens to the wide sea, there's a lighthouse that stands so that ships can find their way to the river even in the darkest night. *You* have always been my lighthouse here in the temple, guiding me back home. You have always been that solid, dependable beam of goodness, reminding all of us why we do what we do. Yorbel, please, tell me what is going on with you. Tell me the truth!"

Yorbel dropped his face into his hands.

There were a dozen truths he could tell her, and perhaps if she'd asked him another day, he would have chosen a different answer. But there was just one dominating his thoughts at the moment his old friend demanded the truth:

Muffled through his hands, he whispered, "I think I may be in love."

The room was absolutely silent, as silent as the old stone that formed the walls and the floor, as silent as the shadows in the corner.

"With whom?" Gissa asked, and the two words sank like stones into still water.

"Trainer Tamra Verlas."

He then heard an odd kind of strangled noise. Raising his head, he saw Gissa was tucking something into a fold in her tunic, and that her face was contorted as she tried to hold in—

"You're laughing at me," Yorbel said.

And Gissa burst out laughing, a full belly laugh, bent

over, with her hands on her knees. "You. Yorbel. That was . . . I was not . . . Oh, by the River . . ." She laughed for a solid minute while Yorbel waited, feeling himself blush to the tips of his ears. She wiped her eyes with the back of her hand. "I'm sorry. It's just . . . I mean, it's not that you aren't lovable . . . You absolutely . . ." She dissolved into laughter again.

"You are not making me feel good about confiding in you." He didn't see the humor in this. He was, as he'd pointed out just a few minutes earlier, a grown man. He had control of his thoughts and emotions, he'd believed. He'd dedicated his life in service to the temple, to higher intellectual causes, which left little time for things like . . .

Things like living in the moment, he thought.

She got ahold of herself and sat down next to him. A giggle escaped her lips, and she swallowed it back. "So this trainer . . . She is the one you brought back to the emperor-to-be? She is who you see when you go to the royal stable? And the racetrack, where you've never set foot in your life?"

"I saw the Becaran Races once," he said defensively.

"And you thought they were barbaric."

"She's not barbaric."

"I'm sure she's not." Her face was contorted with the effort of not laughing.

"She . . . constantly surprises me," Yorbel said. "You would think, given what she does, the choices she's made, that she would be . . . lacking. But, Gissa, when I read her soul, she has this core of strength. She isn't a pillar of light, like the purest souls, like I have been taught to aspire to, but . . . I can't explain it." He shook his head. "I sound ridiculous, don't I? At my age."

Flopping back on the bed, Gissa laughed again.

"You are being a terrible friend," he told her. "At least give me some advice. I want to tell her, or show her, how unique and special she is."

"My intellectual friend is a romantic. I truly had no idea." She sat up. "I am so very relieved that *this* is the explanation. I will spread the word to your concerned friends."

"Gissa!"

"You can't expect me *not* to gossip about this."

He glared at her. "A. Terrible. Friend."

"All right." She composed herself. "You want a grand gesture, to show her how you feel. Traditionally, I'm told sweets, flowers, or jewels work. Poetry." She held up a hand. "Wait. Forget I said that. Please do *not* write her poetry."

He couldn't picture how Tamra would react to sweets, flowers, or jewels. Somehow it didn't feel right. And he sensed it would make him look ridiculous. *She'd laugh at me like Gissa is laughing,* Yorbel thought. "I'm not looking for a way to confess my feelings. She doesn't know how I feel, and she doesn't need to know—she has enough to handle right now. This isn't about me. It's about her. I want her to know she's amazing."

"If you truly care for this woman," Gissa said, "what you should do is obvious: do something that would make her happy."

Of course! Yes! That was perfect advice. And with that, he shot to his feet. Because he knew *exactly* what would make Tamra the most happy. "I take it back. You aren't terrible. Thank you, Gissa." He rushed out of the room.

The sound of her laughter followed him.

CHAPTER 24

While her sponsored rider and racer continued to win during the day, Lady Evara spent her evenings drifting through the palace, twinkling at everyone. That was her personal term for it: a light laugh, a twinkle in the eye. Every so often, she'd toss out a compliment. "Lovely bracelet, darling." Or "Your hair looks divine." Or stop, stare, and then say, "Stunning," before sweeping on. She'd hear in her wake: *That's the woman who sponsored the emperor-to-be's racer! She may have picked the winner!*

As pleasant as that was to hear, she rarely paused long enough for a full conversation. Until she knew who was interested in her, she was careful not to appear interested in anyone.

It was a delightful game. Be accessible, but not too accessible. Aloof, but not too aloof. Charming without seeming insincere. Superficial without seeming inconsequential. And she was good at it, which was proof that, no matter what her darling parents had thought, she could be good at something. It helped that the emperor-to-be frequently summoned her for updates on "their" rider and racer—their mood, their health, their training regime. He sometimes employed musicians for their conversations and sometimes not, presumably to keep any busybodies from guessing that he was fond of hiding important discussions beneath the cacophony of sound. *He's a clever boy,* Lady Evara thought. *I do hope he lives to be emperor.* She liked the idea that she could do something to help ensure that, even though she hadn't uncovered anything useful yet.

She was just about to retire for the evening, though the shrimp being served in the statue hall were divine, when she was approached by an impeccably dressed man with a truly stunning mustache. He had tiny jewels clipped to his mustache and had somehow endeavored to make it curl twice before ending in a three-pronged split capped with diamonds.

"Lady Evara." He bowed. "I am honored."

"You are a work of art," she said. "Let me admire you."

"Sweet lady—" he began.

She laid a finger on his lips and then walked around him in a slow circle, taking in every detail of his outfit, which was at least three layers of silks plus a braided belt that draped from his shoulders, circled his waist, and then vanished within the silks. "All right, you may speak now."

"It has been brought to my attention that, despite your beauty and your many charms, you do not belong among us." This shocking statement was delivered in a soft voice that sounded better suited to reciting lyrics from love songs.

"Excuse me?"

"If my sources are correct, my sweet lady, you are within

months of losing your ancestral home, your title, and your reputation, due to an unfortunate clause in your parents' will that prevents you from accessing your inheritance."

She would not let him have the satisfaction of seeing he'd rattled her. "Your manners, unlike your mustache, are deplorable. You must have mistaken me for someone else." *Sources? What sources?* Her parents' will was a private matter, known only to her and the augurs who handled such matters, and they were honor-bound to silence.

He bowed again. "Please believe me, my lady, I have not said these things to embarrass you. I am, in fact, in the happy position to help you reverse your fortunes. For that is, indeed, why you have come to court, is it not?"

That was so very close to being true, it was disconcerting. *Do not lie to yourself,* she told herself sternly. *That is precisely why I came.* Self-delusion had been her parents' flaw, not hers. In that, she and her rider, Raia, were alike. However he knew, the truth was the truth. "Speak on."

"I am very fond of the Becaran Races. So fond that I have sponsored my own racer and am investing heavily in the fate of several other riders and racers. I believed I had accounted for all variables, but then your rider and racer appeared on the scene . . . and it has thrown a shadow of concern onto all of my careful plans."

A servant bearing a platter of puffed pastries passed by them. The man declined to take one, but Lady Evara made a show of selecting the perfectly puffed pastry, to buy herself a moment to think.

The man's story *could* be the truth. It was plausible. He certainly knew the truth about her own situation, however he obtained it. *My dear mother and father, of course,* she thought. The augurs who knew the truth would have been discreet, but she had no proof that her parents hadn't whispered their little inheritance plan into the ear of a "trusted" friend. Her mustached acquaintance had probably begun researching her when Raia and her racer began winning. Bribe the right people, and you could learn anything about anyone. If the leak wasn't her parents, a servant could have overheard sensitive information and shared it for the right price. Their loyalty would have naturally diminished after she was forced to dismiss them. She tried to hide how much that thought dismayed her. She'd always tried to be kind to them.

She bit into her pastry, and discussed the state of the weather and vague statements about the inconvenience of unrest in the street until the servant was far enough away. When there were no more nearby ears, Lady Evara said, "To the point, then. What are you proposing?"

"If your racer were to come down with an illness, say a permanent illness, I would stand to profit greatly, and I would ensure that *you* were to profit equally greatly."

"You want me to poison my own racer?" This man was lacking in subtlety, so she used none. If their positions were reversed, she would have been much more careful in how she led into this request. Maybe begin with a few innocent conversations, feeling her target out before exposing her plan. *Amateur,* she thought. "Such an action, if detected, could lead to expulsion from the races for life. The race committee frowns on tampering with race results."

"Expose me, and I will expose the fragility of your finances and the . . . ahem . . . state of your soul," the man said quickly. "I am in a position to do so. I am Lord Petalo, cousin to Lady Nori of Griault, whose star is on the rise, and my word carries weight."

Ah, so it was to be blackmail. She was glad she hadn't

retired to her rooms earlier. She wondered if Lord Petalo was motivated by greed, or if it was more sinister—he might not care as much about his chosen kehok's winning as he did about the emperor-to-be's kehok's dying. "I would need to know your definition of 'profit greatly.'"

Lord Petalo leaned forward and whispered a sum in her ear, making it look as if he were whispering a flirtatious compliment.

She played along, with a twinkling laugh and a loud, "Oh my!"

In truth, the sum he named was worthy of an "oh my." It would restore her family fortune. She could not imagine what kind of bets this man could be placing that would result in that kind of payoff for her and still leave a profit for himself. But was he truly that rich?

Well, he was not the only one who could research a peer. She didn't doubt that with the assistance of the emperor-to-be, she could discover whether this man did in fact have the finances to make her such an offer. Or if he had another, wealthier backer behind his request.

"How can I refuse such a very generous offer?" Lady Evara said, fanning herself as if she were swooning at his attention. "But while the reward is substantial, so are the risks. I must wait for an opportunity to present itself."

"Of course. Please know if you were to succeed, it would fill my heart with joy, and both our vaults with gold." Bowing, he excused himself.

She stood for a moment longer in the shadow of a statue.

She *could* go to the emperor-to-be. This was precisely the kind of information that would interest him, especially if her instincts were correct and the bribe money was more than Lord Petalo could afford on his own.

But there was the little matter of the offer itself. It was high enough to make all her problems go away. She did owe it to herself and her future to thoroughly consider all possibilities and ramifications.

No longer the least bit tired, Lady Evara again drifted and twinkled around the room, searching for another helping of shrimp.

If she were the type of person her parents—and the augurs and Lord Petalo and anyone else who knew the truth about her—thought she was, then she'd take the gold, preserve her reputation, and secure her future.

If she wasn't . . . *Well, that's an interesting question, isn't it.*

It was a very large amount of gold.

FIVE DAYS, SIX RACES, AND SIX WINS, THOUGH MORE than one was tight enough to make the hair on the back of Tamra's neck stand up. She kept a close eye on Raia for any signs of exhaustion, but the girl seemed to be floating on the exhilaration of the races. Which was how it should be.

"Race like it's new," Tamra advised her as Raia prepared for the next race. "It has to be a fresh hunger every time." She then sent her to the starting gate yet again.

With the races coming so close together now, there wasn't much for a trainer to do except hope, console, and encourage. She was continuing to make sure Raia slept and ate, and she regularly checked the kehok for any signs of stress or injury.

It didn't make it any easier to have no control.

Taking her spot in the stands, Tamra waited for the start of the next race. She glanced up at the royal box—the emperor-to-be was there, as always, and Lady Evara had woven herself in among the royal courtiers. Tamra hadn't spoken to her lately and wondered what had been keeping her busy. Probably parties with nobles.

"Ready! Prepare! Race!" the announcer cried.

Yanking her mind back into the present, she watched Raia and her racer thunder around the track. She catalogued every stride, thinking of how it could be improved—dig a little deeper there, lean a little into the wind. Raia took the turn flawlessly.

"She's really good, Mama," a familiar voice said beside her.

Tamra's breath caught in her throat. She spun around and there was Shalla! Dropping to her knees, Tamra pulled her in tight until she yelped. "How is this possible? How are you here? Are you all right?" Releasing her, Tamra examined her daughter's face, body, whole self. *She's here!*

Shalla laughed. "I'm good! Nothing's wrong. Don't worry so much, Mama."

"But . . . you're here!"

Then Tamra noticed Yorbel standing behind her with a big, wonderful, goofy smile on his face. "I arranged a transfer. Until the end of the race season, she'll train at the temple in the Heart of Becar."

Tamra, who never cried, felt tears pouring down her face. "Thank you. You are a *good* man." She held Shalla close as, down on the track, Raia raced first across the finish line.

AFTER THE RACE, RAIA DUMPED THE LION'S DINNER into his dish and then flopped down on the ground next to his cage. She knew she should drag herself to her cot and catch a few hours of sleep—and as soon as Trainer Verlas noticed her lying here, she knew her trainer would prod her into the tent for a proper rest—but for right now, this was fine.

She hoped that Shalla wouldn't mind if she greeted her

later. She was grateful to her for distracting Trainer Verlas. It was nice to have a few minutes without anyone fussing over her.

We did it, she thought. She tried to muster up enough energy to feel excited, but she just wanted to collapse on her cot and sleep. They'd won race after race, and it was nearly over. Only one race left: the final championship race. The only one that mattered.

From the cage, the lion huffed.

It was an unusual enough sound that she lifted herself off the ground to peer into the cage. He was sniffing at his dinner, and she suddenly realized she hadn't checked it first. "Wait! Don't eat it yet," she told him.

His head shot up.

Hauling herself up to her feet, she unlatched the cage.

"Excuse me, lady?" one of the guards they'd borrowed from the palace said. "But are you sure you should go in there while he's eating?"

"He won't hurt me." She knew Trainer Verlas would scold her for even thinking that—the second a rider started to trust her racer was the second she opened herself up to disaster. It happened often enough.

But my lion isn't like other kehoks.

"Calm," she said to the kehok. "I have to make sure it's safe to eat." Ever since Lady Evara had reported an attempt to bribe her to poison their racer, Raia had been checking her lion's food. It was easy enough to do—a drop of medicine. If the meat sizzled, it was bad. No reaction, it was fine. She usually remembered to do it *before* she put the dinner into the cage.

The lion growled at her.

"Back," she told him.

He retreated one step.

"Rider Raia, I must insist." The guard clamped his hand on her arm. "He isn't shackled." She had taken to leaving the lion unchained within the cage—he was secure enough within it, and his muscles needed to be able to stretch after all the racing. Plus, she hated seeing him piled underneath all the iron.

The lion growled deep in his throat.

Raia glared at the guard. He was a new one. He must have missed Trainer Verlas's "don't mess with my rider" lecture, which she gave to all the guards sent from the palace. "It's all right."

He was sweating. "You can't risk—"

As she opened her mouth to tell him to let go of her arm, the lion launched himself against the half-open cage door. She was knocked flat on her back, and her kehok landed directly on top of the guard.

The guard screamed.

"No! Stop!" Raia shouted.

But the lion didn't move. He stayed on top of the guard, pinning him with his massive paws. She heard a commotion around her as other guards, trainers, and riders came running. One of them struck at her lion with a spiked whip, and her kehok snapped his jaws fast and hard toward the trainer.

Raia shouted with every bit of strength she had. "Into the cage!"

Growling and resisting, the lion retreated paw by paw.

Another guard tried to strike her kehok, but Raia jumped toward the guard and knocked his club to the side. With her focus broken, the lion surged forward, knocking the same guard—the one who had grabbed Raia—back down again.

Then Trainer Verlas was there. "Back into the cage!"

Together, Trainer Verlas and Raia focused their will on the lion. He made a whimpering kind of sound, eyed the prone guard, and then walked back into the cage calmly, as if he hadn't attacked.

Rushing forward, Raia slammed the cage door shut and latched it.

"What happened?" Trainer Verlas demanded. She glared at all the onlookers who had gathered. "Show's over," she barked at them. "Go back to your tents."

They scattered like gazelle.

"I don't know," Raia said. "He—" She turned to point at the guard, but during all the chaos, he'd slipped away and run. She had a terrible thought. A terrible, wonderful thought.

Turning back to the cage, she unlatched it again.

"Raia, don't!" Trainer Verlas barked.

The lion didn't budge. Raia grabbed the bowl of meat and pulled it out of the cage. Trainer Verlas shut the door and locked it.

Hands shaking, Raia pulled the vial with the poison-testing powder out of her tunic pocket. She sprinkled it on the meat. It sizzled the instant it touched.

Both Raia and Trainer Verlas stared in horror.

He knew! The lion had known—not only had he avoided the poisoned meat, but he'd targeted the one responsible and found a way to communicate all of that to his rider. "You clever boy," she murmured. To Trainer Verlas, she said, "The guard, the one he attacked, tried to keep me from testing it."

Trainer Verlas snarled to the remaining guards, "Who was he? Where did he go?"

One of the guards sputtered, "H-h-he was newly assigned. Came with all the correct paperwork—"

"I suggest you catch him," Trainer Verlas said, with all the coiled fury of a chained kehok. "And hope the emperor-to-be is lenient about this negligence."

Two of the guards immediately sprinted through the crowd, leaving one remaining by the cage. Until they returned, Raia swore she'd stay up and guard the lion. She felt herself begin to shake and didn't know if it was from fear or rage or pride. *He tried to hurt—kill!—my lion!* But her lion had been too smart for him. Luckily. "I won't let anyone hurt you," Raia swore.

Yorbel and Shalla jogged over to join them. "What happened?" Yorbel demanded.

In a low voice, Trainer Verlas explained what had occurred. Raia pressed closer to the cage. As far as she could tell, he looked well. He didn't seem to have eaten any of the poisoned meat. *Somehow he knew. And he was trying to tell me.* He'd kept his claws retracted when he pounced. He could have savaged that guard before anyone could stop him. *But he didn't.*

"You're good," she whispered to him.

He met her eyes with his beautiful, sad golden ones.

"Do you know that?" she asked.

And he, to her shock, nodded his head.

That's impossible, she thought. Kehoks couldn't understand concepts like that. Orders, yes. Verbs. A few nouns. But an idea like "good"? Even though she'd always claimed she had a powerful connection with the black lion, she hadn't thought it was anything like this. And she definitely didn't think he was this aware a few weeks ago. She wondered if it was possible that his mind was growing.

Or that he was remembering who he used to be.

She wanted to ask him more questions, to see how much

he understood about who he was and where he was and what they were trying to do. But there were still too many people around, lingering to see if there was going to be any more drama, gossiping about what they'd seen. She couldn't let other people know he was different.

But she could know it in her heart. *I'm right about him. I know I am.* Somehow a piece of him knew what he was and who he had been, or sensed it. Touching the bronze lion pin on her rider's uniform, she thought of Prince Dar and wished she had a way to tell him that a part of his brother still lived on.

At least until the assassins kill him, Raia thought, her hope dashed once again.

It didn't even occur to her how close she was to her kehok's cage—that, if he wanted to, he could have ended her life right then.

Instead, they both stared out into the night, as if they somehow could see their enemies coming.

CHAPTER 25

Dar hated all the subterfuge. He also hated the musicians he'd hired to obscure his sensitive conversations. Calling today's contingent of personal guards into his throne room, he paced in front of them. "I have a problem," he announced.

The head guard bowed. "We live to serve."

"By the River, I hope not. You should serve to live." He then winced at himself. That was one of those un-emperor-like statements that always made Zarin laugh, right before his brother would caution him never to say that out loud. "Never mind. My problem is that I wish to consult with my racing team about strategy before the final race tomorrow, without fear that someone will overhear and share with my competitors or use that knowledge to help their bets. But spying on me seems to be everyone's favorite hobby. Any thoughts on how I can have a chat without feeling as if my every word is being sold to the highest bidder?"

The horrendous music had worked well for a while, but

by now most of courtiers had caught onto his trick. A few of them had even showed up holding their own instruments, in the hopes of getting close enough to hear something interesting between the squeaks and squeals. Others simply bribed the musicians.

"Vigilance," the guard said. "We will ensure no one comes close enough to overhear."

"So you've been only halfheartedly guarding me until now?" Dar knew that wasn't the case, but honestly, if the man was going to make such a unhelpful suggestion . . . The whole idea behind this conversation was to make his guards feel more personally invested. It was, he thought, a different approach than his brother, but he still thought Zarin would have approved. "Any rooms that my predecessors used that are spy-proof?"

Another guard stepped forward. "Your Excellence, your brother preferred the aviary."

"I know that. He liked to visit the river hawk that was once our mother . . ." He trailed off. The aviary was, by his brother's imperial order, kept empty so Zarin could visit their mother in solitude. *Clever, Zarin.* He felt a pang—his brother was again helping him, even after death. "An excellent idea. I'll visit her as well. Please lead the sweep to ensure it is empty—courtiers, servants, everyone. If I learn afterward that I've been overheard, I will hold you personally responsible."

The guard bowed. "It will be done."

Barking at a contingent of guards, she led them marching out of the room. He stood, smiled at the remaining guards, and said, "The races are thrilling, aren't they? Are you excited for tomorrow's championship race?"

At that, the guards began to chatter, sharing their

thoughts and predictions. Many confessed they'd bet on his racer. It was a pleasant way to spend the minutes while he waited for the aviary to be prepared and his guests to arrive.

When a servant signaled that all was ready, he strolled between his talkative guards out of the throne room and through the halls. Drifting out from where she waited by a pillar, Lady Nori matched pace with him.

He grinned at her. "Sneaky. I didn't even see you there."

"It's impossible to be alone with you these days."

He waved at his guards. "This is hardly alone."

"Closer to alone than we are in the stands, watching the races. Besides, if you can't trust your guards, who can you trust?" But she peeked between them anyway, as if expecting to spot a palace spy, or just one of the court gossips, and then she bowed and said, "Your Excellence, apologies for the interruption."

Dar smiled at her. "You don't need to apologize, and you know I'm not excellent."

"I'm glad to see you looking happy."

"I'd say 'hopeful.' Not happy." He thought of one thing that would make him happy, but it wouldn't be fair to Nori to spring that on her. Not when everything was so complicated. He settled on saying, "I'm happier now that you're here." Then he winced, because he knew better than to be so honest in court. It was a thing that Zarin was always shaking his head at. *You can't just go saying what you feel, Dar,* Zarin used to say. *They'll use it against you, any way they can.*

Nori wrinkled her nose in that way he loved. "I wish I'd cornered you with news that would make you happier." She lowered her voice. "I have heard rumors about the ambassador of Ranir. It's said he's been bribing augurs to delay the search for your late brother's vessel, and it's said he has the full resources of the king of Ranir's treasury to draw from. Far beyond a mere ambassador's typical funds. It's also said that the movement of Raniran troops on the border is more than mere 'military exercises.'"

"Augurs are immune to bribes," Dar said. Their treasury was vast—augurs had no need of personal wealth when they had the vast resources of the temples at their disposal—and they were committed, by both training and temperament, to the purity of their souls. "And I am aware of the troop movements." His generals kept him updated, as well as voicing their increasing frustration at their inability to do anything substantial about the massing army. Without imperial orders, they could do little but increase their standard patrols. He wondered if it would take an invasion for his generals to agree to break with tradition—and law—and defend Becar. Surely, if the threat grew serious enough, they'd rally, even at risk to themselves. In the meantime, he had a real enemy to find, one already within the palace, not across the desert.

"Dar . . . I think it's more than merely flexing their muscles. If Ranir believes we're weak—"

He'd heard Ambassador Usan at the Listening—Ranir was an ever-present threat but not an imminent one. There were many more close-to-home dangers for Dar to worry about, such as unrest within the capital city itself. He didn't deny that Ranir was a threat, but he questioned how much damage one man, far from his home, could do.

But Nori only meant to help. "Thanks for telling me," he said.

She'd taken a risk in talking to him outside the public eye. Until he was crowned emperor, it was a political gamble to be seen as being linked too closely to him. If he failed to be crowned and Lady Nori was known to be loyal to him . . .

She placed her hand on his. Her hand was soft, uncalloused, and warm. "I just . . . worry about Becar."

She said Becar; he heard *you*. He stared into her eyes, barely noticing that he'd stopped walking. "I have every hope that this waiting period will be over soon."

Her stunning smile spread across her face, and she took a step closer to him. "That's wonderful news! You've located your brother's vessel?"

He hated lying to her nearly as much as he hated not talking to her. "Not yet. But I have faith that he will be found. There's a finite number of creatures in Becar, after all. It's merely a matter of time."

Stepping back, Nori withdrew her hand. "Time is something you might not have, if the ambassador is actively working against you to prime Becar for an invasion."

Dar went very still, hating himself for the thought that went through his mind. "Nori—are you asking me to step aside?" He kept his voice as soft as possible, but he still heard the nearest guard hiss.

She looked so appalled that he almost smiled. "Of course not!"

He reached out and took her hand this time. "Sorry. I didn't mean . . . I've been on edge lately. Forgive me?"

She let out a frustrated huff. "I'd *never* ask you to sacrifice yourself. I merely . . . Dar, just watch yourself around Ambassador Usan, all right? He's not to be trusted."

"I will," he promised.

They reached the aviary doors, and she retreated. He watched her go, wishing the conversation had ended differently, wishing he'd had the courage to tell her how he felt—though a piece of him whispered, *She already knows.*

She'd risked her reputation and her future safety to warn him. Wasn't that a sign that she cared? And she wasn't wrong—the ambassador was a threat. Just low on an ever-growing list of them.

It *was* worth considering the fact that Ambassador Usan had access to a vast treasury. That was valuable information he hadn't fully considered. Drawing on a king's funds, Usan could have afforded a charm to turn a man into a kehok.

The more Dar thought about it, the more he believed it to be possible. If the king of Ranir were planning an invasion, destabilizing Becar from the top would be a brilliant move. Dar had studied enough history to know that Becar's strength—an emperor guided by the purity of the augurs—was also its weakness. Becar had never been without a crowned emperor for so long. *We're ripe for conquering.*

Thank you, Nori, he thought. *You may be more right than you know.*

She would make a spectacular wife and empress.

He mulled over Usan's possible treachery as he left his guards and entered the aviary alone. The peaceful quiet, punctuated by birdcalls and the rustling of leaves, descended on him. Centuries old, the aviary used to be his brother's favorite place. It was filled with lush trees and flowers that wouldn't survive outside this glass enclosure. All the winding paths were mosaics, and hidden fountains were tucked into the bushes, creating tiny pools for the birds who lived here.

He missed his brother so terribly that for an instant, he couldn't breathe.

It kept striking like that these days. He'd think he was fine. He'd be moving forward, focusing on the problems of the country or even more simply what to wear that day or whether he liked a particular soup, and a memory would strike him, leaving him feeling as if he'd plunged into a hole.

He walked through the aviary, carrying his grief with him, until he reached a courtyard with a circle of chairs carved to look like waves of water. A river hawk was perched on the back of one.

"Mother," he said.

Startled, the hawk spread her wings as if to take flight. She only managed a sort of hopping fall to the ground, before scurrying in between the bushes. She'd had her wings clipped. She never seemed to remember him as well as she'd remembered Zarin.

"Your Excellence?" a guard called across the aviary. "Your guests have arrived."

"I am here," he called back.

He composed himself, forcing back thoughts of his mother and his brother, as the rider Raia, her trainer, Augur Yorbel, and Lady Evara were led into the courtyard. All of them bowed. He gestured to the chairs. "Please, sit. Make yourselves comfortable. I believe I have found a location where we can, at least for the time being, speak freely."

"It's beautiful," Raia said, looking around. "You could almost believe it wasn't a cage."

"Raia," the trainer muttered.

Raia blushed. "Oh! I didn't mean . . . Forgive me, Your Excellence! It's only . . . My family had an aviary, but you could see the walls and the wire mesh above. With the glass, the birds have the sky. I think that's wonderful."

"My brother loved this place," Dar said, and then his

throat clogged. He cleared it, as if he'd merely swallowed wrong. "But I asked you here for a purpose, not pleasantries. Rider Raia, congratulations on all your wins. Trainer Verlas, how are our prospects for tomorrow's championship race?"

"She can win, if people will stop trying to murder our racer," Trainer Verlas said.

The word "murder" felt like cold water being thrown in his face.

Lady Evara rolled her eyes. "Forgive her, Your Excellence. I've often considered Trainer Verlas's bluntness to be a virtue, but I recognize that not everyone agrees with me."

Dar tried not to look as alarmed as he felt. "Tell me all."

Trainer Verlas described an attempted attack on the lion in the stables. Most of it he'd heard when Lady Evara requested the use of palace guards for the kehok, but he'd assumed it was an accident. The trainer, though, was clear that she did *not* consider it an accident. She suspected that the latches had been weakened on purpose. She believed it was too great a coincidence that the three kehoks with weakened latches also had loose shackles and also aimed their attack at the same target—she believed the attack was orchestrated and guided. After listening to her, Dar was inclined to agree.

"We should arrest the suspect trainer," he said.

"With all due respect," Lady Evara said, "our sneaky little trainer is no longer a threat, and we should be focusing our attention in other directions."

"But we can't let this criminal walk free—not when there's only one race that stands between us and an end to this! We can't allow anything to interfere with tomorrow."

"Precisely my point," Lady Evara said. "The racing commission has been alerted. They view any attempt to tamper with race results as the ultimate crime. She is being interrogated and will be dealt with. At the very least she won't dare make another attempt. But she is not the only threat." Lady Evara related how a courtier had approached her with a threat of blackmail and an offer of riches. She named the man as Lady Nori's cousin, Lord Petalo, a man known for his heavy gambling on the races. She wasn't specific about the details of the blackmail, but Dar considered that a lesser issue.

Lady Evara added: "Just for the record, I did *not* try to poison the kehok." She smiled at them as she said that, as if expecting great praise for not committing treason and murder.

Raia picked up the story, describing how a palace guard, or someone impersonating one, had attempted to poison the black lion. The suspect had fled. "We're watching his food even more carefully now," she said. "It won't happen again. And the lion is helping—he knows not to eat until I've tested his food."

"Uncanny," Trainer Verlas muttered.

Dar heard her. "What do you mean?"

"He's a highly intelligent kehok."

My brother was a highly intelligent man, Dar thought.

"No, Dar," Yorbel said quietly, as if sensing his thoughts. "He may have your brother's soul, but he does not possess his mind. He is *not* your brother. He has the mind of a monster now, with all its limitations."

Raia jumped in. "But he didn't kill a man when he could have."

That's true, Dar thought. Was it so terrible for him to hope that some vestige of his brother survived whatever was done to him? After all, Zarin had come regularly to talk to the river hawk who had been their mother, claiming she carried some of her memories. It was said memories, at least the strongest ones, could return through exposure to past loved ones.

"Details aside, it remains that the poisoner is still out there," Lady Evara said, "as is the one who hired him or her. . . . According to all I've been able to discover, Lord Petalo does not have access to the kind of funds he claims to. I believe that the corrupt trainer, the poisoner, and Lord Petalo are all puppets. Which means there will be other attempts."

Raia let out a gasp.

"As much as I love surprises, perhaps there's something we could do to minimize the effectiveness of our next aspiring assassin," Lady Evara said. "Like, ooh, I know, set a trap!" She said it as if the idea had jumped into her head.

Dar didn't believe for an instant that it was a thought she'd spontaneously had. Lady Evara was far more intelligent than she pretended to be. She'd merely been waiting for the right moment to introduce her idea. "Go on."

"Instead of waiting to be surprised by our puppet master's next move, why not present an appealing opening and see who rushes to claim it?"

"Terrible idea," Trainer Verlas said.

Lady Evara pouted. "I think it's brilliant."

"You want to use my rider and racer as bait!" Trainer Verlas scowled at Lady Evara. "For one, it's too risky. For another, Raia and the lion should be focusing on preparing for the final race, not being distracted by playing bait. I won't permit it."

Lady Evara let out a tinkling laugh. "Darling, you are in the presence of the emperor-to-be. I don't really think it's your place to permit or not permit anything. Besides, worrying about another murder attempt is already quite a distraction." She flashed a charming smile at Dar. "Your Excellence, of course, it's your decision."

He considered it. "Your rider and racer are already targets. If we can anticipate when and where the next attack will be, it would give us a measure of control that we don't currently have." *And it would be nice to control something,* Dar thought. As it was, nothing in his life felt under control. If he could flush the ambassador of Ranir out into the open, it might be enough to convince the generals to act to defend the border even without a formal imperial order. "Yorbel, what are your thoughts?"

Yorbel looked startled, as if he'd hoped to blend into the greenery. "I . . . Couldn't we simply increase security? All we must do is protect the kehok until he wins the final race." His eyes slid over to Trainer Verlas, as if he were looking for her approval.

"This is the best way to protect him," Lady Evara said. "Catching an assassin in the act could even lead to unmasking our puppet master. Wouldn't it be lovely to know who is behind these attempts? It could be separate coincidences, or a pattern that points to one powerful, wealthy enemy. Don't you want to know which? If this all works and you're crowned emperor, your enemies aren't going to—*poof*—vanish."

"She's right," Raia said. "We'll do it."

"Raia!" Trainer Verlas snapped.

"I'm willing," Raia said stubbornly.

Dar admired that. "You have my gratitude." She had it twice now, the first being when she gave him hope that Zarin had been the man he thought he was. "Lady Evara is correct. If there's a chance to identify and stop this enemy, that's what we should do." Especially if it were the same enemy who used a charm against Zarin. If he could expose *that* enemy . . . he could achieve both redemption and revenge for his brother. "Let's discuss specifics."

TAMRA HATED THEIR PLAN.

It was simple, which she was assured by Raia, Yorbel, and the emperor-to-be meant that there were fewer ways it could go wrong. *I do not feel reassured.* All she had to do was leave Raia and the kehok on the racetrack for a few minutes.

By tradition, before the final races, every trainer was granted fifteen minutes with their rider and racer on the racetrack in private. You were supposed to use the time to work out any nerves, refine strategies, practice techniques— you *weren't* supposed to play bait in a trap. But the wheels were already in motion. Lady Evara had spread word, amid her "twinkling," that her rider was so confident of her abilities that she planned to use her time to bond with her racer on the track without her trainer. She'd be alone.

Of course, Tamra was nearby, hidden beneath the stands, ready in case the attack came in the form of other kehoks. And of course, the emperor-to-be had deployed several of his most trusted guards to rush in in case of a human attack. A few of his best archers were hidden in the stands as well. As Lady Evara had put it, "They'll be safer in these fifteen minutes than they are at any other time during the whole Becaran Races."

Tamra had felt even less reassured after that. The races were never safe.

Squeezed into her hiding place with her was Lady Evara herself, though she was blessedly silent now that the fifteen minutes had begun. Peeking out, they watched Raia and the racer run a lap. At the end of the lap, Raia dismounted and came around to her kehok's face.

Lady Evara whispered, "What's she doing now?"

"Talking to him," Tamra whispered back. Wasn't that obvious?

"She's too fond of him," Lady Evara noted. "You should speak to her about that. Augur Yorbel is right—whatever he used to be, he's a monster now."

But Tamra was no longer sure that was true.

Raia backed away from her kehok, then turned and walked slowly down the length of the track. The kehok watched her, motionless.

"Now what's she doing?"

"Testing her control," Tamra said. It was similar to the exercise they'd done on Raia's very first day—call a kehok to her. *Clever girl,* Tamra thought. If she wanted to make the bait more appealing, separating from the kehok was a smart way to do that. Both of them looked even more vulnerable.

But what if this time the killer decided to target Raia instead of the kehok?

If the enemy hated the emperor-to-be, then targeting the kehok was logical. However, if the enemy hated Tamra or simply wanted to fix the races, then—

"Ooh, what's this?" Lady Evara clutched Tamra's arm.

A woman was walking onto the track. Tamra squinted, trying to see who it was. She didn't appear to be armed, and Raia didn't look as though she was afraid. "I'm going out there." Tamra started to stand.

Lady Evara held her back. "See how it unfolds."

"She could have a knife or—"

"She's making the universal sign of *I'm not going to stab you.*" Lady Evara jutted her chin at the track, where the woman was approaching Raia with both hands raised, palms out. The woman halted a few yards away from Raia.

Now that she was closer, Tamra could see—*Yes, I know her.* Or more accurately, Raia did. "It's Raia's mother," Tamra said flatly.

Lady Evara released her arm. "Maybe you *should* go out there. Nothing can mess with a person's head more than family. My dear parents still mess with mine, and they're dead."

"Agreed." Tamra began to move, but Lady Evara caught her arm again.

"Wait, no. Changed my mind. If you go, it wrecks the illusion that Raia's on her own. The killer won't show himself. Just wait and watch. Her mother won't hurt her. Raia's her ticket to wealth."

Looking out, Tamra swore that if Raia looked the least bit distressed, even if Raia didn't signal that she was in danger, she was going out there. *I wish I could hear what they're saying.*

RAIA WALKED AWAY FROM HER LION. SHE FELT HIS EYES on her back, watching her. It was a risk to experiment with how much she could trust him. But with guards watching them from the shadows and Trainer Verlas nearby, she couldn't think of a better time to test her theory.

He won't hurt me, and he won't leave me.

She made it to the end of the track without looking back and turned around. The lion remained where she'd left him. He was still watching her.

She had not used a single command to keep him there. She had merely explained what she wanted him to do. Even now, she wasn't reaching out to control him, and he wasn't trying to flee or fight.

This wasn't how ordinary kehoks behaved.

Smiling, she began to head back to him when she saw a

figure walk onto the track. She tensed, and then she saw who it was and tensed some more: *Mother.*

"I'm training, Mother," Raia said.

"I heard your trainer isn't here. You're just playing."

"This is private training time. You shouldn't be here. Why did the guards let you through?" She wondered if Mother had sneaked past them. Or bribed them. Or . . .

"Because I'm your mother! Raia . . ." She took another step toward Raia, and Raia took a step backward. Mother stopped, a healthy distance away. "I want you to know that your father and I deeply regret our behavior. The truth is we were scared about the future. About your future, and about ours. Our fortunes have always been precarious, and when you left the augur school—"

"When I failed," Raia corrected her.

"Suddenly, all our dreams vanished. You must understand that we thought we were doing what was best for all of us. We never meant to drive you away from us."

Raia wished she could believe her. She'd always wanted the kind of mother who put her children first. But she remembered too many nights when she'd woken screaming from a nightmare, and her mother had come in and told her to be quiet, that children were to be seen and not heard. She remembered the first time her parents had paraded her in front of their friends, as if she were some clever trinket they'd bought, and then shooed her upstairs with orders to stay there until their party was over, forgetting she hadn't eaten and couldn't reach the kitchen without crossing the party room. She'd been hungry while the adults dined on sugar dates and other delicacies. Until Celin, there had never been a moment that tipped the scales into unbearably cruel, but it had been a hundred little things every day that said "we don't love you," even before her parents had tried to sign away her freedom.

"You never cared about me. Only about what I could get you. That hasn't changed."

"Oh, my baby, we want to try to make it up to you," Mother said. She had tears in her eyes, and Raia couldn't help but think they were real. Mother wasn't that good an actress. She believed what she was saying. "Your father and I . . . we see we were terrible parents. You were a sensitive child, and we didn't give you the love and affection you needed. I suppose it took an event like Celin's death for us to realize it—and even then, we realized it too late. We treated you unkindly. We took you for granted and didn't appreciate the fine woman you've become. Seeing you race on that track . . . Raia, we are so very proud of you."

She was saying everything that Raia had always dreamed she'd say. With all her heart, she wanted to run into her mother's arms and say *I forgive you.* But she didn't move. It was too easy. Even if Mother had good intentions, that didn't mean her actions were right. Especially what she'd done, or tried to do, with Raia and her so-called fiancé. "You said I'd be free of you if I won, witnessed by an augur. But you never thought I'd win. And now that I'm one race away from winning the grand championship, you're regretting letting me go."

"That's right," Mother said, more earnest than Raia had ever seen her. Raia felt tears prick her own eyes. "We only agreed because we thought we'd never lose you. Facing that loss now . . . it's made us realize all that we're losing. We want to try again, Raia, to be the parents you deserve."

Raia took a step toward her. "I want to believe you." She ached to believe with all her heart. All the memories, all the times she'd felt unloved—she'd wanted this moment so badly!

Mother crossed to her and clasped her hands. "Then believe us, darling."

Maybe she could believe her. If they wanted to apologize at long last, then shouldn't she at least give them a chance to—*Wait a minute.*

Them.

"Where's Father?"

"We're trying to be the parents you need." Mother's grip on Raia's hands tightened. Raia tried to pull away. "Please understand. Everything we do is for love of you. So you can have the future you should have."

It was as she said those words, so similar to what she'd said when they bargained for her engagement to Celin, that Raia realized this was about more than her mother trying to worm her way out of the agreement they'd made. Twisting, Raia yanked her hands out of her mother's grip.

"*Run!*" she shouted at her kehok, with both her voice and her mind.

Her lion ran.

But he didn't run away, as she'd ordered. He ran *toward* her.

As he did, she heard a *whoosh* and saw an arc of fire burst onto the racetrack. It impacted exactly where the lion had been standing waiting for her, and the flames spread—oil was pouring onto the track, and the fire raced along it.

From the stands, the palace guards were shouting. She saw Trainer Verlas burst out of her hiding place, and without thinking, Raia ran toward her lion.

Smoke billowed.

She couldn't see him!

Flames filled the width of the track, roaring toward the sky. She skidded to a stop as the heat slammed into her, and Trainer Verlas yanked her backward, pulling her away. *No! My lion!* She fought her, trying to get back to the fire.

And then she saw a dark shadow in the middle of the fiery red, and her lion leaped out of the heart of the flames. He landed in the sands and let out a roar.

Fire licked over his metal body, and he shook, shedding sparks in every direction. He then ran toward her. She opened her arms.

"Stop!" Trainer Verlas commanded.

Come! Raia called.

He lowered his head as he ran past her, and Raia jumped. She grabbed on to his mane and swung herself up onto his back. He kept running. His metal body was hot, just short of searing her hands, but there was no way she was letting go.

Reaching the end of the racetrack, he didn't slow. Instead he leaped over the gate. *Faster,* she thought. *Away!* He ran through the camp, past the other riders and trainers and kehoks, and then beyond the crowds gathered to watch the next race.

He kept running into the desert beyond.

Only when she had control again, when the fear wasn't coursing through her veins stronger than blood, did he slow.

"You could have run away," Raia said. "I told you to. But you ran toward me. To save me." Leaning forward, she hugged his neck.

He came to a stop, and she slid off his back. She stood in front of him.

He regarded her with his golden eyes.

"You wanted to protect me," she said.

He inclined his head.

"My parents tried to kill you. And I don't know why. It doesn't even make sense—the more I win, the more gold for them—unless that was just another twisted way to try to control my future? By taking you from me?" She wrapped her arms around his still-hot neck. "No one will take you from me."

Unless we do win, she thought. If they won the victory charm, he'd be killed and reborn as a human baby. He wouldn't know her or remember any of this, and he wouldn't be her lion anymore. "I'll visit you, when you're human again. I can be your crazy aunt Raia who once won the Becaran Races."

He rolled his golden tongue out of his mouth and, like a mother cat, licked her cheek. It felt like sandpaper against her skin. She laughed.

"You know, we could just leave. Run away, you and me. No one would ever catch us, or hurt us, if we ran far enough and fast enough." As she said it, she knew she didn't want that—to never see Trainer Verlas again, to always be living on the run, to be afraid again.

He sat down and curled his tail around himself, as if he didn't plan to run anywhere.

"You don't want to do that," she said. "You want to go back?"

He nodded his head.

So do I, she thought. *They can't make me run away again. I choose to run, on the racetrack, toward the finish line. Not away from anything.* "You understand everything I'm saying, don't you? And everything that's going on?"

Another nod.

"Do you . . ." She licked her lips. It was a crazy question, but she had to ask it. "Do you remember who you were?" No one remembered their past life. It wasn't possible.

He hesitated. Shook his head. Then nodded. Then tilted his head to the side.

"You're not sure? But you might? You were Emperor Zarin, emperor of all the Becar Empire." She held her breath, studying his face. His golden eyes were fixed on her. "Your brother was Dar, who is now the emperor-to-be. He can't be crowned until you're found, but if you're found as a kehok . . . The brother of a kehok can't be emperor. The emperor-to-be's only hope is if you win and are reborn."

He began to trot past her, back toward the racetrack. He then stopped and looked at her, as if he wanted her to follow. She ran to catch up to him. "Do you remember him? Your brother? You called him Dar."

He pawed the sand. Yes? Did that mean yes? She climbed onto him, and he began to walk at a steady pace, not slow but not hurrying either. Saving his energy for the next race?

"You want to race?" she asked him. "You want to win?"

He did keep walking implacably toward the racetrack. She wondered if she'd imagined it when she thought he understood her. Maybe she'd wanted that so badly that she convinced herself they were having a conversation. Or maybe a piece of him knew who he was, or at least knew this wasn't what he was supposed to be.

She'd promised him freedom if he won the races.

Maybe he didn't know who he was, but she thought he knew exactly what that meant: freedom from what he'd become.

If that was what he wanted, then she would do everything in her power to ensure he had that chance. "We will win," Raia promised. "The killers—" She stopped. It felt so strange to refer to her parents that way, but that's what they were. By now, they would be on their way to a jail somewhere, charged with trying to interfere with the championship race. Or maybe even treason. She wondered if they were behind the poison attempt, or even the loose latches in the stable. Her parents could have orchestrated all of it, some convoluted attempt to "save" their daughter. It might have had nothing to do with emperors and successions at all. *If so, we're safe now.*

"The killers have been caught," she said to both the lion and herself. One good thing had come out of this: "No one can stop us now."

CHAPTER 26

Standing at the edge of camp, watching the wind blow sand across the desert dunes, Tamra told herself she was *not* worried.

"You're worried," Yorbel said.

She glared at him. "Raia will come back. She has before."

Tamra went back to staring at the desert, as if that would make Raia and the lion reappear. She was glad she'd sent Shalla to the temple for her lessons. She didn't need to know about any of this. Tamra wished she could have protected Raia too. "Raia shouldn't have to worry about any of this. She should be focused on the races and that's it. She's just a kid!"

After a moment's hesitation, Yorbel reached over and took her hand. He held it lightly, as if he'd never touched a hand before. "It's funny—as an augur, I am supposed to always know the right thing to say. Lately, I never do. Tell me how I can help you."

She wanted to tell him that she didn't need anything

from anyone. But instead she squeezed his hand and said, "Just wait with me."

Both of them waited, hand in hand, standing together on the sand, until at last the silhouette of a girl and a lion appeared on the horizon. Tamra felt as if chains were loosening around her. She could breathe fully again.

When Raia and the kehok reached them, she dismounted, and Tamra crossed the feet between them in two strides and folded Raia into her arms. Stepping back, she examined her— she seemed unharmed. The lion stood quietly beside her like a tame pet.

"My parents?" Raia asked.

"In custody," Tamra said. "They won't be able to hurt you again." She hesitated, unsure how much she should say. It was likely her parents would be imprisoned for many years. "They claimed they wanted to 'save' their daughter from the corrupting influence of kehoks and racing."

Raia laughed, a hollow sound. "Who is going to save me from the corrupting influence of my parents?"

"I am," Tamra said. "And Shalla and Yorbel. Your friends from the training grounds." She wasn't quite sure of their names, but she knew Raia was fond of them. "Even that monster. You aren't alone."

Her lips trembling, Raia still managed to smile. "I know."

She seems all right. Tamra wished she knew what Raia's mother had said to her, how much damage she'd done. She wondered how much more of the truth to tell her—would it hurt her more, or would it help? "They also said it wasn't their idea. They were offered a vast amount of gold—"

"Of course they were."

Beside her, the lion growled.

Tamra shot him a look, wondering if he was responding to her words or to Raia's emotion. He had to be feeding off her emotion; he couldn't understand what was going on. Even as intelligent as he was, there were limits. He wasn't the man he had been. "It was more than they would have received if you'd won."

"Who bought them?" Raia's voice was utterly flat.

She's not all right, Tamra thought. As gently as she could, she answered the question. "They claim they never saw him or her." That was the part that Tamra hadn't wanted to say, to admit that the enemy was still out there, unknown and dangerous.

Raia wrapped one arm around her kehok, as if for comfort. "But it's over for now?"

It's not over. Whoever hired Raia's parents, whoever was behind the attempt to bribe Lady Evara, whoever encouraged the fake guard to try to poison the kehok would try again. It could all be the same enemy, or it could be multiple enemies. All they'd done with their trap and everything they'd risked was remove a few puppets from the stage. "For now."

"Then we should rest before the next race."

Tamra's heart ached for her. "You'll have extra time. The championship race has been delayed so that the track can be fixed. We'll be returning to the royal stables until it's ready."

"Good."

Tamra nodded. But deep down, she was still worried.

Because this delay could have been part of the plan too.

ESCORTED BY THE EMPEROR-TO-BE'S GUARDS, RAIA TRIED not to think about anything as she rode on a cart back to the royal stables. Plenty of gawkers lined the streets, watching them pass, but she barely saw them through the thick column of soldiers.

When they reached the royal stables beside the palace, she let the heavy silence wrap around her, smothering all her thoughts and feelings. Rejecting Trainer Verlas's offer to help, Raia unlatched the cage and guided the kehok into the stable—after the guards had thoroughly checked the building and pronounced it safe. "I want to sleep in the stable tonight," Raia told her trainer.

"I will as well," Trainer Verlas offered.

"I'd rather be alone. Just the lion and me." She didn't know if her trainer would be offended by that, but she didn't want anyone around her tonight.

"Then I'll sleep outside the door. If you need me, all you have to do is call out."

Trainer Verlas excused herself to arrange for cots to be provided, while Raia checked on the lion's food and water. She tested both with the anti-poison powder, even though the guards had already done it. She then shut the lion into his stall without shackling him.

"I don't want to leave you helpless," she told him. "I'm trusting you not to hurt me."

He made a sound that was nearly a meow, and she laughed in spite of herself, in spite of everything. It was such an innocent sound, as if he were trying to say how could anyone think he'd ever hurt anyone. "Yeah, that's right, you're just a sweet kitty cat."

She settled in and tried to think of nothing. The worst part about her parents' betrayal was how surprised she'd been. She *knew* what they were like, knew what they were capable of. They'd shown their true selves time and time again, and she still hoped she was wrong about them. They were never going to be the kind of parents she wanted, the kind who loved her as she was. *They do love me, in their own way,* she thought. *It's just that they love themselves more.*

"Raia?" Trainer Verlas said through the door. "You have a visitor. I . . . don't think I can send him away. I'm sorry."

Raia took a deep breath to steady herself, guessing who her "visitor" was before Trainer Verlas even finished. She touched her bronze lion pin. "It's fine. I'm fine."

"It was a difficult thing that happened today. You don't have to be 'fine.'"

She wished that were true, but now wasn't the time to fall apart and let herself feel things. She told herself that her parents' actions were nothing new. They'd been consistent throughout her whole life, culminating in her engagement to Celin and today's attempt to kill her racer. She couldn't keep letting it surprise and hurt her. But it did every time.

"You can let him in," Raia said.

Opening the door, Trainer Verlas bowed as the emperor-to-be walked into the stables. He hadn't tried to dress as anything other than himself this time. His embroidered robe swept over the muck on the stable floor, and Raia thought about saying something, but she didn't know if that would be appropriate.

"He wasn't hurt?" Prince Dar asked.

"Not at all." She liked that that was his first question.

"And you? Were you hurt?"

"I wasn't . . . because he tried to protect me." She didn't know if he'd understand the significance of that. She knew it didn't match anything she'd ever been told about kehoks and their behavior. "That's not what ordinary kehoks do. I don't know if he remembers anything about who he was, but Your Excellence, he's not a monster."

Prince Dar looked at her as if she'd gifted him with the moon. He was shaking as he approached the stall. "Zarin? Do you know me?"

The lion lifted his head.

"Open the door," Prince Dar commanded.

"He's not shackled," Raia warned. "If he attacks faster than I can react . . . I can't promise he won't hurt you."

"If any part of him is still Zarin, still *good*, I believe he won't."

She believed he wouldn't too. It was nice to have another who saw him the same way. "My trainer would say this is stupid." She then added, "Your Excellence."

He flashed her a smile. "I've done plenty of stupid things."

She was relieved he wasn't offended. She ventured to say, "You know that's a reason to feel lucky, not a reason to do more. Maybe if I come in the stall with you?" She could soothe the lion, watch him carefully, and be ready.

He nodded his permission. "That sounds wise."

Raia unlocked the stable. Murmuring to the lion, she knelt beside him. She stroked his mane, the smooth metal cool under her fingertips. He seemed calm.

The emperor-to-be dropped to one knee in front of the lion. He held out his hand, palm up, as if greeting a dog. The lion stretched his neck, sniffed one finger, and then retreated. "I'm Dar. Your brother. And I miss you."

She couldn't tell if the lion understood or not.

"I miss how you used to tell me to watch my step every time we walked into the throne room together, even though you were the one who always tripped on that River-damned mosaic floor. I miss how you used to insist on a pear with every meal, because Mother told you once it would make you healthy, even though you hated pears. I miss how you used to misquote poets on purpose, to make me laugh at the expressions on our tutor's face. I miss how you'd slip away after meetings and come find me—you said it was because you needed someone that you could talk to, and I was that someone. I miss being your someone."

The lion was listening.

Raia held still, not sure if Prince Dar had forgotten she was there or simply didn't care. She kept her hands on the lion's mane, ready in case he suddenly snapped. She trusted the lion not to hurt her, but this man was a stranger to him. Or he should have been.

Prince Dar buried his face in his hands.

The lion stood, and Raia tensed, ready. But the lion merely stepped forward and pressed his forehead against the emperor-to-be's, as if comforting him. The emperor-to-be lifted his head.

Raia held her breath.

They were inches away, face-to-face.

"Zarin?"

Prince Dar wrapped his arms around the lion's mane, like Raia had done, and the lion let him for several long minutes. Then the lion stepped backward, retreating to the corner of his stall, and sat, watching and silent.

"He remembers me," Prince Dar said, almost more of a question than a statement. "He's still my brother. At least a part of him."

Gently, Raia guided him out of the stall and shut and locked the door. Only then did she let her muscles unknot and her breathing return to normal. "He's special." He shouldn't be able to feel loyalty to her or to understand the need to win the races, and yet he clearly did. Maybe it was because a part of him did remember who he'd been.

"I'm going to find who did this to him," Prince Dar promised. Laying his hand on the stall door, he said, "I'll make this right, Zarin. I swear I will, by the Lady, by the River, by the souls of our parents . . . I swear I will."

The lion did not respond.

Maybe he remembers only sometimes? she wondered. *Like a dream? Or he remembers pieces?* She took a step backward, not wanting to interfere. It felt like such a private moment, and she was intruding. But she also didn't dare leave.

"Your parents," Prince Dar began, facing Raia.

Raia tensed. She wondered if he was about to blame her.

"I am sorry for how they treated you."

She blinked. That was unexpectedly kind. He was wrapped up in his own grief and misery, yet still managed to think of her. "Thank you, Your Excellence. I am glad they can't do any more harm." That was as much as she could say without her voice breaking. She knew it was wrong to be happy her parents would be jailed, and she wasn't *happy* precisely. . . . Relieved, maybe. Vindicated? Always, they'd blamed her for everything that happened, but it was their own choices that caused this, their own shortsighted selfishness that warped their view of reality.

"Mine died a long time ago," Prince Dar said. "It was just Zarin and me. And an entire empire's worth of people, I suppose, but it felt like just Zarin and me."

"Your Excellence . . ."

"Dar."

She hesitated.

He gave her a lopsided smile. "You've seen me bare my heart. I think that puts us on a first-name basis. You call me Dar, and I'll call you Raia, if that's all right with you."

"Dar," she repeated.

"You may be the bravest person I've ever met."

She felt herself blush. "Trainer Verlas has been teaching me. . . ."

"Not only on the racetrack. Here. Every day. You could have run, after the attack this afternoon. I'm told you escaped into the desert, but then you came back. Why did you come back?"

"Because . . ." There were at least a half-dozen reasons. Because of her future. Because of the lion. Because of Trainer Verlas and her daughter, Shalla. Because she didn't want to run away anymore. Because if she stayed, if she raced, if she won, then she was doing something extraordinary with her life, saving a dead emperor and helping crown a living one. "I wanted to."

He smiled. "That's a good enough reason." Stepping toward her, he took her hand and raised it to his heart. He held it there for a moment. "Thank you, brave Raia." Then the emperor-to-be of the great Becaran Empire bowed to her.

CHAPTER 27

Shortly before dawn on the day of the championship race, Ambassador Usan prepared a messenger wight. He'd been sending dozens of them over the past week, all with innocuous complaints about the sand or the food or the heat or the atrocious manners of the Becarans. *All true,* he thought. But all of them were designed to conceal the important updates. Namely, that Becar was on the brink.

He was confident that there would be riots after the final race, when people went to collect their winnings. Emotions were running high, and it would take only the slightest spark to ignite the fire. He'd bribed enough people to start that spark one way or another, and he'd bribed others to spread it once it started. There were always those who wanted to take advantage of chaos, even in a country as uptight as Becar.

Everything is in place, he thought.

Years of planning. Months of careful maneuvering, judicious bribes, and outright lawbreaking—and soon it would all pay off.

Carefully, he spoke the name of the recipient: his lover, Captain Sarna of the Third Battalion. She would see his message was relayed to the appropriate people, in particular the general himself. While the kehoks raced and the Becarans cheered, the Raniran army would be on the move. They'd cross the desert while the riots raged, and they'd surround the capital, a noose around the Heart of Becar. Meanwhile, the Becarans would be so involved in their own race-and-riot combo, they wouldn't even be aware—and those who were aware would be unable to act without an emperor to issue the proper orders. By dawn, while the Becarans stood in the wreckage of a nightlong riot, the Ranirans would be ready.

He released the messenger wight from the window and watched it soar smoothly over the Aur River, buoyed by the ever-present wind. It receded to a dot of white on the horizon. In it, he'd mentioned the exact time of the final race, all the while complaining about the barbarism of the vicious event.

What kind of people harnessed monsters for gambling?

In Ranir, you killed kehoks. You rounded them up and slaughtered them, for the safety of all. Certainly you didn't bring them in close proximity to your capital city and surround them with your wives, husbands, children, and elders. You didn't gather them in a single location within a few mere miles of your palace and temples. *Idiocy*, he thought. Any sensible Raniran knew that you kept kehoks *away* from your cities. You built towering walls and fortresses. You watched your borders. You didn't play with them, any more than you'd play with fire, and you certainly didn't bring hundreds of them together for sport; you hunted them down and destroyed them.

Fools, he thought.

But he had no choice but to attend. It was important that he be visible and therefore above reproach. He allowed his servants to dress him, and then he, with an escort, joined the thousands of spectators flowing toward the racetrack in the predawn light.

When my king comes, all of this will end.

IGNORING THE FLOOD OF SPECTATORS, RAIA SLIPPED behind the stands, toward the healer's tent. She wore her old tunic, the one she'd run away in, in hopes it would keep the crowd from recognizing her as one of the finalists, and was able to reach the tent without anyone stopping her.

Tucked away, the healer's tent was one of the few places within the racetrack grounds that qualified as quiet. There were no campsites nearby, no bleachers, no food stands. It was on the opposite side of the tracks as the holding area, yet close enough that emergencies could be funneled to it as quickly as possible.

Like Silar had been.

Raia gave her name to the gray-clad man at the door, as well as the name of the patient. He consulted his notes and waved her inside. She was grateful he didn't ask about the upcoming championship race or wish her luck—it was the last thing she wanted to talk about right now.

The tent was divided into rooms, with tarps separating them, and she heard murmurs from behind the heavy fabric. Sometimes she caught glimpses of patients: one covered in bandages from their waist down, one with burns over half his face, one missing an arm. Raia had been so focused on her own races, she hadn't realized how many riders got hurt each season. And these weren't even all of them. Plenty had been hurt earlier, in the qualifiers. It also didn't include the dead, like Fetran.

"Silar?" she called softly.

"Down here," a boy's voice called back. Jalimo stuck his head out from between tarps. "Hey, you should be preparing for your race."

"Don't stop her from being nice," Silar scolded from inside the room.

Her voice sounded fine. Raia slowed, bracing herself for what she'd find on the other side of the tarp. Silar had been injured a few days ago. For her to still be in the healer's tent meant that it hadn't been a minor injury.

With Jalimo holding the tarp door open, Raia ducked inside.

Silar lay on a cot, propped up by pillows. "He does have a point. These other losers don't have anything better to do, but you . . ." She pumped her fist into the air. "Go, champion-to-be!"

Beside her, seated on a stool, Algana said, "We're planning on cheering for you. As soon as the doctors find her a chair she can travel in."

Raia took a deep breath, trying to find the right words to ask how she was, what her prognosis was, and whether—

"Broken back," Silar said lightly, as if she were reporting on the weather. "It's permanent. I won't race again."

"Will you—"

"Or walk. It's all connected, you see."

"I'm so sorry." If she had been paying more attention to the racers behind her . . . if she hadn't been so focused on her own race . . . there might have been something she could have done. As it was, she hadn't even known until it was all over. "I should have—"

"Not won? Don't think that." Silar struggled to sit up higher. Algana leaned over to help her, and Silar batted her away. "You didn't cause this. I lost control of my kehok when some idiot lost control of his. It happens." Her face twisted, belying her nonchalance, but she kept her voice even. "Your job now is to make sure it doesn't happen to you."

"She won't lose control," Algana said. "She's got some kind of freakish connection with her monster." She made wiggling motions with her fingers.

Raia didn't deny it. Instead, a question burst out of her: "Was it worth it?" As soon as she asked it, she winced. She hadn't meant it the way it sounded. "Sorry. I didn't mean—"

"Obviously it wasn't. For me. But you—"

Algana was studying Raia with narrowed eyes. She interrupted Silar. "You're not here to check on Silar. Or not *just* to check on her. You could have done that after the race. What is it? Nerves? Second thoughts? Completely understandable, since this is the championship. Endless luxury and fame if you win, and all that."

"What happened?" Silar asked.

"I'm fine. The lion's fine."

Silar pressed her lips into a line. "Raia. What. Happened."

She couldn't look at them as she said, "My parents tried to murder my kehok." Fixing her eyes on a tray of bandages, she tried not to see the flames roaring through her memory.

"So?" Jalimo said. "You already knew they were shit people."

And with that, he so easily dismissed the central pain of her entire life. She stared at him for a moment, and then she laughed. She didn't know why she was laughing—it wasn't funny, either what her parents had done or what had happened to Silar—but she couldn't seem to stop. Her friends laughed with her.

She spent the next precious few minutes with them, as long as she could spare, talking and laughing, and by the time she left, she knew she was going to win this race. She held tight to that confidence as she strode through the camps, past the holding areas, and through the crowds that were shouting and pointing at her, calling out to her to wish her luck, either good or bad.

She'd nearly reached her campsite when Gette caught up to her.

"Told you we'd race together again," the prior grand champion said. "I know a competitor when I see one."

"You told me to quit racing," Raia reminded him.

He flashed a smile that he must have thought was charming. "It was a test. You passed!"

"You didn't. Highly likely you'll be reborn as a hyena."

"Ouch."

"Are you trying again to get in my head? Because it won't work. I'm ready to race, and I'm ready to win." She smiled as she said it. "And do you know why?"

"Because you're arrogant after all your wins and have forgotten what it feels like to confront a proven champion? From one rider to another, I only came to tell you that you should feel proud of what you've accomplished and not let today's inevitable loss diminish that pride."

Raia quit walking. He could be right. He was last year's champion, and like her, he was undefeated in all his races so far this season. Worse, he'd already beaten her once. Easily. "I have so many reasons to win. Important reasons. But the real reason I'll win isn't any of them. Actually, they're all too terrifying to even think about." She looked him straight in the eye. "The real reason is because it will be fun to beat you. So thanks for that. And thanks on behalf of my kehok. He'll enjoy his rebirth."

Without waiting for him to respond, she pivoted and marched toward her camp, where her kehok and trainer waited for her. In the distance, on the stands, the spectators continued to fill in every bit of available space, all of them eager for the final race to begin.

At last, she was eager too.

And for a brief instant, the excitement outweighed the terror.

BY MIDMORNING, THE RACING GROUNDS WERE PACKED tighter than ever before. The stench of kehoks permeated the air, and the sound of several hundred kehoks screaming, bellowing, and screeching at one another was phenomenal.

Tamra loved it.

They'd done it: the championship race!

Or we almost *did it. One more race. Just one, and then we'll have everything we want and need.* She thought of Shalla and what this win would mean to their lives, and what it would mean to Raia and her life.

Tamra shooed Raia into the tent to dress in her riding uniform. She checked over the kehok—he looked healthy, strong, and fast. She hummed to herself. *Today is going to be a great day. And Shalla will be by my side to see it!*

Augur Yorbel promised to bring her when he came from the temple. Lots of augurs came to watch the championship race, and the high augurs would of course be here to drape the victory charm around the winning kehok's neck. At sundown, they'd bring the kehok back to the temple to be reborn into his or her second chance at life.

It will be better than great, she thought. *It will be glorious!*

Raia dressed quickly and emerged to coax her racer out of his cage. All around, the other finalists were doing the same. Tamra checked both Raia and the lion over once, twice, three times, and then they made their way to the holding area.

As one of the top twenty, she had well-wishers all around her, shouting at her to run fast, as well as those who were rooting against her, calling out insults. Tamra cheerfully made rude gestures at all of them. "Block it all out," Tamra told Raia. "Or drink it all in. Whatever will fill you the most. Isn't this amazing?"

"I think it's making him nervous," Raia said.

"Is it making *you* nervous? That's what matters most."

Tamra saw Raia glance at the other competitors, each with his or her own racer. Nearby was Gette with his silver spider. He gave Raia a mocking salute.

"I'm not nervous," Raia said.

It was, Tamra thought, a lie. But it was a good one. Raia was getting better at telling them.

At last, a few hours past dawn, the last of the undercard heats were completed, and the horn was blown for the top twenty to get into position for the final championship race. Tamra felt as if her body was humming with excitement.

Her ears were buzzing with the cheers and screams as Raia rode the lion to the starting gate, where Tamra was allowed to give her rider one last piece of advice. She thought of what she'd told last year's rider, before things went so disastrously wrong: to own the track, to swallow every moment and make it his, to use his hunger for victory to propel him faster. *That* was why the race commission had fined her, because of that advice. With difficulty, Tamra pushed that memory out of her mind. Raia was different. She ran for her own reasons. She wouldn't suffer the same fate.

Tamra chose different advice for her: "Run with joy."

Raia smiled—all the hours, days, even years of worry and fear disappearing as her whole face brightened. "Yes. I can do that."

At the race official's signal, Tamra retreated from the track with the other trainers. Other officials herded up into the stands, on the opposite side of the psychic shield. She craned her neck to see over the throngs of people—*There! Shalla!* She waved at Augur Yorbel. He was standing with a woman augur, with Shalla between them. Shalla was wearing her training robes, one of her braids had slipped out of its ribbon, and she was dancing from foot to foot.

Pushing through the crowd, Tamra reached them. She scooped Shalla up against her, helping her stand on a bench for a better view. "Isn't this exciting?"

Shalla laughed. "I'm so excited I think I'll burst!"

"Thank you for bringing her," Tamra said to Yorbel. She then greeted the other augur, an elegant woman with silver braids and a welcoming smile. "I'm Trainer Tamra Verlas."

"Tamra, this is one of my oldest and dearest friends, High Augur Gissa," Yorbel said.

A high augur! Tamra tried to think of what to say, and words failed her. She hadn't been close to such a luminary in years, not since she'd been a champion racer, and she'd never met one in the stands.

"Pleasure to meet you," High Augur Gissa said. She clasped Tamra's hand warmly, and Tamra was surprised to feel callouses on her palms. Yorbel's hands were as soft as cotton. She wondered what work High Augur Gissa did in the temple, aside from continuously being good and holy. She couldn't imagine a high augur doing common chores.

"Yorbel has spoken highly of you," High Augur Gissa continued. "And I am told your daughter is a gift to our temple. We are pleased to have her as a student."

"Thank you, Your Grace." Tamra told herself not to be awed by the fact that they were standing with a high augur. After all, Tamra had talked with an emperor-to-be, and Yorbel himself was an augur. She shouldn't be so starstruck. But a *high augur*, the holiest of holies! "Honored to meet you."

Then there was no more time to be impressed with the lofty company she and Shalla were keeping.

The race announcer shouted, "Ready!"

Her heart felt as if it was pounding so fast that it would drown out the cheers.

"Prepare!"

She joined the cheering, yelling so loud that her voice scraped her throat. Shalla cheered with her, and Tamra braced her so she could stand on the bench and see better.

"*RACE!*"

The starting gates exploded open, and the kehoks shot out like blurs.

The twenty riders and racers were the best in Becar. Most had been racing for years. Only a few were newer. And none were as new as Raia and her lion—to be in the first heat in your first season was extraordinary, and she knew others were waiting for her to falter.

But Tamra had no fear.

She felt as if she were running along with Raia and the lion. Her heart, mind, and soul were with them as they charged toward the first turn, picking up speed. The lion dug his paws into the turn, attacking it, and gained speed for the straightaway.

"Mama! She's catching up to the lead!" Shalla cried.

"Run," Tamra whispered. "Just run."

RAIA FELT THE WIND ON HER FACE AND TASTED THE sweat that dripped off her lip. The roar of the crowd was distant thunder, a storm that didn't touch her. She felt as if nothing could touch her. She was flying, on the back of her lion.

"*Faster, my love,*" she called to him with her mind, heart, and soul.

She was aware of the other racers: a red lizard who breathed fire, a silver-and-black jackal with a snake's tail, a winged crocodile, a beetle the size of a hippo, an elephant that looked as if it were made of rocks. . . . All of them were racing with her, kicking sand into the sky. She felt as if she were buoyed by them, by their speed, as they careened along the first straightaway.

Ahead of her was Gette, whipping his silver spider kehok.

She saw every movement with clarity. Beside her the rock elephant bashed against the shoulder of the beetle. It bashed back, biting. Sand clouded the air, thrown upward in the clash, and she felt as if she could see every grain.

The crowd's cheers roared louder as Raia saw the first turn ahead. *Own the turn,* she thought. *Use the turn.* She felt the lion run faster, his paws digging into the sand, shoveling it behind him. She was shoulder-to-shoulder with the red lizard. Flames ringed its neck, and Raia breathed in the heat. She lay flat against her lion's cool metal mane.

Another racer slammed hard into her side—the silver-

and-black jackal. She slipped an inch to the side, then righted herself. Her lion shouldered the jackal back and kept running. Now the red lizard was ahead of them.

Next straightaway.

She was speed. She was wind. She was a sandstorm. The lion ran faster than he'd ever run before, gaining on the lizard. Raia heard the pounding of racers' hooves and paws behind them, as if the sound was pushing them forward. As they neared the next turn, the lion ran low, his strides so smooth that Raia could barely feel the impact of his paws on the sand.

They whipped around the turn, and they passed the red lizard. She heard its rider screaming and saw him in a frenzy, beating the lizard with a spiked club as they fell behind.

Only Gette and the spider were left in front of her. He twisted in his saddle to look at the competitors behind him, and their eyes met. His lips quirked into a smile, and he faced forward, rose up in his saddle, and hit the spider so fast and hard that his arm was a blur.

Beneath her, she felt her lion's growl build. It vibrated her legs until she felt herself growling with him. Her focus narrowed to Gette, and she felt a strange kind of hunger, sharp and predatory.

Faster, Raia and the lion closed the distance between them.

Closer. Closer.

They were inches behind them, with the spider's many legs stabbing the sand in front. Her kehok roared, his jaws open, snapping at the spider's legs, and Gette steered sharply left. The lion's teeth closed on empty air. For an instant, she thought she saw fear in Gette's eyes. She now snarled at him and in that instant he was everyone who had ever let her down: her parents, the augurs who turned her away, all the people who had never cared but were supposed to.

In the stands beyond Gette, Raia caught a glimpse of three familiar faces: Jalimo and Algana, with Silar hoisted between them on their shoulders. Their mouths were open, screaming for Raia and cheering her on as they'd promised they would. Silar was punching the sky.

Raia saw the scene in a millisecond, and it wiped all thought of Gette from her mind. He no longer mattered. And he had no power to stop her.

As the spider lunged to attack, the lion spurted ahead, and Gette faltered as their target suddenly disengaged. She heard his kehok scream in rage, but Raia didn't look back. As she and the lion took the lead, everything and everyone faded behind them until there was only her and her kehok. They ran as one.

"Fly, my love," Raia whispered to the lion.

Smooth, fast, and strong as wind, they flew through the final lap.

Alone in the lead, they surged across the finish line.

CHAPTER 28

As the crowd cheered, Raia soothed her lion, "Slow, slow, it's over. Breathe."

Flowers were tossed onto the racetrack, as the other racers were led back to the stable. Soon, Raia and the lion were the only rider-and-racer pair left on the track. She felt enveloped in cheers, as if the excitement of the crowd were lifting her into the sky. She raised her arms and, with her thoughts alone, guided the lion back to the finish line.

Guards and race officials swarmed around them, clamping shackles on him.

Don't fight them, she thought at him. *You won! We won!* She didn't know if he could feel her thoughts beneath the barrage of others, but he didn't resist.

Trainer Verlas appeared at her side, as if by magic. She hauled Raia off the lion's back and hugged her. "You did it!" she shouted. "I knew you would!"

Raia felt as if she'd never stop smiling. She'd never felt this kind of overflowing joy, as if she wanted to wrap the whole city, the whole desert, the whole empire, and everyone in it in her arms. Joy had replaced her blood, coursing through her and making her laugh and cry all at once. She was lifted up on the shoulders of riders and trainers. Cheering, they carried her to the base of the royal viewing box and set her down.

Smoothing her tunic, she smiled up at Dar. With palace guards on either side of him, he approached her.

"Congratulations, Rider Raia!" His voice rang across the sands. "Grand champion!"

The crowd roared loud enough to shake the sky. She thought they'd be heard across the desert. The cheers rang in her skull, and she thought she'd never, ever forget this moment.

Carrying an ornate black box, the high augurs filed onto the sands, and Dar led Raia to a dais that had been constructed during the chaos under the finish line banner. Trainer Verlas was already standing on it, beaming at her.

Where's my lion?

Raia scanned the crowd—if he wasn't with Trainer Verlas . . .

"Steady," Trainer Verlas whispered. "First you, then the kehok. It's how it's done."

Squashing her worries, Raia waved at the spectators as Dar led her up the steps and presented her to the stands. "Your grand champion, Rider Raia!"

She waved at the crowd as Dar presented her with a medallion. It was stamped with the symbol of the Becaran Races, the victory charm, and it hung from a blue silk ribbon. He lowered the ribbon around her neck. She felt the heavy weight of the medal. She waved again, and in the sea of faces, she saw Silar, still on the shoulders of Jalimo and

Algana. As the others cheered for her, Silar clapped her hands together and shook them in victory.

As Raia came off the dais, Trainer Verlas wrapped an arm around her shoulders. Shalla hugged her waist. Lady Evara fluttered around them, proclaiming how she always knew, she always believed in them, and she was so very proud.

Next, it was her kehok's turn.

The crowd hushed as her lion was led in shackles by guards and trainers toward the dais. Growling, he was trying to snap at them through the chain muzzle. Raia broke away from her friends and ran toward him. As soon as he saw her, he calmed. She knelt in front of him.

"You don't need the chains," she told the guards.

"He can't approach the emperor-to-be unchained."

She didn't argue with them. *This will all be over soon,* she thought at him. At sundown, he'd be reborn and have no more need of chains or cages. Clasping the lion's face in her hands, she said out loud, "It's all right. You did it. Everything's going to be fine now. Very soon, you'll be free."

She then walked alongside him up to the dais.

Dar bowed to the kehok.

The lion knelt and inclined his head.

Around Raia, she heard gasps and then whispers—people were amazed at the control she had over the lion, that she could make him bow. She didn't say that she hadn't done it. The lion had bowed on his own.

Soon, he'll be free.

I'll miss him.

She kept that voice inside her very quiet. This was a joyous day, and she wanted the kehok to know she was proud of him and happy for him.

Then the high augurs stepped forward, and one of the

high augurs, an ancient man with a face as weathered as a rock in the wind, addressed the crowd. "As the winner of the Becaran Races, this kehok is to be redeemed."

Beside Raia, the lion tensed.

She laid a hand on his mane. *It's all right,* she soothed him.

The high augur went on with his speech, and Raia sensed the lion becoming more and more agitated. She whispered, "What's wrong?"

This didn't make sense. The lion understood what was going on, at least she thought he did. He wanted this! She wondered if he was afraid of *how* it would happen. To be reborn, he would have to die. But after that, he wouldn't be a monster anymore. He'd have a chance to start over, and his death and rebirth would save his brother.

"Don't be afraid," she whispered.

She knew they'd take him to the temple and perform the ritual at sundown. She wished she'd asked if she could go with him. He'd be alone, and frightened.

For the first time, she wondered if winning was what she'd wanted after all. *They're going to kill him,* she realized, *in order to free him.* And she wouldn't be able to help or comfort him or even be nearby. She wouldn't be allowed in the inner sanctum of the temple.

Maybe we should have run.

She told herself to stop thinking like this. It was just a selfish fear, because she'd miss him and miss racing the sands with him. "Go to them," she told the lion. "They'll set you free."

Stepping back, she let him walk forward toward the dais.

A high augur, a woman who had been standing near Augur Yorbel, stepped forward. Seeing her, the lion halted.

Raia saw his gaze fix on each of the high augurs. His growl intensified.

Raia had a sudden terrible thought. What if it wasn't death he feared? What if it was them?

As a kehok, he'd never seen the high augurs before. He shouldn't have recognized them as anything but strangers. He should have no reason to feel threatened by them, but he was acting as if they were a source of danger.

The soldiers tried to prod the lion forward as the high augurs formed a line, blocking the lion's view of Dar. As soon as Dar disappeared behind them, the lion reacted.

He charged toward the high augurs.

The soldiers reacted, seizing his chains.

Raia cried, "No! Stop! They're not your enemies!"

As the lion was subdued by the will of the nearby trainers and the strength of the guards, he continued to thrash and try to bite, and Raia thought, *What if they are?*

She looked at the high augurs.

Impossible.

The high augurs were the most pure beings in Becar. They guarded and guided the souls of everyone. *Except not all augurs are kind,* a little part of her whispered. She knew how much Trainer Verlas feared they'd take Shalla from her. Granted, that was entirely different—the augurs at Shalla's temple believed they were doing the right thing for Shalla and for Becar.

But was it all that different? Because her parents believed they were doing the right thing too.

It was a horrible thing to think, that the augurs could have played a role in Zarin becoming a kehok.

But she trusted her lion, and he feared them as if he

remembered them. She watched him whimper as one of the high augurs approached him. Giving a command, the high augur gestured at a cage. The guards and race officials hauled the kehok into it. A red velvet cloth was tossed over it, and the final thing Raia saw was her lion's sad, beautiful, frightened eyes.

She heard a voice inside her head—a voice she'd heard only once before. His voice.

Pain, his voice said. *Death.*

And then: *They killed me.*

He was afraid because he remembered them. He remembered his death!

"Wait!" She pushed through the crowd and ran to the cage.

Behind her, Trainer Verlas called, "Raia, what are you doing?"

"Let me in the cage. I need to fix his chains," she lied to the nearest guards. "He's shackled wrong—he'll break free if I don't fix it."

Believing her, they opened the cage. She threw herself inside. Hands shaking and heart pounding, she unlatched his shackles and loosened his chains. He lunged out past her.

Trainer Verlas rushed to block him. "Stop!" She was flanked by other trainers and riders, all of them bearing down with their will on the lion.

He halted as if he'd been frozen.

Raia ran to his side. "Please! I have to save him."

"We're trying to save him!" Trainer Verlas said. More calmly, she said, "This is what has to happen. You have to let the high augurs take him. They'll use the victory charm, and then he'll be saved."

"They won't!" Raia knew she was crying—she felt the

tears on her cheeks, tasted them on her lips. "Please, Trainer Verlas—if you won't trust him, then trust me!"

On the dais, she saw Prince Dar stride toward her, flanked by his imperial guards. In his robes, with a circlet of gold on his head, he was nothing like the boy who had wept for his brother. He was as radiant as a legend. "Rider Raia, I demand you stop at once! This kehok must receive his reward!"

She sprang onto the lion's back. He was snarling and snapping but wasn't attacking, held in place by the will of the riders and trainers. Wrapping her arms around his neck, she cried, "I can't! They won't! Dar, the high augurs killed your brother! They murdered the emperor!"

She'd shocked the riders and trainers—she felt it the second their will faltered, like a spring released. "Run," she ordered the lion. As the crowd exploded into shouting around them, the lion pivoted and carried Raia off the racetrack.

CHAPTER 29

Tamra shielded Shalla as chaos erupted all around them. The palace guards, the augurs' soldiers, and the track officials marched through the crowd, shoving people back toward the stands. Closing ranks, the high augurs filed out of the racetrack, while the emperor-to-be's personal guards spirited him safely out of sight.

"Follow me," Lady Evara commanded.

Herding Shalla with her, Tamra said, "Come on."

All around them people were shouting at each other. She saw one man punch another, and a fight broke out to their right. *I have to get Shalla out of here! And find Raia!* She felt a hand on her elbow and saw Yorbel was there, helping shield Shalla from the crowd.

The tension that everyone had been bottling up during race season, the passion that had built up during the races themselves—all of it was bursting out. It was as if the people were transforming into monsters right in front of her. Every bit of rage that they'd held in was exploding out of them.

Fights were erupting in the stands and on the racetrack. Everyone was screaming louder than a horde of kehoks, as if they'd been just waiting for the right moment to unleash all their anger and frustration at life.

The only saving grace was that the actual monsters, the kehoks, were locked in the stable, as was protocol after every race. *The stable!* Tamra thought. It was the one place that the rioters wouldn't enter, no matter how inflamed they were. If Raia had any sense, she'd run there. It was the next best thing to fleeing into the desert, which was the opposite direction from where she'd fled. "To the kehok stable!" she shouted at Lady Evara.

Lady Evara nodded once, to show she'd heard, and led the way, wading through shouting people, elbowing them aside. Her enormous hat was easy to see and follow as they pushed through the panicking crowd.

Beside Tamra, Shalla stumbled as a woman crashed against her. Tamra and Yorbel immediately flanked Shalla, protecting her on either side. "Stay close!" Tamra shouted at the others.

It felt like an eternity of pressing through the crowd, but at last Tamra saw the stable ahead of them. She could hear the shrieks of the kehoks inside, echoing the mood of the rioters behind them.

Reaching the stable, Tamra expected to find a knot of guards, but they'd been drawn away toward the thick of the fighting. Lady Evara yanked open the door and shooed them inside. There was none of the flighty aristocrat about her now. She looked more like a soldier, her eyes darting around, taking stock of their situation. The bulk of the chaos was by the track, but it could easily spread here. "Quickly!"

I never thought I'd feel better having Lady Evara with me, Tamra thought.

They ducked inside, and together Tamra and Lady Evara slammed the door behind them and lowered the lock, a thick iron bar. It was a door designed to keep kehoks in; it would keep a horde of people out. Plus the walls of the stable were thick stone.

Inside, the noise was like being within a tornado. There were hundreds of kehoks, shrieking inside their stalls, bashing at the walls and doors. Wincing from aches she was just starting to feel, Tamra turned and saw Shalla retreating, her eyes locked on the face of a jackal-like kehok that snapped its jaws at her. Behind her, a hulking rhino-like brute bashed its stall door so hard that it shook. "Shalla, watch out!"

Shalla jumped away, her mouth open in a scream that Tamra couldn't hear because of the kehok shrieks. In the next stall over, another kehok, a monkey-like creature with sword-length claws, swiped at her.

"*Back!*" Tamra ordered with both her voice and mind. "*Down!*"

The two kehoks skittered back and then lay, cowed, in their stalls.

"*Silence!*"

The nearest dozen kehoks also quieted. She felt Yorbel staring at her. "I won't let anyone hurt my girl," Tamra said as an explanation. "Either of my girls."

She strode through the stable. Halfway down, she found the stall that had been assigned to their kehok. As she hoped, inside was Raia, with her lion. Standing in front of the lion as if she were protecting him, Raia was stroking his mane and murmuring to him.

Seeing her, Tamra felt as if she could breathe again. She'd been imagining Raia swept into the crowd, trampled, battered, crushed beneath feet and fists. Quickly, Tamra examined Raia. She looked unhurt.

Shalla rushed toward her. "Raia!"

Blocking her, Tamra said, "Stay outside the stall." Shalla halted, as did Yorbel.

Also stopping outside the stall door, Lady Evara snapped at Raia, "What were you thinking? Accusing the high augurs of murder and treason? You started a riot, girl!"

Raia stood her ground, even in the face of Lady Evara's fury. "He remembered them. He was afraid of them. Because they killed him!"

"Impossible," Yorbel said gently. "Raia, I know how hard this is for you. You've become close to your kehok, and it's understandable. You've been through a lot together. It's human nature to—"

Tamra cut him off. "If she says the high augurs killed him, I believe her."

Yorbel's mouth dropped open.

If he expected me to always agree with him just because he's been nice . . . "You can't say it's impossible. Think about it: they have access to all the gold in the temples. More than enough to attempt to bribe Lady Evara, pay off Raia's parents, and hire that false guard to poison the kehok. And if anyone could create an anti-victory charm, it's them. Am I right about that?"

She could see truth and belief warring on his face. "I do say it's impossible," Yorbel said firmly. "The high augurs are the purest of the pure!"

Shalla, to Tamra's surprise, spoke up. "How would you know?"

"I . . . In order to become a high augur . . ." Yorbel began.

"But you can't read an augur's aura," Shalla said. "I learned that. Once you become skilled enough to read auras, no one can read yours. Augur Clari herself told me that."

"Smart girl," Lady Evara said. "A very valid point. Well, Augur Yorbel, do you *know* that the high augurs are still as pure as they were the day they were chosen for their rank, or could their souls possibly be stained with regicide and worse?"

He looked sick. "No augur would—"

Tamra laid a hand on his arm. She knew this had to be a terrible thing for him to contemplate. "*You* wouldn't, because you're a good man."

Raia said with no trace of doubt in her voice, "They'll kill him! And they won't use the charm. He'll be a kehok again, but he won't remember me, and I won't be able to find him. And then Dar . . . he won't become emperor. I don't know what will happen to Dar!"

Yorbel swayed, and Tamra wondered if he was going to faint. He looked as if all the blood had drained out of him. "Sweet Lady," he whispered. "I *do* know what will happen to him. But . . . No! It won't come to that! Raia won. Zarin will be given the victory charm."

"Can you be certain?" Lady Evara asked.

"The high augurs would never—"

"Ugh, *you're* impossible," Lady Evara said. "Expand your mind! Raia, you know that monster best. Is there any chance that he was wrong? Or is there any chance that you misread what he was trying to say? Can you ask him again?"

Raia knelt by the lion's face and began to murmur at him, stroking his mane. He leaned against her as if exhausted. *No ordinary kehok would ever act like this*, Tamra thought. With this kehok, she could believe virtually anything.

"I don't . . . know," Raia said. "I think his memories come and go. I think . . . I think he recognized Dar . . . the emperor-to-be, I mean . . . the other night. He seemed like he might have, but I wasn't sure. Prince Dar was sure, though. And then today, as soon as he saw the high augurs . . . he . . ." She stopped as if there was something more she wanted to say but wasn't sure she'd be believed. She pleaded with Tamra. "You know he's always understood more than any kehok could! Tell them, Trainer Verlas!"

"He has shown an understanding of what we say and what we do," Tamra agreed.

Yorbel pushed. "Are you certain he was reacting in fear of the high augurs? Couldn't he have been reacting to fear of what would happen to him next?"

"It's possible . . ." Raia said. She had tears pooling in her eyes, but she didn't let them fall.

"Yes!" Yorbel said, seizing on that ray of hope. "Every being fears death, even knowing there is life on the other side. It means the end of your current existence, and an adventure into the unknown. Perhaps he feared the unknown!"

"He could have been afraid of dying," Raia whispered. "I was . . . I was thinking how I was afraid of him being killed. And of how much I'll miss him." She looked at the lion as if he were a dear friend, not a murderous monster. "Could he . . . Could he have been reacting to *me*?"

"Maybe," Tamra said. In which case, speaking out against the high augurs would be the worst thing they could do. The best would be to wait out the riot, then bring the kehok to the temple, let things proceed, and have the emperor-to-be find his brother's new vessel and be crowned emperor. Exactly as they'd planned.

But if we're wrong . . .

Out by the dais, Raia had reacted so strongly. And she knew the kehok better than anyone. If that was what she felt he was trying to say, and if all they were doing now was making her doubt herself . . . *I trust her.* "You sounded certain out there." And all the arguments were still valid—the augurs could have made the anti-victory charm and used it. Or paid someone to use it on the late emperor.

"I was. I am!"

"What are even our choices here?" Lady Evara asked. "Do nothing, or lob unproveable accusations at the most powerful people in our land until they decide to squash us like bugs?"

"He needs to be killed and reborn as human," Tamra said. *That's how we all win,* she thought. "No one knows the lion is Emperor Zarin. This can still work." As soon as Zarin was reborn, Prince Dar could announce he'd found his late brother's vessel and be coronated. Then as emperor, he could deal with the mess that was the high augurs and whether or not they were guilty. *It will cease to be my problem.*

"But how can we be sure the high augurs will follow through with the ritual?" Raia asked. "If they're guilty, all they have to do is *not* use the victory charm, and they'll escape unscathed."

Tamra had an idea. "What if it doesn't happen behind sealed doors? What if the emperor-to-be were to insist that the grand champion kehok be killed in public, with the victory charm visible for all to see?"

Looking immensely relieved, Yorbel nodded. "That's not too much to ask. The augurs can prove their innocence, and the wrong that was done to Zarin and Dar will be fixed, at least as much as it can be. Right will prevail, and goodness will be restored."

Lady Evara waved her hand. "Yes, yes. All of that. Very relieved we didn't reach the conclusion that we needed to raise an army, storm the temple, and lay siege to the city, because I have to host a celebratory party later tonight. So . . . we just waltz out of here with the racer and rider who just caused a riot and say oops, sorry, but can you slaughter this lion for us where we can see the blood? Yes?"

The lion growled.

Tamra thought he might have understood *that*. "We need to get him to the emperor-to-be, explain the situation and Raia's suspicions, and then have Prince Dar tell the high augurs what they need to do to prove their innocence. If they're innocent, they'll do it. If they're not . . . what choice will they have? They'll have to, or they'll be admitting their guilt."

"Lovely! I see no holes in your plan!" Lady Evara clapped enthusiastically. "I'm sure the guards will be thrilled to let us see the emperor-to-be now. Or as our rider so familiarly calls him, *Dar*. Especially if we come in the company of the girl who accused the most holy people in the empire of depravity, the monster whose disobedience started a riot, and their trainer, infamous for last year's disaster at finals."

Tamra crossed to one of the narrow slit windows and peered out. It was worse than she expected. More soldiers had arrived, drawn from the local battalion, and were marching through, trying to stop the riot without harming any Becarans, but the spectators were rushing past them, wrecking the camp. The augurs had fanned out, calming people where they could, but they couldn't be everywhere . . . and they were now part of the problem too. She wondered if people had been killed, trampled, or attacked. She looked back at Shalla and Raia.

Shalla was kneeling next to Raia with her arm around her. Raia was in too deep. She couldn't be sent away. But Shalla . . . Tamra didn't want her anywhere near the racetrack or the palace or any of this mess. She certainly didn't want her to witness the high augurs killing the kehok, if that was where this led. *And that's the best-case scenario. Worst . . . we're arrested for Raia's accusation.* Or was it worst case if Raia was right, and the high augurs were the emperor's enemy? She didn't know what she was hoping for. She just knew that their victory had turned into disaster, and her first responsibility was to protect Shalla and Raia as best she could. *Raia and I can't go out there. We'd be recognized. But an innocent bystander could, with an innocent girl.* "Yorbel, you've masqueraded as an ordinary citizen before. Can you do it again and get Shalla to safety?"

"Yes, of course," Yorbel said.

"Hide somewhere in the city," Tamra said. "As far from the riots as you can get. Don't come out until this is all over."

"But, Mama!" Shalla cried. "I can help!"

Tamra knelt beside her. "You can help by being away from danger, while Lady Evara, Raia, and I save Raia's racer, okay?"

Shalla continued to protest, but Tamra overruled her. She hugged her tight.

"I swear I'll protect her," Yorbel said.

"I trust you," Tamra said, both as a statement and a threat.

"And where will you be?" Yorbel asked. "Lady Evara is right—you and Raia cannot approach the palace. You'll be held responsible for starting the chaos outside."

Lady Evara sighed dramatically. "Very well, I nominate myself."

Tamra nodded. It wasn't a terrible idea. Lady Evara was

far more likely to be admitted to the palace on her own, and Tamra, to her own surprise, trusted her. "We'll hide here and wait for you to send word."

"Good," Lady Evara said. "And don't hesitate to use the charming brutes around you to defend yourselves, if need be. No one will dare come near a stable full of rampaging kehoks. If you can keep them from goring you, you should be perfectly safe. I will send word as soon as I can, and then you bring the kehok. With luck, this will all be resolved by sundown."

While Raia stayed with her lion, Tamra shepherded Lady Evara, Yorbel, and Shalla to the door. She hefted up the bar that locked it. Hugging Shalla one more time, Tamra shooed them all out. She then retreated, barred the door again, and watched out one of the tiny windows. Lady Evara, with all her self-confidence wrapped around her like armor, plowed through the crowd in the direction of the palace, while Yorbel, without his robes and with his augur pendant hidden, spirited Shalla off in the opposite direction, away from the racetrack.

And then they were out of sight, and Tamra was left with Raia and several hundred kehoks, as well as a slew of regrets. *Should I have gone with Lady Evara? Should I have kept Shalla here?* But it was too late now. The decisions were made, the plans enacted, and all that was left for her to do was hope that nothing else went wrong.

DAR EYED THE EMPEROR'S THRONE. *YOU SHOULD BE sitting here, Zarin.* None of this should have ever happened. He lowered himself into the chair one step down on the dais and smoothed his robes. He told himself he had to remain calm.

Raia's words were ringing in his head.

Could she be right?

He'd summoned the high augurs to the palace. If the allegations were true, then the high augurs had to be removed from their temple, stripped of any political power, and imprisoned. If they were false, then he needed to clear their names as quickly as possible and calm the riots that were erupting all over the city.

The high augurs filed into the throne room in a solemn line. Palace guards flanked them, then split to take their positions in a semicircle. All eight high augurs wore their hoods up and had their hands clasped in front of them, and Dar tried to remind himself that he wasn't a child being judged—they were the ones whose integrity was in question.

The eldest high augur stepped forward. Dar noted that he did not bow. "We have come on a serious matter," High Augur Etar said.

"Yes," Dar said heavily. *I don't want to do this.* The augurs, especially the high augurs, were supposed to be as pure as the stars, the guiding lights of their people. If Raia's allegation was true, this was going to gut so many Becarans. How could it be true? There had to be another explanation. "I was shocked and distressed by the serious allegations—"

High Augur Etar cut him off. "It is our belief that the late emperor Zarin, long may his soul thrive, did not die a natural death."

Dar hadn't been interrupted since Zarin died. And was the high augur admitting involvement? Dar's hands curled around the armrests of his chair, gripping them hard, as the augur continued. He met the eyes of the nearest guard, who tightened her grip on her spear.

"It is a suspicion we have held for some time, but our resources did not lead us to the one responsible until today."

"A credible source named you—" Dar began.

"A desperate attempt to cast blame elsewhere," High Augur Etar interrupted. "She will be dealt with. The fact, however, remains that her outburst did direct us to examine one we previously considered above blame."

Dar rose. "One of your own?" Perhaps this crime was the actions of one rogue high augur. Perhaps the council had been unaware of his or her actions. That could be the best-case scenario here. "I am deeply saddened—"

"Your Excellence, we examined your aura and have found you guilty of the murder of your brother, guilty of high treason against the Empire of Becar." All the high augurs bowed their heads, their hands clasped in front of them in a sign of mourning.

Dar heard a kind of roaring in his ears. He felt himself begin to shake. *This is absurd! Me? Of course I didn't kill my brother!* He heard gasps from his guards. "How dare you—"

"Your soul has been stained beyond recognition." High Augur Etar signaled to the guards. "I myself have borne witness to its corruption."

Dar backed up, thumping against his chair. "There's been a mistake! Guards!" But there hadn't been a mistake, he realized. This was intentional. Well planned, even. The palace guards were loyal to him, but only to a point. In matters of morality, the high augurs outranked him, and the guards would listen to them. He hadn't expected them to flip the tables like this. "*You* killed Zarin. Or had him killed. Why? Zarin was a good man! A great emperor!"

As if on cue, the high augurs parted, and Lady Nori was

standing there, framed between them. She had tears streaking her cheeks, blurring her eye paint. "Dar, how could you? Zarin loved you! He practically raised you! To turn on him because of your design for power—I didn't think it of you."

He stared at her. This felt like a second knife strike to the heart. "You too? Are you involved in this? I never thought you would betray me." It was difficult to even say the words. Nori . . .

"You betrayed yourself," Nori said sadly. "Your jealousy of your brother undid you. But your plan failed, Dar. The high augurs were clever enough to hide your brother's vessel. Without him, you couldn't be legitimized."

"But . . . it's a lie!" *I found him!* he wanted to scream, but he stopped himself. It was still possible that they didn't know the black lion was Zarin. If he could keep that knowledge from the augurs, he could at least keep Zarin safe. And Raia, who would try to protect him. He hoped they'd fled far away by now.

"The high augurs do not lie," Nori said. "Dar, please don't make this more difficult than it already is. You know as well as I do that the high augurs are incapable of such an atrocity."

She was right. Yet he knew they had done it.

He backed up to the edge of the dais. There was nowhere to run. The palace guards and high augurs were between him and every exit, and the aristocrats of the court were beginning to drift closer, listening and whispering. *I trapped myself.* He'd been so sure he was safe, here in his palace. *Foolish.* He'd been oh-so-cleverly outmaneuvered. "I did not kill my brother," he said firmly. "I loved him deeply, and I never wanted to be emperor. You know that, Nori. You know *me.*"

"I used to think I did. But now . . . Believe me, this is the last thing that I wanted. But we cannot hesitate, if Becar is to be saved. An army approaches from Ranir, and a riot rages in our streets. You, I fear, are beyond saving." She drew herself upright, looking regal. "Guards, take him away."

The guards marched as one toward him. He froze. He could not believe this was happening—the high augurs, Nori . . . A second before they reached him, he spun, scanning the windows, looking for an escape. But there wasn't one.

"Lady Nori," High Augur Etar said, "it is our recommendation that your coronation ceremony be conducted at sundown—word of it will calm the citizens, and a fast coronation will enable the military to respond to the external threat."

"You are wise," Nori said. "It shall be done."

It was all absurd. It was all just flimsy words. And if it had just been Nori, this would have been easily dismissed. But for the high augurs to say them—it was too much. There was nothing he could say that would convince others of his innocence when the ones who confirm such innocence had already spoken against him.

He seized on another thought that didn't make sense. "Your coronation?"

Nori bowed her head.

And suddenly he realized what should have been clear before. Lady Nori of Griault was of noble birth and beloved by the court. In the absence of any direct heirs, she had a viable claim on the throne.

Especially if she were seen choosing the good of Becar over her feelings for Dar.

It was a brilliant move.

"Nori . . . how could you? I loved you."

Nori didn't speak. She wouldn't even meet his eyes. He wanted to be wrong, to believe that she was deceived by the high augurs, that she was as innocent and good as he'd believed, that she loved him the way he loved her, but the high augur's words about the coronation and Nori's lack of surprise . . .

She had planned this, with them.

The guards clapped their hands on Dar's arms. Some were guards he'd joked with only a few days before, who'd helped him secure musicians to drown out spies, who had accompanied him to the aviary. "I didn't do this," Dar pleaded with them. "The high augurs are lying!"

The nearest guard, one he knew, who had stood outside his chambers and protected him, said in a broken voice, "I believed in you. I thought you were *good*."

That hit him straight in the heart. "I am. And so was Zarin. I don't know why the high augurs wanted him dead, but you need to get word to my rider that she needs to flee. She accused the high augurs. They'll target her next." *And the lion.* "Please. Say you'll warn her."

But the guards refused to speak with him again or even meet his eyes. They marched him out of the throne room and through the court. He heard the whispers, saw tears on the faces of the lords and ladies, saw the disbelief and the pain—*Everyone believes them!* he realized. He tried again. "I didn't kill my brother! The high augurs murdered him!" But even he knew how crazy that sounded. Still, he kept shouting when they pulled a velvet bag over his head, bound his arms, and threw him into a kehok cage. He fell when the cage lurched forward, hauling him out of the palace. His shouts were drowned beneath the screams of his citizens as they fought one another in the streets.

CHAPTER 30

Yorbel led Shalla to the safest place he knew: his own quarters within the augur temple. It took only a word to the temple guards, explaining she was a temple student who had been caught in the riots at the racetrack, and he'd been allowed inside with her.

The girl hadn't spoken a word as they'd crossed the city, and they had slipped through anonymously, with no one suspecting he was an augur. Oddly, the farther from the tracks they got, the less the riots seemed to be about Raia's accusation. He didn't know how the violence had spread so far so fast. It felt as if everyone had simply been waiting to let all their frustration, fear, and anger explode, and the fuse lit at the racetrack had outrun reason. He wished he could have stayed and done something to protect Tamra and her rider, as well as Shalla. *But she asked me to take her daughter to safety,* Yorbel thought. *She trusts me, and I couldn't say no.*

He hadn't even questioned it.

Opening his door, he welcomed Shalla in. She scanned

the mostly empty room: a cot, a desk, a table where he ate solitary meals. He had a few books on a shelf, and his robes hung in his closet. A plant sat on his windowsill. "It isn't much, but you'll be safe here."

"And my mother? Will she be safe?"

"Knowing you're safe will help her," Yorbel said. "She'll be able to focus on protecting the kehok until Lady Evara is able to reach the emperor-to-be." He thought of the way she'd quieted multiple kehoks at once. She was one of the most powerful people he'd ever met.

"And if the high augurs come for her?" Shalla asked.

"The high augurs are a force for good in Becar." He believed that with all his heart and being. "I don't believe Raia lied, not knowingly, but she must have misinterpreted. There must be more to what is going on than what we know."

"Then find out." Shalla crossed her arms. In that instant, she looked so exactly like her mother that Yorbel nearly smiled. "Ask your augur friends. Before the truth gets my mother killed."

It was a brilliant idea. And now he had a way to help Tamra, even from a distance: discover the truth and share it. Once he knew why the emperor kehok had reacted the way he did, Yorbel could spread the word and save them all. He had the potential to know both sides of the story. In fact, as the only augur who was privy to all the details of the kehok's relationship with Prince Dar, he was uniquely suited to this task. "Stay here," he told Shalla. "I have a friend who is a high augur. I'll speak to her."

"Speak well," Shalla demanded. "Mama thinks she can fix everything if she works hard enough, and sometimes that's not true. She needs help, even if she won't ask for it. Promise me you'll try to help her."

"I promise."

She was scowling at him as he let himself out of his quarters. He swore silently that he wouldn't let her down, either of them. If there was anything he could do to help, he'd do it.

He hurried through the corridors. It would be a supreme stroke of luck if Gissa were in her quarters, but it wasn't impossible. She could have returned after the riots on the racetrack—seeking safety was a sensible course of action, and Gissa was sensible. He was crossing a courtyard, heading toward the east wing of the temple, when he heard a clatter from the front gate. Veering, he followed the sounds.

The temple soldiers were returning with a prisoner. He didn't see who it was, but he saw they were within a cage—and there was Gissa! She was with other high augurs, accompanying the cage as it crossed the courtyard between the pillars.

Lurking in the shadows so he wouldn't be drawn into extraneous conversations, he waited as they maneuvered the prisoner into the temple, and then he intercepted Gissa as she split off from the others. "Gissa, it's urgent that I—"

Grabbing his arm, she yanked him into a side corridor. "Yorbel, you shouldn't be here! These are matters for the high augurs." She shot a look back at where the prisoner had disappeared through a doorway. Yorbel briefly wondered who the prisoner was, then dismissed it as irrelevant. He had to stay focused on his purpose.

"This is a matter for the high augurs too—matters that affect all of Becar. Gissa . . . I was there when the grand champion accused you all. I know it was a misunderstanding, but if you could help me sort out the truth, then we could end the violence that's sweeping our fair city."

She shot a look back at the courtyard, and then she sighed.

"Yorbel. Oh, Yorbel. So innocent. So foolish. You had to get yourself mixed up in this, didn't you? Why couldn't you have stayed in your quarters, done your readings, continued your studies, and not ventured out into the world? The world eats those like you."

"Gissa?" He didn't know why she was talking like this, but it wasn't helpful. "You can't expect me not to care about the turmoil in Becar. There's rioting in the streets!"

"And an invading army nearly on our doorstep," Gissa said. "Seal yourself in your room. Ignore it all. Come out in the morning when the world is pure and fresh again." She put her hands on Yorbel's shoulders and turned him, giving him a little shove toward the rooms.

He heard footsteps clip-clop on the stone. A deep voice said, "High Augur Gissa."

Yorbel turned and bowed low to High Augur Etar.

"You're needed for securing the prisoner," High Augur Etar said. He then hesitated. "Who is this? Your friend who found the kehok?"

"High Augur Etar, may I present Augur Yorbel," Gissa said. He thought he heard a strange note in her voice, but he couldn't identify it, and he didn't dare rise from his bow until High Augur Etar acknowledged him. He'd never been in the presence of the most holy of augurs before.

"Rise, Augur Yorbel. High Augur Gissa has spoken highly of you."

He straightened his back. The high augur looked as he'd imagined him: serene and wise, with gentle eyes. "High Augur Gissa is kind."

Gissa gave a light snort.

High Augur Etar actually smiled.

Yorbel felt as if the moon had peeked through the clouds.

The high augur knows I exist! It was one thing to know Gissa was a high augur. It was quite another to be talking to the most revered elder. He wanted to ask him a thousand questions about the nature of souls and their place in the universe, but his tongue couldn't seem to form a single coherent sentence. He dragged his thoughts back to Tamra, whom he'd sworn to help.

"You would not happen to know the location of the emperor-to-be's kehok and its rider, would you?" High Augur Etar asked. "We were separated from them at the tracks and are concerned about their well-being."

"They're safe," Yorbel reassured him, "though I am deeply worried for their continued safety. Your Pureness, I overheard the accusation made by the grand champion, and if I could but know the truth of the matter . . ."

"The truth of the matter is that emperor-to-be Dar has been arrested on charges of high treason," High Augur Etar said. "He is accused of the murder of his brother, the late emperor Zarin. This will be known to all soon enough."

Yorbel felt as if all the air had left his lungs. He gaped at the high augur, then found his voice. "With all due respect, Your Holiness, but that is impossible. To murder an emperor . . . one's own brother . . . it would leave an unmistakable stain on the soul, and Prince Dar showed no such corruption. I read him as recently as a few days ago."

He thought he heard Gissa make a small, sad noise, but when he glanced at her, her expression was impassive. He remembered the prisoner he'd seen brought in through the courtyard—had that been Dar? Was his friend imprisoned here, right now?

High Augur Etar was regarding him with far more interest. "You will swear to this?"

"By the Lady, by the River, by all I hold dear, I swear it."

Another almost-imperceptible sigh from Gissa, and Yorbel wondered if he'd misspoken. Surely, honor compelled him to defend his friend and their prince. If nothing else, the truth ruled in Becar, and for all his recent, smaller obfuscations, he was a servant of that truth.

"You were never approved to read the emperor-to-be," High Augur Etar said sternly. "Only a select few are permitted to view the auras of the royal family. How did such a thing come to be?" He then held up a hand before Yorbel could explain and apologize—it had never been Yorbel's intent to read Dar. His second sight often manifested on its own accord. But even if that wasn't true, Dar was his friend, and he never would have objected to Yorbel reading him. "That is of no consequence. What matters is what you saw."

A little voice inside Yorbel whispered that he may have misread the situation very, very badly. He looked from Etar to Gissa and back again.

"High Augur Gissa, you know what must be done."

Yorbel felt a chill chase over his skin. *Surely, he doesn't mean—*

"Obtain the answers we need, and then do what you must."

Gissa bowed. "Yes, Divine One."

They both watched as High Augur Etar strode after where the cart had disappeared. "You're an idiot, Yorbel. You know that? You mean well, but . . ."

"Gissa . . ." Yorbel began. *He didn't truly order Gissa to interrogate me, did he?*

And kill him.

Yorbel couldn't forget about that part. He thought back to a conversation that he and Gissa had had—he'd looked up to see her sliding something back into her robes. He wondered now if it had been a knife. *I have been so very trusting.*

I have been so very sheltered.

"Shush, not a word more. I will do what I can to save you, but you must trust me."

He did, of course. She was his oldest friend.

And it wasn't as if High Augur Etar had given either of them much choice. At least if he was able to talk with Gissa alone, he'd be able to explain all he knew. She could then speak to High Augur Etar and convince him that the augurs had made a terrible mistake in arresting Dar.

She clamped a hand on his arm and pulled him after her. She didn't speak again until they were deep within the interior of the temple. He heard the sound of jackals baying and wondered where she was leading him. He wasn't familiar with this part of the temple. Here, the stone walls were old, pockmarked with the passage of time, and the floor was smooth from centuries of sandaled feet.

"Keep your hand on my shoulder," Gissa said. She placed his hand on her shoulder and stepped forward toward a simple stone archway. Beyond the archway was darkness, and on either side were chained jackals. "And do not touch the walls."

He'd heard the stories about the High Augurs' Chamber, the poisoned walls, the jackal guards, but he'd never thought he would visit the place himself. He felt himself begin to sweat beneath his robes.

Perhaps following Gissa hadn't been wise.

But she was still his best chance of helping Dar and stopping the violence. If he could make sense of it all and work with Gissa to find a solution . . . It would be worth it.

He thought of Tamra and Shalla.

This was bigger than all of them now, if the augurs had imprisoned the emperor-to-be.

Deeper into the maze, the silence pressed on him. It felt as if it were a living creature, filling his ears with nothingness. He strained to hear anything beyond their footsteps and their breathing. His eyes tried to form shapes out of the blackness.

At last, they stepped into a chamber lit by torches. Eight massive chairs, ancient and decorated with carvings, dominated the room. "Do not touch, and do not sit," Gissa told him. "We are here because it is the one place in the temple, perhaps in all of Becar, where we can speak freely." She crossed to a throne that was devoid of carvings or markings of any kind, and she sat.

It became harder to see her as his friend Gissa. Here, she was more than that. She was a high augur. The holy assassin. Without even deciding to do so, Yorbel knelt. "Dar is innocent of the crime he's accused of. His soul is uncorrupted, and I will vouch for that in front of any and all."

If he could just make them understand that Dar wasn't a murderer, then he could fix everything. They'd see the truth, release Dar, and crown him, solving all of Becar's problems. That was worth any cost.

Even my life, Yorbel thought.

Gissa drummed her fingers on the armrest of her noble chair. "Mmm. You can't do that, Yorbel. The people *must* believe in his guilt. He *must* be executed. And a new empress must be crowned tonight, before the Raniran army reaches the Heart of Becar."

He didn't understand. "Gissa, he's innocent."

"We act for the good of Becar. Innocence is irrelevant."

He rose to his feet, unable to believe what he was hearing. "You don't mean that. We are the custodians of the light, the keepers of virtue, the protectors of goodness. Innocence is the most relevant metric of all!"

"So stunningly naive," Gissa said. "And I wish I could leave you this way, but you had to go and . . . Yorbel. Oh, Yorbel, did you lie to me? You read the kehok, didn't you? You knew all along what he was!"

He opened his mouth to confess that yes, he knew, when the realization struck him: *She knows too.* She, and perhaps the other high augurs, knew that the black lion was the vessel for the late emperor. "How long have *you* known?"

"I am impressed." She flopped back against her throne, not answering his question. "There may be hope for you yet. If you know the late Emperor Zarin is the kehok, then you understand why Prince Dar must die." She sounded almost pleading, as if she wanted to beg for his forgiveness.

Yorbel hated every thought that was pummeling his brain. *Gissa knew. And if Gissa knew, all the high augurs must have known. Raia was right.* He repeated his question: "How long have you known that the lion was Emperor Zarin?"

"Only since the final race."

And then he asked a more terrible question: "How long have you known that the late emperor was reborn as a kehok?"

Gissa was silent for a moment. In this chamber, where all other sound had been erased, the silence had weight and meaning. "Do you want the answer to that question, Yorbel? Think carefully. You may not like what you hear."

He already hated everything he'd heard so far. It felt as if his world had been ripped open and turned inside-out. He felt numb, stunned by the sense that one of the foundation stones of his life had crumbled to sand.

The high augurs were supposed to be good. The holiest of holies.

But he didn't need to read her or any of the others to know that was no longer the truth.

He wondered if it had ever been true.

"Did the high augurs use a charm to ensure that Emperor Zarin was reborn as a kehok?" The question felt as if it burned his tongue. It was inconceivable that he could even suspect them. There was no rational reason they'd want the late emperor dead, and no reason to arrange events so that Dar would fail and the empire would suffer.

He heard a shuffling behind him.

Gissa intoned, "You are known to us."

High Augur Etar entered the chamber. "High Augur Gissa, I question your methods. You are supposed to be questioning the witness, not vice versa. Have you obtained the information? Where is the kehok?" The last question was aimed at Yorbel.

Yorbel felt as if he was reeling, but he pulled himself upright and answered the high augur, the most holy of holies. "As I told you, Illustrious One. Safe."

The high augur snorted and then sank into his throne, the one decorated with carvings of men and women. Yorbel wondered briefly what the carvings signified, his scholar's mind wanting to categorize all he saw.

"You do not understand the gravity of the situation," High Augur Etar said with a heavy sigh.

Gissa inclined her head. "He is an intelligent man. I had thought to explain it to him. Once he understands, he will help us willingly."

"If he doesn't, he will die."

The casual indifference in his voice was chilling. The way they talked about him as if he wasn't even there was perhaps even scarier. Yorbel thought of Shalla, asking if he knew the high augurs' souls were pure, since no one could read them. *I have been so very wrong about so many things.* He met Gissa's eyes, hoping against hope to see some drop of compassion, some hint that he could have misunderstood.

More shuffling from the labyrinth beyond. One by one, the other high augurs entered the room, each greeted with the same phrase: "You are known to us." At last, five of the eight chairs were filled.

"We have before us Augur Yorbel," High Augur Etar said. "He has graciously agreed to share with us the location of our errant kehok." All the augurs present murmured their approval.

Yorbel wet his lips and tried to think quickly and clearly.

He would not lie to the high augurs, even knowing what he did about them now. But he also would not betray Tamra. "He's well guarded. You will not be able to force him from his position. But there may be another way. If you confess the truth to the people, explain *why*—"

High Augur Teron said, "You are ignorant of what is at stake here."

Gissa cut in. "Then enlighten him. Augur Yorbel is a good man, concerned with the future of Becar. He has already compromised his soul to protect the kehok; he may be willing to go further to protect all of Becar."

The high augurs regarded Gissa as if she were a unique bug specimen. Yorbel realized she was going out on a limb, defending him. He also realized it was likely he wouldn't walk out of this chamber alive, and that no one would ever know. *Either this ends in the death of my body or the corruption of my soul,* he thought. He couldn't see any other possible outcome.

I should have left Shalla with her mother. If he never returned, what would happen to the girl? With luck, she would simply be sent back to the training temple when everything had blown over, her connection to this corruption deemed tangential at best. Without luck . . . He tried not to worry about her, or about other mistakes he may have made.

There had to be a way he could still help them. And the people of Becar.

"You favor this man," another of the high augurs said. Yorbel didn't know her name.

"He is a good man," Gissa argued. Sweat beaded on her forehead. He'd never seen her look so unsettled before, and he wondered what it was costing her to stand up for him. He knew, though, it was hopeless. He was dead the moment he'd walked into the maze. He just hadn't realized it until now. "Becar needs such as him."

High Augur Etar spoke to Yorbel in a teacher's voice. "Several months ago, Emperor Zarin came to me with a discovery. He had studied the ancient tomes, combed through old legends, and believed he had unearthed a long-lost secret: anyone can learn to read auras. It is a myth that an augur's ability requires a pure soul. It merely requires the proper training."

Yorbel gaped. "But . . ."

"Of course, we immediately realized the danger of such knowledge," High Augur Etar said. "It would disturb the world order. Rip open the very fabric of our society. Becar functions because its people trust augurs to guide them—if they ceased to view us as superior, the result would be chaos and despair. So we had to remove the emperor."

He shook his head, as if he could shake out the horrible things he was hearing. "You murdered him. And had him reborn as a kehok?"

Another high augur explained, "Given that it was possible he'd retain at least some of his memories, we needed to ensure he was reborn as the one creature whom no one would ever trust."

"I don't understand how this revelation would destroy Becar," Yorbel said. It didn't sound so dire. Perhaps augurs were less special than he'd believed, but surely the world could adjust. "Yes, it would cause change. Our role would change." The augurs would lose some fraction of their power. . . .

Was that what this was all about? Power?

Augurs weren't supposed to covet power.

Augurs aren't supposed to be a lot of things. Like murderers.

They killed Zarin to hide the fact that they themselves weren't pure. To prevent anyone from suspecting their depravity, they committed an act of utmost depravity.

They made a monster, in order to hide that they're monsters, Yorbel thought. It was suddenly clear why the high augurs discouraged other augurs from interacting with kehoks—they saw too much of themselves in them.

"This is pointless," High Augur Nolak cut in. "The longer we wait, the closer the Raniran army marches. It is not altogether certain that the Becaran army can be repositioned in the time we have as it is. Emperor-to-be Dar must be executed, the kehok must be neutralized, and a new empress must be crowned. Delays cost all of Becar."

Gissa bowed her head, refusing to meet Yorbel's eyes, and he knew it was over. Now Dar would die. And the decay in the heart of Becar would fester, unseen and uncured.

The high augurs had become corrupt, or corrupted themselves. *That* much he understood clearly. *And no one will know. I'll die here, before or after Dar, and they will descend on Tamra, Raia, and what remains of Zarin.*

Great wrongs were being done here, in the name of good.

Unless there was a better explanation . . .

"I understand why you feel Zarin had to die." He didn't. But he would say so, if it helped. "Please just tell me why Dar must as well. He knows nothing of his brother's discovery."

Gissa sighed heavily. "Emperor-to-be Dar was doomed from the moment Emperor Zarin died. You know this. At least with a public execution, his death serves two purposes: allowing the empire to continue, and allowing the high augurs to do their work."

He's a scapegoat, Yorbel realized.

Bad enough that Gissa had been assigned to assassinate Dar for the sake of succession, but the fact that they were falsely accusing Dar in order to hide their own crimes . . .

None of them are worthy of being high augurs. Even Gissa.

They had corrupted Becar with their thoughts and actions. They were a rot in the heart of the country he loved. They had to be stopped. Excised from the body of Becar.

But what could he do?

He thought of Tamra. And Raia, her almost-adopted second daughter. "The rider who accused you—what will happen to her?" Yorbel looked only at Gissa.

"She'll die in the riots," Gissa said. "It is the simplest solution."

"We do not know what the kehok-emperor has been able to communicate to her," High Augur Etar said. "She is a risk we cannot take."

He bowed his head. "And the trainer."

"I am sorry, Yorbel," Gissa said quietly. "It is for the good of Becar. I know you are fond of the trainer woman, but our duty and responsibility is to the people and the empire as a whole."

High Augur Etar spoke again. "There is one alternative. If you could convince this trainer and her rider to bring the kehok to us, and if we are able to determine they have no knowledge of Emperor Zarin's discovery . . . we may be able to spare them."

Yorbel's head snapped up.

He had an idea.

A terrible idea.

Gissa was watching him closely. "You know how to convince her to come to the temple, with both her racer and rider, don't you? I can see it in your eyes."

I do, he thought. *But Tamra will never forgive me for it.*

There was one chance to stop the high augurs, to save the emperor-to-be and Becar. But it was a risk. It could end in the deaths of the ones he held dear. He couldn't be certain that Tamra would understand what needed to be done. He had, though, read her soul, and he believed in her. Moreover, he believed he knew what she'd risk if she had to and . . . what she was capable of doing.

"You will not be able to reach the kehok where he is without causing the kind of spectacle that I believe you want to avoid. But there is a way to convince Trainer Tamra Verlas to come to the temple." He took a deep breath and said a silent prayer to the Lady. *For the good of Becar,* he thought.

"She has a daughter named Shalla whom she would do anything to protect. That daughter is in my quarters right now. Send a messenger wight to the racetrack stable, directed to Trainer Tamra Verlas, and tell her she must bring the lion here if she ever wishes her daughter returned to her. I guarantee she will come—and she will bring the kehok with her."

He prayed that Tamra would understand. And that someday she'd forgive him.

"Thank you, Augur Yorbel," High Augur Etar said. "High Augur Gissa was correct about you. You are a good man, and Becar thanks you for your service." He nodded at Gissa.

Gissa stepped forward and slit Yorbel's throat.

CHAPTER 31

Raia crouched inside the lion's stall. She kept one hand on his smooth metal mane, while Trainer Verlas strode through the stable. She was unlocking the stall doors and loosening the shackles of three of the nearest kehoks.

"Are you certain that's a good idea?" Raia asked.

"Oh, yes," Trainer Verlas said grimly.

After she'd finished, she retreated to join Raia and the lion in theirs. She shut the stall door, secured the lock, and stood like a soldier at attention, watching while the three nearby kehoks yanked on their chains.

SNAP.

Crash.

One after another, the three kehoks broke through their bindings and battered open their doors. They raced up and down the stable, screaming at one another. Raia cowered against the lion.

"If someone enters who shouldn't, they will regret it," Trainer Verlas said.

Raia knew she should feel reassured, but she just felt terrified. Outside, she could hear that the riots hadn't calmed—there was still shouting and screaming. Every few minutes, she heard a loud crash, as if something large had collapsed. "I didn't mean for this to happen."

"I know you didn't. It wasn't your fault."

Yes, it was. If she'd not spoken, if she'd found a way to quietly free the lion . . . She didn't regret saving him. She just regretted that she hadn't done it in secret.

"The city was ripe for this," Trainer Verlas said. "Honestly, I doubt it was your proclamation that truly sparked this anyway. We've never gone so long without an emperor, and it was wearing on everyone. You could tell. They were just looking for an excuse to explode. I bet that ninety percent of the people out there have no idea what you said or why the fights started."

"Do you think Lady Evara made it safely through?" Raia asked.

Trainer Verlas snorted. "I think it would take an army to stop Lady Evara."

Raia smiled briefly, and then went back to worrying. If Lady Evara weren't able to reach the emperor-to-be . . . If he didn't agree . . . If the high augurs refused to cooperate . . . "I wish there were something we could do."

"Me too." Trainer Verlas laid her hand on Raia's shoulder.

They waited, as the kehoks raged through the stable and the people of Becar raged outside. Raia thought this was worse than when she ran away from home. At least then she was *doing* something. But this . . . She hated this. The not knowing was like a constant pressure on her mind.

She saw a flutter of white by one of the windows. "Trainer Verlas?"

Trainer Verlas did not switch her focus from the kehoks. She was eyeing the three of them, clearly ready to restrain them if they tried to attack the lion's stall or tried to force their way out of the stable. So far, they hadn't. "Yes?"

"The window. I think . . . It looks like a messenger wight!"

The delicate white shape was fluttering against the windowsill.

One of the loose kehoks, a muscular brute that looked like a cross between a bull and a crocodile, lunged for it, pawing at the wall. "It could be from Lady Evara!" Raia said.

Trainer Verlas nodded once, then vaulted over the stall door.

Raia saw her wince as she landed on the other side. But then Trainer Verlas straightened as the three loose kehoks all targeted her. They charged across the stable.

Trainer Verlas, however, was having none of it. She raised her hands. "Stop." She didn't even raise her voice, and they skidded to a trembling halt. They pawed the ground and snorted, but none of them moved. She walked between them to the windowsill. Gingerly, she lifted the wight off the sill and unfolded it.

She turned back toward Raia as her eyes flickered over the silken paper.

Raia saw Trainer Verlas's face harden.

And then every kehok in the stable, all three hundred of them, screamed at once.

TAMRA READ THE RANSOM NOTE.

There could be no other interpretation for the message, despite all the flowery language. She crossed the stable, and the three loose kehoks cowered away from her. She handed the message to Raia, who read it, let out a gasp, and then read it again.

"The high augurs have Shalla," Tamra said flatly.

She felt her throat close up as she said the words.

Raia's eyes widened in alarm. "Trainer Verlas! The kehoks!"

Tamra pivoted. She fixed the three kehoks in their place. Slowly, they knelt and then lay down, submissive. Her will was implacable. She felt as if she were holding an ocean within her. "Tell me I read it wrong."

"You . . . you aren't wrong. I trusted Augur Yorbel."

"So did I." She felt as if her heart were being pierced by a thousand claws and talons. *He betrayed me. And Shalla. And Raia, Emperor Zarin, and Prince Dar.* Closing her eyes, she felt as if a sandstorm were battering within her.

"How could they blame Dar?" Raia asked. "He didn't kill his brother! They're lying!"

"Of course they're lying. But even if they were saying the sky is green, it wouldn't matter to the people. Trusting augurs is our national pastime. As soon as the riots die down, everyone will remember how much they revere the high augurs. They're the purest of the pure—or so they told us," Tamra said, opening her eyes again. Her hands were clenched so hard that her nails bit her palms. Even if she were to show this message to anyone, it was written cryptically enough that it wouldn't be proof of anything. The high augurs were too clever for that. "You were right. They killed Emperor Zarin, and they're using Emperor-to-be Dar—" She stopped. He wasn't emperor-to-be anymore. "They are using Prince Dar to cover their tracks."

The lion and Raia . . . We're loose ends they want to tie up.

"I believed in them," Raia said. "The high augurs. They're

supposed to guide us. They're the heart of Becar, within the Heart of Becar—that's what my teachers always said. Do you . . . do you think they'll kill Shalla if we don't go?"

"I think they'll kill us if we do," Tamra said.

She felt cold, as cold as the metal in the black lion's mane. She felt as if silver were flowing through her veins instead of blood, hardening her.

Raia swallowed but did not cry. She merely trembled as she reviewed the message once again, as if on a third read, it would give her different answers. "It says we need to come by sundown. Maybe . . . Maybe they'll make the trade. Me and the lion for Shalla. Maybe we *should* make that trade. I . . . had my freedom. I raced, and I had everything I ever wanted. Shalla . . . she should have a chance to live. If this is the only choice . . . Trainer Verlas, is this the only choice?"

Tamra sank onto the floor of the stable, her back to the stable wall. The three loose kehoks were staring at her, their golden eyes unreadable. She breathed. That was what she did. She drank in the moment. And the moment was this:

The high augurs had souls worse than kehoks.

The high augurs were the monsters.

"I don't believe they'll honor the trade." Tamra felt the truth of it as she said it. "I think they'll kill us all. Shalla included." It's what a monster would do. It was the practical solution. If they wanted to hide their sins, the logical choice was to destroy every bit of evidence. "They'll say we died in the riots. Or at the claws of the kehok."

"You think it's a trap." Raia's voice shook but didn't break. And she wasn't asking.

The augurs never failed to act "for the good of Becar." It was their excuse for choosing Shalla's future for her. It was their excuse for continually pushing to take Shalla from

Tamra. It had been their excuse for how they'd treated Raia, first taking her from her family then tossing her back like unwanted garbage. "I'm not letting you sacrifice yourself," Tamra said.

"But your daughter . . ."

"We set her free."

Tamra stared into the golden eyes of the kehoks. Brave words, but how could she free Shalla? And Prince Dar? And keep the lion and Raia safe? How could she fight people who were monsters inside . . . ?

"How?" Raia asked. "They're the high augurs!"

Her back twinging, Tamra pushed herself to standing again. An idea was forming in her mind. A terrible idea. "We fight monsters with monsters." Her hands were curled into fists.

So the high augurs wanted her to bring a kehok. Oh, she'd do that. And so much more. Tamra turned to face Raia. "You can stay here, if you want. Stay safe."

Raia shook her head. "You can't attack the temple alone."

Tamra smiled, stretching her scar. "Oh, I won't be alone."

Kneeling, Raia whispered to the black lion. She tilted her head as if listening to the lion reply, which Tamra would have thought was impossible, except she would have also thought it was impossible for the high augurs to be this corrupt.

She wondered what other atrocities the high augurs had committed over the years. *There's rot in the heart of the empire. It must be rooted out.*

"He wants to save his brother," Raia said. "He . . . told me."

Tamra didn't question it. There would be time to wonder at the miracle of that later. And she had no interest in wasting time arguing—Raia was old enough to make her own decisions. Besides, Raia could help. *I can't do this alone.* "I will go for Shalla. You and the lion free Prince Dar. Can you do that?"

"Yes," Raia said.

"Help me unlock the stalls."

Raia came out of the kehok's stall, with the lion close behind her. "How many?"

Tamra felt her anger and fear rolling inside her. It was a power unlike anything she'd ever felt before. All the sorrows and humiliations and struggles of the past were colliding inside her with all her fears and dreams for the future—she felt the moment, even more intensely than she used to on the racetrack. Her will stretched through the stable, unstoppable.

"All of them."

CHAPTER 32

Ambassador Usan needed to delay the coronation, or everything would be ruined. His king's army wasn't close enough yet! Just a few more hours, and they'd be in position. If Prince Dar were executed and Lady Nori crowned before they arrived . . . the Becaran military could be redeployed to defend the capital city, and the invasion could fail. He'd never imagined the Becarans would act so quickly.

My timing should have been perfect!

He'd been right about the riots. They'd begun as soon as the races ended, and the spectators he'd paid to escalate any conflict had done their job admirably. It had blossomed into full-fledged chaos, with violence spilling out into the streets and across the city, as perfectly as if he'd orchestrated it all. Which he'd done. Mostly. He hadn't been the one to strike the spark, but he had been the one in position to take advantage.

The city was supposed to be distracted by the riots. They weren't supposed to crown a new empress. He hadn't counted on Lady Nori working so effectively and efficiently in coordination the high augurs, and that was a grave error. *It's her fault,* he thought. *And mine, for underestimating her.* Plastering a smile on his face, he swept into Lady Nori's chambers, escorted by her family's guards. "Your Excellence-to-Be." He bowed.

Lady Nori was seated on a velvet chair so ornate it resembled a throne. Usan was positive that was intentional. Lady Nori knew how to play this game. She'd project an air of competence and sorrow as she claimed power. *Oh, she's good.* Make a show of reluctance, of only doing her duty. But his spies had reported conversations between her and the high augurs prior to the arrest of the emperor-to-be. He had no proof, of course, but he had little doubt that she was involved. If only he'd realized the significance of those meetings sooner . . . But he hadn't. *That's on me.* So he swallowed his pride and said grandly, "I offer the congratulations of my king."

"All is not resolved yet." Lady Nori gestured with an elegant hand toward the window, where the sounds of chaos in the streets still drifted in. The city guards had called on any available soldiers, the few who were already assigned to the city, to aid with subduing the citizens, but there was still the sound of shouts and screams. He normally would have been pleased about this. Fracturing the city's defenses was excellent, leaving the city wide open for the Raniran army. "But I will accept your congratulations, as well as your fealty."

"As ambassador, I cannot swear my allegiance to a foreign—"

"Usan," Lady Nori purred. "We both know you have been acting far beyond the limits of an ordinary ambassador.

I will have your oath, or I will have you arrested for attempting to ignite a war."

He then saw how disastrous his mistake of timing was. He'd counted on more days between the riots and the crowning of a new emperor. Plenty of time for his king to swoop in and establish rule. As it was, Usan was alone, with the Raniran army too far away to help him. Not only was his plan in jeopardy, but his life was as well.

He dropped to his knees. "All I want is to go home."

"This will be your home," Lady Nori said with a smile.

He was to be a prisoner then, forced to divulge whatever Raniran secrets they thought he held. He saw his future stretching out bleakly before him. How had she moved so fast to outmaneuver him? She must have been planning this for some time, perhaps since Emperor Zarin's death. Or before. He wondered if she'd had a hand in his death as well. At this point, it wouldn't have surprised him.

There was, as he saw it, only one option left to him. He'd lost his chance to go home, but perhaps he hadn't yet lost his chance to complete his mission. He could still ensure that Becar was ripe for the plucking when his love arrived within his king's army.

Bowing his head, he crossed his arms as if intending to swear fealty. Instead he used the movement to draw a small knife from within his tunic.

Rising from her throne-like chair, Lady Nori approached him to receive his oath.

He sprang up and buried the knife in her heart.

Her eyes flew open.

The guards sprang at him, tossing him onto the ground and pinning him down. He heard one of them calling for a healer, who would arrive too late. *It's all about timing,* he thought. The healer would be too late, and now his army would be right on time.

The Becarans would never be able to unite to choose a new emperor or empress by sundown.

I win, he thought, as the guards bound his hands, arresting him.

LADY EVARA HAD PLANNED TO MARCH DIRECTLY TO the palace when she left the kehok stable, but that proved to be impossible. The rioting had spread beyond the racetrack and through the streets of the city. Fires had broken out in several shops, and she was forced to shelter in an alleyway as a shouting mob stomped by.

"Now how do I reach the palace?" Lady Evara asked herself.

Luckily, she was always her own best resource. She spotted a column of palace soldiers marching through the street. *Excellent,* she thought. *They'll do nicely.*

Lady Evara scurried out of the alley, then straightened her hat, grateful she'd worn one so ridiculous that it identified her as an obvious aristocrat, and strode beside the column. "Thank you for the escort," she told the nearest soldier.

He shot her a look, but since she was dressed as a noble and was unarmed, he did not object. She walked with them to the gates of the palace, and then she swept forward to present herself to the guard. She schooled herself to ignore the way her heart thumped hard in her chest.

"Lady Evara," she said in her most imperious tone. "I must have an audience with the emperor-to-be as quickly as possible. I come on urgent matters."

"You come too late," the guard informed her. "Prince Dar has been arrested on charges of high treason for the murder of Emperor Zarin."

For once, Lady Evara was speechless.

Dismissing her, the guard inspected the soldiers, admitting them into the palace.

All right. This . . . changes things. Lady Evara prided herself on being able to quickly grasp a situation.

Either Prince Dar had indeed murdered his brother and sent his soul into a kehok, or the high augurs had orchestrated the murder and were seeking to hide their guilt by framing Prince Dar. Either way, she possessed dangerous knowledge. Only a few knew that the black lion held Emperor Zarin's soul. If anyone found out that she was one of those few . . . If Prince Dar were guilty, she'd be branded a traitor for keeping his secret, potentially condemned to suffer the same fate. And if the high augurs were secretly evil, they'd seek to silence her. Her wealth would be the least of her worries.

I should flee.

It was the obvious choice.

Sell whatever possessions she could, and start a new life somewhere else in Becar. Or even outside of Becar. There were lovely lands beyond the desert, if she could scrape up enough gold to buy passage on one of the trade caravans. She was simply not in the position to make enemies as powerful as the ones involved in this game.

Her parents would have expected her to, as the lesser Becarans would say, cut bait and run. She was used to looking out for herself. After all, no one else would.

But . . . But . . .

What if Prince Dar were innocent?

Augur Yorbel would have known if he wasn't. She was certain of that.

Which meant the high augurs were *not* innocent. And she was in possession of information that could help expose them, if she were willing to use it, thus potentially freeing all of Becar from the influence of duplicitous murderers.

That, of course, meant *not* fleeing and instead choosing to endanger herself.

Ironically, she wished she had an augur to consult about this moral dilemma.

No one is going to help me make this choice, she thought.

Maybe there was a way to protect herself *and* do the right thing, if she played this correctly. She'd have to handle it carefully . . . Yes, she could do it.

Plopping herself back in front of the guard, she said imperiously, "I need to see Lord Petalo on a matter of utmost importance."

Others were clamoring for the harried guard's attention. He glanced again at her, at her ridiculous hat, and waved her through. Quickly, before he could change his mind, she hurried through the arch and up the steps. Her heart felt as if it were pattering faster than a kehok could run. She tried to keep her expression smooth and walk without running toward the heart of the palace, the vast courtyards where the aristocrats commonly gathered. She then settled herself and strode through the court.

Everything was in chaos.

Some of the lords and ladies were weeping, collapsed in an undignified manner beside the statues. A few wounded soldiers were being treated out in the open. Lifting her skirts to increase her mobility, Lady Evara hurried through. She passed a clot of guards in the hallways and heard whispers: a lady had been murdered. Lady Nori.

But Lady Nori wasn't her concern. She had one goal: the mustached blackmailer.

It took her far longer than she would have liked to locate Lord Petalo. He was in an office, hiding bravely from the riots and chaos of the court by barricading himself behind a door and a layer of servants. "Announce me," she told a servant. "And tell him I have news that will profit him."

After a few moments, she was permitted into the office. Steeling herself, she swept inside.

He was seated at his desk, his papers arranged as if this were an ordinary day he'd devoted to paperwork, instead of a day when the city was falling apart. She noticed, though, that the windows behind him were shuttered and barred. Plus, his glorious mustache was slightly less coiffed. It drooped instead of curled.

"You surprise me, Lady Evara. I didn't think you would dare show your face here, in my office. You know we had an agreement, and you did not follow through. The lion not only lives, but he won."

"Mmm, a few other events have occurred since then. You may be aware?"

He snorted. "I'm aware of everything."

She doubted that. But she knew that as a gambler, he was considered to be an expert on the Becaran Races. And she was certain that every other member of the palace court knew that as well. They'd expect him to know every detail of the racers he bet on and to be privy to the most exclusive information. Such as a the nugget she was about to share. "I have discovered that the kehok who won the Becaran Races bears none other than the soul of the late emperor Zarin. That is why Prince Dar obtained him."

He gawked at her, which was satisfying.

"You know this . . . how?"

"The augur who purchased him from me confided in me, before Prince Dar's arrest."

He shook his head. "Not possible. Emperor Zarin was a good man."

"He was," she agreed. "Which is why it took an artifact that functions as the opposite of a victory charm to influence his rebirth. As you may have heard, the high augurs used it on Emperor Zarin when they murdered him."

"You can't possibly believe that nonsense your rider spouted."

"If you doubt that an augur can be corrupt, then tell me: Who told you that I'd failed to meet the stipulation in my parents' will? Only the augurs and I knew." It was a risk. She couldn't be certain that the augurs were to blame. But it seemed likely. If the augurs were behind all the murder attempts, it explained quite a bit.

"I cannot reveal my sources." But his mustache twitched.

"Then let me reveal what I know: Emperor Zarin was murdered and reborn as a kehok. You tried to blackmail me into killing the kehok so that this fact would never be discovered. Which means that you were in on the plot. Either you were working with Prince Dar to help hide his crime, or you were working with the high augurs to hide theirs."

"But—but I wasn't!"

"Of course you weren't." She flounced into a chair and spread her skirts wide, as if she planned to stay for a while. "You and I both know that you couldn't have afforded to pay me the amount you promised. You were working for someone. Your 'sources.' But the people of Becar don't know that. They'll blame you."

His eyes bulged as the implications of what she was saying sunk in. "It was Lady Nori. Her idea. Her information, obtained from the augurs."

"What a pity she's dead and can't confirm or deny that."

He was sweating. "She's . . ."

"Oh my, Lord Petalo," Lady Evara mocked. "I thought you were aware of everything!"

"Are you trying to blackmail me? I already have info on you—"

She gasped as if offended. "I wouldn't dream of spreading unsavory rumors about you! Unless, of course, you were to spread unsavory ones about me . . . But truly, there's no need for us to threaten each other. I have come to you with a gift of information."

He narrowed his eyes. "What do you want from me?"

Goodness, he was dense.

"Spread the truth as widely as you can, as quickly as you can." She smiled at him, knowing the power of her smile. She'd charmed much more intelligent men than Lord Petalo before. "You're a clever, resourceful man. You have connections throughout both the court and the racing community, which makes you the perfect mouthpiece for such news . . ." She trailed off, letting her request sink in, along with the compliments.

His eyes widened, as if understanding were blossoming. "Ah, so you are giving me this information, in exchange for my secrecy about your personal situation?"

She was fine with him thinking that was the reason. Even her own parents hadn't been capable of seeing anything virtuous in her.

"It's a win for you," Lady Evara promised. "Reveal the truth about the kehok-emperor. Expose the fact that Lady Nori tried to have him killed, at the bequest of the high augurs or in coordination with the high augurs. Let people draw the obvious conclusions they wish, and you become blameless."

He was nodding. "Lady Nori was supposedly present when the high augurs arrested Prince Dar. She *could* have orchestrated all of it."

"If you expose her crimes, you'll be a hero."

He liked that. She could tell.

She smiled encouragingly as he began to pace and plan. A person who could provide information like that would be valued. He'd curry favor with whomever stepped forward to fill the power void. He suddenly frowned. "But . . . proof? What proof do I have?"

"This isn't a trial," Lady Evara pointed out. "This is a riot. You don't need proof. You only need gossip. I'm sure you know the right ears to whisper into."

"I do!"

"Right now, people are hungry for facts, whether they're true or not. Feed that hunger, and they will be grateful to you." She laid a hand on his arm. "As am I."

"And I am grateful to you, Lady Evara. You did indeed have news that will profit me. I will forget our prior conversations ever happened."

Calling to his servants, he scurried out of his chambers. She surveyed the room and spotted a fat pouch hastily shoved between tunics. She lifted it out and checked its contents: gold coins. Glancing at the open doorway, Lady Evara pocketed it.

If everything went wrong, she was not going to be penniless.

She then sailed out of the room with an aristocratic nod to the guards. Before giving up and fleeing with a stolen pouch of coins, though, she was going to do what she could to make sure that nothing more went wrong—*At least not for me.*

She wasn't going to make any bets on the fate of Becar itself.

IN HIS CELL WITHIN THE AUGUR TEMPLE, DAR DESPAIRED.

He sat on a bare cot. Through the one tiny slit of a window, he could see the sky, a mottled orange and rose—it was near sundown, the time when Zarin's vessel should have been killed so he could be reborn. *It had been such a good plan,* he thought.

But he realized now he'd never had a chance. The high augurs had always had all the power, and today they'd proved that. He could almost admire how thoroughly they had outmaneuvered first his brother and then himself, and no one had ever suspected them. Until Raia.

He wondered if the high augurs had caught her yet. He didn't doubt she was on their list, as one who knew the truth. It was too dangerous to leave her be. She may be publicly executed as well, accused of high treason, or it could be done quietly. The augurs might not even have to sully their own hands. Certainly they had enough gold to ensure it happened.

How could he have misjudged them so badly? All of Becar had. Everyone trusted the augurs, completely and absolutely, to guide them toward the right and good. But all the while . . . And now the people would never know the truth. Lady Nori would be crowned empress, and Zarin and Dar would be forgotten, intentionally, as an embarrassing disaster that they'd escaped.

What he didn't understand was why. But he doubted anyone would explain that to him.

He wished he'd had a chance to talk more with Zarin. He would have liked to say goodbye. And Raia . . . He'd never met anyone as brave as her. He knew what had happened with her parents, and how she'd gone on to race and win.

There were a thousand things he wished he'd said or done. Alone in a room with stone walls, he thought through them all. *If I had a second chance, I wouldn't let so many moments pass me by. I'd say what I felt. And do what I thought was right.*

But he'd used up all his chances.

His fate was sealed. No one was more powerful than the high augurs.

He wondered what he'd come back as.

CHAPTER 33

Tamra strode through the stable, unlatching lock after lock on the stall doors and loosening the chains that held the monsters at bay. She could feel the agitation of the kehoks on her skin and taste it in the air. Every nerve in her body hummed in response. She held the monsters still with her mind, as if she were a dam holding back a river.

The pressure was enormous, but she would not break.

Behind her, the kehoks pawed the floor. She felt them strain at the weakened chains, inches from freeing themselves. *Not yet,* she ordered them. And they waited.

She felt as if she were expanding, her skin stretching, her blood pulsing through a thousand veins, her heartbeat magnified—she was them, and they were her. She breathed with them. Every kehok in the stable, hundreds of them, breathing together as one, with Tamra.

"How are you doing this?" Raia whispered. Her eyes were wide.

"They are me, and I am them." She heard her own voice, distant and hard. *My rage is their rage.* She felt focused in a way that exceeded anything she'd ever felt before. Crystallized. In this moment, with Shalla at stake, with every fear and every failure culminating inside her, her will smothered theirs. As she finished with the final stall, she pivoted and marched straight toward the stable door. "Get on your lion. Rescue Prince Dar. And most important, keep yourself alive."

Raia scurried to the black lion and mounted. "What are you going to do?"

"We are going to destroy the high augurs," Tamra said.

"But . . . but . . . Trainer Verlas! You can't!"

"I can. And I will. I'm tearing it all down."

And with that, she released the monsters.

They screamed as one, yanked their chains, and broke free. Behind her, they burst through the doors to their stalls. Tamra lifted the bar over the stable door and pushed it open. The black lion ran out first, carrying Raia. In their wake, Tamra strode out. The monsters followed her, fanning out to either side.

Outside, people were still fighting. A fire burned in the stands. Most of the tents had been torn apart, and debris littered the campsites. Several bodies lay prone, and the city guards were still trying to quell the violence.

Tamra selected a silver jaguar the size of a rhino and forced it to stop in front of her. Climbing onto his back, she ordered, "Run!"

All the hundreds of kehoks ran. She was in the front, leading the way as they thundered through the crowd that had spilled beyond the racetrack, breaking apart the riot, leaving the people stunned.

Her army poured into the city, filling the streets. Statues that had stood for hundreds of years were knocked over. Palm trees snapped and fell beneath the onslaught. The kehoks flattened everything in their path: carts, fruit stands, benches. . . . People ran screaming into buildings and alleyways. Controlled tightly by Tamra, the kehoks didn't chase them. United, Tamra and the monsters had one goal: the temple.

As they ran through the streets, Tamra saw the augur temple perched on the hillside, a hundred times more glorious than the temple in Peron. Every dome was sheathed in gold, and every wall was made of a brilliant white marble. A blue stone path led to an arched gate that had been painted in blue and gold. It had stood for hundreds of years.

She led her monster army to the front gate and then halted.

Behind her, the kehoks screamed. She stayed on the back of the silver jaguar and let them scream. When the augurs' guards rushed to fill the archway, Tamra silenced the kehoks. She spoke into the eerie quiet. "Evacuate the temple, and bring me my daughter and the high augurs."

"You can't come here with *them*!" one of the guards shouted.

She fixed her gaze on him. "I can, and I have. Empty the temple."

The guard blustered. "No one dares attack the augur temple! It is the bastion of goodness and light and hope for the Becar Empire! This temple has stood for hundreds of years—"

Enough, she thought. "And it will fall today," Tamra said.

She murmured to her army, "Chase them. Herd them.

Frighten them. Force them all outside. And then pull the buildings down behind them. Destroy everything."

Tamra released the monsters.

RAIA AND THE BLACK LION HID BEHIND A PILLAR AS Trainer Verlas faced down the temple guards. Wearing black armor with jackal-shaped helmets and carrying eight-foot spears, the guards looked terrifying. Raia had always avoided them as much as possible when she was a student. But Trainer Verlas, with her army of kehoks, regarded them as if they were unruly children.

She felt the lion's eagerness. His muscles were quivering beneath her. Leaning forward, she stroked the smooth metal of his mane. "Wait for our moment," she murmured.

It came.

Trainer Verlas unleashed the monsters.

Urging the lion forward, Raia kept low on his back. She joined the surge as the monsters rushed in through the archway. The guards fell beneath their paws and hooves. As sand stirred around them, Raia couldn't see whether the guards lived or died. *They'd been warned,* she thought, trying not to feel sick.

As the kehoks bashed through doors and plunged inside the temple, Raia guided her lion deeper through the courtyards. She knew the layout of the temple, and she wasn't distracted by the need to destroy everything in their path. She and the lion quickly left the other kehoks behind.

The screams and crashes faded, muffled by the thick stone. Prince Dar would be in the old prison cells. They had been used in ancient times to hold those likely to be reborn as kehoks, in hopes of rehabilitation before their fate was sealed. All old temples had them, she'd learned from her lessons. The high augurs of several generations ago had determined that their efforts were better spent persuading the vast swathes of the public to living holy lives, than in trying to save the handful of the doomed, and the prisons were left unused. But she didn't doubt that they'd been maintained. Everything in the temple was kept in perfect order.

She and the lion ran past quiet reflection pools and statues of birds and animals in a chain of courtyards, before they were enveloped by the cool shadows of the inner corridors. She caught glimpses of augurs, fleeing with their belongings clutched to their chests. Seeing her, they'd flee in the other direction. She didn't bother to tell them she wasn't here for them. Or that there were even worse kehoks the way they were now running.

She wasn't sure what to do about the guards that would almost certainly be protecting such an important prisoner. She wished that she had some of Trainer Verlas's courage. It suddenly occurred to her that her thoughts weren't focused— she was feeling self-doubt, worrying about the future, all the things she wasn't supposed to do near a kehok—but the lion hadn't slowed or veered. He seemed to be following a map in his memory, with no prompting from her. *It's as if he knows we're trying to rescue his brother,* she thought.

Maybe he does.

She wondered if he'd ever speak to her again, in her mind.

As they neared the prison cells, Raia regained her focus and encouraged the lion to slow. He padded silently through the corridor. Ahead she heard voices, barking orders to stand firm.

Two voices, she thought. *Two guards.*

And then a third voice, a woman.

Three guards. She felt the lion tense. She wasn't sure what to tell him to do. She was certain this was the place—or maybe they should make certain?

"What's going on?" That was Prince Dar!

Hearing his voice was all it took. The lion, with Raia clinging to him, leaped out of the shadows. He plowed directly into the first guard, knocking him back against a wall, and then spun to bat away a second guard.

Raia realized what it meant that she didn't have to guide him: she'd take care of herself. And she could free Prince Dar. She immediately slid off the lion's back, leaving him to fight the guards. She crossed to the nearest fallen guard, who'd been thrown into the wall. Kneeling, she yanked the keys from his belt.

She hurried to the prison cell door. Her hands shook as she slid a key into the lock.

With any other kehok, she couldn't have turned her back to him. She couldn't have trusted that he wouldn't attack her too. But she trusted the lion absolutely.

"Prince Dar? Don't worry. We're getting you out."

"Raia? Is that you? What are you doing here? You can't be here! You'll be arrested. They'll kill you!"

"Only if we're caught."

The first key failed. She tried the second. There were over a dozen on the key ring, and her hands were shaking so badly it was hard to hold them. Behind her, she heard the guards scream but she refused to look. She kept trying the keys, one after another, until the second to last key turned.

She felt her heart thud hard against her chest. She was *not* going to look behind her. If the lion had killed anyone . . . she didn't want to know. Raia yanked the door open, and Dar stumbled out—he'd been pushing from the opposite side.

"What . . ." he began. "Zarin?"

Raia turned. Two guards were prone—she didn't know if one was alive or not, but the other was screaming. The third had fled. The lion had his massive paw on the screaming guard's chest, pinning him to the stone floor. Zarin growled as he looked back at Dar and Raia.

"You came to rescue me?" Dar said to Raia.

"We both did." Raia pulled Dar with her to the lion. Climbing on, she scooted forward so that there was room for Dar behind her. He climbed on and wrapped his arms around her waist. He smelled faintly of mildew mixed with incense, the scent of the older parts of the temple.

"The high augurs won't let us just leave," Dar said.

"The high augurs are distracted right now," Raia told him. She leaned forward and asked the kehok. "Please take us away from here."

It was a vague order—the kind that no ordinary kehok could obey—but the lion leaped forward, kicking the downed guard with his hind paws, and raced through the corridors. He ran as if he knew the way, which was either due to Raia's knowledge of the temple layout or whatever he remembered from his life as Emperor Zarin.

As they neared the front of the temple, Raia heard noises. Crashing. The walls were crumbling up ahead. A pillar had fallen. Dust choked the air. She saw people, augurs, running from the building, where they were herded by kehoks, who kept them pinned nearby.

The lion didn't slow, even when Dar called out to him.

Trainer Verlas will take care of it, Raia thought. Her trainer often talked about how she was too old, that now was the time for the young. But Raia didn't want anything to do with this. She'd happily leave it to Trainer Verlas to finish what she'd come here to do. Raia had one goal: escape to safety with Prince Dar. That was enough for her.

She'd face tomorrow when it came. For now . . . safety was all she wanted.

And safety meant running.

They ran through the streets of the city, toward the palace, and then beyond it. The racetrack loomed ahead of them, but the lion didn't slow. He kept running, carrying them out into the desert. As the chaos of the city faded behind them, Raia felt she was back to doing what she did best: running away. Except this time, she wasn't alone.

"FIND SHALLA."

Tamra planted the image of her daughter into the mind of the nearest dozen kehoks, and she sent them plunging into the temple. *"Save her."*

She mounted the silver jaguar and ran with them. Ahead of her, clearing the way, the kehoks plowed down the guards in their path and tore tapestries off the walls and knocked through pillars.

Not all the kehoks understood the word "save," but she kept tight control over them, as well as the ones that were holding the augurs who'd spilled out of the building. Killing them wasn't the goal, and she refused to allow the monsters to turn this into an indiscriminate bloodbath. She wasn't after ordinary augurs; it was the high augurs she wanted. And she'd seen none of them.

The temple was a warren of countless corridors filled with exquisite tapestries and ancient mosaics. But Tamra wasn't interested in the architecture or its history. *This is too slow,* she thought. "Topple it."

She reached to the kehoks outside, and they began to

wreck the temple around them—slamming into pillars, clawing apart the walls, puncturing the roofs. If the high augurs were here, this would flush them out.

But she heard only crashing. There were no human voices. The high augurs were hiding her somewhere. She had to be close!

"Stop," she ordered them. "Keep searching."

Deeper inside the temple, she heard the howl of jackals. An archway of darkness lay in front of them. She knew this . . . she'd heard legends about the labyrinth in the heart of the temple, where the high augurs met in secret. *This is where they are,* she decided.

She slowed the kehoks and stared at the opening. Two jackals were chained on opposite sides of the doorway. They cowered in the face of her monsters. She'd heard the walls were coated in poison, and the darkness was absolute. She had no torch. If she proceeded, she would have to wander through a poisonous maze in the dark in hopes that luck led her to her daughter.

Screw that, she thought. *I'm done playing by their rules.*

"Break the walls," Tamra ordered.

The kehoks hurled themselves at the stone. Again and again, until the ancient stone began to crack. Fissures ran through the stone, and along the ceiling, until at last the ceiling broke apart and sunlight poured through. The kehoks kept battering the walls until they crumbled. The outer labyrinth walls crashed down,in a cloud of dust. Tamra urged the silver jaguar forward, and they climbed over the rubble. She kept the other kehoks fanned out around her on either side as they picked their way over the crushed labyrinth.

She faced a doorway, shrouded by the dust-choked air. "Shalla?" she called.

"Mama?" a voice called back, and then was muffled.

A deeper voice said, "This is the point where we compromise. We have your daughter, as you can see. Cease your destruction."

Stop, she ordered the kehoks.

The deep voice began to list out demands, beginning with her immediate surrender of the black lion kehok—

"And if I refuse?" Tamra called out. Her heart was hammering hard within her chest. She felt every beat. Her skin tingled. She'd never felt more tied to a moment. *My Shalla is within that room. With them.*

A woman's voice said flatly, "Then your daughter dies, crushed by falling rock. A tragedy that you caused with the damage to the temple."

"You cannot hope to win," another chimed in. "Any moment now, the temple guards will descend. You and your black lion atrocity cannot prevail. You will be outnumbered."

They don't know I have an army, Tamra realized.

"Is this the verdict of all the high augurs?" she asked. "Is there none of you who will defend an innocent child?"

The deeper voice again. "There is more at stake than one life. You do not understand what the cost will be to Becar."

"The cost of what? The cost of people knowing the high augurs are as corrupt as a kehok?" Tamra asked. "Are you afraid they'll realize you murdered their emperor and arranged for his soul to be eternally tormented, purely for whatever political power play you wanted? That they'll know you condemned Prince Dar to die for reasons you've engineered?"

"All for the good of Becar," another voice said. "You have a child. You understand the lengths one would go to to protect it. The Becaran Empire is our child."

"Bullshit," Tamra said. "You don't lie to your child." Raising her voice, she said, "Shalla, are you all right? Did they hurt you?"

There were murmured voices again. Beside her, the kehoks pawed at the rubble. But under her tight control, they stayed silent. She knew the others on the edges of the temple were also paused in their destruction. She could sense them coiled like a spring.

She tried again. "Shalla? Are you there?"

From within the chamber she heard murmured voices, and then she heard Shalla's sweet voice. "I'm here! Mama . . . Augur Yorbel . . . he's dead."

She didn't expect to feel grief at that, but she did. *I trusted him before, and he betrayed me,* she thought. But she'd never wanted him dead.

"You see, then," one of the high augurs said, "how serious we are."

"Sweetheart, close your eyes," she told Shalla. "No matter what happens. Keep them shut." And then she took a deep breath.

Past and future didn't exist.

Consequences didn't matter.

There was only this moment, like she'd told Raia when she raced. She had this one moment to change the world. "Do not touch my daughter," she said.

The high augur within the chamber replied, "We will not harm her if you—"

But she wasn't talking to him. "Kill the rest."

She released her mental grip on the nearest monsters. They threw themselves through the door. Tamra rode the silver jaguar through the doorway. Surveying the chamber, she stayed mounted on the silver jaguar as the high augurs screamed.

Screamed and died.

She felt the screams inside her, welcomed them.

In one corner, Shalla was huddled beside the body of Augur Yorbel. Her eyes were squeezed shut, and her hands were pressed over her ears. Controlling the kehoks, Tamra kept them away from Shalla. But she let her monsters do as they wished with the rest.

Blood sprayed on the walls, on the ceiling, on Tamra, on Shalla's student robes, and Tamra bore witness to it all. The head high augur died when a spider kehok tore his head from his body. An elderly man was impaled by the horn of rhino with a hide like a crocodile. A lizard kehok gnawed on the body of a third. Watching, Tamra felt as if she were fraying apart inside, as the images embedded themselves deep in what would become her nightmares. But she did not let herself look away. She was causing this; she had to bear witness.

When all eight high augurs lay dead, Tamra sent the kehoks to join the others, rounding them up as if they were within a corral, circling the other augurs. *Stay*, she told them.

They stayed.

Still with her hands shielding her face, Shalla was sobbing.

Tamra slid off the back of the silver jaguar. She walked forward, trying to feel nothing but feeling everything. She smelled the bitter tang of blood in the air and walked into the chamber. Between Tamra and Shalla were the bodies of the high augurs. Or what remained of them.

"Keep your eyes closed," Tamra told Shalla.

Crossing to her, Tamra wrapped her arm around her.

She led her out of the chamber, and Tamra instructed a few kehoks to collapse its walls. While Shalla clung to her, Tamra picked her way across the rubble of the temple, back to where her army of kehoks surrounded the augurs.

All several hundred kehoks turned to look at her with their beautiful golden eyes, awaiting her next command. And she didn't know who was the monster anymore—them or her.

CHAPTER 34

Raia, with Dar, rode on the black lion across the sands. It was nearing sunset on what felt like the longest day of her life. The whole desert glowed amber, and the wind tasted sun-warmed. She knew they couldn't run forever, but for now, it felt right.

"What's that?" Dar called in her ear.

"Where?"

"On the horizon!" He pointed past her toward a darkened cloud.

"Desert wraiths?" she guessed. She'd never seen any up close but they were known for lurking around the edges of sandstorms. Wisps of souls, like the messenger wights, who never found their way to their new vessel. Parents used to scare their kids by saying if they didn't stick close to home, they'd be lost and become a desert wraith. *My mother once said she hoped I'd become a wraith*, Raia thought.

But that time was long behind her. She'd rescued a

prince, who was a kind man who missed his brother. She'd never imagined doing anything like this.

"I don't think it's wraiths," Dar said in her ear.

"Sandstorm?" It didn't look like a sandstorm, at least not exactly. A gray billowing cloud of sand, it seemed to have shapes inside.

They ran toward it, the black lion carrying them without any instruction from her, as if it were something he wanted to see as well. She wasn't certain this was wise. Shouldn't they run away *from* a sandstorm, not *toward* it?

The shadows within the cloud of sand began to take shape: figures. People. *Soldiers,* she thought. Rows and rows of soldiers. The lion slowed. "It's an army," Dar said. "From Ranir. And no emperor sits on the Becaran throne."

"I saw Becaran soldiers in the city, subduing the riots," Raia said.

He nodded grimly. "One battalion, scattered and distracted. No one is guarding the city borders while the center is imploding."

Everything we've done, and we could still lose it all, Raia thought. Staring at the coming army, she felt as if she'd merely delayed her fate. *Maybe I was always destined to fail. Maybe my parents were right . . .*

"Without an army at the ready, the Heart of Becar will fall," Dar said flatly.

He had to be seeing his dreams dissolve in front of them too. And they were so close to having everything! Raia ached for him, as well as herself.

The lion made a huffing noise and pawed the ground.

Dar let out a slightly hysterical laugh. "Zarin, I know you have teeth and claws now, but you can't take on an army by yourself. You're only one."

Raia had an idea. Another terrible, wonderful idea. She didn't know if it would work. She didn't know what was happening back at the temple—the guards could have rallied to fight the kehoks, the high augurs could have captured Trainer Verlas, and she could have been outmaneuvered. It was also possible that Trainer Verlas had already lost control of the kehoks. But Raia didn't believe any of that was true. "I know where there is an army."

Dar went still, and she knew he'd guessed what she meant. "No. That's impossible. Kehoks are never used for war. They're too unpredictable. Too hard to control for an extended amount of time."

"We don't need them for an extended time," Raia pointed out. "Only long enough to convince the Ranirans to turn around."

Dar was silent for a long moment. "I think I love you."

Raia smiled, and they turned and ran back toward the temple. Behind them, the enemy army advanced on the Heart of Becar—far more slowly than the Grand Champion of the Becaran Races could run.

TAMRA RODE THE SILVER JAGUAR TO THE TOP OF A fallen pillar and shouted to the augurs, "Prince Dar did not kill his brother! He is innocent!"

The augurs began to yell back at her and at one another.

In her mind, she called to the kehoks to scream—they cried out as one, silencing the augurs. She shouted, "Emperor Zarin was murdered by the high augurs and forced to be reborn as a kehok!"

More muttering from the augurs that grew again into shouting. "Proof!" someone yelled. "Show us proof of their corruption!"

Tamra didn't know how to do that. The kehoks sensed her agitation and began to strain to escape her hold. With Shalla safe, it was becoming more difficult to focus on them.

If I lose control of them, in the Heart of Becar . . .

She refused to let herself finish that thought. She *couldn't* lose control. There were hundreds of thousands of innocents in the capital city.

Shalla squeezed her hand. "Mama! It's Raia!"

The black lion was riding toward them, with Raia and Prince Dar on his back. All the augurs' attention shifted to them. The kehoks around Tamra strained against her. It was getting harder and harder to hold them.

"Read their auras!" Shalla shouted. "You'll see your proof!"

Yes! Tamra thought. *That's my smart girl!* These augurs could all read the black lion and see the truth—that the kehok was once Emperor Zarin—and read Prince Dar and see that he was not a murderer. His soul was unstained by his brother's murder. They'd see the high augurs had lied to them. They'd know the truth.

The gasps from the augurs told Tamra that those who could were doing exactly that, as the black lion galloped toward them with its riders.

We can win this, Tamra thought, feeling dizzy at the thought. Prince Dar could become emperor, and Raia and Shalla could be kept safe. . . .

Beside Tamra, one of the kehoks screamed and burst forward. "*Stop!*" Tamra ordered. She had to get them back to the stables and shackled. She could leave the political mess to the augurs to sort out. Now that they knew the truth, now that the late emperor's vessel had been found and identified, Prince Dar would once again be the emperor-to-be and be crowned as emperor.

We did it, Tamra thought. *It's over. Isn't it?*

Prince Dar reached them. "The Raniran army approaches."

One of the augurs stepped forward and bowed to him. "My emperor-to-be. We have read you and will attest that you have found your late brother's vessel and that you are innocent of all accused crimes. You can be immediately coronated. Once the ceremony is complete, you can summon our army and send them out onto the sands."

"Even immediately isn't fast enough," Dar said. "Our army is stationed across Becar, and the one battalion positioned here is scattered through the city. It will take time we do not have to gather them and reposition them, and more time to call for reinforcements from elsewhere in the empire. Our soldiers can only travel as fast as humans." He met Tamra's eyes. "But *your* army can travel faster."

"I . . ." Tamra couldn't find the words.

"Becar will fall," Dar said, "if you do not."

She looked at Shalla. She'd done this only for her daughter, and now her daughter was safe. Both daughters, Shalla and Raia. She hadn't meant to raise an army, and she didn't know how much longer she could control them. Already she could feel her focus fraying.

But the threat isn't over just because the high augurs are gone, Tamra realized.

"You can do it, Mama," Shalla said.

Tamra looked at her daughter. Her eyes were full of trust. If she didn't stop this invasion, her daughter would be in danger again. She couldn't allow an enemy army anywhere near her. She'd just saved Shalla! She would not allow her to be in danger again! "I'm not leaving you again."

"Then take me with you."

"But—"

"I'll be brave," Shalla promised. "And I'll do everything you tell me to."

She didn't see that she had any other choice. She wasn't going to leave Shalla with the augurs, even if the worst of them were gone. "Hold on tight."

Do you want to run? Tamra asked her kehok army silently.

In answer, they broke from the augurs and began to stream away from the temple, running at full speed.

Lady with the Sword, keep us all safe, Tamra prayed.

Wrapping one arm around her daughter's waist and holding on to the kehok's fur with her other hand, Tamra urged the silver jaguar forward, and ran with her army toward the desert, Raia with Prince Dar beside them on the black lion.

DAR HAD NEVER FELT LIKE AN EMPEROR BEFORE, BUT AS he waited with their army of kehoks for the Ranirans several miles outside of the Heart of Becar, he thought for the first time, *I can do this.*

Seeing them, the army slowed, and a man on a horse walked forward. The horse's flanks were coated in sweat so thick that it looked as if he was shimmering. The man looked like the perfect soldier: arm muscles as thick as Dar's thighs, armor that had seen plenty of battles, a scar above his right eye. A general, judging from the colors on his helmet. He halted several yards from Dar.

"This is new," the general said. "Also, foolish."

"Becar is not for the taking," Dar said.

The general flashed what was most likely intended as a charming smile. "We aren't here to take. We're here to help! I was under the impression that you needed assistance with civilian unrest. Our information said the empire was faltering due to the lack of an emperor." He sounded urbane, as if they were meeting for tea in a garden, not under the hot sun with armies at their backs.

"Your information is out-of-date," Dar said. "Take your army and go home."

"You realize that it's not possible to hold this many kehoks for an extended battle," the man said, as if he were scolding them. "History is rife with such failures."

As if on cue, all the kehoks screamed simultaneously. Dar saw the enemy army shuffle nervously. The front lines inched backward, and the soldiers whispered to one another.

Softly, Raia whispered, "Trainer Verlas, can you control them?"

"Mama can do it," Shalla said.

Tamra shuddered, sweat glistening on her skin. Dar wondered briefly what it was doing to her, controlling so many kehoks at once. History might be full of failures, but it said little about successes. He knew of no one who had led this many kehoks for this length of time. *This has to end now,* he thought. He glanced at Tamra and her daughter. The young girl's eyes were wide, terrified, but she hadn't let a hint of fear color her voice. *Brave child,* he thought. He needed to be brave now too.

He had to end this, for all the children of Becar.

"I am Prince Dar, soon to be emperor of Becar, and I tell

you we are not in need of your 'assistance.' Again, take your army and leave. You are not welcome here."

"I am General Sambian of the Raniran Empire, and I say whether I am welcome, boy-king. You do not yet wear a crown, and you wield an army you cannot hope to control."

Through gritted teeth, Tamra said, "I. Can't. Hold. Them. All."

Raia grabbed her hand and said, "Let me help."

Dar looked at the stretch of soldiers in front of him, and then down the line at the kehoks. There was one simple fact that the general had overlooked. This wasn't a battle of two human armies; there was only one army here. "We do not need to control our army. All we need to do is set them free. We have no one here to lose. You do."

The general paled.

"I can't . . ." Tamra whispered. "The deaths on my soul . . . Already so many . . ."

"These will be on mine," Dar said firmly. "As emperor-to-be, I take responsibility for protecting my people, in any way that I can." This was the best he could hope for: to release the monsters out here, in the desert, where they'd harm only their enemy. His people would be safe within their city. Raising his voice so the general could hear, he said, "We ride the fastest racer in the empire. The kehoks will not catch us if we run. Can you say the same?"

The soldiers began to mutter to one another.

"Surrender, General Sambian," Dar said calmly.

"Our orders are to take Becar, and a pack of mongrels will not prevent the great kingdom of Ranir from claiming the weak and corrupt empire of Becar, as is our destiny," the general said. "We will not surrender to a boy who will never be crowned."

The kehoks howled, pawing at the sand.

"So be it," Dar said.

TAMRA COULDN'T KEEP HOLD OF THE RAGE AND FEAR that had fueled her through the attack on the temple. Her mind was beginning to fray—thinking about the high augur's deaths, about Shalla, about the future, about what would happen to all of them now.

A few kehoks burst free of her control and loped toward the army.

"No!" Tamra cried. She tried to focus harder, feeling sweat bead on her forehead. She breathed in the heat of the desert, tasting it in the back of her throat. The sun made the air over the sand shimmer, making the army waver as if it were a mirage.

"Dar . . ." Raia said, as more kehoks overrode Tamra's and Raia's control and began tearing into one another. As the first kehoks to break free reached the enemy army, the soldiers tried to defend themselves. Shalla whimpered and clung tighter to her mother.

"Let them go," Prince Dar said calmly. "All of them."

"But . . ." Tamra began. She couldn't complete the sentence. It took too much to focus on the kehoks. They wanted so badly to be free, to run, to destroy, to kill. She felt as if their rage was stuffed down her throat. It was hard to breathe.

"You can't hold them forever," Prince Dar said. "Release them here, far from the city. Our people will be safe."

"But the Ranirans . . ." She didn't know them. She couldn't hold them in her heart to steady her, the way she could with Shalla. Especially since they had come to attack her home and seize it for themselves.

"The Ranirans came to conquer us," Prince Dar said.

"Their orders were to kill and enslave. They would have destroyed our cities and our way of life. If they hadn't made the choice to do this, they would not face the consequences now."

More monsters broke free. *Stop! Do not kill!*

His voice was gentle, even kind. "You've saved us. You can let go now. Be free."

Prince Dar was right—she couldn't maintain her focus forever. Already, she felt as if the world was tipping, tilting, spinning. She hoped that the Raniran army had retreated far enough fast enough. She hoped no one innocent was hurt. She hoped . . .

"Close your eyes," she whispered to Shalla.

She lost consciousness. Blackness swallowed her vision, and the last thing she heard was the joyous, wild screams of the kehoks as they plunged across the sand.

WHEN TAMRA WOKE, SHE WAS LEANING AGAINST THE metal mane of the lion. Raia and Prince Dar were behind her, and they were running smoothly across the sand toward the Heart of Becar. She didn't hear or see any other kehoks around them.

"The kehoks?" she asked.

"Gone," Raia said.

"You did it, Mama! You scared the bad people away."

"The kehoks will hunt our people, once they've finished chasing the army across the desert," Tamra worried. "Travelers . . . People in small villages . . . Our people won't be safe from them, even if they stop the army . . ." Her mind shied away from thinking about what had happened to the soldiers in the Raniran army. It was possible they'd fled fast enough. She didn't think that was likely.

"That's not a problem for today," Prince Dar said firmly. "Today you saved Becar, twice over. Today you are a hero."

How nice, Tamra thought. It was difficult to pull her thoughts together. She felt as if her mind had been shredded. "Don't want to be a hero. Just want . . . to save my daughters."

Someone spoke—she didn't know who; the voice was deep and gravelly in her mind. She thought, oddly, impossibly, that it was the lion.

You saved us all, he said.

CHAPTER 35

Everyone in the palace, the fallen temple, and the city scrambled to organize the coronation of Prince Dar as quickly as possible. By the very next day, all was ready, or ready enough. Raia had never seen a coronation—she was stunned at how quickly the decorations were unfurled. Flowers everywhere. Ribbons and banners strewn across every pillar, building, and bridge. Musicians were playing on every street. Dancers and acrobats performed in every open square, in the shadows of broken statues and damaged structures. It all felt forced and frantic, but no one said so. Everyone just smiled harder, determined to make this joyous even if it killed them. Per Dar's instructions, Raia watched from the steps of the palace, beside her black lion.

Her role in the coronation was simple: stay with the kehok-emperor.

She was to keep anyone from harming him and keep him from harming anyone. Prince Dar had asked her to remain visible, so that anyone who wanted to confirm the legitimacy of his claims, that the kehok had once been Zarin, could do so. It had already been sworn to by the augurs of the fallen temple, but other augurs were pouring in from other cities and they too wished to see with their own eyes. Thanks to Lady Evara, even those without the training to see auras were adding credence to the claim that this kehok was the late Emperor Zarin, falsely reborn as a monster. She had, apparently, been busy spreading the truth among the powerful men and women in the palace, and now everyone was curious to see this wonder.

And the woman who had tamed him.

Raia had been draped in silks and jewels, and she felt like an ornament standing next to the gleaming black metal lion. Over the last several hours, she thought she'd been stared at by every single person in Becar. She tried to remember not to fidget or scratch her nose or look as uncomfortable as she felt.

In addition to the finery, she also wore a heavy amulet around her neck, proclaiming her the Grand Champion of the Becaran Races—as if there was anyone in the entire empire who didn't know who she was. She'd never meant to become famous. But in a way, she'd become as famous as the emperor-to-be himself.

My life will never be the same.

Certainly she'd never be able to hide in plain sight anymore. She wasn't forgettable the way she had been when she first ran from home, so very long ago. She wondered if anyone had told her parents about her new status: handler of the late emperor's vessel, grand champion, and friend to the emperor-to-be, and she wondered what they'd think. She told herself she should no longer care, though that was easier to say than believe.

She touched the one piece of jewelry she'd been allowed to choose herself—the pin that Dar had given her, in the shape of a lion. It calmed her.

Bells began to ring all over the Heart of Becar. High and low notes blended together into a cacophony. She twisted to look up at the great entrance. Prince Dar had emerged, weighed down in more finery than she'd ever seen. He carried it with no sign of its weight as he crossed to the clear pool of water in front of the palace. She immediately stopped feeling bad about all that she was wearing.

Poor Dar, she thought.

The new head augur carried the symbols of coronation. She projected an air of calm dignity.

A steward beckoned frantically at Raia. *Our cue,* she thought at the black lion. With her hand on his mane, Raia walked the lion down the steps.

The audience was packed into the streets. They backed up as she walked past them and took her place on the opposite side of the mirror pool. Her and the lion's reflections appeared in the clear water. The emperor and the augur were reflected in the opposite side.

One by one, various courtiers spoke. In an unrushed coronation, these would have been the governors of the various districts and cities of Becar, but there wasn't time for the travel, and so they'd chosen representatives to read speeches sent by messenger wights.

Raia heard little of the speeches. Most of her concentration was on the lion, keeping him calm, and on Prince Dar. He was listening, seemingly intently, as he was lectured on the noble duty of the emperor to his people. The words were traditional, but the emotion in them wasn't. She heard a mix of fear and relief—the people needed an emperor, but few had ever seen a succession like this.

At last it was Raia's turn.

She cleared her throat and said the official words: "I present the late emperor's vessel and certify that Prince Dar has fulfilled his duty to his family, our history, and our traditions." Her voice didn't shake, and she kept her eyes fixed on Dar.

He smiled at her, and that was all she needed. She heard a roar of ragged cheers from the crowd behind her, which was answered by the black lion roaring at the sky. She grinned at Dar, then at her lion. Then she tilted back her head and roared too.

The augur presented the symbols of the emperor: blue beads that draped over Dar's shoulders to symbolize the river, a gold pendant in the shape of a stylized sun, and a simple circlet of silver that had been worn by the very first empress, thousands of years ago, when the Becaran Empire was born.

By the time the circlet was placed on Prince Dar's head, tears were pouring openly down his cheeks.

The black lion stirred beside Raia.

"What is it?" she asked in a whisper. "Our part is done."

But the lion rose and walked around the edge of the pool. The soldiers gripped their spears, but Raia held out her hands and followed beside the lion.

Silence had fallen over the packed street. All eyes were on her and the kehok.

The kehok halted in front of Dar. Raia held her breath,

ready to intervene if she had to, if the kehok was more in control than the memory of the man.

Lowering onto his front knees, the lion bowed to the emperor.

This time, the cheers of the people were loud and full of joy.

ady Evara wasn't used to being called a hero. In fact, the first time it happened, she overheard a whisper in the palace court. "I heard she knew from the beginning—that's why she sent her trainer to the market to buy him."

She opened her mouth to correct the rumor. *Of course, I hadn't known,* she was prepared to say. *I was as shocked as anyone.*

But then the whisperer continued. "She's the true hero behind it all. If she hadn't had the vision to instruct her rider to purchase that kehok . . . well, imagine where we'd be. Slaves to the Ranirans!"

Pretending she hadn't overheard, she'd glided toward the speakers, introduced herself, and let them fawn over her as they introduced her to their social circle. When they asked her direct questions, she demurred, which they took for humility.

From them, she gleaned that Lord Petalo had taken a few liberties with his retelling of what had happened. Instead of leaving her out of the tale, or revealing the sordid mess with her inheritance, he'd painted her as some kind of wise heroine.

Which her parents would have thought was hilarious.

Frankly, *she* thought it was hilarious. Also, bewildering.

Why would mustache man enhance her reputation? If she was a heroine, then he had no leverage over her—who cared about her past when she'd helped save the empire? But after she talked with a few more fawning nobles, she realized that Lord Petalo had *also* inserted himself into the tale, as the brave double-agent who alerted the wise Lady Evara to the murder attempts. She let his lie slide. After all, in a way, he had helped.

And he *had* been the one to make sure the entire court knew the truth, which had softened them up for the official verification from the augurs. With the support of both the augurs and the court, Prince Dar had sailed through his coronation.

It also helped that the prince, Trainer Verlas, and the rider Raia had stopped an invasion. Just the three of them, with an army of monsters, against one of the largest invasion forces Becar had ever seen—the size of the invasion force tripled every time the story was retold, Lady Evara noticed. The exact numbers were unknown. But the story caught the imagination, and it spread far and wide. Lady Evara fanned its flames as often as she could.

Of course, she wasn't foolish enough to believe all the praise being heaped on her. Her soul had yet to be read by an augur, at least not since the last time she'd tried (and failed) to obtain her inheritance—what was the point? Her soul was still very much whatever it was. She didn't think it was likely to have changed. She'd never even returned the gold pouch she'd lifted from Lord Petalo. She tried not to let her nerves show, though, when she was at last summoned to the aviary to speak with Emperor Dar.

If he knew the truth, he could still have her cast out of the palace as unworthy, no matter what lovely rumors were circulating.

The guards recognized her at the doorway and escorted her inside. She heard the soothing waterfalls and the pleasant chirp of birds and did not feel calm. What if he objected to the rumors? What if he thought she was trying to claim glory for herself by not refuting them? *I wasn't. Well, only as a side benefit.*

She picked her way through the winding path, between the lush flowers and the tranquil corners, until she reached the center mosaic. Emperor Dar was seated on a throne of white marble. The black lion was with him, as he always seemed to be, accompanied by Raia. The three were inseparable these days, which Lady Evara approved of. The emperor's enemies would think twice if he was perpetually protected by a vicious monster.

With a flourish, Lady Evara bowed. "Your Excellence, how may I serve you?"

"You are already serving your empire, Lady Evara," Emperor Dar said.

He did not seem displeased. In fact, he was smiling. Perhaps this wasn't going to be a disaster? It would be lovely not to be forced to leave the Heart of Becar in disgrace and poverty. "Always," Lady Evara said smoothly. "Your coronation was a joy and blessing to all."

"Your efforts to ensure that have not gone unnoticed,"

Emperor Dar said, and then he wrinkled his nose. To Raia he said, "Am I sounding appropriately pompous? I feel like I'm overdoing it."

Raia laughed. "You're doing great."

Lady Evara noticed how relaxed they were and began to hope. If he was going to send her away, he would be more serious, wouldn't he? "May I ask why you have summoned me, Your Excellence?"

"I'd like you to keep doing what you're doing," Emperor Dar said.

"Oh?" That sounded promising, though she wasn't exactly sure what he was referring to. *Keep doing what?* she wondered. The threat to the kehok had been removed, and she'd neutralized Lord Petalo.

"My brother had friends among the court. . . ." The emperor laid his hand on the lion's metal mane. "Friends who smoothed the way for him. They'd put in a good word for policies he wanted to be supported. And they'd watch the temperature of the court."

"You want me to keep spying for you," Lady Evara clarified.

"Precisely."

Lady Evara felt like dancing a little victory lap, but she kept her expression smooth as if she were considering it. "My affairs in Peron have been calling to me. I was intending to return home. . . . My finances have suffered a blow since my time away." She hoped that was a subtle enough hint. If not, she'd be more blunt.

"You will be compensated," Emperor Dar said. *Music to my ears,* Lady Evara thought. "I need allies, Lady Evara. Every new emperor does. Will you be my ally in the court?"

"Yes, Your Excellence," Lady Evara said with another bow. "I would be honored."

"Splendid. Then let's begin now. What have you learned?"

She dove into relating her conversation with Lord Petalo, excluding the unflattering bits, but including everything he'd said about Lady Nori.

That seemed to sadden him. "I suppose I never did see her true soul."

She also told how Lord Petalo was altering the story to paint her as a heroine. "I am your loyal spy," she told the emperor. "But I'm not a heroine. If you wish, I could correct the record. . . ."

She hoped he'd say no, and to her relief, he did. "It's useful to have you admired by the court. Leave it be. My concern, though, is whether you will be vulnerable to blackmail again."

Quickly, Lady Evara weighed her options. He already knew about the attempted blackmail, so there was zero point in trying to deny it. She should have suspected he'd ask. For all she knew, he'd already investigated and this was some kind of test. "It relates to my parents."

Raia spoke up. "You already have my sympathy."

She flashed the girl a grateful smile, and then she launched into the messy tale. The will, the failed readings, the humiliation. As she talked, the kehok watched her with his golden eyes, which oddly enough made her feel better.

Maybe she wasn't worthy enough of her inheritance. But she *had* done some good here.

When she finished, she noticed a river hawk had settled on a branch above Prince Dar. It was the only bird anywhere in the vicinity of the lion.

"Thank you for trusting me with your secret," Prince Dar said gravely.

It wasn't as if she'd had much choice.

"Do I still have the position?" Her voice was stiff as she asked, but mercifully didn't crack.

"Of course."

Lady Evara inclined her head in gratitude. Inside she cheered.

"You should have an augur read you now," Raia said. "Maybe this time it will have a different result."

Prince Dar held up his hand. "You could. But consider: you have already proven yourself to me and to all of Becar. Perhaps it isn't necessary."

Lady Evara mulled over his words. *He's right,* she thought. With a promise of a position at the palace, she didn't need her inheritance. Given that, why submit to a reading? So she could secure her late parents' approval? She didn't need to prove to anyone that she was worthy of the kind of future she wanted.

I make my own destiny and determine my own worth.

And I am worth quite a lot.

RAIA WAS SILENT AS LADY EVARA LEFT THE AVIARY. When the door closed, she said, "You didn't want her to win her inheritance, did you? You wanted her to need you."

"I meant what I said: I need allies," Dar said. "I let my brother down once—his murderers almost succeeded. I will not leave the empire so vulnerable again."

Rising, the lion pressed against her side. She placed a hand on his smooth metal mane. She could guess what her kehok wanted to say. "You didn't let him down. And we're your allies. You can count on us."

"I *am* counting on that. Are you ready?"

When she nodded, he signaled the guard, who let augurs file into the aviary. There were six of them, four women and two men, in robes and wearing pendants. Raia guessed they were the new high council—she'd heard elections had been held across the temples. An unusual move, but then there had never been another time in history when all the high augurs needed to be replaced at the same time.

They halted, formed a semicircle, and bowed in unison.

They've been practicing, she thought, and buried a smile.

"Your update," Emperor Dar commanded.

One of the augurs stepped forward and began reciting a litany of facts: the cost to rebuild the temple, the number of workers they'd already employed, the impact of the riots on various professions and how the augurs were assisting. . . . Raia stroked the kehok's smooth mane while Dar listened to the augur drone on.

At last, she wound down, and Dar said, "I am delighted to hear the augurs are offering so much aid to the people of Becar."

"The old high augurs strayed from the path," the new head of the high augurs said. "We wish to restore the people's faith in us."

"Excellent," Dar said, nodding. "Then you will be open to restructuring of the role of augurs in Becaran society."

The high augur blinked. "The—"

"I have prepared the proclamation that my brother wanted. The one that he died for." He smiled, and Raia could tell it was a fake smile. She was beginning to notice the nuances between his always well-controlled expressions. "I know you're not your predecessors, but in the interest of the stability of the empire, I have already had multiple copies written. If I die unexpectedly, they will be distributed."

The head augur managed to stutter, "P-p-proclamation?"

"My brother uncovered the truth that all people have the capacity to read auras. It is not limited to 'the purest of the pure,' which is how it was possible for corruption to sneak into your ranks. Now the truth will be known: anyone can be an augur. I imagine your temples will want to prepare themselves for an influx of volunteers. And an exodus of those who never wanted to be augurs in the first place."

He said all of this calmly, as if he weren't upending a basic tenet of what the augurs believed about themselves and their power. Raia kept her face expressionless—she had heard all of this as the one who had helped the kehok and the emperor communicate with each other over many, many sessions—but it was new to the augurs.

New and unwelcome.

"Only the purest *should* become augurs," Prince Dar said. "This is very different from only the purest *can* become augurs."

The augurs murmured to one another, and the second from the left, a man with a braided black beard and bald head, said, "This will undermine people's faith in us!"

"There will be ramifications," Prince Dar agreed. "You may, in fact, find people relying on themselves more, once they know we are all the same: equally human, with our own choices to make."

"It will shake the core of how people see themselves, as well as us!" the bearded augur said. "Becarans are not prepared for this. You cannot issue this proclamation!"

The black lion began to growl. She felt the rumble vibrate through his mane.

The bearded man swallowed hard but pushed on. "I only mean that such an unsubstantiated claim could cause great harm, especially with no proof that it's true. . . ."

The kehok bared his teeth, continuing to growl. *Easy,* Raia thought at him. The people might not be so forgiving if kehoks slaughtered a second set of high augurs.

"My brother was murdered to keep this secret," Dar said blandly, as if sharing news of the weather. "I believe that in and of itself proves its validity."

"With all due respect, Your Excellence," the head augur said, bowing, "it merely proves that our predecessors considered it dangerous."

Dangerous and true, the kehok's voice echoed in Raia's head. She was startled—she heard him only rarely. She repeated his words: "Dangerous and true." She added, "I was chosen to be an augur. I'm proof that who we were doesn't determine who we become."

"You are but one person," the head augur objected.

"Then study this," Dar said. "I am giving you the chance to prepare for the questions, the confusion, and the changes this announcement will cause. You have two months."

All the augurs began to babble, objecting.

Convince them, Raia told her kehok.

He paced toward them with measured steps. His paws were silent on the sandy path, the birds were silent in the presence of the kehok, and as soon as the augurs noticed he was moving, they fell silent too.

"Two months," Dar repeated. "This is a gift that your temples do not deserve, after what befell my brother. What almost befell our nation. Do not make me regret it."

Eyes on the kehok, the new head augur stepped forward and bowed. "Release your proclamation now."

The other augurs behind her gasped.

"Secrecy is the enemy of trust," she said. "Let all Becarans face this revelation together."

The bearded augur objected. "But we don't know if it's true—"

"The people are afraid because they have seen the purest of the pure be corrupted. They do not know how they can continue to make the right choices if those who should have been incorruptible could not. At least this gives them an explanation: the old high augurs were not special. They were not better. All I ask, Your Excellence, is that you call it a theory, and together all Becarans will explore its truth."

"Very well," Dar said. "It will be done."

The head augur bowed, and the others followed suit before retreating.

Raia waited for the door to shut before she sagged against the kehok. She'd held her breath for much of that conversation—just thinking of the ways in which this revelation could change Becar, most especially the lives of everyone like her who'd never wanted to be an augur but thought they'd had no choice. . . . It made her head feel as if it were whirling.

"Did that go the way you wished it to?" Dar asked the kehok.

The lion looked up at the river hawk perched above them.

Raia answered for him. "I believe it did."

RAIA AND THE KEHOK MOSTLY KEPT TO THE BACK-ground while Dar continued his day, meeting with various nobles and advisers. He heard updates on the rebuilding of the city, signed various documents, refused to sign a few others, and delegated tasks as necessary.

After a while, Raia and the kehok drifted away, wandering the paths of the aviary. She followed the sound of a man-made stream that trickled between the trees. A few statues decorated the paths.

The kehok remembered who he had been for most of the time now. Raia wasn't sure if it was because they were in his old home or spending so much time with his brother, but walking through the aviary, she felt as though she was with a friend, not a beast she'd tamed. The spectators at the races would have been stunned to see them.

Beside her, the kehok stopped.

A river hawk was perched on top of one of the statues. It watched them for a moment, and then inclined its head before spreading its wings and disappearing into the tops of the trees.

Raia didn't know what it meant, but she sensed peacefulness from the kehok. She hadn't felt that from him before. Resting her hand on his back, she meandered with him back to Dar.

"One more left for today," Dar said when they returned, "and I would like you here with me for this." He looked into the kehok's eyes. "You'll tell me if I make a mistake, right?"

That sounded worrying. "Who is it?"

"The ambassador from Ranir."

"I thought you'd imprisoned him." *As well as my parents,* Raia thought.

His gaze shifted to her. "I did. But it's time for him to deliver a message."

Raia swallowed. "You don't think destroying their army was message enough?"

Dar didn't reply. Instead he straightened in his throne as the guards crossed the aviary, escorting a disheveled man in chains. He was unshaven, and he looked as if he hadn't bathed in weeks. But his expression was peaceful—he looked, Raia thought, like a man prepared to face his own death.

She inched closer to the kehok and hoped that they wouldn't be the cause of that death.

"Ambassador Usan," Dar greeted him.

"I don't think I still have the right to that title," the man said, holding up his shackled wrists. "My king has most likely decided I failed in my duties."

"That is his right to decide," Dar said. "You can ask him when you see him."

The man cocked his head, as if mildly interested. "You aren't executing me? Curious. You know I murdered the woman you reportedly loved. Like you murdered mine."

Dar looked taken aback by that—most wouldn't have noticed, but Raia saw the tightening of his hands on the arms of his throne. She felt the kehok stiffen beside her.

"She was in the army that was supposed to invade. A captain in the third battalion."

"She may have survived," Dar said. "The extent of the losses aren't known."

"You unleashed an army of several hundred murderous beasts," Usan said with a shrug. "After so much time listening to your nobles discuss betting on your sun-blasted races, I know bad odds when I hear them."

"We are returning you to Ranir, for the good of Becar," Dar said. "The invasion, as well as your actions here, were an act of aggression we cannot and will not ignore. You will carry treaties that your king will sign."

"And if he does not?"

"Kehoks can travel across the desert. I do not think your king would like to find an army of them on his doorstep." Dar adopted the same casual tone as the ambassador, but Raia could feel the underlying tension.

"To warn you, my king may take it as a sign of weakness that you allowed me to live."

Raia burst out, "Are you asking to die?"

He shrugged again. "I'd prefer to die someplace where I'm not so thirsty all the time. I don't know how you Becarans can stand it here. People aren't meant to be surrounded by so much sand. So, if you're offering me a chance to live long enough to leave this place, I'll take it."

"You will be provided with an escort, as well as a written list of demands for your king. And you will deliver a special message." Dar nodded to the kehok.

Standing, the lion walked toward the ambassador.

For the first time, Usan looked frightened. Shrinking back, he began to tremble. Raia didn't know what the kehok was doing, but she didn't sense rage. Perhaps this was something Dar and the kehok had worked out between them. Often, Dar talked with his brother, and Raia gave them space, moving herself out of earshot but staying close enough to control the kehok, if necessary. They'd managed to find their own ways to communicate.

She was musing over this when the lion swiped his claws diagonally across Usan's body. Usan cried out as the metal tips gouged his skin. Blood sprang from the long gash, and Usan fell hard onto his knees.

To the guards, Dar said, "Make sure it scars. Then send him home." To Usan he said, "If you return, the claws will cut through your heart. And if your kingdom moves against us again, it will be your king's heart."

The bleeding man was carried out of the aviary.

RAIA AND THE KEHOK MET THE EMPEROR IN THE AVIARY the next day, and the next. The emperor wanted his brother present, and it was unsafe for the kehok to be without her—she couldn't guarantee he would hold on to his memories, and his guards wouldn't allow the risk.

Sometimes the meetings were fascinating, sometimes boring. None were as monumental as either the meeting with the new high augurs or with the former ambassador from Ranir . . . at least until the day when no one walked through the aviary doors for the next meeting.

"Isn't there anyone coming?" Raia asked.

"This time is reserved for you," Dar said. He drew a roll of parchment out of a pocket in his tunic. "These were made official just this morning."

She took it, unsure what it could be. It was tied with a gold ribbon, as if it were a new law or a proclamation. Feeling Dar watching her, she untied it—there were two papers. She flattened them on her lap.

As she read the first one, she felt her throat clog. It was a release statement from her parents, obtained from them in prison, admitting they had no claim over her, that she owed them nothing, and that all debt and relations between them were canceled.

A hot tear landed on the parchment.

It was what she wanted, but it still tore her up to read. Her parents had disowned her in a statement that was fully legal. They had no claim to her, nor she to them. *I'm free.* She didn't know why that didn't make her happier.

The black lion nudged her hand, and she stroked his metallic muzzle. He laid his head on her lap, comforting her.

"Read the second," Dar urged.

She flipped to the second paper and read. This one was an adoption certificate. Even though she was a full legal adult, this paper claimed her as part of the family Verlas. Daughter of Trainer Tamra Verlas, sister to augur-in-training Shalla Verlas. If she chose to accept. There were no financial ties within it—no obligations from either the family to her, or her to the family.

But they were legally bound, if she wished to be.

Now she was crying in earnest.

"I can't tell if you're happy or not," Dar said.

"I can't either," she admitted.

He gestured to the papers. "Do you want this?"

"Yes! Oh, yes!" She clutched both to her chest. Free from the family who never loved her. And tied to a family who did. Yes, she wanted this very much. She'd never imagined it was possible to change something that felt as immutable as the family she was born into. *But I did. I changed my life, my future, my destiny.*

The kehok leaned against her, and she heard the words in her head: *You changed mine.*

She wrapped her arms around his neck, as far as they would reach, and wept into his mane.

CHAPTER 37

S halla sat next to her mother, looking out at the desert. She rested her head against her mother's shoulder and breathed in the familiar scent: a little sand, a little sweat, a little hibiscus, and a little wildness. It was a smell that always made Shalla feel safe.

"You have a choice now," Mama said. "The new high augurs promised you would. All students can choose whether they want to continue to train to become augurs."

Ever since the emperor had issued his proclamation, she'd known this was coming: Mama would ask her what she wanted. What she didn't know was what Mama wanted her to choose. "Emperor Dar is making a lot of changes."

"Yes, he is. And not everyone likes that. But sometimes the world has to change." Mama paused as if considering her words. "Or be changed."

Shalla thought about that. So much of what she understood about the world she'd thought *couldn't* change, and that had been proven wrong. Because Mama had changed it. Shalla looked out at the wind dancing over the sand and wondered if she dared ask the question that had been haunting her for days now. "Are you sorry for what happened?"

"You mean am I sorry I saved you? No. Am I sorry I used the monsters to stop the invasion? No. Am I sorry it's my fault all those people died? I . . . don't know. Because I can't have one without the other. I did a terrible thing at the same time I did the best thing I've ever done. And if I had to do it all over again . . . I would do the same."

Shalla absorbed that.

"Do you understand, my star? I would destroy the world for you."

Shalla didn't know if that was right, as Augur Clari would consider it, but it made her feel warm and safe. She wished, though, she could forget what she'd seen and heard in that chamber. It woke her in the night, and for a few seconds, she'd be convinced she was still there. But then she'd remember her mother had come to save her and had kept her safe when the monsters attacked, and it would be okay again. "I love you, Mama."

She heard her mother make a small hiccup, and she tilted her head to see Mama's face. There were tears on Mama's cheeks. *Did I say the wrong thing?* she wondered.

But Mama just squeezed her tighter and said, "I love you too, my star."

"I still want to be an augur," Shalla said. "Like Augur Yorbel was." Even if being able to read auras didn't mean she was inherently special, she was still good at it. And she liked the idea of helping people be better. "Are you mad at me, for wanting to keep training?"

"I'm proud of you," Mama said. "After what they did . . . After what you saw . . . No one would have blamed you if you said no."

"I thought you might want me to say no. Because of the high augurs."

Mama hugged her again. "I only want you to be happy. And you . . . should have something in your life that's separate from me. Because I have a lot to atone for."

"You saved me," Shalla said firmly. "And Emperor Dar. And everyone in the entire empire." And then, to be honest, she added, "Except for the ones who died."

Mama gave a tight laugh, and Shalla thought maybe she shouldn't have said the "except for the ones who died" part. "You're right. But, Shalla, I want you to know that if you still want to be an augur, you can be. I promise I'm not mad at you."

Shalla felt the bit of nervousness that had been inside her belly unknot. She smiled, and they sat together quietly for a while. Then Shalla thought of something else she'd been wanting to say. "You shouldn't be mad at Augur Yorbel either."

Her mother stiffened. "I'm not. He's dead."

"That doesn't mean you can't still be mad."

Mama laughed again, a little freer, though Shalla didn't think what she'd said was funny. "My wise little star. I think I believe he was a good man. He wanted to make the right choices. . . . Sometimes I even think he might have meant for me to do what I did."

Shalla studied her mother for a minute. "You have to forgive yourself too."

Mama's laughter faded, and she looked out across the desert again. "Perhaps I do."

TAMRA CAUGHT THE SILVER JAGUAR FIRST.

He was lurking on the outskirts of the Heart of Becar. She'd taken to living at the now-deserted stables out at the racetrack, even though Emperor Dar had offered her and Shalla a place in the palace. Shalla swore she didn't mind, and Tamra felt more at home there.

During the day, while Shalla was at the temporary temple for her augur training, Tamra felt like she was paying penance by cleaning the massive kehok stables by herself, fixing the broken doors, and strengthening the chains and shackles. All the temporary tents from the campsite were gone, but the permanent structures that remained were massive and in need of work, after the damage they'd sustained in the riots. She refused every worker that Emperor Dar sent, and she was blessedly alone when she heard the growl outside the door.

She crept out, still holding the wrench she'd been using, and saw the silver jaguar pawing through the wreckage of the campsite. "Come," Tamra ordered.

The jaguar froze, and then he trotted toward her, as if that had been his plan all along. She stared into his golden eyes and knew this monster wasn't like the black lion—he hadn't been a pure soul tricked and trapped in a fate he didn't deserve. This soul deserved his fate. *And maybe I deserve him,* she thought.

She contemplated him for a moment. He shuddered, and his silver scales rustled as the shudder traveled down his back. "We ride," she decided.

He knelt at her command, and she climbed onto his back.

"Let's find the others," she said, then made it an order: "Find the other kehoks."

They ran across the former campsite and past the racetrack. That afternoon, they found three. She corralled them with the force of her will back to the stable and locked each of them in stalls.

There were hundreds still out there, roving the desert, hunting people who couldn't protect themselves, destroying fields and houses and anything they could find.

But I can bring them back.

She started shortly after dawn the next morning, after Shalla was escorted, by palace guards, to her lessons. Taking the silver jaguar as her mount, Tamra rode out into the desert and returned by nighttime with another five kehoks.

She felt happier than she had since the coronation. She hummed to herself as she latched the locks on the stable doors. *I have a purpose. There's good I can do.*

Every day, she hunted kehoks, sometimes returning with several, sometimes returning with none. It occurred to her that she'd be more effective if she wasn't working alone. Plus she'd be able to stay out longer, if she had someone in the stable taking care of feeding and watering the kehoks she'd already caught.

When Raia came to visit for dinner with Tamra and Shalla, Tamra told them what she'd been doing. Shalla clapped in approval, and Raia said, "I'll go with you."

"You can't," Tamra said. "Emperor Dar needs you—if he keeps insisting on having his brother with him all the time, he needs someone who can control him if the kehok forgets his humanity. We didn't do everything we did to lose our emperor in an accident."

"Then who do you want?"

Tamra thought about it. "Riders and trainers who want to help. And hunters." She thought of the man who had sold her the black lion—he'd be perfect for this. "I'll also need people who can feed and water the kehoks while I'm out finding more."

Raia nodded. "I'll talk to Dar."

Shalla giggled. "You call the emperor of all Becar just 'Dar.' Like he's an ordinary person."

"He is!" Raia insisted. "He worries about things, like ordinary people. He likes some people and doesn't like others, even though he has to be fair to all of them. He hates mushrooms and loves mangoes. He thinks his official robes itch too much, and the many-generations-old crown is too small and gives him a headache. He . . ."

Tamra grinned as Raia continued on. And on.

She wondered if Raia was even aware of how fond she was of the emperor. *She'll figure it out,* Tamra thought. *As will he.* They made a formidable trio: the emperor, the kehok, and the girl who linked them together.

Within a few days, Tamra had her crew. The hunter from the Gea Market was one of them, as were a handful of trainers she recognized, plus a few riders who were friends with Raia—they introduced themselves as Jalimo, Silar, and Algana, and this time she made a point of remembering their names. Silar rode with Algana, strapping herself into the saddle. She couldn't ride solo anymore, due to the paralysis in her legs, which meant she couldn't race, but nothing prevented her from wielding a weapon, a net, and her will. Together the two girls made an effective team.

Thankfully, none of the riders and trainers she couldn't stand volunteered. *It's possible they can't stand me either,* she thought.

On the back of the silver jaguar, she issued orders. "You"— she pointed to the hunter, who called himself Lormat (and his sword Ebzer)—"track any kehoks outside the city. We'll start north and work our way around. You and you"—she pointed to two trainers, an older woman named Yelna and a younger man named Jacrin—"be bait. After Lormat finds the kehoks, you draw them closer to me. I'll hold them while Silar nets them. Got it?"

All of them nodded.

"Remember—these kehoks have known captivity and freedom. They're going to fight hard for freedom. We work together, and we can bring them in." She paced in front of them on the silver jaguar. He snapped at the bit in his mouth. "This isn't a race. You falter, they will kill you! You lose focus, they will kill you!"

Unlike her rich students, she was certain these people believed her and understood.

They rode out, and by the end of the day, they'd captured nine more kehoks. For the first time in a long while, Tamra was able to greet Shalla with an unforced smile, and she slept without waking until dawn.

It was going well until the day they ventured far enough into the desert to trip over what was left of the Raniran army. The wind and sand had buried many of the remains, and scavengers, possibly even kehoks, had picked the bones clean. But there were hundreds of them. A desert of bones.

I did this, Tamra thought.

She slid off the back of the silver jaguar. It had been easy to avoid thinking of what had happened. She'd lost consciousness when she lost control of the monsters. She could fool herself into thinking the Raniran army had fled and the kehoks were merely reveling in their new freedom, far away from any humans. But the kehoks' thirst for destruction had been too great, especially after being contained at the temple. They had run down the Raniran army. She couldn't tell if any soldiers had escaped. She could see that most hadn't.

Tamra sank to her knees. Wind brushed sand over the bones, the armor, and the trampled banners. She felt the others staring at her.

"It's true, then," Algana said, awe in her voice. "What they call you."

What do they call me? Monster? She couldn't stop seeing the bones. *Bringer of death?*

"The Defender of Becar," the girl said.

The young trainer, Jacrin, said, "You saved us all."

Tamra tore her gaze away from the grave before her and stared at them, her team. "I caused so many deaths."

"And saved so many lives." Silar waved back at the city, at the Heart of Becar. "They came to kill and enslave us. You stopped them."

Lormat held out his hand toward Tamra to help her stand.

She stared at it for a moment, trying to accept what they were saying. They didn't see a monster when they looked at her. That wasn't the story that was told about what she'd done.

"Come, Defender of Becar," Lormat said. "We need to find the rest of your army."

Tamra took his hand and, leaning on him, stood. She remounted the silver jaguar, and they rode away from the fallen soldiers. She didn't look back.

ALONE, THE DEFENDER OF BECAR RODE THE SILVER jaguar onto the racetrack. The other hunters were on a well-deserved day off, visiting their families or the markets. Shalla was at the training temple for her lessons. Raia was with the emperor and her kehok, as always, when she wasn't spending time with her friends, the three young riders who had joined Tamra's kehok-hunting crew.

Tamra's old injuries ached, as they often did, but they weren't as bad as they used to be, thanks to all the regular riding she was doing. She'd strengthened old muscles and had also been seen by the palace healers, who had helped.

The silver jaguar pawed the ground. Absently, Tamra patted his neck. He twisted and snapped his jaws at her, but she was quick enough to avoid his bite.

"Ready?" she asked him.

He snorted and then tensed. Ahead of them lay the racetrack, sand smoothed by wind. It stretched along the stands and then curved for the turn.

"Prepare," she said.

She felt the sun on her back, the sand on her skin. She smelled the acrid scent of the kehok mixed with the smell of her own sweat. She felt the beating of her heart, faster and faster.

"Race!" she cried.

The kehok surged forward, and Tamra felt wind hit her face. She heard the shriek of it in her ears. She felt the power of the jaguar beneath her, his muscles reaching and straining as his paws swallowed the ground. And she felt joy inside her, filling her, pushing aside all else.

On the back of the silver jaguar, Tamra ran faster and faster until she was one with the wind, the sun, the sky, and the sand. She ran until she understood in a bone-deep way that *this* was who she was and who she'd become.

She was the one who would destroy the world, if that was what it took to save it.

She was the one who would race fate. And win.

ACKNOWLEDGMENTS

I decided I wanted to become a writer when I was ten years old. (Before that, I wanted to be Wonder Woman.) I didn't know any writers, though, and wasn't sure it was possible for an ordinary person to become a writer. In my mind, all writers were mythical. Or dead.

And then my friend loaned me a book with a girl holding a glowing sword on the cover. "You'll love this," she said. It was *Alanna: The First Adventure* by Tamora Pierce, a fantasy adventure about a girl who disguises herself as a boy in order to become the first female knight in her medieval land.

When I closed that book, I remember having one very clear thought: "If Alanna can become a knight, then *I* can become a writer."

That book changed my life.

Fast forward to 1999, and I had the chance to meet Tamora Pierce at Boskone, a Boston-based SF/fantasy convention. And I discovered that she is as awesome, great-hearted, and badass as any of her characters. We became friends after that, and when my first book was published in 2007, Tammy was the first person to send me flowers.

So that's why this book is dedicated to her. And that's

why Tamra is named Tamra, after Tamora. I wanted to write a character as badass as she is.

I believe that fantasy is a literature of hope and empowerment. It can serve as a light in the darkness, as a guide toward strength, and as an escape from pain. It is my secret hope that someone will read Tamra and Raia's story and realize that they can be who they want to be, that they can shape the world, that they can race the sands—and win.

I'd like to thank my phenomenal editor, David Pomerico, for taming the kehoks with me, and my incredible agent, Andrea Somberg, for racing with me from the start. I'd also like to thank Jennifer Brehl, Mireya Chiriboga, Chris Connolly, Kathleen Cook, Kara Coughlin, Angela Craft, Michelle Forde, Pam Jaffee, Ronnie Kutys, Lainey Mays, Debbie Mercer, Virginia Stanley, Kayleigh Webb, and all the other amazing people at HarperCollins who brought this book to life!

And a special thank-you to my husband, my children, my family, and my friends. You make life worth living and races worth running (in a metaphorical way, of course—we all know I'd rather be reading than running). If I were to be reborn, I'd hope to be reborn with you.

ABOUT THE AUTHOR

Sarah Beth Durst is the award-winning author of twenty fantasy books for adults, teens, and kids, including the Queens of Renthia series; *Drink, Slay, Love*; and *Spark*. She won an ALA Alex Award and a Mythopoeic Fantasy Award and has been a finalist for SFWA's Andre Norton Award three times. She is a graduate of Princeton University, where she spent four years studying English, writing about dragons, and wondering what the campus gargoyles would say if they could talk. Sarah lives in Stony Brook, New York, with her husband, her children, and her ill-mannered cat.

More titles from Sarah Beth Durst

The Queen of Blood
Book One of The Queens of Renthia
The spirits that reside within this land want to rid it of all humans. One woman stands between these malevolent spirits and the end of humankind: the queen. She alone has the magical power to prevent the spirits from destroying every man, woman, and child. But queens are still only human, and no matter how strong or good they are, the threat of danger always looms.

The Reluctant Queen
Book Two of The Queens of Renthia
In T*he Queen of Blood*, Daleina used her strength and skill to survive the malevolent nature spirits of Renthia and claim the crown. But now she is hiding a terrible secret: she is dying. If she leaves the world before a new heir is ready, the spirits that inhabit her realm will once again run wild, destroying her cities and slaughtering her people.

The Queen of Sorrow
Book Three of the Queens of Renthia
The battle between vicious spirits and strong-willed queens that started in the award-winning *The Queen of Blood* and continued in the stunning *The Reluctant Queen* comes to a gripping conclusion in the final volume of Sarah Beth Durst's Queens of Renthia trilogy . . .

The Deepest Blue
Tales of Renthia
The natural magic of the classic *The Island of the Blue Dolphins* meets the danger and courage of *The Hunger Games* in this dazzling, intricate stand-alone fantasy novel set in award-winning author Sarah Beth Durst's beloved world of Renthia.

Race the Sands
A Novel
In this epic standalone fantasy, the acclaimed author of the Queens of Renthia series introduces an imaginative new world in which a pair of strong and determined women risk their lives battling injustice, corruption, and deadly enemies in their quest to become monster racing champions.